I0652163

Images courtesy of Shutterstock.

This book is a work of fiction. Any resemblance to actual events or persons, living or dead, is entirely coincidental.

"Havana, a Novel," by Douglas Clark. ISBN 978-1-63868-040-6 (softcover); 978-1-63868-041-3 (hardcover); 978-1-63868-042-0 (electronic).

By Douglas Clark

To Josie for all that she is and what she means to me.

HAVANA

A NOVEL

DOUGLAS CLARK

Chapter 1

Sitting in a bar in a small village forty miles northwest of Managua, Nicaragua, Bartolo Landeira was in a dark mood. A fetid late afternoon in sweltering heat following a rain. Soaked in sweat drinking lukewarm lousy local beer. His third week in this shithole. Waiting for his team of four U.S. marine instructors to join him. Their day spent setting up for tomorrow's exercise. The marines painted a bleak picture about the fighting quality of the Guatemalan rebel force. After two weeks of making his own evaluation, Landeira shared their assessment. Rather than trying to explain the problem, he chose to stage a realistic exercise to simulate the rebel's military objective. Landeira demanded the CIA team leader and the Guatemalan rebel commander in Managua arrive in the early morning to observe the exercise.

The cause of his misery neither the oppressive climate nor anything immediate for that matter. Festering circumstances years in the making. Guatemala only the inflection point in a long arch of a developing existential crisis. The year is 1954. Feelings of service to his country since in 1942 progressively deteriorated over the years since the end of the World War Two. His present circumstances now ethically repugnant. How had things come so far?

Going to war following Pearl Harbor seemed a natural response as it was for so many Americans. World War Two left no ambiguity. Every American felt a personal identification with

1

the threat to the United States by the Axis powers of Germany, Italy, and Japan. Spending almost four years as a field operative in the clandestine Office of Strategic Services, the OSS proved a violent experience for Bart Landeira. Yet one of clarity of purpose.

Following Allied victory in 1945, communism in the form of the Soviet Union loomed as the next threat to America's security. Valued for his wartime work in American intelligence, the offer to continue working in peacetime intelligence work appeared attractive. Admittedly, engaging in a form of foreign adventurism and intrigue proved more attractive than his civilian alternatives.

Following an undergraduate degree in journalism, he pursued a law degree unenthusiastically and joined his father's law firm in Tampa, Florida in 1940. Eighteen months of dealing with contracts and investment consulting while working closely with his father left him disenchanted about his career choice. America's entry into World War provided escape. With the war over, difficult to reconcile a return to practicing law given those prewar memories. Having never held a job in journalism made that earlier career aspiration now seemingly out of reach with the passing of too many years since earning his undergraduate degree. Whether practicing law or journalism, skills in guerrilla warfare provided no basis for a civilian career.

The prospects of returning to a normal civilian life also held uncertainty. Like tens of thousands of American demobilized servicemen, it meant restarting an interrupted career. A seismic shift from combat to peacetime normality. Although in constant danger, serving in the OSS proved an intense endeavor in which he excelled. Surviving behind enemy lines by your wits and skills proved a unique wartime experience. Often terrifying, always exhilarating, he prevailed by his own devices. The normality of a civilian career could never match the effects of those life or death experiences.

In his case, he had no close family ties to facilitate a comforting return to civilian life in the States. His mother died just before the United States joined the war. A largely distant family other than his father. Two older married sisters lived in Florida. A remote extended family living in Cuba. As to his father, they respected each other, but their relationship held little warmth. Equally strong-willed, tensions flared into argument. The elder Landeira was a product of the strong Latin patriarchal family-centered environment. His son viewed his relationship different-ly. Too independent to conform to rigid cultural protocols simp-ly because of ethnic background.

Therefore, the offer to remain in the clandestine world of U.S. intelligence with its intrigue and international travel held the draw of something familiar. World War Two may have ended in 1945, yet world peace remained an illusion. The new enemy of international communism produced a collective threat to West-ern democracies giving intelligence work a new purpose.

Unfortunately, the Cold War lacked the clarity of World War Two from the onset. The hysteria wrought by the threat of com-munism distorted both the domestic and international political climate of the United States. The Cold War warrior waged un-conventional warfare against an indistinct enemy. They enemy those pulling the levers of power in the Soviet Union. For the warrior, an enemy taken largely on faith. The threat either indi-rect or obscure. Of course, that was not immediately evident to Landeira as the post-World War Two era unfolded.

The violence of his war service in the OSS left no ambiguity. From his first assignment accompanying Allied forces in North Africa in November 1942 to German surrender in May 1945, he engaged in sabotage and killing Germans and Italians behind enemy lines. Circumstances changed with the end of war.

President Truman disbanded the OSS following the end of the war. A premature reaction by siding with critics warning of the ultra-secretive organization as unnecessary in peacetime and a possible domestic threat. However, necessity allowed for the secret intelligence and counterespionage branches of the war-time OSS to survive, becoming the Strategic Services Unit. With-in months, the SSU became the Office of Special Operations within the newly formed Central Intelligence Group. In 1947, the

CIG transformed into the Central Intelligence Agency under the National Securities Act of 1947.

Within the National Security Act was an obscure buried sub clause. Subsection D of Section 102 stated in deliberately vague language, the CIA might be tasked *to perform such other functions and duties related to intelligence gathering affecting the national security as the National Security Council may from time to time direct.* In effect, it authorized the NSC to conduct any action deemed necessary, including covert operations with no limitations or oversight. With his recognized wartime exploits in the field, Landeira became part of the newly created semi-autonomous section called the Office of Policy Coordination. The OPC became the covert operations section of the CIA headed by former senior OSS officer Frank Wisner in 1948. Purposely set apart from the intelligence gathering operations, the OPC afforded the fig leaf of plausible deniability for the President, Secretary of State, and even the Director of the CIA for clandestine activities conducted in foreign countries.

Landeira then followed his OSS boss in wartime Italy in a seamless transition into American peacetime foreign intelligence engaging in covert operations. A new American governmental institution, nonexistent prior to World War Two. From the onset, its agents had only wartime experiences to fall back on. The Cold War presented entirely new challenges. The singular enemy identified as international communism. Actual military confrontations took the form of proxy wars between the superpower adversaries of the United States and Soviet Union.

From the onset, American covert intelligence fixed on using right wing proxies to counter any political movement deemed socialistic, or even with progressive objectives. Political thought harboring policies of land reform, labor organization, and social justice, or anything threatening to the conservative status quo, appeared as foundations for communist infiltration. Such political circumstances in strategic locations provided justification to interfere by any means necessary, no matter how contrary to American democratic ideals.

When Landeira arrived in Nicaragua in 1954, he had served in a succession of clandestine operations beginning with staying on in post-war Italy to thwart the Italian Communist Party's election chances. The CIA arranged for him to secure a position as foreign correspondent with the Miami Herald as his cover. Not exactly his idea of a career in journalism, but it provided a start.

In Greece from 1949 to 1950, he represented American interests supporting the heavily U.S.-subsidized government. The CIA mission was to prevent a largely non-existent Communist threat in securing a forward position close to the Balkans. From Greece, Landeira engaged in running agents into Communist Albania.

Egypt in 1952 followed with Landeira participating in engineering a coup d'état as part of the CIA's *Project Fat Fucker*. The derogatory name for Egyptian King Farouk stemmed from his wide girth, a product of a lavish lifestyle. His regime a holdover from the old Ottoman Empire, the Eisenhower administration feared the developing internal revolutionary political instability might invite communism. The U.S. pressured Farouk to make political reforms to replace the corrupt political system in Egypt with a government more internationally acceptable. With efforts unsuccessful, the CIA reverted to regime change by backing a military takeover by General Mohammed Naguib and Colonel Gamal Abdel Nasser. A regrettable move that would carry unintended consequences in succeeding years.

Using *Project Fat Fucker* as a template, the CIA engineered a coup d'état with *Project Ajax* in Iran in 1953. Here the issue was control of petroleum reserves and the democratically elected Prime Minister Mohammad Mosaddegh of a constitutional monarchy. After the Iranian parliament nationalized the British Anglo-Iranian Oil Company, concern arose of Iran turning toward the Soviet Union. Joining forces with British MI6, the CIA orchestrated the removal of Mosaddegh. A new government formed under an Iranian army general allowed Shah Mohammad Reza Pahlavi, to acquire the real power as monarch, relying heavily on U.S. support.

From its creation, the CIA began engaging widely in covert operations as the intelligence arm of the world's singular superpower. There was scant history of intelligence gathering of its predecessor agency in the wartime OSS. The OSS was predominately a clandestine operational organization. Populated with many OSS veterans, the CIA inclination tended to pursue active subversion over passive intelligence gathering.

Dispatched to Nicaragua in the spring of 1954 directly from Tehran, Landeira was a proven asset in CIA coup d'état subversive operations. This new project in Guatemala code-named *Project Success* was to be a repeat of Egypt and Iran. Landeira's assignment was to train a proxy ragtag rebel army. Staging took place in nearby Nicaragua under the CIA-friendly cooperation of dictator Anastasio Somoza. This time the mission was to force regime change of a democratically elected Guatemalan government feared leaning too far toward communism. The evidence against Guatemalan President Jacobo Árbenz was however exceedingly thin.

Through Landeira's nine years of post-war participation in covert subversive operations, his personal feelings about his work progressed from unease, to distaste, to outright disgust. Not how he envisioned service to his country. Landeira saw America repudiating its core values once its interests moved outside its territorial boundaries. The CIA becoming a tool of American imperialism leaving in its wake corrupt totalitarian regimes holding power through force. In every developing country touched by the United States, the result was the same. Oppression by inflicting every form of brutality to suppress political opposition.

Nothing intended to foster democracy. Simply a counter to the other post-war superpower the Soviet Union. Furthering American interests by extending control over smaller proxy states became strategical important.

****

What astounded Landeira about CIA covert operations were crackpot methods built around flawed expectations then compounded by poor planning. During World War Two, you did not survive as a field operative by engaging in such ill-conceived adventurism. The difference seemed to stem from the CIA using proxy combatants for the dirty work. Deficient planning risked only the lives of expendable functionaries rather than CIA agents.

Project Success was another such amateurish mission. A successor operation to *Project Fortune* of 1952 under the Truman administration. The plan therefore evolving as a continually changing work in progress. Landeira's role in Nicaragua just one part in a collection of ad hoc moves directed toward coercing the Guatemalan army to depose the Árbenz government and replace it with one acceptable to the United States.

Arriving first in Miami, Deputy Director Frank Wisner briefed Landeira on the mission. Wisner made a case for Árbenz reshaping Guatemala into a communist state. The first in the United States' backyard. A threat that could then spread throughout Central America. The Panama Canal potentially placed in jeopardy. Without knowing the true facts, Wisner expected his operatives to buy into the program. Already skeptical of CIA propaganda, Landeira soon learned Wisner's portrayal of circumstances in Guatemala was entirely bullshit. Bullshit however with an ulterior motive.

Landeira learned this from none other than his boss in Nicaragua, William Campbell after arriving in Managua. While not some sort of CIA heretic, Campbell simply held no concerns about the ethical relevance. Campbell loved the life of intrigue. A dirty business but necessary. A soldier serving his country by following orders. A part of a larger struggle of international politics.

Campbell's candor explaining the real background of this mission nothing more than enjoying the game of double-dealing. A former officer in U.S. Naval Intelligence during the war, Campbell lacked field experience. Telling Landeira of the various tactical aspects of *Project Success*, he did not even recognize just how bizarre this mission sounded to someone with Landeira's experience.

At his first meeting with Campbell in the U.S. Embassy in Managua, Landeira said, "My cover as a journalist gives me a lot of access to other journalists. There is no public evidence that Árbenz is a closet communist. Educated at a military academy, a former army officer, and national defense minister. Hardly a left-leaning background."

Campbell shrugged. "Some say his Marxist leanings come from his wife. Doesn't really matter. Árbenz stepped on the wrong toes. His land reform policies included confiscating unused land owned by United Fruit of Boston. In Central America, United Fruit is the 800-pound economic guerrilla. They enjoy a powerful lobby in Washington. Portraying Guatemala as ripe for communist takeover, they played to the receptive Eisenhower administration."

Landeira said, "With that asshole McCarthy conducting his theatrical senate hearings, a perfect environment. A communist behind every banana plant."

"Perhaps. Anyway, Árbenz sufficiently concerns the Eisenhower administration. Secretary of State John Foster Dulles and his brother Allen Dulles our CIA Director have their sights set on changing the current regime governing Guatemala."

"Wisner said my job is to train an army of mercenaries to invade Guatemala. Why Nicaragua which doesn't border Guatemala?"

Campbell smiled. "An invasion of course must come from bordering Mexico, Honduras, or El Salvador. Honduras is the best prospect. Training started there but relocated to Nicaragua after becoming too obvious. Needs some sorting out since United Fruit workers there just went on a general strike over pay. Honduras will eventually come around and we will launch operations from there. The operation is getting material cooperation from Nicaraguan President Somoza and Dominican Republic President Trujillo."

Landeira made an expression of disgust. Both repressive brutal dictatorships. "Who makes up this invasion army?"

"Mostly former Guatemalan soldiers. Following officers loyal to a right wing Guatemalan colonel named Carlos Castillo Armas. Paid mercenaries. Armas participated in a failed coup in 1949 then fled into exile in Honduras. The United States nominated him to front this regime change."

"So our mission is to install another dictator in the Americas," Landeira commented.

Campbell responded, "You have a problem doing this work, Landeira?"

"I'll do what I do best. Don't have to like it." Landeira needed to reserve his antagonism for a different audience. "How big is this rebel force?"

"Right now a few hundred."

"Jesus Christ. You intend to invade Guatemala with such an insignificant force? To accomplish what?"

"Didn't Wisner tell you the mission objective is to force the Guatemalan military to overthrow Árbenz? The invasion of rebel forces is just another means of exerting pressure."

"Wisner mentioned arms sanctions, the implied threat of U.S. invasion, a propaganda campaign, and a rebel invasion force. He never mentioned this invasion force only amounted to a few hundred. A bunch of unmotivated mercenaries does not constitute a viable force capable of achieving any military objective. Do I assume they are also not going to engage in guerilla tactics?"

"Only to the extent of targeting small Guatemalan remote garrisons. Capture weapons and destroy tanks and trucks. Avoiding any major engagement. The expectation is to demoralize the Guatemalan Army with simultaneous air and ground attacks sufficient for them depose Árbenz and install Armas."

"Why should the Army do that? Wisner even said Árbenz enjoys strong support among the officer corps."

"Because the Army by this point will be convinced that if they do not act to depose Árbenz clearly demanded by the United States, they invite invasion by the U.S. Marines."

Not that farfetched. The United States had a history of invading its small southern neighboring countries that did not bend to U.S. foreign policy interests.

* * * *

In the morning, Campbell arrived with Colonel Armas and another officer. Campbell was in a sour mood. As a deskbound intelligence officer, the rigors of the tropical climate left him sweating profusely. An entire day spent outside with the temperature climbing. Worse yet, Landeira was presenting him with a problem. Campbell resented Landeira insisting he come and view the situation. Also demanding he bring along Colonel Armas the rebel commander to explain the sorry state of his forces' readiness.

Arriving at the field headquarters in a jeep driven by a Nicaraguan sergeant, Campbell introduced Colonel Armas. Sharply dressed in starched battle dress with the U.S. insignia of a full colonel. Sidearm in a polished leather holster and belt. Polished boots. In contrast, Campbell looked wilted with his shirt clinging, mopping his forehead with a damp handkerchief.

"This better be goddamn important, Landeira. What exactly is the problem?"

Campbell spoke no Spanish, so in English Landeira said, "It's an exaggeration to call these troops soldiers. They cannot follow even basic instructions. Live fire scares the shit out them. The Guatemalan officers expected to lead this rabble know nothing of tactics."

"Well that's why you are here to turn them into a fighting force."

"You do not understand. Even with months of training, these guys will never become an effective military force. The marine instructors are first-rate. They feel the same way. You need to talk to them yourself."

Armas took offense at Landeira's remarks. "These are former Guatemalan soldiers and officers. You make them sound like raw recruits."

10

Switching to Spanish, "Sorry if this offends your professional pride, Colonel. I fought with Italian partisans with no military training during World War Two. They would cut your troops to pieces. Your officers are incompetent. Your soldiers do not represent a fighting force capable of taking on even small units of the Guatemalan army."

Campbell uttered, "Shit. What are you suggesting, Landeira?"

"Not suggesting anything. I didn't create this problem. Just telling you it cannot be fixed without months of intensive training and many more trainers."

Campbell shook his head. "We don't have that kind of time."

"Like I said, that is your problem. Tomorrow you and Colonel Armas can see for yourself. Draw your own conclusions. I have set up a live action simulation of a mission to attack a Guatemalan border garrison."

"Christ, I am not a military expert. That's your job."

Landeira could no longer contain his disgust. The larger issue was his falling out with the CIA. Putting an incompetent like Campbell in charge of a military operation another manifestation of the CIA's hubris.

"This is a stupid cockup. Whether Dulles or Wisner's idea, if this turns to shit, they will blame you, Campbell. I am trying to protect you."

"Protect me? Really? I didn't request you. They said you were highly experienced at this sort of thing. If you can't pull this off, it will be your head, Landeira, not my doing."

* * * *

The same four marine sergeant instructors worked with the small Guatemalan rebel force earlier for over two months when in Honduras. Circumventing the U.S. arms embargo, the Árbenz regime landed 2000 tons of weapons from Czechoslovakia on the *SS Alfhem* on May 15.

Landeira's predecessor CIA officer received instructions to destroy the weapons shipment. He hastily assembled a ten-man rebel demolition team from among the rebels. Without direct operational involvement by the U.S. marine instructors, the rebels botched the attempt to blow up the train carrying the weapons from the port of Puerto Barrios on the Caribbean coast to Guatemala City. The massive stock of weapons served instead to strengthen the capability of the Guatemalan regular army.

The political environment of a general strike in Honduras by United Fruit workers then forced the rebels to withdraw eastward to continue training in more politically friendly Nicaragua. The CIA reassigned Bart Landeira to assess the effectivity of the 480-man rebel force. After three weeks observation he concluded the small force was totally unreliable even for small-scale operations against even minor Guatemalan objectives.

Landeira's demonstration exercise consisted of a 90-man force attacking a defended position of 25 men. The target an abandoned barn the U.S. marines configured to simulate a Guatemalan border garrison signified by a Guatemalan flag. Landeira ordered the exercise without the marine instructors coordinating. A test of the capabilities of this questionable rebel force using only their own officers.

The attack plan called for three attacking forces converging on the target from different directions. The theory being infiltration of the Guatemalan border accomplished best using smaller units. Reading maps and navigating was a critical component along with radio communications. Demonstrating those capabilities represented the expectation of the exercise.

Landeira, Campbell, Armas, and the four marines followed in two jeeps behind one column designated Baker platoon. The purpose to act only as observers. Landeira intentionally chose this unit rather than Alpha platoon under the overall Guatemalan commander as a test of the leadership. The starting point for each 30-man platoon placed each a two-hour march from the objective. The area unfamiliar to all the Guatemalans but selected to simulate conditions expected when penetrating the Guatemalan border for real.

Baker platoon arrived within sight of the objective on schedule.

An unhappy Campbell said, "What's the big deal, Landeira? These guys navigated to the objective with no problem."

From there the situation deteriorated.

The officer in overall command of the operation a captain radioed his position from Alpha platoon. "Alpha platoon is in sight of objective to our west. Baker and Charlie platoons report your position."

The lieutenant commanding Baker platoon responded they were in position facing the objective to the north.

After repeated attempts to raise Charlie platoon, a minute later came a confusing response. "Charlie platoon reporting. Arrived at target."

"Signal your position relative to the objective," The captain radioed.

"Directly in front of the building facing north."

Landeira and the four marines looked at each other with questioning expressions. That was *their* position. Charlie platoon was nowhere in sight.

The background sound of heavy small arms firing suddenly came through the radio. "Taking heavy fire!"

"What the fuck?" The senior marine exclaimed, bewildered by the radio message. They were standing two hundred meters from the abandoned barn flying the Guatemalan flag. Where was Charlie platoon? *Taking fire?*

After a confused back and forth radio exchange, the sound of gunfire over the radio intensified. Even without the radio, they heard the sound in the distance.

Landeira immediately realized what likely happened. Grabbing the radio, he yelled, "The flag! The flag! What flag do you see?"

Moments later came the reply. "The Nicaraguan flag."

"Christ. The stupid fuckers attacked a Nicaraguan border garrison!" Landeira took out a map and pointed, "Here according to the sound of gunfire."

Landeira rushed to a jeep followed by Campbell and Armas.

"What the hell happened, Landeira?" Campbell shouted frantically as Landeira drove as fast as possible on the dirt road.

"Shut up, Campbell. I warned you about these guys."

"Did you set this up to fail?" Campbell said.

Landeira pulled the jeep to a skidding stop. "Open your mouth again and I'll dump you out of the jeep you stupid desk-jockey."

Landeira found his way to the Nicaraguan garrison. By now hearing no gunfire.

He pulled up on a slight rise of the dirt road. The marines in a second jeep stopped behind. The sight told the story. Disarmed Guatemalans stood in a tight group surrounded by a half dozen Nicaraguan border guards.

Approaching on foot, Landeira observed just how far the exercise went awry. Five Guatemalans lay in the tall grass. A Nicaraguan soldier applying a bandage to one.

Landeira recognized the Nicaraguan lieutenant he met days earlier when making arrangements accompanied by a senior Nicaraguan officer for the exercise to take place north of this garrison position.

The lieutenant angrily approached Landeira. "What the hell is this? Two of my men are seriously wounded."

"I will let the Guatemalan commander explain."

After telling Campbell and Armas to deal with the Nicaraguan officer, he joined the marines already shouting at the Guatemalan officer responsible for the disaster."

Landeira pushed the marines aside to deal with the officer personally. "You cannot even read a map, you stupid shit. Five of your men casualties against friendlies."

He intended the exercise to demonstrate to Campbell the lack of capabilities of the rebels to undertake basic military logistical operations. Never fathomed a catastrophe like this. His anger getting the best of him, he struck the Guatemalan lieutenant in the jaw knocking him to the ground.

Campbell, Armas, and the Nicaraguan lieutenant approached while witnessing Landeira's action. Armas made the mistake of confronting Landeira.

Armas said, "You struck one of my officers."

"Should have shot him. You command idiots not soldiers, Colonel."

Armas turned to Campbell, "I demand you arrest Landeira."

Now incensed, Landeira stepped aggressively toward Armas as Campbell attempted to intervene fearing what Landeira might do. Campbell's mistake.

Landeira grabbed Campbell's arm and dumped him hard to the ground using a judo move. Immediately Landeira turned on the startled Armas grabbing him by his fatigue shirt. With his face inches from Armas, he screamed, "You pompous shithead. Somebody should shoot you and save these idiots from dying for your stupidity. You have an undisciplined rabble not a fighting force."

"Jesus, Landeira have you gone nuts?" Campbell yelled while getting up with sand clinging to his sweat-soaked shirt. "Release the Colonel."

The aftermath left three dead Guatemalans, two others wounded, and two wounded Nicaraguans. The practice location and the Nicaraguan garrison were two miles apart. Landeira previously alerted the Nicaraguans to the exercise using the abandoned barn as a practice target to avoid just this type of misunderstanding.

Distressed over the catastrophe, Landeira felt a measure of responsibility. They were not ready for this exercise without their marine instructors supervising. The practice location, a barn with a collapsed roof displayed a makeshift flagpole with a Guatemalan flag. The marines rigged the target with simulated defenders using helmets sitting atop wood planks. All this fully explained to the rebel officers. The objective was to assess tactical proficiency. Map reading and navigation, communications coordination, and assault tactics.

Looking up at the Nicaraguan flag, Landeira realized something he did not previously consider. The Nicaraguan flag consists of two *horizontal* blue stripes separated by white. The Guatemalan flag flying over the simulated exercise target has two *vertical* blue stripes separated by white. A seemingly obvious difference, but maybe not to an inexperienced officer in command under stress to perform well.

Regardless why the outcome proved a deadly disaster, Landeira's pent up dissatisfaction pushed him over the edge. "You can have this mess, Campbell. Everything about this entire operation disgusts me. Wisner's folly from the beginning. He does not understand operations any more than you do. If you idiots use this miserable rabble led by this asshole colonel and his cashiered Guatemalan officers, you are nothing more than criminals. I'm out of here."

Campbell responded, "What the hell does that mean?"

"Means I quit. Fuck the CIA. I will call Wisner myself but feel free to get to him first."

With that, Landeira took one of the jeeps leaving Campbell and Armas and the four marines to deal with the aftermath. Landeira drove nonstop to Managua. After checking into a hotel, he made a flight reservation to Miami for the following morning. Settling into the hotel bar he felt a sense of relief. This was not simply a rash emotion move. No regrets. Too long in coming. Should have quit after Egypt. Certainly after Iran. Joining the CIA became a protracted existential crisis.

* * * *

The fiasco in Nicaragua did not deter Frank Wisner from pursuing *Project Success* to conclusion. Wisner attributed Landeira's warnings and expletive laced telephone call to a mental breakdown of a good field operative. Yet the overall efforts of the CIA played out as dark tragicomedy.

Relocated to Honduras and El Salvador, the 480-man rebel force split into four formations planning to cross the Guatemalan border at widely separated locations. The objective to conduct harassing raids and sow panic in the capital. Simultaneously, rebel aircraft would buzz government buildings in Guatemala City and drop small bombs.

Before the planned day to begin the invasion, Salvadoran police spotted the formation deployed in the south and arrested all the rebels. They confiscated a large cache of weapons including 21 machineguns and jailed the rebels. Another formation of 122 rebels encountered a garrison of 30 police. After a 36-hour battle, the rebels lost 92 men as causalities or captured. The following day, the largest force of 170 rebels suffered a similar defeat while attacking the port city of Puerto Barrios. Police aided by dock-workers arrested a large number of rebels and drove off the remainder who fled back across the border into Honduras, refusing to take up arms again.

A formation led personally by Armas struggled in taking their objective a few miles from the border while encountering only light resistance. Another formation succeeded in capturing a small Guatemalan police garrison three miles from the border. These meager results

on the ground and random air assaults failed to inflict real damage, nor induce panic in the Guatemalan population.

U.S. combined overt and covert actions eventually made clear the United States would not back off without regime change. With the loss of Guatemalan military support, President Árbenz bowed to the inevitable and resigned ten days later, seeking asylum in the Mexican Embassy in Guatemala City. After turning over his presidential powers over to Col. Enrique Diaz. In a final act of defiance to the U.S., Diaz refused to negotiate with Armas.

On the same day that Árbenz left office, a P-38 without markings, operated by the CIA and piloted by an American, bombed the British registered freighter *SS Springfjord* in Puerto San José with napalm. The freighter was loading a mixed cargo including mostly coffee. Guatemala claimed the aircraft frown from Nicaragua belonged to the insurgency. The reason for the attack unclear. Another piece of damning evidence in America's obvious heavy-handed interference in Central America.

Landeira followed events in Guatemala from a hotel in Miami. Nothing surprising, just disappointing. Guatemala would soon join the fraternity of dictatorships in the Americas. Now free of the CIA, introspection followed in an attempt to discover where he went wrong for so long.

Blaming his anxiety and depression on the excesses of the CIA was a flawed excuse. He could have left long before Guatemala. In truth, he never directed his future. Undecided about pursuing a career in journalism following his undergraduate degree, he let his father persuade him to consider corporate law. That poor choice abruptly altered by World War Two.

Even after the war ended, he opted to take the easier path of the job offer to remain in peacetime U.S. intelligence. In retrospect, a choice of convenience when he saw no viable alternative other than returning to a pre-war legal career in his father's law practice.

Now set adrift, introspection prompted a more candid assessment. Roaming about the world doing secretive work served his avoidance of close relationships. Easy enough with estrangement from family. Although possessing a normal sex drive, his profession became an excuse for avoiding sustained romantic involvements. Skilled in social environments, he accumulated acquaintances but no real friends. In a moment of clarity, he saw himself too much like his father. A disturbing conclusion.

Although arriving in Florida weeks earlier, he avoided contacting his father. He wanted first to position his next move to deflect renewed pressure to join the law firm. Still accredited by the Miami Herald, journalism seemed the most attractive prospect. Although senior management of the Miami Herald unofficially knew of his association with the CIA, his journalism role was real and substantive. Tell them he was relocating to Havana as his base of operations to cover the Caribbean. Havana seemed a familiar refuge from his past.

The thought occurred that he might do an investigative piece on United Fruit Corporation. Campbell alluded to their involvement in the political turmoil in Guatemala. How far did their influence extend to other banana producing countries in the Americas? What was the role of United Fruit with repeated U.S. military interventions in the *Banana Wars* of the early part of the 20th century?

18

Chapter 2

Having left the CIA over a year ago, life was good. Not perfect. Not entirely settled into a new life but free of doing something he despised. Happy with his choice to come to Havana, Cuba. An unlikely decision that immediately proved a welcome oasis after years of far-flung government assignments.

Although Cuban-American, he grew up in Tampa, Florida. Memories of Cuba came largely from occasional trips and summers during his youth. The last trip with his father was in 1940. Fresh out of law school, the trip more than just visiting extended family in Cuba. During that trip, Bart Landeira began to understand the unconventional role his father played in shuttling back and forth between Miami and Havana. His father's work went beyond managing the financial affairs of the family's Cuban enterprises. As a way of impressing his son, he told of his unrelated legal consulting work involving foreign investment and public finance. Without divulging details, he bragged of his relationship with the newly elected Cuban president, Fulgencio Batista. A former army officer with a colorful past in Cuban politics.

Only since settling in Havana while taking up a journalistic career in earnest as a foreign correspondent for the Miami Herald did Bart Landeira began to suspect the scope of his father's influence in Havana.

Maximiliano Landeira became acquainted with Fulgencio Batista during the war years after Batista's election as president in 1940. In a bloodless coup in 1952, Batista returned to power, but under different governing circumstances. Batista now ruled Cuba by decree as a dictator firmly backed by the Cuban military. Max Landeira deftly exploited his earlier connections.

Delighted with his son leaving government work, Max remained disappointed that he still rejected his overtures to join the law firm. Pleasantly surprised when his son declared his intent to set up residence in Havana as a news correspondent, the elder Landeira insisted on accompanying him to visit family. Ever hopeful of still enticing his son to join him, his son's decision to reside in Havana might possibly be a start in that direction. Although still guarded about revealing any details, Max could not resist boasting of his stature in the affairs of Cuba. Given the current questionable reputation of the Cuban government, a dubious admission.

While closely supported by the United States government, the world recognized the Batista regime as corrupt and repressive. Often compared to the dictatorship of Rafael Trujillo of the Dominican Republic. A populist revolutionary movement continued to gain traction in the rural areas of Cuba. Yet Havana had become the world's pleasure destination of the Western hemisphere. The favored venue of the rich and famous. Gambling, sex, drugs. Showcased with an exotic backdrop of a subtropical climate, beautiful beaches, and a lively friendly culture. Only 228 air miles from Miami, Florida with multiple daily scheduled commercial flights made Havana seem almost a part of the United States.

While finding Batista's authoritarian rule of Cuba distressing, Landeira intended to report on the goings on without investing personal feelings. No longer was he a paid mercenary replacing regimes on questionable orders from others. Now just an observer. He might not like what he sees, but this is Cuba's unfortunate history since independence from foreign rule in 1902. In many ways, still a colony suffering economic dependence on the United States and plagued by successive corrupt governments.

Returning after fifteen years, Bart Landeira increasingly found himself feeling Cuban. In his youth, he thought himself a *Yanqui,* the Spanish variant for Yankee, or North American. After all, he lived in Florida, educated in America, and fought for America. Cuba was someplace he occasionally visited with his father. An exotic yet foreign place. The cultural connection more that of his father's generation.

Now matured and disgusted with his participation in U.S. international misconduct, Cuba seemed a refuge to reset his bearings on life. Arriving by plane in Havana in early April, the weather was spectacular. A bright sunny day in the seventies. Springtime. Before the beginning of the steamy summer and the hurricane season. As the Pan Am DC-6 made its approach for landing at José Martí Airport southwest of the center of Havana, Landeira looked down on the majestic northern coastline of Cuba. Beautiful beaches and an archipelago of offshore barrier islands stretching to the east. As an avid sailor, Cuba's connection with the sea confirmed his decision.

Although Landeira had no interest in gambling, the luxurious hotels and casinos gave Havana a distinctive elegance balanced against the charm of old-world Spanish influence. Different from his memories, yet a pleasant surprise. Landeira was an urban creature. Havana was no backwater. While the length of Cuba stretched for hundreds of miles into a varied rural topography, cosmopolitan Havana remained distinctly vibrant.

Havana also proved a good fit. As the center of power and Cuba's tourism trade, it proved a logical base of operation from which to cover Latin America. A city with a population of 1.4 million, it possessed a varied character. Dominated by magnificent views of the Gulf of Mexico, the northern seacoast sector displayed the city's wealth. Here were the newly constructed grand hotels and casinos. International visitors rarely left this part of Havana. Expensive restaurants competed with colorful local eating establishments and bars. The affluent tourist could choose his pleasures. Luxury accommodations, dining, high-stakes gambling, or more debauched diversions. Sex and drugs available for any taste or wallet. Safety assured by a police state

21

protecting its economic interests. The American Mafia-controlled casinos provided a safe gambling environment free from cheating. Tourists could experience Havana's exotic luxury while titillated by its reputation as sin city.

Along Havana's seashore ran the Malecón, the great boulevard protected by a seawall from seasonal storms lashing sea. A popular promenade for everyone, including locals. It ran from Old Havana to the wealthy Vedado district of expensive homes and apartments, many with breathtaking views of the Gulf of Mexico.

Landeira occupied a fourth floor apartment in the Vedado. According to his father, one of the family business subsidiaries owned the apartment building. Landeira was initially reluctant to accept the largess knowing it was another inducement to join the family business. One look at the well-decorated apartment with a grand view of the sea overcame his reluctance.

While Landeira family enterprises spanned the breadth of Cuba from sugarcane production and sugarcane mills in the eastern province of Camagüey to tobacco cultivation in the most western province of Pinar del Rio, they also diversified from their agrarian roots. In Havana, they produced rum and cigars. Led by Maximiliano, the family heavily invested in Havana commercial real estate before the start of the hotel and casino boom.

Like any great city, moving away from the waterfront revealed greater Havana spread out to include middleclass and poor neighborhoods. Self-contained enclaves with commercial establishments. Ethnically Cuban, fluent in Cuban-Spanish, Landeira immediately gravitated to this truer character of Havana in these neighbors. The authentic food, the natural conviviality, and the Cuban love of life.

Soon after arriving in Havana in early 1955, Bart Landeira fell under the spell of *La Habana Vieja*, Old Havana. The uniquely Cuban architecture of Old Havana provided a perfect backdrop for the spirit of the true *personas de la Habana*. The *Destilerias de Ron Landeira* and *Habanos de Landeira* factories were located in the southern sector of the Old Havana district, east of the central railway station. As a foreigner, his immersion into Havana life came about in large part because of his Uncle Tomás.

Bart Landeira was not close to his father's extended family. For that matter, his relationship with his father was often contentious. A lifelong contest between two strong-willed individuals. His father a product of his culture and personal success. Bart blamed himself for not resisting his father's pressure to attend law school. While rationalizing the usefulness of a law degree, the reality of practicing law as a profession never held interest. World War Two saved him.

As for the extended family on his father's side, even at an early age, Landeira found the atmosphere foreign. The three sons of the aging patriarch ran the family's extensive land holdings since the death of Bart's paternal grandfather in 1936. The dynasty founded originally by his namesake and great-great grandfather in the mid-19th century. An immigrant from Spain, he acquired land, planted sugarcane, continually expanding his holdings with a growing slave workforce. A hundred years later by the 1950s, the family was among the wealthiest in Cuba.

As so often the situation in family business dynasties, management succession becomes a serious problem. The three aging elder brothers had only two sons between them. Wives and daughters played no part in Landeira business affairs.

Suffering serious health problems, the oldest brother Enrique relinquished management of the vast sugar plantations and sugar mills in Camagüey to his son several years earlier. With Maximiliano managing financial affairs from Tampa and Tomás running rum and cigar operations in Havana, that added pressure for inducing Bartolo to join the business having left government service.

At best ambivalent to Landeira Cuban business enterprises, Bart did not find his uncles or cousins particularly inviting. Uncle Tomás the exception.

Tomás Landeira took an immediate liking to his nephew. None of the overt pressure cloaked as familial obligation by his father, Uncle Enrique, and Enrique's son Rafael. Uncle Tomás instead displayed a genuine affection for his nephew Bartolo.

Having three daughters, Bartolo's unexpected arrival in Havana was like discovering a son he never had.

* * * *

On that first trip back to Havana, Bart fell under the spell of Old Havana when Uncle Tomás took him to the rum distillery and cigar manufacturing operations. A delightful experience after a week of his father's shepherding him first to Havana's acclaimed new glamour attractions followed by a flight to Camagüey to the family enclave on the original sugarcane plantation.

Visiting Camagüey brought back disturbing memories. Once old enough to understand, the visible contrast of the wrenching poverty of field workers contrasted with the elegance of the enormous plantation house. Asking impolite questions, he understood the sugarcane cutters, the *macheteros*, only worked four months out of the year at harvest time. Unemployed the rest of the year was a constant struggle on the margins for survival. There was no other work other than sugarcane. It reminded impressionable Bart Landeira of photos of the American South. Back breaking, dangerous work. Few schools to educate their children. The predominantly illiterate Cuban sugarcane cutters of the 20th century little better off from African slaves of a hundred years earlier.

The contrast with Havana and even other major Cuban urban centers was profound. The literacy rate in Havana was one of the highest in Latin America. A thriving middleclass. A highly advanced medical care system that regrettably did not extend to the vast rural areas. Cuba society sharply divided between urban and rural.

Once his father returned to Tampa, genial Uncle Tomás took a special interest in his nephew. Anxious to show Bart Old Havana, he took him to his office in the Landeira cigar factory.

"These narrow streets and the decaying elegance remind me of old towns in Italy," Bart said to his uncle. Old Havana was not far from the fabulous new hotels and casinos and playground of the rich and famous, yet a venerable city with a rich past.

"Well Old Havana is old," Tomás said as he drove the narrow streets with its brightly painted buildings. "Not as old as Italy but going back to the 16th century. Interesting that you see elegance in these crumbling buildings. Yet I feel comfortable here. I would prefer living here instead of the Vedado. Inez however would not agree."

Tomás knew only that his nephew served in Italy during the war then some sort of government service during the intervening years, but knew few details.

Tomás Landeira lived with his wife Inez in the same building where Max Landeira offered his son a furnished luxury apartment. The Vedado district was upscale Havana close to the sea. Too good for Bart to turn down at least until he got settled. Close to the political and economic center of Havana. Ideal for his journalistic work. Convenient for resuming his passion for sailing.

"I can see why you like this part of Havana, Uncle. The sounds and smells are uniquely Cuban. Where we live is cosmopolitan. Too many tourists. Noisy. But for me with my love of sailing, being close to the water is enough reason to live there."

"Sailor? I thought you were in the army."

Bart smiled. "I was in the army. Sailing is something I enjoyed since a kid. Had my own sailboat growing up in Tampa. Learned to sail from an old expatriate Cuban my father hired."

Bart learned the old Cuban was a former rumrunner during Prohibition. Likely, someone his father knew as Bart later pieced together various bits of information about his father's past.

"Little opportunity for sailing these last fifteen years."

"What have you been doing since the end of the war? Your father was rather vague. Even vague about what you did during the war."

Vague, because Bart never revealed his employment in the CIA. As to his wartime service in the OSS, he avoided discussing details even with his father. Impossible to convey the circumstances of surviving under constant danger behind enemy lines and repeatedly killing the enemy silently.

"I worked for the American foreign service after the war. Classified work so I can never talk about it."

"Classified?"

"Secret government work. My public identity was a journalist. Allowed me to travel without raising questions. All I do now is journalism."

Arriving at the cigar factory, Bart was less than enthusiastic but wanted to appear gracious to his uncle. Having observed the grueling demands of sugarcane harvesting, he expected the work of rolling cigars another example of the hard life of working class Cubans.

Entering the industrial building, the pungent aroma of tobacco dominated the air. Unexpectedly, music played from speakers. The factory floor consisted of long rows of tables populated mostly by women of all ages. Sadly, an expression of another form of sweatshop.

Yet the seemingly mind-numbing work of rolling cigars belied the attitude of these women. They talked while their fingers moved almost automatically to produce uniform hand-rolled cigars. The environment gave the impression of a social gathering.

Puffing away on his cigar, several women greeted Tomás. Not only as the boss, but someone to which they felt affection. One middle-aged woman said, "Good morning, Don Tomás. And who is this handsome gentleman?"

Tomás Landeira beamed, "My nephew, Bartolo. Came from Florida to work here in Havana."

Mischievously she replied, "Wonderful. Perhaps I could show him the delights of Havana."

"Behave yourself, Ursula. You are a married woman," Tomás responded to her banter with a broad smile.

"My husband is very understanding, Don Tomás."

Walking down the rows of women, the warm personal relationship between his uncle and his employees struck Bart as a remarkably friendly work environment. His uncle knew each by name, stopping to exchange a few words. Asked about family. The interaction genuine.

Stopping by one woman in her thirties, his uncle said, "This is Zamora. She can roll perfect cigars faster than anyone can. Watch her hands."

Her hands literally a blur as she performed the same intricate moves as the others but at mesmerizing speed. Intrigued, Bart bent down trying to follow her fingers. Zamora slowed her work to demonstrate the rolling technique then returned to her accelerated pace.

"Amazing. Truly amazing, Señora."

Leaving the factory, his uncle suggested lunch before visiting the rum distillery. Although wealthy, Tomás preferred a favorite Old Havana neighborhood modest establishment. Here again, his uncle received a warm welcome, embracing the owner and proudly introducing Bart.

Tomás exhibited a distinctly different personality from his two brothers. Bart's father Maximiliano and older uncle Enrique manifested their patrician status in every aspect of personal and professional life. In contrast, Tomás was engaging with genuine warmth toward everyone. Bart wondered if having only daughters might have added to his easy-going demeanor in contrast to his domineering brothers and Bart's only male cousin.

"My favorite restaurant, Bartolo. Authentic food. A favorite of Cuban professionals. No tourists."

Obviously, a regular as his uncle made the rounds of greeting staff and even a couple of patrons. Considering his uncle's girth, probably his usual lunch location. Uncle Tomás enjoyed food.

"They make the best mojo criollo sauce served over chicken, pork, or fish. I recommend the pork."

The waitress immediately brought over two bottles of Cuban Hatuey beer without asking.

"Go ahead and order for me, Uncle."

Lunch arrived like a feast along with more beer. A hearty portion of pork covered in sauce with rice and black beans. Crusty bread similar in texture to a French baguette. Flavors invoking long forgotten memories.

"Does Tia Inez know you take lunch like this, Uncle?"

Among forkfuls of food, "She will understand today is special. My nephew I have not seen for so many years. Now coming to live in Havana. Having you here is wonderful, Bartolo. So much to talk about." He laid a hand on Bart's forearm.

After a two-hour lunch and several beers, Bart was ready for a nap. He hoped his uncle did not indulge this way every day. His appearance suggested otherwise. With a cigar continuously in his mouth, an unhealthy lifestyle for a man of sixty-five.

Arriving at the rum distillery, the thought struck Bart this likely played into another vice for his uncle. For a man who enjoyed his pleasures, work involving manufacturing liquor and cigars while out of reach each workday from the moderating influence of wife and dotting daughters was perfect.

While touring the distillery, Uncle Tomás provided a general explanation of the rum distillation process. The stainless steel vats turned the sugar in the molasses sugarcane gruel into alcohol by fermentation with the addition of yeast. The tall distillation pot stills cooked the fermented base then cooled the vapor condensing into a high-alcohol raw product. Finally, endless rows of wooden barrels on racks and much larger wooden barrels for blending and aging into finished product ready for bottling.

"If you are interested, I will let my master distiller explain the finer points of rum making."

"I am a Scotch and Bourbon drinker, Uncle. I know nothing about rum. Isn't rum used mostly in mixed drinks like Cuba Libre?" Bart said.

"Not necessarily. My aged Landeira Rum is excellent when enjoyed straight. Come, we shall go to my office and I shall show you."

Bart was right about rum being probably another of his uncle's vices. Unlike the business-like office at the cigar factory, his office at the distillery was a man's hideaway. Two French doors opened out on a balcony with ornate wrought iron railings. Covering the textured plaster office walls were several brightly colored quality paintings by Cuban artists. One wall contained a beautiful antique desk next to a small bar with shelves fashioned from wood matching the desk.

On the bar was a service of cut crystal glasses and a cigar humidor. On the shelves behind the bar, were rows of rum of many different labels.

Bart declined the offer of a cigar as he settled into a comfortable leather chair. After lighting up another fresh cigar, his uncle said, "Let me introduce you to unadorned aged rum. You might be surprised."

Bart smiled to indulge his uncle.

"First let me introduce our family's rum." He brought two bottles to the small round table between the two easy chairs. "I age my rum for at least several years before bottling. Aging in wooden barrels is what gives the color to rum. Cheaper rum is not barrel-aged."

"The difference between these two labels is the aging?"

"Precisely. The bottle simply labeled aged Cuban rum is good quality rum. Accounts for eighty percent of our sales. Now the other labelled *reserva* aged ten years is much better. Here take a sip of the lesser aged product."

Bart took a sip and rolled it around in his mouth. Never having tried rum neat, he was surprised.

"Now try the reserve. Note the darker caramel color."

"Yes. Almost the color of my favorite Scotch."

After taking a sip, he looked at his uncle and smiled. "Excellent. I taste the difference. A pleasant sweet note in the finish, undoubtedly because its origin is sugarcane. But you are right, complexities of taste just like whiskey."

"Most definitely. Now I want to show you something. You see I have a number of bottles of rum on the shelf. Rums from all over the Caribbean. Barbados, Martinique, Antigua, Dominican Republic, Jamaica, and of course Cuba. Important to understand the competition you know."

Tomás got up and pulled a bottle from the shelf. "My reserve is very good aged rum. Now try this. Everyone has different tastes, but I for one find this rum exceptional. Cuban. A distillery here in Havana. Give me your opinion, Bartolo."

Tomás poured a measure into a fresh glass handing it Bart.

Even as a newcomer to rum, this rum tasted markedly different. A well-practiced palate for the subtleties of Scotch and Bourbon, he could appreciate this rum as something spectacular.

"I see what you mean, Uncle. This is extraordinary. Hard to describe other than to say I like this very much. Let me see the label."

"So this is your main competitor for your high-end label?"

"Not necessarily. Too small a producer. The owner, Augustin Montero, is the master distiller. Third generation. Same as my distilling master Gustavo Rodriguez. They are both experts but Montero has the magic. You see, everyone makes rum the same way. However, the devil is in the details. Everything from where the sugarcane comes from to the unique characteristics of the distillation pots, to aging, and blending. More art than science."

Bart took another sip of the Montero rum, appreciating the subtleties.

His uncle said, "I met Augustin Montero a couple of times. Tried to feel him out about selling his distillery and working for me. Complimented me on Landeira reserve rum, but politely said his family business was not for sale."

"Well, according to my father, *Destilerias de Ron Landeira* is very profitable."

"Yes. With these new hotels and the casinos, our business has grown in the last couple of years. The wealthy American tourist trade. Much of that business is your father's doing."

"How's that?"

"Because your father knows everyone in Havana. Put the word out to the casino managers and all the best restaurants. Makes my work as salesman easy."

Bart's expression prompted his uncle to reply. "I know you and your father have your difficulties. I could see that when he was here. But you know he is proud of you though, Bartolo. He worried terribly about your safety during the war. Knowing little about what you did, he understood it was dangerous. Harder yet because he received so few letters from you."

"Not by my choice, Uncle. Still not allowed to reveal what I did during the war. I can only say that much of the time I operated behind enemy lines. I was not in the regular army. Communicating back home often impossible.

"Even when I was young, Father and I fought. He wants to run things his way and I want to run my own affairs."

Tomás sighed deeply. "Yes, I understand. Maximiliano was always strong-willed. Our father, your grandfather, thought him the smartest. Sent him off to the United States to get an education. Largely because of his work shuttling between Tampa and Havana, our family enterprises have flourished. He understands how to make money by investments. Knows both the United States and Cuba. How to use laws in both countries to create opportunity. Told me once the business people he deals with in the States think he is a Yanqui."

"No question about Father being smart. I did not leave government work however to go into business with him. I tried that before the war. It didn't work out. Before getting a law degree, I studied journalism. Worked as a journalist for many years while also doing secret work for the government. A way of staying in the shadows. Journalism is what I want to continue doing. That's why I came to Havana. To cover the Caribbean and Central America for the Miami Herald."

Chapter 3

A fter arriving in Havana, Bart Landeira settled into a new life as a correspondent for the Miami Herald. This time fully devoted to reporting on the Caribbean and Central America. The Herald like many major newspapers knew their foreign correspondents worked closely with the CIA. Public hysteria over communism remained high, despite the discrediting of Senator Joseph McCarthy's headline making accusations of communist infiltration in U.S. governmental institutions. Landeira told the managing editor he is no longer active with the CIA. Without elaborating, he left the implication of some remaining association with the CIA. It might prove useful in the future.

Spending considerable research effort, he submitted a series of investigative pieces titled *The Sordid History of United Fruit*. It went beyond his routine reporting work for the Herald. A project intended as an act of rebellion. Easy enough to paint United Fruit as a villain. Its aggressive business tactics created a monopoly in the banana trade. In the process, it depressed wages of the agricultural workforce. Always hypersensitive to land reform movements and threats of unionization, they used their economic clout to coerce governments. What interested him more was collusion with U.S. foreign policy. An overarching policy of imperialism cloaked in the anti-communism hysteria of the time.

An opportunity to slam U.S. foreign policy. He must avoid revealing American clandestine activities related to his personal experience, therefore, he could not directly condemn the covert methods of the CIA. Everything he did in the CIA remained classified. Exposing such detail risked prosecution. He could only use those experiences as a blueprint for exposing interference in the affairs of other countries to bolster U.S. objectives in the Cold War. Everywhere in the world, each country chose sides, or one of the superpowers attempted to choose for them.

Landeira selected United Fruit as the proxy villain with which to tar U.S. foreign policy with the same brush. American intrusive foreign policy in the Western hemisphere ran parallel to the interests of United Fruit.

Landeira titled a serialized series of articles *Banana Politics – The Unholy Partnership of United Fruit and the Government of the United States*. The introductory opening set the background.

Associated Press International
Bart Landeira of the Miami Herald

The story of United Fruit parallels the rise of the United States in becoming the most powerful country in the world by the turn of the 20th century. Stemming from the Monroe Doctrine of 1823, the young United States declared to European powers that the Americas were the sole sphere of the United States. A warning against European colonialism.

Historians arguably cite the Spanish-American War of 1898 as the first major exercise of U.S. imperialism. A contrived war backed by support of the American populace for military intervention following reports of Spanish concentration camps in Cuba and Puerto Rico with likely exaggerated death tolls. Sending the battleship USS Maine into Havana harbor intended as a show of strength. When the Maine exploded with significant loss of U.S. naval personnel, it ignited hostilities. The United States military quickly overwhelmed the inferior Spanish army and naval forces capturing Cuba, Puerto Rico, Guam, and the Philippines. America had its first colonies.

The United States solidified these new acquisitions through occupation and recurring military interventions throughout the Caribbean and Central America during the

20th century. Nicaragua, the Dominican Republic, Haiti, and Guatemala. Actions directed at controlling the affairs of these small agrarian countries to advantage U.S. political hegemony in the Americas.

In the Roosevelt Corollary of 1904, President Theodore Roosevelt stated the right for the United States to intervene in conflicts should Europe consider military measures to force repayment of Latin American debt. In 1912, President William Howard Taft explained his concept of exercising financial power instead of military force to further U.S. foreign interests. Dollar Diplomacy simply became an adjunct to military intervention rather than an alternative. The exercise of economic power became a cornerstone of U.S. foreign policy of subsequent administrations continuing to this day. A perfect pretext for United Fruit to participate as an integral part of American economic imperialism.

From the time of its formation, United Fruit found their interests aligned with regional American foreign policy. The pejorative label *Banana Republic* stemmed largely from the actions of the United Fruit Company in Honduras, Costa Rica, and Guatemala.

To exert economic power, United Fruit employed proven tactics. Establish monopolies of such economic importance it allowed for pressuring local government for preferential tax treatment. Purchasing extensive tracts of land for future cultivation while denying it to competition including even small indigenous farmers controlled prices.

The company formed in 1899 with the merger of two competitors, Tropical Trading and Transport Company and Boston Fruit Company. The new corporation combined plantations, logistics, and markets in the United States for bananas. Tropical Trading and Transport brought to the corporation its plantations and railroads in Central America along with its markets in the American south and southeast. Boston Fruit provided its plantations in the West Indies, a fleet of steamships, and the Northeast American Market.

The merger architected by creative business lawyer Bradley Palmer resolved cash flow problems of the separate enterprises while simultaneously combining their respective holdings into a powerful corporation. With their control of transport logistics, United Fruit aggressively continued establishing monopolies in the entire supply chain of bananas. Palmer proceeded to enlarge their banana monopoly by acquiring or buying shares in fourteen smaller competitors. The assurance of a continuing market with United Fruit controlling 80 percent of banana imports into the United States provided sufficient inducement. If small producers did not join United Fruit, the economic implications became clear.

An influential American corporation headquartered in Boston, United Fruit maintains a strong lobby in Washington. The interests of United Fruit and the government of the United States converge in the practice of installing right wing totalitarian regimes. Any political movement espousing social reforms raises the specter of socialism. Socialism of any form stokes fear of communism. For United Fruit, totalitarian regimes mean receptivity to control by corruption. As a major American corporation with economic clout, ensuring monopolies depresses wages offsetting the cost of bribes. A marriage of mutual self-interest ignoring the human cost of those effected in underdeveloped countries.

From setting this background in the initial piece, Landeira launched a series of articles on specific examples of abusive practices of United Fruit. Each episode of the corporation's sordid history appeared as a serialized newspaper feature over a period of many Sundays. Following its newspaper run, Colliers Magazine picked up his lengthier unabridged manuscript for serialization.

Well-researched and footnoted, the articles portrayed the United States in unflattering terms. Detailing official collusion with a greedy corporation to oppress the poorest workers of these struggling countries subtly suggested Washington corruption. The third leg of this unholy trinity was the brutal dictatorships brought into power.

An artfully constructed body of work sharply poking U.S. foreign policy in the eye. One reviewer apply characterized it, *'The master villain of Bart Landeira's investigative series of wrongdoing in the Americas is United States foreign policy, overshadowing the crude corporate greed of United Fruit.'*

Landeira was careful to sight public sources for the messy Guatemala intervention where he possessed access to classified information. No details of his experiences in the Guatemalan regime change appeared in print. As a closing to that first article, he did however sight United Fruit's most recent exercise in banana politics.

> Regime change in Guatemala is the latest act of United Fruit's political interference in the affairs of a Latin American country. United Fruit deemed modest land reform policies of Guatemalan President Árbenz unfavorable to their corporate interests. Consistent with their past excesses, United Fruit conspired to convince the Eisenhower administration that Árbenz was tilting Guatemala toward communism. Buying into the communism hysteria, the full weight of the United States government conspired to force the Guatemalan Army to depose the democratically elected Árbenz. The result, a right wing military junta under the thumb of the United States. The obvious heavy-handed involvement widely condemned by the international community.

The expected backlash from the political right in Washington meant his material hit a nerve. Exactly his intention. Landeira concluded his series of articles on United Fruit with another jab at the United States.

> In the early part of the century, United Fruit ceased growing bananas in Cuba and transitioned their acreage to sugarcane. Populated with too many small growers, they could not create the monopolies that afforded them leverage. They began moving to better opportunities in Central America. They instead leased their Cuban land holdings becoming the largest distributor of Cuban sugar with their logistical investments in railroads and shipping.
>
> The rebel Fidel Castro grew up in relative privilege. While not part of the elite large landowner Cuban society, Castro's father did very well growing sugarcane on 23,000 acres of land leased from United Fruit and selling the harvest to the Company. It afforded the young Castro a Jesuit education. Two years ago, Castro led a small group of rebels in an attack on the Cuban Army Moncada Barracks in Santiago de Cuba on July 26, 1953. A desperate ill-fated action with hopes of igniting a popular uprising to overthrow Fulgencio Ba-

tista. In an ironic twist, strongman Batista was born into the poverty of the sugarcane working class.

Imprisoned, Batista pardoned Castro last year as part of a general amnesty. A move he may regret later. Castro fled to Mexico but reports indicate he continues fomenting a Cuban revolution. In exile, Castro memorialized his nascent rebellion in the name *Movimiento 26 Julio* or M 26-7. Good marketing for a resistance movement with as yet no organized following.

Living in a police state, Cubans may empathize with Castro's resistance but are not yet ready to take to the streets in active support. The only exception perhaps a group of university students known as the *Directorio Revolucionario Estudiantil.*

* * * *

Sitting in his son's apartment, Max Landeira said, "I read your series of articles appearing these past weeks in the Herald. Did you come here to make trouble?"

It had been over a month since his father's last trip to Havana. Max Landeira knew his son worked for the CIA rather than the State Department. With Batista closely supported by American intelligence, Max Landeira became closely acquainted with the U.S. ambassador. As a Batista confidant and financial adviser deeply involved with American investment, shuttling between Tampa and Havana, Max Landeira avoided revealing the extent of his association with the Batista regime to this son.

"Whatever pissed you off enough to leave government I hoped you left that behind? I envisioned you possibly joining the law firm in Tampa. I understand your coming instead to Havana to pursue a career in journalism. Apparently, you are still angry. This material you are writing is editorializing, not reporting."

Historically, their interaction frequently turned into argument.

"Are you just being a critic of the press or does my perspective bother you, Father?"

"Of course it bothers me. You are an American citizen. You even worked for the American government in a confidential capacity. Yet you make the United States government out to be gangsters."

"That's because they operate as gangsters beyond U.S. borders. I know that first-hand. That includes here in Cuba. Although I do not know details, the level of Cuban corruption is pervasive. Batista is just another petty dictator. A 40,000-man army keeps him in power, courtesy of the United States. The same military and economic benevolence the United States uses in Central America and other places around the world to advance its political interests."

"You need to be careful with talk like that."

"Yes, I am aware I am living in a police state. Political opposition and troublesome journalists often disappear."

"Come now, you exaggerate. That may describe Trujillo in the Dominican Republic but Cuba is different. It does not operate like the United States, but circumstances here are no different from a U.S. territory like Puerto Rico. A much more varied economic environment in fact. Look at what Havana is becoming as the luxury getaway for wealthy Americans. The growth spurred by American investment."

"Like the American Mafia?"

Max Landeira shook his head in frustration. "Come on, Son. You know the way the world functions. Money is the lubricant that drives everything. Money is amoral. By that, I mean morally neutral. Only people are immoral. It is public knowledge the Mafia is financing much of the new hotel and casino projects. Do you expect Cuba to reject investment fueling Cuba's economic boom? Look at the thousands of jobs created. Good jobs. Diversifying the Cuban economy."

"Likely fueling corruption of the Batista regime."

"Unfortunately, corruption is a fact of life in Cuba. An inevitable result of sudden economic opportunity. The Havana hospitality industry is like finding gold or oil."

"Journalism is about looking for facts. Hidden facts," Bart said. "Those that hide facts do so for their own self-serving reasons knowing disclosure can be damaging. It does not matter the motivation of those hiding information. It is discovery of previously unknown information that is news. When you discover incriminating information about bad characters that is the most satisfying work. The Mafia and Fulgencio Batista are newsworthy. Police state excesses are news.

"I did not come to Cuba however to conduct investigative journalism on Batista. I came here to decompress from years of stress bred from disgust. Things I cannot discuss. Things fundamentally I disagreed with. Things I could no longer live with. Coming to Cuba is a way of starting a new life. Journalism is intense work if it has meaning. I am not interested in covering Havana nightlife. Corruption, injustice, murder, social unrest have serious consequences. That's what makes journalism meaningful.

"I am here as an observer to report facts. I will report information unflattering to the governing regime but I am not unmindful of the circumstances, Father."

Max replied, "It is more than just Cuba. You must be cautious. Some of the countries you cover in Latin America are exceedingly dangerous for journalists poking into the shadows. Cuba not so much. But even Cuba is not the United States."

"I appreciate that, Father. Having survived the war, I have an acute sense for danger. I am neither a crusader nor martyr. Yet I am unwilling however to turn a blind eye to criminal activity."

Sensing the last comment directed toward him, Max decided to tone down the argument. They were never going to agree philosophically. It was time he took some ownership in improving the relationship with his only son.

"Well I came to Havana this trip to spend some quality time with you. I did not see you for three years during the war. After that, only infrequently as you wandered the world doing whatever secret work you did for the government. I am sixty-two. Want to make up for all the time I missed with my son.

"Happy you are living in the same building as Tomás and Inez. They speak fondly of the time you spend together. Having only daughters, both are especially fond of you, Bart."

As opportunity to make a new beginning with his father through their shared affection with Tomás, Bart said, "Perhaps we could all go sailing. Aunt Inez was hesitant at first, but I even got her go out a couple of times. I don't think I told you I bought a sailboat. A thirty-six footer with a cabin. Not very old, in great shape, newly outfitted. Even rigged with winches to allow me to sail singlehanded without leaving the wheel to adjust the sheets. Large enough for all of us to be comfortable."

Max Landeira recalled his son's passion for sailing in Tampa Bay from a young age. Although he had no interest in sailing, he was intent on rehabilitating relations with his son.

"If Tomás and Inez are willing, count me in, Son."

* * * *

Maximiliano Landeira inherited his personality from his father Enrique. A patriarch of the old school, Enrique Landeira advanced the family dynasty through intellect and drive. A second-generation immigrant, he enlarged the family sugarcane and tobacco holdings as Cuba transitioned from slavery. A difficult undertaking since Cuba did not abolish slavery until 1886.

Enrique Landeira's father began importing Chinese and Mexican Indian contract workers to replace slaves. Itself an ugly system of exploitation where working conditions were little better than those of slaves. Coming of age, Enrique Landeira convinced his father to invest in machination to reduce reliance on manpower. Steam-powered mills and narrow-gauge railroads. With this, Landeira land holdings exponentially increased as they bought out smaller farmers and increased cultivation acreage by clear cutting hardwood forests.

Enrique Landeira died in 1936. He lived long enough to hand the reins of the expanded family business to his three sons. A true entrepreneur, he recognized the exceptional intellect of his youngest son Maximiliano. Rather than directly grooming him into the business, he shipped Max off to the University of Florida. After Maximiliano acquired a law degree and passed the American bar, Enrique encouraged his son to remain in the

United States and cultivate influential associations. American government officials and American business interests important to Cuba.

Taking a page from his father's history, Maximiliano found his first entrepreneurial venture in bootlegging when Prohibition came into effect in the United States in 1920. Circumstances aligned offering opportunities for expanding sales of Landeira rum. From a modest sized producer of quality rum predominately for the Cuban market, sales exploded exponentially within a few years through illegal sales to the United States. Max Landeira promoted it as a top-quality liquor to compete with European spirits coming through the Bahamas. With rum's capacity for mixing well in a range of cocktails, it was a sure product where many average speakeasies served moonshine of dubious providence.

The windfall profits spanning the Prohibition period provided capital for continued investment in acquiring additional sugarcane and tobacco cultivation acreage. Eventually the Landeiras became one of the largest sugarcane growers in Cuba where most other large producers were American-owned.

Making his law office in Tampa with its large Cuban immigrant population afforded the perfect opportunity to partner with bootleggers. With a large Italian immigrant population of predominately Sicilian descent in the Ybor City district, Prohibition provided the perfect opportunity to supplement meager wages. Tampa instantly became the wettest city in the country. Public sales of illegal liquor became openly permissive in Tampa. Police and judges even benefited in the trade. A cottage industry providing the principal source of income for possibly half the families in Ybor City making or transporting bootleg alcohol.

Landeira approached a local Sicilian criminal figure involved with the popular bolita lotteries. The career of Santo Trafficante Sr. was on the rise in the 1920s. A long partnership ensued with Trafficante providing smuggling boats and U.S. distribution. The partnership also yielded long-term benefits even after the repeal of Prohibition in 1933.

The years of Prohibition, providing staggering profits from illegal alcohol, gave rise to organized crime in the United States on a national scale. Trafficante became the boss in Tampa with close ties to Charles "Lucky" Luciano and Thomas Lucchese in New York. Although Traffacante Sr. died in 1954, Max Landeira remained associated with his son Santo Trafficante Jr. who took over the Tampa Mafia family. That association provided Max Landeira the opportunity to become a central player in the financial structuring of the Mafia-financed Havana hotel and casino boom. That further expanded to his establishing an intimate connection with President Fulgencio Batista, personally benefiting from Mafia investment.

No question about Max Landeira being brilliant. Circumstances perfectly positioned him to advance family business interests and pursue lucrative personal opportunities. Important connections in both Cuba and the United States opened infinite possibilities for someone expert in business law with American capital flowing into Cuban investment. Someone also willing to work outside legal constraints devising creative financial solutions. With the regime of Fulgencio Batista, Max Landeira found a capable and corrupt politician. One with an astounding history of longevity in politically unstable Cuba. Batista currently exercised control over a large well-equipped army courtesy of United States foreign aid.

Yet in 1956, Max Landeira began reflecting on his mortality. His wife died twenty years ago. Little in the way of family life. Two married daughters and several grandchildren that he saw occasionally. His only son virtually a stranger since 1942. Although he would never admit to it, he was lonely. A mistress in Tampa did not alleviate a growing sense of malaise. His two older brothers only increased his feelings of encroaching age. Enrique was ten years older and suffering health issues. Max's only nephew Rafael ran the extensive sugarcane growing and mill operations in Camaguey while Rafael's son Carlos managed the tobacco growing in the western province of Pinar del Rio. Max's other brother Tomás, managed the rum and cigar manufacturing operations in Havana. He was only two years older but did not take care of himself.

None of the daughters and only a couple of their husbands held middle management positions in the family Cuban enterprises. The scope of the immense cultivated acreage stretched Rafael to the limit. Max had little use for Rafael's son Carlos. The young man in his early twenties was geographically too close to the temptations of Havana. Carlos spent considerable money at the Havana gaming tables most weekends. Max suspected Carlos also indulged in drugs and prostitutes.

Not only was the advancing age of the brothers an issue, but a viable succession plan was long overdue. Of all those involved with the family business, Max Landeira felt that the present success of Landeira Grupo was largely due to his efforts. His creative financial leadership fueled the corporation's success of the last twenty-five years by expanding beyond its core agricultural origins.

Feeling the weight of time, the prospect of his son joining the family business became pressing. Settling in Havana proved too good an opportunity to pass up. He must repair their estrangement of the last years. Make a concerted effort to change how he interacted with his son. Establishing an emotional relationship with Bart the only resolution for his loneliness.

Chapter 4

In June of 1956, the issue of long-term senior management from within the Landeira family suddenly became immediate. Tomás Landeira died of a massive coronary in his sleep.

Living in the same building, Bart was the first to learn of his death. Aunt Inez pounded on his door early in the morning hysterical and crying. Finding no pulse, he touched his uncle's cheek with the back of his hand. Cold. With a peaceful expression on his uncle's face, he turned to embrace his aunt. "I am so sorry, Tia Inez, he is gone." As she sobbed on his shoulder, he added, "He passed peacefully. Look at his face."

Having known his uncle for only a brief time, his death affected him profoundly. Bart Landeira felt little family attachment. With the loss of his mother almost twenty years ago, her family in Cuba played no part in his life. Nor was he close to his father's extended family. Living his whole life in the United States he felt more American than Cuban.

His affection for Uncle Tomás proved the exception making his passing all the more painful. Tomás and Inez were warm and generous people. They enjoyed life and others. Unlike Tomás' brothers, business did not consume their lives. They treated their nephew as if he were their own son. For the first time since the untimely death of his mother, Bart Landeira felt the pain of personal loss. After wandering the world, Tomás and Inez gave Havana a sense of belonging.

It was Bart who made the difficult phone calls informing the family. His father's overwhelming expression of grief surprised him. For someone seemingly aloof and self-absorbed, it added a human dimension that Bart found gratifying. What drew him close to Tomás obviously also affected his father.

His father arrived in Havana later that afternoon to take charge of making funeral arrangements. A week later, Max Landeira chartered a DC-3 to fly the body of his brother and family members living in Havana to Camagüey over three hundred miles to the east. Although having flown to Camagüey on his first trip to Cuba with his father after leaving the CIA, he spent no time in the city. This time, out of town visitors for the funeral would stay at the elegant Gran Hotel within the city. The diocese bishop would deliver a requiem mass in the 18th century Baroque church Iglesia de Nuestra Señora de la Soledad. Following mass, the funeral procession would travel by automobile to the family estate fifteen miles to the southwest. Internment to take place in the family cemetery near the great house. The burial place of the earliest Landeiras in Cuba.

Although the City of Camagüey was a sizeable urban center, its character was of another world compared to Havana. This was Cuba of the last century. A confusing layout of short narrow streets turning in random directions. Bart remarked about the street layout to a local shopkeeper after becoming lost while walking. The man related the story of the pirate Henry Morgan sacking and burning the city in the 17th century. Rebuilding designed intentionally as a maze to make it more difficult for any attacking force to maneuver inside the city. Not sure that he believed this as the reason for purposely constructing a city with a confusing pattern of streets, but it made for a good story. Cuba did have a colorful violent past plagued by pirates.

Following the funeral, Bart and his father stayed on at the Camagüey estate.

The morning after burying Tomás Landeira, Bart returned to the cemetery. A private time of contemplation. He remained unsettled by the depth of his grief. Perhaps never to return to this place. Even remaining in Havana now felt questionable.

Bart was standing in front of the weathered headstone of the founding patriarch of the Cuban Landeira dynasty. His great-great grandfather and namesake, Bartolo Landeira, 1825-1881.

His father approached and placed a hand on his back. "Been twenty years since I last came out here to the family cemetery. My father's funeral, your grandfather Enrique. Just over there. The plots are arranged according to generation starting here with the founder of the Landeira Cuban dynasty, your namesake, Bartolo. Emigrated from Spain a hundred years ago. It was his vision that created the foundation for the family business you see today.

"I have a favor to ask of you, Son. Even before the passing of Tomás, the size and complexity of our enterprises today represents a management challenge. This is a family business. Those with the name Landeira must be in charge. We have many competent mid-level managers but they are not Landeiras by blood."

Bart suspected what was coming. Some role in the business since he was already here in Havana.

"I need your help to oversee the rum and cigar operations."

Bart expected his father to use the death of Tomás as a tactic to entice him joining the Havana law office to support his father's financial management activities from Tampa. This was something far different. He knew nothing of managing manufacturing operations.

He shook his head, "I would like to help out, Father, but that is not a good idea. I know nothing of those businesses. I made a difficult career change leaving government service. Selfishly I cannot sacrifice my journalism career for something that holds no future career interest for me."

"Believe me, I understand. All I am asking is to for you hold things together until we can fix on a long-term management solution. We have competent managers and foremen to run operations. We need someone though at the helm. You can keep a close eye on financial performance and help us find that long-term solution. I can trust you. You're smart and you are a Landeira."

Shit. Bart felt genuinely empathetic to his father's plight, but equally determined to forge his own path forward rather than dictated by circumstances. He came to Havana as a place to decompress and realign his life. He never thought of Havana as likely to be long-term.

"Look, Father. I can't make that kind of commitment without first seriously considering what it means to me. That probably sounds selfish but I must consider the rest of my life. The war changed everything. I never told you details of what I did. An ugly experience. I still experience recurring nightmares. My own fault for then accepting a job in secret government work after the war rather than coming back to the States and finding a real job. Involvement in business in Cuba is not what I have in mind."

The expression of sadness on his father's face suggested something more profound than his refusal to join the family business even temporarily. Could it be pain over their estrangement for so many years?

The elder Landeira nodded without commenting further.

Bart said, "Look, Father. I don't want to leave you in a lurch. Painful enough losing your brother unexpectedly. When we get back to Havana, we can look into the situation at those operations managed by Tomás. Give me a sense of what is involved then we can go from there."

His father awarded him a smile and embraced him. "Thank you. It will help me immensely. Enrique's health will not permit him to leave Camagüey. Rafael must remain here to run sugarcane operations. Without you, business demands in our Havana operations will prove difficult for me manage. Everything will suffer as a consequence."

Bart believed his father's sentiment genuine. While not happy about unexpectedly drawn into family affairs, worth the detour if it improved his relationship with his father.

* * * *

Before departing Camagüey, Max Landeira convened the equivalent to a family board meeting. Seventy-four year old Enrique, his son Rafael a couple of years older than Bart, and the youngest, Carlos, Rafael's only son. Following tradition, male family members always ran the business. Enrique and Tomás both had two daughters. They possessed non-voting shares in the holding company set up Maximiliano. The board consisted of the remaining two senior brothers Max and Enrique, Marta their sister, and Enrique's son Rafael. Now reduced from five to four board members. An awkward number by the possibility of tie votes on motions.

By reason of birth, Bart was a shareholder holding a modest block of voting shares but declined the invitation to join the board. That much of a commitment went too far. With Bart's consent, Max however announced his son's willingness to look into how he might help temporarily shore up the management void with the passing of Tomás.

Enrique spoke up, "Excellent. Bartolo is a lawyer like you Max and already settled in Havana. Tomás ran Havana operations for more than thirty years. None of us knows anything about making rum or cigars."

Rafael offered, "Certainly meaning no offense, but neither does Bartolo."

Bart responded, "You are correct, Rafael. I can only be of assistance in an oversight capacity. My father understands the financial aspects of these enterprises. He can direct how I can be of service. Remember, I only said I would look into helping temporarily if my father feels I can be of meaningful service. I came to Havana as a journalist not to run a business."

Max said, "The operations managers at both plants have been with us a long time but know nothing beyond working production. Bartolo would be there to act as my eyes and ears. The real problem is finding a permanent solution. That probably means looking outside the family."

The unspoken problem was Rafael's son Carlos. A business degree from Havana University, and for the last two years in charge of tobacco growing in the province of Pinar del Río west of Havana. Specifically the Vuelta Abajo Region. Because of a unique combination of climate and soil, some of the world's best tobacco is grown there. A perfect opportunity for the youngest male family member to develop professionally.

Unfortunately too rural for a rich young man. Even the city of Pinar del Río was a provincial backwater. Unlike the sugarcane operations in the faraway eastern end of the island, glamorous Havana was only a 100 miles to the west. An easy drive or train ride. For a twenty-five year old with money, the lure of sex and drugs proved overpowering. The distance also offered escape from the stern hand of his father. Carlos spent most weekends in Havana. Returning with enough cocaine to fuel his habit for the week.

The elder Landeiras had little choice but manage as best possible. With his uncle Tomás geographically closer and connected by cigar manufacturing, some measure of senior oversight was possible. With the death of Tomás, Carlos only added to the family's management problems.

**** ****

The days spent at the family estate following the funeral provided an opportunity to view the uglier side of life in Cuba with a more critical eye. The route from Camagüey City passed by clusters of homes of cane workers. Shacks. Earthen floors, windows without glass. No running water. Half-naked dirty children chasing chickens. Slum dwellings as found among the world's most impoverished people. Little wonder Fidel Castro found sympathy for his social revolutionary movement among the working class of rural eastern Cuba. Although sympathetic, those same peasants did not respond to Castro's call for armed rebellion in significant numbers.

Three years earlier on 26 July 1953, Castro and a band of 135 poorly armed men made an ill-fated attack on the second largest Cuban army garrison 200 miles to the east. It spectacularly failed. The Army killed or captured most of the rebels. Many of the captured executed in reprisal. Only a handful of rebels including Castro escaped but captured soon after.

Nor did the attack bring about a popular uprising. Imprisoned, Castro's nascent revolution seemed relegated to a minor historical footnote. Castro's eventual release from prison in an amnesty and exile to Mexico should have removed him as a serious threat.

Rural Cuba was little different from the impoverished places Bart Landeira saw in Greece, Egypt, Iran, and Guatemala. Places where working class people suffered under the yoke of corrupt rule. Right wing totalitarian rule enforced by military force. Governments he helped to install.

Living in Havana as part of an elite family was worlds apart from rural Cuba. He knew that when he came to Cuba. Leaving the CIA because of choosing not to perpetuate in injustice did not draw him to become a crusader. Poverty existed in every country in the world. Communism was not the solution. Democracy does not disenfranchise the poor. Market economies and totalitarian regimes however both do that. Society everywhere divides everyone by economic opportunity.

His personal choice to confront intractable larger economic and social problems was that of observer. His activism extended only as far as exposing those responsible for inflicting harm. Political ideologies, no matter their professed reason for existence, invariably suffered serious shortcomings. Universally true for specific governmental institutions often acting in their own self-interest.

Regardless his empathy for the impoverished Cuban peasant, he was glad to return to Havana. Unfortunately under changed circumstances. The loss of Uncle Tomás was particularly distressing with their special relationship cut short. Now the unwanted obligation to help out with management of the family Havana businesses. This could only interfere with time otherwise devoted to journalistic work. Working with his father an unknown. They appeared getting along better than he remembered from before their long estrangement however, the demands of business would likely raise issues of conflict.

For Bart, all this was just temporary. Remaining in Havana indefinitely uncertain. With what he learned since the death of his uncle, his father must be more anxious than ever to entice him to join him in the financial and legal management of Landeira Grupo. In this patriarchal family, there were no more suitable male candidates to take over from the last generation.

Father and son enjoyed an excellent dinner at the Club Parisién in the iconic Hotel Nacional. Opened in 1930, it stood as an imposing large gleaming white building sitting atop a hill on the sea front of the Vedado district. Most rooms offered a commanding view of the city or the sea with the 16th century Castillo del Morro sitting on a cliff guarding the entrance to Havana harbor.

The recently renovated restaurant showroom offered subdued lighting, tropical plants, and plush seating intended to convey the same intimacy of the Copacabana and Stork Club in New York City. Everything targeted to the affluent American tourist.

Max said, "Let's enjoy a good dinner. Tomorrow we can get down to work. Introduce you to the operations managers and administrative staff at both factories."

Both ordered drinks. Very good Scotch. Something they both had in common. Father wanted to talk.

"I am not expecting you to work this full-time, Bart. You already have a job. I just need you to keep an eye on critical matters that I will point out. That's my most pressing problem. The unexpected passing of Tomás leaves a real void with our management already stretched thin."

"Welcome, Max. The maître d' told me you were here. Good to see you," A dapper man dressed in tuxedo said walking up to their table. Both Max and Bart stood up.

"How are things, Wilbur?" Max said.

"Shaping up to be our best year ever. Look around. Like our remodeled décor?"

"Impressive. Let me introduce my son. Bart, this is Wilbur Clark, the entertainment director. He runs the casino."

"Bart has been wandering the world reporting for the Miami Herald. Settled now in Havana to cover the Caribbean and Central America."

"Good to meet you Mr. Landeira. Hope to see more of you. We are not as large as the San Souci or the Tropicana so we don't have the same ambitious floorshows. However, our refined elegance is enough to attract the most famous entertainers. We have Eartha Kitt performing tonight and for another week."

Wilbur Clark worked for Tampa Mafia family boss Santo Trafficante Jr. The most visible face of organized crime in Havana and a close associate of Max Landeira. Bart Landeira would learn all this only later as he probed deeper into the dictatorship of Fulgencio Batista and his partnership with the American Mafia.

As they enjoyed their drinks before dinner, Bart said, "Since you run the financial side of Landeira Grupo S.A., how is it you work out of Tampa? Seems much easier to work in Havana."

Max said, "I agree, however my law practice offers other business services. My clients located in investment and commerce centers in the United States. Trade with the U.S. is 90% of Cuba's economy. I serve as a facilitator to foster Cuban investment. All about networking. American, investors feel more comfortable dealing with an American attorney on American soil. I provide the added benefit of legal expertise in both countries.

"Part of that networking is maintaining close relationships with influential Cuban government officials involved with economic development. Cuban tax law, commercial licensing, government contracting, corporate law, and so on. Means shuttling back and forth between Tampa and Havana."

"Some of your time is then spent on matters other than family business?"

Max nodded. "Comingled might be a better characterization. Running the financial aspects of a business the size of Landeira Grupo is complex. It benefits indirectly by my activities outside the corporation."

"What makes it financially complex? Isn't that largely a matter of running operations profitably?"

"Not entirely. Landeira Grupo got to where it is today through seizing opportunities for strategic advantage."

Bart hailed a waiter to order another round of drinks. He was enjoying this rare personal interaction with his father. An opportunity to learn more about his father after isolating himself for some many years.

"Sugarcane formed the foundation of what is today a diversified collection of enterprises. Sugar dominates Cuban trade even today. Yet it is a tough business. Harvesting is a seasonal labor-intensive endeavor. Profitability is a function of the amount of land devoted to growing. Devastating hurricanes are an annual threat. Sugar mill efficiency and transport logistics influence profits. Only the largest growers can be profitable. The majority of large sugarcane operations are American-owned. Landeira is one of the largest Cuban-owner growers in Cuba.

"The founding patriarch, your namesake Bartolo Landeira, your great-great-grandfather came from Spain. Prospered and eventually employed hundreds of African slaves. It was his only surviving son Rafael, your great-grandfather that brought our sugarcane operations through difficult times in the last century.

"The Ten Years War to achieve independence from Spain almost a century ago was the first great upheaval. A rebellion fueled by a broad abolitionist movement despite increased importations of African slaves about the time of American Civil War. Neither Bartolo or Rafael joined the rebellion thereby avoiding harsh Spanish reprisal."

"During that difficult period of Spanish oppression until the Spanish-American War, Rafael survived the economic downturn by rethinking the business of producing sugar. The African slave trade was an anachronism, increasing costly and not sustainable, yet it persisted in Cuba until 1886.

"Taking over from his aging father, Rafael invested in technology to move away from labor-intensive practices requiring cheap labor whether slaves or low-cost immigrant laborers. He invested in steam powered mills to lower production costs, and narrow-gauge railroads to efficiently move harvested sugarcane to the mills then transport the refined sugar to the shipyards."

Bart interrupted, "Not sure I understand how sugar cane is transformed into granulated sugar. Where does steam power come in?"

"The heart of sugar production is the mill. Works much like making flat rolled steel. Sugarcane stalks are fed into a succession of large tandem rollers exerting pressure to squeeze the juice from the pulp. Requires tremendous energy to power the mills. Before steam, the power came from slave manpower, oxen, or mules. Steam automated the process. Increasing production output while reducing labor costs.

"When your grandfather took over following Cuban independence in 1902, Landeira sugarcane mills became the most advanced in the Camagüey region.

"Our success always stemmed from astute money management. Aversion to debt. Taking advantage of land purchase opportunities. However, capital demands of the 20th century made banks essential. I learned what your grandfather learned intuitively about the value of leveraging assets to fuel growth while managing risk. The cost of capital became a significant expense.

"Here is the best example of what I mean. A life lesson not taught in universities. The year was 1920. I was twenty-eight. World War One ended two years earlier. As a commodity, all countries imposed price controls during the war. The world supply of sugar also fell throughout the war years by 20% due largely to the loss of French sugar beets because of fighting on the Western Front. After signing the Armistice in November 1918, price controls lifted. The price rose sharply to 6.6 cents per pound in 1919. By May of 1920, sugar hit a high of 22.5 cents. By Christmas, it fell to 3.7 cents. Descending further to 1.8 cents in 1921."

"Sounds worse than the Wall Street crash of '29."

"If you were a Cuban sugar grower, or a Cuban bank, just as bad. Before the crash, Cuban owned mills produced 40% of the Cuban crop. Cut in half after the crash. Wild borrowing and lending on margin took down small producers and many Cuban banks. Opened the floodgates for American investment to buy up land and mills at depressed liquidation prices. Branches of

American banks expanded and still dominate the Cuban financial sector."

"So my grandfather was running Landeira at this time. How did he manage to survive the bank failures and the depression aftermath?"

"Aversion to debit. He never borrowed on margin. Did not trust banks. Always conservative. Managed operations on cash flow. Only borrowed when necessary for major capital expenditures like mill equipment. If he bought land, it was from cash reserves."

"Let me guess. He used his saved cash to buy up acreage at distressed prices."

Max smiled broadly. "Right you are. Your grandfather significantly grew the business not through luck but through discipline.

"I could tell you more stories about your forbearers, but enough of history for tonight. My point being our success today did not come by chance. Each successive generation of the Landeira bloodline contributing. I am equally proud of my contributions.

"But just one more piece of more recent history you might find interesting. In 1950, I took us into another bold venture. In the 20th century, banking relationships are necessary for large businesses because of sustaining demands for capital. Growth, investment opportunities, seasonal and market fluctuations all require operating lines of credit. Maintaining large cash reserves became counterproductive. I therefore created Banco Crédito Industrial y Mercantil de Habana. Landeira Grupo's own bank."

"Our own bank? What does the family know about banking?"

"I understand banking, Bart. That's why your grandfather sent me to the United States. Not only for the education but to understand American business practices. Everything about Cuban economics centers on the United States. Landeira Grupo functions financially like an American corporation."

"Is the banking profitable?"

"Of course. Now a lucrative additional Landeira profit center. For Landeira's own operational capital needs alone, it returns a significant cost savings. We are no longer dependent on American bank branches dominating Cuban financial affairs. Banco Crédito has a direct relationship with Banco National de Cuba, the Cuban central bank. Less red tape without the arrogance and restrictions imposed by American banking regulations."

Max did not share with his son the larger benefit of Banco Crédito. The ability to conceal financial transactions from American law enforcement access to banking records. An essential prerequisite for banking services of clients operating outside of legitimate business areas.

Beyond the benefits to Landeira Grupo, the Bank became a perfect vehicle for managing the flow of Mafia investment money. Offering unrestrained financial transactions through the range of shell companies he set up for investment clients. Investment, tax sheltering, and preferential licensing for legitimate American corporations. Money laundering and concealing of identities for Mafia clients. The Bank could deliver on all three of the elements of money laundering: receiving the *dirty* money, obscuring it through layers of seemingly legitimate transactions, and then reintroducing it into circulation after transformation into *clean* money. It also afforded the means to conceal corrupt funds flowing to the Batista regime. A conduit for bribes and kickbacks from managing the flow of funds for governmental contracts and preferential licensing concealed from public scrutiny.

Under his control, Banco Crédito provided the means for Max Landeira to offer a full range of financial services for Mafia investment in Havana.

Chapter 5

The following day after dinner and the show at the Club Pa-risién, Max Landeira was anxious to introduce Bart to the rum and cigar manufacturing enterprises. Bart had not yet agreed to oversee these business units without first understanding his father's expectations. He was a fulltime correspondent so this sideline must not command significant time. *Temporary* was too open-ended.

For Bart, one thing was certain. He intended to move from the luxury apartment in Vedado to Old Havana. The only time he frequented the five-star restaurants in the area was during periodic visits with his father. The garish nightlife did not appeal to him. Not a gambler. Disliking crowds, loud American tourists letting loose in sin city was not his idea of Havana. They frequented the casinos until the early hours of the next morning then spilled out into the streets disturbing the dawn peace. For him, the attraction of Cuba was the Latin rhythm for the pleasures in life. The same cultural feeling he experienced in Italy after the war.

For experiencing Cuba of an earlier time, its other larger cities were probably better suited than Havana. Yet Havana remained Cuba's heart and soul. Historically its center long before the Yanqui invasion. The high-end hotels and casinos at least relegated mostly to the Vedado district.

Moving to Old Havana placed him at least five miles east of his sailboat dock. A perfectly sheltered small inlet where the Rio Almendares River emptied into the Gulf. In sight of the 17th century fortification Torreon de la Chorrera. The location of the dock provided as much shelter as possible against damaging winds for a boat sitting in the water. Although spared devastating hurricanes since 1940, a small but deadly category-five storm made landfall in Cuba in 1952. Growing up in Tampa on the Gulf of Mexico, he learned to respect hurricanes. Nonetheless, getting away from the perpetual party location to Old Havana suited Bart. With the passing of his uncle, no reason to remain in the company-owned apartment.

Arriving at the rum distillery, Max and Bart entered the office. One of the small office staff went to locate Gustavo Rodriguez somewhere on the factory floor.

Seated in Tomás' office, Rodriguez joined them within a few minutes. He embraced Max and Bart. "So sad losing Tomás. A wonderful man. He loved life. Loved people. We were like brothers. Worked together over forty years."

"Thank you, Gustavo. All three of us grew up in the Landeira rum business."

Rodriguez said, "Señor Bart. Tomás was so happy when you came to live in Havana. Your time together sadly so short."

Bart nodded. Rodriguez had tears in his eyes. The passing of his uncle affected many people.

"Please sit down, Gustavo," Max said. "I would like Bart to oversee the financial side of the business until we can sort out how to manage without Tomás. Of course, we know it is you that makes the rum with your many years of experience. Bart is not here to interfere with your running of operations." Turning to Bart, "Gustavo is a third generation master distiller."

"My father is right, Gustavo. I am just here to help the accounting staff. I know nothing about making rum. Would like you to show me about and at least explain the basics though."

"My pleasure, Señor Bart."

"How about now?" Bart said.

58

"Excellent," Max said. "After Gustavo shows us around, we can look in on the office staff."

Once out on the floor of the distillery, Rodriguez began to explain the process of making rum. The pride of a craftsman from living his life producing what was arguably very good aged rum.

"Most rum is made from molasses. That is how I make Landeira rum. Your Uncle Tomás joked about how we make something of beauty from something so ugly. Molasses is the black intermediate product of refining sugarcane into sugar.

"The molasses comes from our mills in Camagüey. Just like making wine from grapes or whiskey from grain, the soil where the sugarcane grows is important. Different soil produces subtle differences. I blend our rum from molasses from all four of the Landeira sugar mills."

Bart smiled at his father rolling his eyes as Rodriguez relished explaining the detail of his craft.

"We turn the sugar in the molasses to alcohol in these stainless steel fermentation tanks. This is where we introduce yeast. The yeast I prefer takes a week for the fermentation process. The smell in here is the yeast doing its work."

Moving into another area, Bart looked out on rows of gleaming copper pot stills.

"This is the second step in rum making. We cook the fermented juice to about 175 degrees. The alcohol evaporates from the juice then condenses in these cooling pipes. Out comes the raw beginning of rum. 70-95% alcohol by volume. This raw fiery cheap rum is sometimes bottled straight from the still. Drinkable only with something to dilute the alcohol and the harsh taste. Not our kind of rum."

Walking into another separate large building, inside were row upon row of wooden barrels stacked two-high.

"This is where Landeira rum matures. Oak barrels previously used in whiskey making. You might say your father built this building."

Bart first looked at his father with a questioning expression then turned to Rodriguez, "What do you mean, Gustavo?"

"Because of Maximiliano's efforts, we could not produce enough rum to ship to the United States thirty years ago. The time of their Prohibition against selling liquor.

Max said, "When you were very young, Bart. A foolish American law. The majority of Americans wanted beer and liquor. Too many state legislators knuckled under to temperance pressure groups. Legal to produce alcohol spirits in Cuba. I saw it as an exceptional business opportunity."

"You were a bootlegger, Father?" Bart remarked with a grin at his father's slight embarrassment.

Max shook his head vigorously. "No. I wasn't a bootlegger. I was what you might call a facilitator. As a member of the American Bar Association practicing in Tampa, I was careful to avoid any involvement in illegal activity. I simply directed the bootleggers how to make contact with Tomás.

"The bootleggers handled the smuggling and distribution in the United States. My role was making sure we received payment before the rum left our Havana warehouse. I'll tell more about it over lunch."

Bart said to Rodriguez, "So selling rum in the United States during Prohibition increased demand enough to warrant a larger building?"

Rodriguez replied, "Oh yes. Your father bought this building next to the distillery and we converted it into our warehouse. You will notice the crane system for maneuvering barrels in and out of the storage racks. Even different locations within the warehouse are part of the art of aging. The final step in creating great rum."

Max was getting anxious to leave but the artistry of making good rum intrigued Bart. Perhaps interesting enough to appease his father and oversee its administration. He liked the feel of the distillery. A product of generational artistry like making Scotch. A part of Cuban culture. The ninety-year history of Landeira Rum proudly part of that heritage.

After a brief introduction to the office staff, they left for lunch. Bart suggested Tomás' favorite lunchtime restaurant.

After ordering beers, Bart raised the issue of his father's bootlegging.

"You never mentioned your involvement in Prohibition bootlegging to any of us. How did that come about?"

"Tampa was one of the wettest places in the United States during Prohibition. Smuggled liquor flowed into Tampa Bay with its tradition of flaunting the law. A large Sicilian immigrant community fostered early organized criminal elements engaged in illegal gambling, particularly the popular bolita lottery. Prohibition immediately provided a vastly more lucrative trade in illegal alcohol. Locals even began distilling moonshine.

"Legal everywhere else, liquor began coming in from all over the Caribbean. An economic windfall for impoverished British crown colonies. Gin and Scotch came in from the Bahamas. Rum from Jamaica, Barbados, and of course Cuba. Miami was the closest, but Tampa enjoyed a particular advantage. Corrupt local politicians and police turned a blind eye to the illegal alcohol trade for a percentage of the profits."

"So you saw the opportunity for Landeira Rum. Makes sense but don't you think you were getting your hands dirty dealing with organized crime?"

Max shrugged his shoulders. "Business often involves dealing with those circumventing the law. A good many Wall Street lawyers regularly construct investment deals to circumvent regulations, avoid taxes, or remove competition. Prohibition was a stupid law. A perfect opportunity for criminal enterprise just like any black market. Selling rum was not illegal in Cuba."

Bart thought that was a telling distinction for an American attorney.

"Who did you partner with in Tampa to smuggle the rum?"

"An Italian named Santo Trafficante."

"Trafficante? Isn't he the Mafia boss in Tampa named in the news as investing in the Havana casinos?"

"No. That is his son, Santo Jr. The old man died two years ago."

"Are you doing business with his son?"

"Like I told you before, I am a business consultant. I facilitate investment deals in Cuba. If Santo Trafficante Jr. is an investor, it is only indirectly. Most of my investment clients are syndicated groups. Individuals usually never identified by name."

Bullshit thought Bart. His father knew far more than he was willing to reveal. He keeps alluding to his investment counseling practice. In Cuba, that means hotels and casinos. Common knowledge the major investors are American organized crime. Bart has been reporting on the hotel and casino construction boom in Havana since he arrived two years ago in Havana. Common knowledge the Mafia is providing the majority of capital. Santo Trafficante and Meyer Lansky the names most mentioned. Yet theirs or any other known members of organized crime do not appear in public ownership documents. He knew that from his own research.

His father also boasts of setting up shell companies for tax and liability reasons. Also useful for concealing all sorts of information. A necessity for the Mafia and corrupt Cuban officials. Bart chose not to press the matter at this time. Well connected within the financial sectors of the Cuban government, his father was likely involved in unsavory dealings given his professed role as a financial *facilitator*.

"Okay. Forgetting the legal semantics of your role in bootlegging, how lucrative was this for Landeira Rum?"

Max smiled proud of his first major business coup. "Beyond all expectations. Sales rose so rapidly the need for expansion became obvious from the beginning. More stills obviously required. Therefore, I purchased the warehouse building next door. Relocating the barrel storage to the new building freed space for new stills. Kept a crew of coppersmiths busy for a year fabricating the additional stills.

"The profits were sufficient to fund the expansion out of cash flow. Sales never fell off until the repeal of Prohibition in '33. Trafficante moved all the rum we could provide."

"What happened when Prohibition ended?"

"Although liquor was again legal in the U.S. the Depression caused several lean years of reduced sales. Prohibition era profits sustained us until I did a deal with a Canadian named Samuel Bronfman. His liquor distribution company acquired Seagram's in 1928. Bronfman was a bootlegger during Prohibition with his product crossing into the U.S. from Canada.

"Bronfman knew Landeira Rum as marketable to high-end retailers. Even made an offer to buy us before the war. I liked the diversification it gave to our family enterprises so I declined. Instead, he offered to distribute for us. A successful partnership from the beginning. Since that time, Seagram distributes Landeira Rum worldwide. Distribution is their core business not ours. Business success comes from staying focused on what you do best and contracting the rest."

After a traditional Cuban lunch, Max was anxious to learn Bart's reaction to overseeing the rum business. "So what do think, Son? Willing to help out?"

Bart felt an obligation to help his father if for no other reason than to further their renewed relationship. Rum making stirred his interest. Tomás and Gustavo portrayed it as more art than production. Whatever they did, they made good rum.

"Yes. I can appreciate your bind with the unexpected death of Tomás."

Max squeezed Bart's forearm. His expression of gratitude confirmed Bart had done the right thing.

"Gustavo is the reason for the quality of Landeira Rum, but he cannot run the business. He is my age, which also means you must look for his successor. With you involved, you can help me resolve both those long-term personnel problems."

"Do I assume you are not open to selling the rum business?"

"Not yet. I have too much personally invested to see it go to a Seagram or Bacardi."

* * * *

Following lunch, they went to the cigar factory. A tearful reception from the predominately women employees hand-rolling cigars. The operations manager Alejandro Ruiz impressed both Max and Bart. Holding a college degree, Tomás hired him for his management skills. With several years prior work experience, he had been with Habanos de Landeira for ten years. As a protégé, Tomás gradually turned over more and more responsibility to Ruiz. In his mid-thirties, the perfect choice for promotion to general manager according to Max. No oversight required just monthly reviews of financial performance according to Max.

For Bart, the visit made his decision by limiting his involvement to Landeira Rum manageable. The task appeared more one of searching for an experienced general manager.

Their final visit was to the Havana administrative office that doubled as Max's satellite law office with two attorneys and a small clerical staff. The larger Landeira Grupo staff consisted of accounting and the staff of Landeira Servicios de Logistica, the shipping and customs brokerage division.

At dinner that evening at the Parisién, Max was in an uncharacteristically relaxed mood. "A very good day. Particularly impressed with Alejandro. With Tomás gone, obviously we should promote him to general manager. Rafael also says Carlos respects him. Since Carlos' growing operations in Pinar del Rio furnishes the cured tobacco leaves for the cigar production, they work closely together. Alejandro also understands the process of curing the tobacco leaves. Provides a measure of management depth given Carlos' bouts of instability. Making cigars is simpler than making sugar or rum.

"But the best outcome of today was you agreeing to help. Especially gratifying to know we shall see more of each other. Since you went off to war, we have been strangers for too many years. Good to have you back, Son."

After drinks, dinner, and sharing a bottle of good French wine, Max appeared feeling the effects of the alcohol. Coffees and Landeira rum further loosen his tongue.

"I am one of three sons that inherited management of the Landeira enterprises with the death of your grandfather in 1936. Tomás is now gone. Enrique is no longer active in the business because of poor health. Your cousin Rafael manages the sugar business competently but that is all he knows and constitutes a major responsibility. His son Carlos is a drug addict. A looser with no future. The demands of running Landeira Grupo now outstrip our bloodline.

"I explained where Landeira Grupo is invested outside its core business units. Legal identities I conceived to increase profits in diversified investments delivering excellent returns. Banco Crédito, Servicios de Logistica, and a construction management business Construcción Landeira are examples. I created Landeira Grupo as a holding company in 1949 to leverage our collective net worth. Enrique and Rafael have no understanding of corporate finance. They function no differently than your grandfather's generation. Good instincts but no substitute for understanding the fiscal workings of a modern corporation in today's complex financial world.

"I am largely responsible for the success of Landeira Grupo since the 1920s. I don't mean to sound boastful, but that is the reality. Yet I can also be self-critical. This current predicament of managerial succession is my fault. I should have addressed the issue years ago."

A rare admission out of character that surprised Bart. "Why did you not at least raise the question with Enrique and Tomás?"

"Hard to look back and see how I missed what is now obvious. Probably too caught up in my separate legal practice outside my role within Landeira Grupo. The seduction of creating complex legal entities to make money without delivering products or services is what I do best."

"Not sure what you mean, Father."

Bart had a good idea though. The public records of ownership of new hotels and casinos showed only the names of investment companies with untraceable ownership trails. Was this his father's handiwork? If so, it went deeper. The hidden Mafia investors needed a way to invest money from criminal activities in the United States into legitimate business. Outside the United States avoided U.S. tax fraud laws. What better place than a corrupt police state? Carrying the thought further, the same mechanism of shell companies used domestically could conceal preferential government contracts and kickbacks. Was Landeira Grupo also benefiting by complex unlawful financial practices created by Maximiliano Landeira?

Bart thought it a good time to understand exactly what his father did outside of Landeira Grupo. Every time Bart raised the question, his father was evasive or vague. Fond of referring to himself as a facilitator, Bart wanted to understand what that meant in specific terms.

Bootlegging during Prohibition introduced him to American organized crime. The partnership proving mutually profitable. Likely his involvement continued. What better place than to offer his services for investing in politically unstable Cuba now governed by a corrupt dictator. Ideally positioned with his ties in both the United States and Cuba.

With his father in a talkative mood, a good time to exercise constraint and just listen without interjecting challenging remarks causing argument.

"You mention your active legal practice often. What exactly is your involvement in American investment consulting? Acting as a facilitator as you call it."

"Doing business in Cuba is not the same as in the United States."

"Of course not. This is a corrupt dictatorship."

"Most governments are corrupt to some degree. Depends on your definition of corruption. You claim the United States is corrupt for acting in its own self-interest in foreign policy with no regard to the damage caused. That is the reason you left government service was it not?"

Bart nodded. "I would characterize it as something different from corruption though."

"Well my point is that all of us must contend with circumstances beyond our control. Those circumstances dictate how business functions. No matter where, it is rarely fair or an equal playing field. In Cuba, money changing hands is a necessary business reality.

"I am not justifying corruption, just explaining my role. Which is to find investment opportunities and create the legal framework whereby my clients can generate a return. To do that requires understanding the playing field. In Cuba, that means developing close working relationships with those influential government officials involved with public finance and commercial interests. Banking, taxation, licensing, trade, public works.

"My function brings together the interests of the Cuban public sector and American private sector investor clients. Negotiating licensing, tax incentives, preferential access to capital, joint investment with public funding participation are among the services I provide.

"But don't you do more than that, Father?"

"What do you mean?"

"I have been reporting about the hospitality boom in hotels and casinos since I arrived in Havana. Rumors abound that the American Mafia is the principal source of financing. Yet the public ownership records reveal only names of obscure companies. American and Cuban companies. None identified as subsidiaries of known American corporations or financial institutions. My guess is these are front companies. Am I correct?"

"In substance yes. I disagree though with your characterization as *front companies*. You see, these companies typically represent a group of investors. Some are individuals but most are legal entities as corporations or LLCs forming a consortium for participating in larger projects. I form an investment corporation with each investor holding shares proportional to their invested capital. Shareholders are not a matter of public record in Cuba."

"Have you created many of these investment companies for the purpose of investing in hotel and casino projects?"

With a broad smile, Max answered, "A good many."

"Do these involve Mafia money?"

"The truthful answer is I do not know. None of the names at least seen in newspapers."

"What about Santo Trafficante Jr."

"I do not know. I know he frequents Havana but he is not directly a client. He might be a silent investor in one of my syndicate clients.

"Listen, Bart. The Mafia is certainly invested in Havana hotels and casinos. Same as in Las Vegas. They know how to launder their money and evade paper trails. Their names never appear as owning anything. They do not come to me to create Cuban companies as cover. Lawyers come to me to put together syndicate entities for the ability to participate in developing large-scale projects. To the extent American organized crime capital flows into Havana, it likely exists among the many obscure legal entities invested in various U.S. and Cuban companies. Individual identities of known criminal figures probably buried in multiple layers of false identities or proxies. My role is to secure financing, licensing, and provide business related legal services. I do not research the identities of individual underlying investors."

"What about the bribes and kickbacks to the Batista regime?"

Max shook his head. "Of course that goes on. Naïve to think otherwise. But that is out of my hands. I just do the legal framework of creating companies and offering professional advice. I do not negotiate bribes. Nor do I manage these Cuban companies I create. What money changes hands as a part of doing business is the affairs of others."

Bart retreated from pressing his father any further. He did not believe his father whitewashing his role. Too many circumstances pointed to complicity in funding of the brutal dictatorship of Fulgencio Batista. Likely earning fees for devising methods to conceal Mafia investment and buying off Batista. Those invested funds the product of unlawful criminal activities in the United States. Gambling, drugs, prostitution, extortion. Functioning like a corporation, the Mafia corrupted American institutions by bribing police and judges while enforcing their interests by intimidation and murder.

He knew his father functioned in partnership with the Batista regime and the Mafia. Longstanding relationships with both. Clients that paid lucrative fees for his special services.

"I don't want you to think my work is entirely centered on the Havana hospitality boom. I set up Cuban subsidiaries for public-traded American corporations. Tax advantages exist from operating in Cuba compared to the high corporate tax rate in the United States. For those companies doing business in Latin

America, Havana can be a tax haven. Close to the U.S. mainland. Knowing tax law in both countries, I structure arrangements that legally reduce U.S. taxes by sheltering profits offshore."

Trying to move to less contentious ground, Bart said, "You said your legal services have also benefited Landeira Grupo. In what way?"

"For example, our construction management business, Construcción Landeira. We bid on commercial projects. If awarded the contract, we finance construction through our own bank, Banco Crédito. Acting as the general contractor, we manage subcontractors doing the construction. With the Havana building boom, we have multiple projects currently under contract."

If Bart thought his father complicit in facilitating the unholy marriage of Batista with the Mafia for fees, this meant directly participating in the graft. With his connections, he could bid on government contracts while possibly seeing the other bids, ensure the building permits favored Construcción Landeira, and the cost of the kickback figured into his bid.

"Our logistics company, Landeira Servicios de Logistica, brokers shipping transport and provides export and import U.S. and Cuban customs transactions services. We have offices in Havana, Miami, and New York."

"Impressive, Father."

"Bart. This is what I want for you. You have a law degree. I can teach you everything I do. It is an interesting and lucrative career. You can eventually take over."

"Please, Father. You do not count on that. I am a journalist, not a lawyer or businessman. I tolerate Batista's totalitarian regime only because I am not personally affected. Just an observer though it troubles me. Havana does not suffer as does the working poor in the rural regions. So living here in prosperous Havana, I do not feel the weight of Batista's oppression. In contrast, the Army's rural garrisons in Oriente Province brutalize the peasants. Revolution will eventually come from there. Or until Batista falls out of favor with the military and succumbs to a coup."

His father replied, "Although making my base of operation Tampa, I am Cuban. Perhaps cynically, I am also a realist. I fully recognize the character of Fulgencio Batista. Yet under his rule, Cuba has generally prospered. It is more functional than any regime since gaining independence from Spain."

Bart responded, "Cuba is hardly independent from the United States. Its entire economy so intertwined with the U.S. that it is a colony in all but name."

"That is true. Cuba should have become an American protectorate like Puerto Rico. Yet all the same, Cuba's economic dependence on the U.S. with its strategic importance to the U.S. will insure what you call quasi-colonial status. The United States has not hesitated in using military force to enforce regional stability in the Caribbean, as they did in the Dominican Republic and Haiti."

Bart said, "And look how that turned out. Trujillo is no different from Batista. U.S. Marines occupied some portion of Hispaniola since before World War One. Haiti for almost twenty years. Once the Marines left Haiti, Trujillo murdered over 20,000 Haitians living in the Dominican Republic a couple of years later. Since then, Haiti became a failed state in continual political chaos. Trujillo's been in power for twenty-five years. By all accounts his regime has become even more murderous."

Max responded, "My point is Cuba's future depends on relations with the United States. I must work within that framework. Regardless the nature of the relationship, Cuba is the most prosperous country in Latin America."

Chapter 6

For the first time in years, Bart Landeira felt strangely comfortable. An unusual assessment living in a dictatorship. Simultaneously, he felt some guilt associated with his privileged circumstances while opposition to the Batista regime mounted. Cuba was now a police state since Fulgencio Batista seized power in a bloodless takeover backed by the Cuban military four years earlier.

Easy to feel comfortable while living well in Havana. Havana was a separate world from the rest of Cuba. A sharp distinction between urban and rural. Yet the stark comparison held even with other sizable Cuban cities considered provincial by those of Havana. Havana was not only Cuba's historical center but now an international glamour location. Sun, sea, gambling, a freewheeling exotic getaway reachable by regular commercial airline flights from mainland United States.

The most overtly violent expression of the regime's repression came in the rural eastern provinces. The region of the poorest of Cuba's citizens working the sugarcane industry. Here the Army exercised extrajudicial violence on those suspected of subversive activities. This region is the origin of Fidel Castro's revolutionary movement. Known as continuing his efforts to organize rebellion from exile in Mexico, substantial support existed among the rural Cuban peasantry.

Havana however was not without political opposition to Batista. The student federation of the venerable University of Havana demanded restoration of the 1940 constitution, leading to formation of a clandestine subversive organization, the Directorio Revolucionario Estudiantil. The militancy of the DRE caused Batista to suspend classes at the University of Havana indefinitely.

Reshaping Havana from a quaint Caribbean city to a cosmopolitan international attraction, Batista's repression went largely unnoticed. Closure of the University and nighttime patrols of the secret police in areas blocks away from the casinos did not affect the tourists or prosperous Cubans.

Landeira's family name placed him among the elite of Cuban society giving him certain impunity from police harassment even as a journalist often publishing material critical to the government. That reality allowed him to live without the fear of a knock on the door in the early hours of the morning by the secret police. Yet that superficial security did foster uncomfortable emotions. Why did he deserve to live in this illusionary paradise while thousands suffered violent injustice?

His newspaper reporting since coming to Havana was routine at best. Mostly centered on the hotel and casino boom. Like other reporters, he could mention the presence of organized crime figures such as Lansky and Trafficante but unable to uncover corroborating evidence of Mafia investment diminished the impact. For a group of violent thugs, the Mafia did remarkably well in obscuring their tracks from legal documents. Being in bed with the Batista government thwarted any intrusive investigation by the U.S. FBI. According to editorial speculation, that was the fundamental reason Meyer Lansky promoted Mafia investment in Havana.

No outsiders knew any details, however the Mafia summit meeting of 1946 held at the Hotel Nacional became common knowledge. Too many Mafiosi attending to conceal. The meeting was Meyer "The Little Man" Lansky's idea. Lansky headed the Jewish crime syndicate and more broadly served as the top financial adviser to the larger Italian Mafia. Lansky's particular specialty was gambling. Las Vegas, Cuba, the Bahamas. Chief among the attendees and acting as host was Charlie "Lucky" Luciano, former chairman and co-founder of the *Commission*, the ruling body of the loose American Mafia confederation. Deported from the United States, now living in Naples, Luciano still held paramount power over the other provisional bosses of the various *families* in the United States.

Prominent representatives from the New York and New Jersey families included: Frank "The Prime Minister" Costello, Luciano family boss, Vito "Don Vito" Genovese, Luciano Family caporegime, Giuseppe "Joe Adonis" Doto, Luciano Family caporegime, Albert "The Mad Hatter" Anastasia, Mangano Family underboss, Joseph "Joe Bananas" Bonanno, Bonanno Family boss, Gaetano "Tommy Brown" Lucchese, Gagliano Family underboss, Giuseppe "The Old Man" Profaci, Profaci Family boss.

From other cities: Anthony "Joe Batters" Accardo, Chicago Outfit boss, Commission member Charles "Trigger Happy" Fischetti, Sam Giancana, Chicago Outfit front boss, Stefano "The Undertaker" Magaddino, Buffalo Family boss, Carlos "Little Man" Marcello, New Orleans Family boss, and Santo "Louie Santos" Trafficante Jr., Tampa Family caporegime. The younger Trafficante now a fixture in Havana after moving here to oversee Tampa Family casino and business interests. In 1954, he became boss of the Tampa Family following the death of his father.

The Jewish Syndicate represented the organized crime's expertise in running gambling operations. Joining Lansky in Havana were Abner "Longy" Zwillman, New Jersey Jewish Syndicate boss, Morris "Moe" Dalitz, Cleveland Jewish Syndicate boss and casino front man for the Desert Inn, Las Vegas, Joseph "Doc" Stacher, New Jersey Jewish Syndicate boss, casino front man for the Sands Hotel in Las Vegas, and Philip "Dandy Phil" Kastel, Frank Costello's Louisiana slots operations and Tropicana Casino, Las Vegas partner.

Frank Sinatra provided stellar entertainment for the gala Mob event.

From that meeting in 1946, circumstances changed dramatically for the Mafia when Batista seized power in 1952. In Batista, they had a dictator as full partner, albeit for a large cut of the action.

With his father's longstanding connection with Batista and the Trafficantes, Bart Landeira felt certain of his father's involvement with Mafia investment in Havana. To determine that required creative investigation. Publishing names and details would be front-page news in the United States. Dangerous in Havana.

Reporting stories of substance with real news value centered on the dictatorships of Latin America. In Cuba, the overt expressions of repression came mostly from military actions in remote rural regions in the eastern half of the island. Difficult and dangerous for reporters. In Havana, the Cuban National Police kept a low profile in the upscale tourist sectors. The rumored disappearances and bodies found in the streets happened in the poorer quarters of the city. As yet Bart had not found a mechanism to enter this alternative Havana juxtaposed with the extravagant casino environment to discover hard-hitting news.

Landeira needed to deliver pieces of more dramatic content. With his coverage territory extended across Latin America, the most often cited brutal regime was arguably that of Rafael Trujillo in the Dominican Republic. A dictator in power since 1930. Best known for the notorious murder of 20,000 Haitians residing in the northwestern frontier region of Dominican Republic in 1937. Killed by machete to instill terror. In six days, the Dominican Army killed or forced the entire Haitian population living on the Dominican frontier to flee across the border into Haiti. The current Dominican environment was one of pervasive fear. Denunciation encouraged turning neighbors into *chivatos*, informers. A climate not unlike the Soviet Union during the Stalin era. People feared loss of social prestige, loss of livelihood, or possibly disappearance if accusations suggested subversion.

The instrument of state terror was the *Servicio de Inteligencia Militar*, the dreaded SIM. They patrolled the streets of Ciudad Trujillo in black Volkswagen Beetles. In whispers, Dominicans called them *caliés*, thugs. It was common knowledge the two in-

74

famous detention centers known as *La Nueve* and *La Cuarenta* were places of torture and murder.

In terms of organized state-sponsored violence to foster a climate of fear, the Dominican Republic was the epicenter. Some suggested Trujillo felt sufficiently emboldened to go after dissidents abroad. The American press reported the disappearance of Columbia University international law professor Jesús Galindez in March of this year in Manhattan. Circumstances suggested kidnapping and probable murder. Galindezes' doctoral thesis centered on Trujillo's rule. He lectured on international law using Trujillo's excesses as prominent examples.

A more recent disappearance appeared in the San Juan, Puerto Rico newspaper El Mundo. The byline by Gaspar Toussaint. Landeira regularly read his column. Toussaint was a virulent Trujillo critic. This incident involved the disappearance of a lawyer and civil rights advocate along with his wife and two teenage children. Landeira understood the need for extreme caution. Unlikely his status as an American journalist offered any security if Trujillo felt emboldened enough to go after a university professor in Manhattan.

Ciudad Trujillo was not like cosmopolitan Havana with its international tourist crowd. Functioning under constant fear, the city was somber by comparison. Rafael Trujillo was an unsophisticated monster from an earlier era. Consumed with a need for power and money, Trujillo's family monopolized control of sugar, tobacco, lumber, and salt industries along with the popular national lottery. The capital city Santo Domingo even renamed to Ciudad Trujillo.

Toussaint's articles in El Mundo described an escalation in state-perpetrated violence during the 1950s. Landeira flew into this snake pit of the Caribbean with no illusion about the dangers. His objective was to investigate the official police version of the disappearance of anti-Trujillo activist Daniel Cabrera and his family. The government version claimed the Cabreras fled the Dominican Republic as passengers on a freighter with several stops in Latin America. Speculation suggested that Cabrera might be in Veracruz, Mexico, a stop on the freighter's itinerary.

Relations between the two countries were currently cold owing to Mexico harboring other Dominican dissidents as they did with Batista's principal antagonist Fidel Castro. Cabrera remaining incognito in exile possibly to sustain publicity related to his disappearance.

Leaving the country by voluntarily would leave clues. The Cabreras more likely languished in one of the notorious prisons in the city, if not already dead. Landeira also knew it unlikely people would offer useful insights through fear of talking to a foreign reporter. Even so, the trip could prove useful in gathering antidotal material illustrating the pervasive climate of fear Gaspar Toussaint wrote about. He planned to populate his article with photographs. Expecting little in the way of useful information from those interviewed, photographs could at least provide a visual sense of Ciudad Trujillo.

As he left the airport in a taxi for his hotel, the contrast between Ciudad Trujillo and Havana was striking. The airport a relic from earlier times well outside the city. Earthwork visibly started with signs advertising construction of a new modern airport.

Armed with a map, Landeira marked a point of interest on this highway into the city. One of two notorious prisons operated by Trujillo's secret police. This prison simply named *La Nueve*. Nine kilometers east of the city on the coast highway to the airport.

Anticipating taking pictures of the prison might alarm the taxi driver, Landeira began snapping shots of the countryside with his Leica well before the prison came into sight. The driver still reacted nervously. "Señor, you must be careful taking pictures!"

"Why is that? You have a pretty country. Very beautiful from the air."

"Yes, but there are many things not so beautiful. That building in the distance is a prison. Something we never talk about."

"Well, every country has prisons. Criminals must be removed from any society."

"That is not that kind of prison, Señor. I wish to say no more."

The reporter Toussaint already reported on what went on at *La Nueve* and another facility named *La Cuarenta* on 40th Street. Survivors described grisly tortures inflicted by the SIM. Horrors rivaling the worst of the Nazi Gestapo.

The Hotel Hodelpa Nicolás de Ovando in the old colonial sector proved an excellent selection. A perfect choice for someone that liked history. Part of the building constructed in 1502 was once the home of the Spanish colonial governor. Hard to envision much of its centuries-old grandeur with modernized bathrooms and furniture, but the lobby and restaurant preserved a certain old world charm. A welcome retreat from what he expected to be difficult days ahead.

Toussaint's article identified the name of the ship on which Cabrera reportedly booked passage. Landeira had not yet attempted to track down the vessel's owner or its passenger manifest. That might take considerable effort. He wanted first to get to Ciudad Trujillo while the issue was still newsworthy and in the minds of possible witnesses. Highly doubtful that the family even left the country by ship.

Tomorrow morning his first stop was to the docks at the harbor. Only a ten-minute walk and the reason he selected this hotel. That evening he would play tourist by roaming the colonial zone neighborhoods and visiting a couple of bars to gather background material. Even in a police state, people often talked indiscreetly at bars.

It was Friday night. Mostly men with a few women occupied what appeared to be a popular bar. Compared with Havana, still unusually subdued for the start of the weekend.

Taking a seat at the bar, the bartender smiled, "Americano?" Probably because of his manner of dress.

"Yes. Cuban-American. From Miami," Landeira answered in Spanish.

"Welcome. What is your pleasure?"

"What is your best aged rum?"

"Several," He said pointing to an upper shelf behind the bar.

"I will leave it to your judgment. Just straight with no ice."

A minute later, the bartender set down the glass. A dark amber-hued rum. "This is the best Dominican rum."

Landeira took a sip. No aficionado yet of rum but he liked Landeira rum better. He smiled giving a nod to the bartender. With a drink, he settled into listening to the conversations at the bar.

Into his second drink, a disturbance erupted at the far end of the bar. He could only hear snatches. A man feeling the effects of alcohol began making angry statements intermixed with emotional outbursts. Something about his brother.

"…they took him…middle of the … No reason. In their black cars."

The bartender managed to settle the man down while two friends hustled him out of the bar. Landeira observed the patrons. Everyone stopped talking. The curious looked at the man. Others kept their heads down or turned away.

Landeira said to the bartender, "What was that about?"

"Just a customer with too much to drink. Some sort of family manner."

"Sounded more serious. Something about men in black cars."

"Señor. You are not from here. It is best never to speak of the special *policia* in the black cars."

The incident impressed on him the real dangers of Trujillo's Dominican Republic. He must be careful. The rumors of a pervasive culture of denunciation meant informers were everywhere. He decided it best not to attempt to play tourist. He did not look the part, nor was there anything newsworthy to gain. Stumbling on the incident at the bar just a random occurrence. Best to stick with asking questions related to the disappearance of the Cabrera family. Probably also dangerous but at least explainable since the story already appeared in the foreign press.

Best to return to his hotel and enjoy a quiet dinner.

The next morning he walked the short distance to the docks. The harbor of Santo Domingo, now renamed Ciudad Trujillo, was comparatively small. Introducing himself at the office of the harbormaster as a foreign newspaper reporter, Landeira said he was trying to track down a freighter named the *Princesa del Caribe*. Sailed from here on August 28.

The clerk at the office returned with a file bulging with papers.

"Yes. Left port on the 28th of last month at 0900," the clerk said.

"Does the manifest give the itinerary?"

"Caracas, Kingston, and then Veracruz."

"Its cargo?"

"Lumber and tractors."

"What about passengers?"

"Passengers?" The clerk made a grunting sound. "This is a small 2500 ton rust-bucket thirty years old. No accommodations for passengers. The manifest does not mention any passengers."

The Dominican SIM confident enough with controlling the false narrative they did not even bother to falsify the most basic documentation. The harbormaster office seemingly unaware of the reason for the press inquiring.

His next stop, the building where Cabrera leased office space. A longer walk in the oppressive August heat, but better to minimize the use of taxis. In a police state, taxi drivers became informers, either willingly or coerced.

The building directory listed Cabrera's law office on the second floor. The glass door stenciled with his name was locked. Landeira entered the office next door, an import-export firm. The reception much different from harbor office.

To the receptionist, he asked, "I am looking for Daniel Cabrera, the lawyer next door. The door is locked. Would you know how I might contact him?"

The young woman made no reply but her expression clearly exhibited fear as she shook her head. "Let me get my manager."

Two other women at their desks stopped working and looked up with expressions of alarm. A minute later, a man came up to the reception counter. His look displayed the same anxiety. "I am afraid we cannot help you. I believe Señor Cabrera no longer occupies that office."

"Really? How long has he been gone?"

"I could not say. At least a week." For a Dominican native, the man was sweating profusely.

"Did he vacate his office?"

"Señor, I am afraid we cannot help you. Now I must return to my work."

With that, the man disappeared into a back office. The women starred at Landeira transfixed as he walked out. In the hallway, he snapped several photos.

After lunch and a couple of beers, Landeira took stock. The fear palatable among the next-door office staff. Leaving the small local restaurant a twinge of unease as the other patrons followed him with their eyes. Perhaps just his paranoia. As a foreigner, everything about Ciudad Trujillo gave you the creeps.

Although he was certain as to the fate of the Cabreras, he still must check off the last items of his agenda before filing a story. First, the family home. Fortunately a manageable walk. The address turned out to be an apartment building in a modest neighborhood.

Cabrera's mailbox still displayed his name. Third floor. Unlike Cabrera's office, no pretense about what happened here. The door stood ajar. The doorjamb splintered.

Landeira gently pushed the battered door wide open. A living room in violent disarray. Furniture not only overturned but destroyed. Without venturing inside, he could see a kitchen table. Food spilled on the floor now consumed with the buzzing of a swarm of flies with cockroaches crawling about. He clicked off a roll of film.

Perhaps an abandoned apartment looted by neighbors. Yet he doubted that. It was not that sort of neighborhood. This was also not looting. The occupants hastily removed undoubtedly by the secret police.

A woman tenant exited the apartment down the hall. Taking a step toward her, "Señora, do you know what ..." She hurriedly reentered her apartment slamming the door closed.

He quickly left the area. She might be alerting the police. No need not pursue this further. His next stop was to have been the children's high school to ask students leaving for the day if they knew the Cabrera children. All that too dangerous now. Better to pursue the story tracking down the *Princesa del Caribe* and debunk the government's official explanation from a safe distance. The Cabrera family will obviously never resurface. When their fate eventually becomes obvious, the lapse of time will diminish the newsworthy impact of their murders. Trujillo is constantly committing political murders. The Cabreras will become just another footnote.

Combined with photos and antidotal material, there was enough to assemble his intended article. While Batista and Trujillo shared much in the way of statistical brutality in their repressive regimes, the climate in Havana bore little resemblance to the ubiquitous fear affecting everyone in Ciudad Trujillo. However, Landeira had yet to experience firsthand Batista's violence in eastern Cuba where murders by the Army were commonplace.

He would cut his Dominican visit short. Nothing more to gain here. Making further inquiries flirted with drawing the attention of Trujillo's secret police.

His apprehension proved correct with a knock on his door at three o'clock the next morning.

Out of bed wearing only underwear, he went to the door. "Who is it?"

"Police. Open the door."

"Just a moment. Let me get dressed."

The police responded by knocking more insistently after more than a minute passed, "Open the door immediately!"

With his pants on, he opened the door. He uttered an expletive under his breath as three men dressed in civilian clothes pushed their way into the room and closed the door.

"Let me see your badges," Landeira said assertively. This was not good. All three dressed casually with shirts untucked. Obviously concealing handguns at their waist.

One man pulled a leather flip-fold from his pocket revealing a badge. As Landeira feared, Servicio de Inteligencia Militar, Dominican military intelligence. Trujillo's secret police.

"Your name?" one asked.

81

"Bartolo Landeira. American. What is the reason for this intrusion?"

The man said, "Your passport."

After handing over his passport, the man in charge said, "You are being detained, Señor Landeira." The SIM agent put the passport in his shirt pocket.

"For what reason?"

"That I do not know. Only that it is a matter of state security. My orders are to escort you to the airport and place you on the first available flight leaving the country. You are being deported."

"I wish to call the American embassy. I am a newspaper correspondent for the Miami Herald. You are creating an international incident."

Landeira said that only for bluster. In absolute power since 1930, Trujillo ignored international pressure. The U.S. was already tiring of their long-standing support for this butcher. Deporting a journalist a trivial matter compared to the body count mounting in the Dominican Republic.

"Get dressed and pack your belongings," the man in charge ordered. "Quickly."

One of the men watched closely as Landeira pack his suitcase after making sure there were no weapons inside.

Five minutes later, they were downstairs at the hotel desk.

"The SIM agent said to the night clerk, "Señor Landeira is checking out. Prepare his bill immediately."

The clerk's hands were shaking as he took the room key from Landeira. A minute later in a cracking voice, he stated the owing amount. The frightened clerk knew who the three men were.

As they stepped outside Landeira saw the dreaded black VW Beetle. Cramped in the back seat of the two-door vehicle with one of the agents left no means of maneuver. If truly a deportation, he was getting off easy. Makes for a perfect closing entry when he files his story. However, this could instead be a ride to the notorious prison *La Cuarenta* not far from the hotel. Perhaps to disappear like Cabrera.

82

The VW headed north through the darkened streets of the city old quarter. Details of the memorized map told Landeira the junction with the highway he came in from the airport was not far. Fear heightened with anticipation. Kept in control by training and wartime experience.

Arriving at the junction, the VW turned left. A sign indicated turning right for the route to the airport. Landeira looked at the agent sitting next to him. The bastard actually appeared to display a slight grin.

The agent in charge in the front passenger seat turned and said, "We must make a stop before proceeding to the airport. A formality to report your arrest to my superiors."

Bullshit. Landeira remained outwardly calm by simply nodding. This was now about survival. Look for an opportunity to escape these thugs. If successful, worry later about escaping the country. Better to die quickly taking some of these fuckers with him rather than subjecting him to torture and a protracted death.

Nothing he could do while cramped in the back seat of the small VW.

His worst fears confirmed as the car turned into a bleak industrial area. Should have realized something amiss at the hotel when they did not confiscate his camera from his suitcase. They knew he was not leaving the country.

The driver stopped with the headlights illuminating a building. After unlocking and getting out, he unlocked a personnel door and entered. Seconds later a rollup door opened. Returning to the car, he drove the VW into the unlit building interior.

Leaving the headlights on, the driver and lead agent in the front seat exited the car. Landeira heard the rollup door closing.

After the driver returned, the lead agent tilted the front seat of the VW down to allow the agent in the back to exit and motioned with a revolver for Landeira to get out.

The VW headlights illuminated a large open area. Several chains hung from a low beam. Underneath the chains was a large dark area covering the concrete floor surrounding what appeared to be a drain in a depression area covered with a cast iron grill. On a nearby post was a fire hose attached to a pipe with a valve. In the background a row of 55-gallon steel drums. Landeira could hear the squealing of what sounded like rats.

Instinctively he understood what this was. A place of torture. A slaughterhouse. For humans not livestock. An industrialized process for making people disappear. Likely hung from the chains then dismembered. The remains placed inside barrels for disposal. The blood and gore washed down the drain.

Ignoring the disturbing images, Landeira's training focused his mind on looking for an opportunity to attack. Had this been a prison, he stood no chance. So far, no one other than the three SIM agents appeared to be in the building. No lights ever came on. Only the headlights of the VW offered illumination. He had been in equally dire circumstances during the war. Taught to act without hesitation at the first opportunity without hesitation. Do not over think the consequences.

His adversaries in this situation were likely untrained in close quarter combat. Landeira trained with the best. A long time ago but thoroughly ingrained through practice, how to kill an instinctive response even after all these years.

The SIM agent in charge moved Landeira forward by pushing the revolver into his back. A careless move getting that close. Accustomed to his usual victims incapacitated by fear. The other two agents walking ahead represented the real danger. Fortunately, neither held a weapon in their hand although certainly they carried guns.

Landeira holding his hands above his head spun rapidly to his left facing the surprised SIM lead agent. The move passed his left arm over the assailant's right arm holding the revolver while clamping the man's arm firmly against his own body. Landeira immediately brought his right knee into the man's groin, simultaneously driving the heel of his right hand under his chin. The entire sequence lasted less than two seconds.

Landeira then closed the distance on another agent fumbling to extract his revolver from his hip holster as the gun caught under his shirt. Grabbing the man's right wrist before he was able to withdraw his weapon, he dropped the man to the floor on his back using a classic wrist throw maneuver. Still holding the wrist with both hands, he stomped down with his left foot on the man's exposed throat.

The remaining agent successfully drew his gun. From only a few feet away, Landeira instinctively stepped close to the man following the cardinal close quarter combat edict of sustaining your attack without pause. The surprised assailant took a step backwards almost losing his balance and wildly fired a shot.

The shot missed wide as Landeira deflected the man's arm. He then seized the man's hand holding the revolver with his right hand, simultaneously seizing the man's forearm with his left hand. Jerking the man's hand upward, he twisted it backwards while pivoting on his left foot to add the full force of his body. The move broke the man's trigger finger freeing the revolver into Landeira's hand.

Disarmed, Landeira kneed him in the groin and delivered a judo blow with the edge of his hand to the side of the neck.

Since Landeira commenced these attacks, only ten seconds elapsed.

While retrieving the guns, Landeira checked the condition of the assailants. One had no pulse. The blow to the chin possibly breaking his neck. Another was conscious but gasping for air with blood coughing out of his mouth from damage by the blow to his throat. The third man getting off the shot remained unconscious.

Landeira forced himself to ease his breathing. He must get away from here quickly but methodically focused on covering his tracks as much as possible. From the pockets of the dead, he retrieved his passport, took their SIM identifications, and the keys used by the driver to enter the building. From the Volkswagen he retrieved his suitcase.

Landeira stuck one revolver in his waist and pocketed a handful of additional bullets. Escaping the country now a major problem. These bastards no different from the Waffen SS. Do not allow them to take you alive after what he just did. Unlikely to prevail in a gunfight, the weapon could provide a final bullet to the head if faced with capture.

One final task remained. He needed to buy time to improve his chances for escaping the country. Leaving behind wounded to talk was not an option.

Raising his pant leg revealed a leather ankle holster holding a folded knife with a five-inch blade. Pressing a button actuated a spring unfolding a stiletto blade. Shorter than his commando combat killing knife during the war, the blade sufficient to inflict a quick death by someone well trained like Landeira.

The switchblade a holdover from his CIA days where carrying a gun was not always possible. He certainly was not coming to the Dominican Republic unarmed.

Without hesitation, Landeira dispatched the two wounded men. Unpleasant but he killed many of the enemy in this manner during the war. For the victim, a quick death. A penetration of the sharp-tipped narrow blade into the lower neck under the clavicle to sever one of the pair of subclavian arteries. The loss of blood flow causes loss of consciousness in two seconds with death in four. The brutal act necessary for survival. *If you hesitate to think, you are dead. Revert instinctively to your training. Act aggressively.*

He took photographs of the warehouse interior and the three dead SIM agents before turning off the VW headlights. After locking the door behind him and discarding the key ring, he set off down the street. No street lights in this industrial sector offered concealment, while moonlight proved adequate to navigate. The map imprinted in his mind another skill learned from wartime OSS training.

His objective was to reach the hotel quarter and get a taxi to the airport at first light. A long walk but at least in the predawn, the heat was tolerable. If his luck held, the dead agents possibly not discovered for hours.

Having waited outside at an upscale hotel not far from the hotel he left just a couple of hours ago, the bell captain emerged at first light. With no taxis waiting this early, he asked the man to call a taxi, giving him a good tip. "An early flight to catch."

No surprises yet. Everything depended on how soon the first available flight departed. It did not matter where. Time was now critical. His only option to escape the country before identified as a wanted fugitive was by air.

Arriving at the airport, his luck appeared holding. There was a flight leaving in thirty minutes for Kingston, Jamaica.

In English, he asked at the ticket desk, "Is there a seat available on the seven o'clock flight to Kingston?"

He had his passport out, not his real passport but one of several U.S. passports in false names. Holdovers from his CIA days. This one hidden in a concealed bottom compartment of his suitcase.

"Yes, Señor Delgado. Will that be round trip?"

"No. Just one way. I need to go to Miami after Kingston but I am not sure of my schedule."

As the reservation clerk took his money and prepared the boarding pass, her telephone rang.

"Policia?" The surprised clerk said.

Landeira turned his head pretending indifference and appearing as if he did not understand Spanish while concentrating on trying to hear the caller.

"Let me check." After checking reservation lists, the young woman said, "No reservation for an Americano named Landeira booked on any of our flights today. Yes, we check the passports of all passengers departing for other countries."

She smiled and handed him his passport and boarding pass. "Have a pleasant flight Señor Delgado."

Chapter 7

Landeira temporarily recovered from the violent encounter by the time the plane set down in Kingston, Jamaica. It would take longer to compartmentalize it. He reflected over several Scotches at the airport bar waiting for a flight to Havana. An experience reminiscent from his war years. Killing then so commonplace it eventually became more existential than emotional. Executing the SIM agents a disgusting necessity. The calluses to his psyche left from his brutal wartime experiences however remained in place. Lacking the reaction of a *normal* person was the only troubling emotion.

The attack unexpected but not surprising. Journalism is a high-risk profession when venturing into dangerous places like Trujillo's Dominican Republic. He knew that yet he still stuck his neck out. Anxious to practice real journalism instead of the insipid crap forced to produce since coming to Havana because of censorship. This was genuine reporting rather than the journalism practiced while a cover for his CIA activities.

The Dominican experience was the perfect story to illustrate the horrors of living in an oppressive police state. It required careful construction to portray in print without making himself the subject of the story.

Although a harrowing incident, it confirmed his abiding interest in pursuing investigative journalism. Journalism and writing his earliest interests. Obtained his undergraduate degree intending to pursue a journalism career. Made the mistake of allowing his father to persuade him to pursue a law degree. The brief time spent practicing law with his father made certain that was not his chosen career path. The war then changed far more than the arch of his career.

Sitting at the bar reflecting on his violent encounters during the war, Landeira attempted to make comparisons with the Dominican incident. Killing in cold blood justified by the same circumstances of survival.

Every soldier seeing combat is changed. The fear, the emotional scarring of taking lives. Operating behind enemy lines placed him in a unique group. Repeated close quarter combat encounters resulted in killing the enemy with a knife. Close enough to smell the victim. The need for silence. Missions of assassination or sabotage. Dispatching enemy wounded necessary to fulfill the mission and insure escape.

The Dominican situation brought back a nearly identical incident in Italy in 1944 when captured by the Waffen SS with four Italian partisans. The scars of a bullet wound to his left hand and knife wound to his left cheek forever reminders of that traumatic event.

Now as then, he attributed escape to his training. Credit given to Major Fairbairn of the British SOE. Camp 103, also known as Camp X, in Ontario, Canada in 1942. Sent their as part of the first United States OSS recruits for training by the established British program.

Fairbairn was the most dangerous man imaginable. Experienced in boxing, wrestling, savate French foot fighting, jujutsu, and various Chinese martial arts. His rule, *There's no fair play, no rules except one: kill or be killed.* Fairbairn honed those skills as instructor to the Shanghai Municipal Police and by extensive combat experience confronting the violent Tong gangs.

Fairbairn co-designed the commando knife Landeira used during the war. Taught its use in efficient killing. Fairbairn continually reinforced technique and muscle memory through repetition to override emotion. *No different from shooting the enemy at a distance, except just a more personal experience. War is a function of killing the enemy efficiently. Forget everything else.*

As disturbing as the Dominican encounter was, Landeira philosophically placed it in perspective. Violent experiences like Italy in 1944 taught him to tamp down the emotional repercussions of doing something so alien to normal human experience.

Regardless of events in Ciudad Trujillo, the experience confirmed his career choice to pursue investigative journalism. Meaningful work with clear purpose. Worth taking risks. It also pointed to avoid complacency of living in seemingly safe Havana. Fulgencio Batista was an equivalent bloodstained dictator as Rafael Trujillo. Currently, that bloodletting relegated largely to the rural eastern provinces of Cuba. Repression in Havana carefully selective to avoid damaging the lucrative American gambling tourist trade.

* * * *

Although Fidel Castro remained in Mexico, political opposition to Batista remained active in early 1956. Having retaken the presidency of Cuba by coup d'état instead of democratic election in 1952, Fulgencio Batista was highly unpopular among the Cuban people. Since coming to power, he suspended the constitution and governed by decree. A dictator by any definition. He made no commitments for calling new elections while increasing suppression of political dissent.

In April, popular Cuban Army officer Colonel Ramón Barquín organized a coup consisting of other army officers opposed to Batista's illegal rule. The coup failed. The officers all court marshalled and removed from the military. Batista imprisoned Barquín in the same prison as Fidel Castro three years earlier. The incident resulted in Batista purging the Army senior ranks of officers that might threaten his hold of the Cuban military.

At the end of April, another organized revolutionary movement known as the Directorio Revolucionario Estudiantil attacked the Domingo Goicuría army barracks in the city of Matanzas. The attack by 100 rebels failed disastrously. The incident was similar to the failed attack on the Moncado Barracks in Santiago by Fidel Castro's 26 July Movement three years earlier. The threat of small-scale attack by armed rebels caused little military concern given the superior strength of the Cuban Army. However, the larger concern for the regime was the apparent widespread expression of revolutionary sentiment among the population sufficient to produce an armed attack by an urban insurgency group unrelated to Castro.

The Revolutionary Directorate evolved from a dissident group of students from the University of Havana. Batista's closure of the university was in response to anti-government demonstrations instigated by the DRE. As with Castro's revolt originating in rural Cuba, frustration eventually led to the armed insurrection by the urban intellectuals of the DRE. While neither group yet presented a military threat to Batista's 40,000 strong military, they fanned the embers of a universally growing opposition to Batista with support among the Cuban people.

****

The following morning after returning to Havana, Landeira went for a day sail down the coast. A beautiful sky with only scattered high clouds. A light breeze out of the northwest as he sailed east. A longer trip back against the wind requiring tacking. A lunch of sandwiches and beer. A chance to settle his thoughts. No better place than the sea. The sounds of a good sailboat performing. The sails taking the wind. The strain on the sheets. The sound of the hull slicing through the water. A beautiful marriage of nature's grandeur and man's engineering mastery. For Landeira, the noise of motorized boats disturbed the contemplative joy of being on the water.

A week later, he filed his story with the Miami Herald. No need to pull punches. With what happened, any return to the Dominican Republic became impossible as long as Trujillo remained in power. However, even then, he was not about to admit in print to killing three secret police agents. Though contrary to journalistic ethics, better instead to portray the photographs of the dead agents and their chamber of horrors as SIM murder victims delivered as intimidation rather than his own photography.

Fear in Trujillo's Dominican Republic
Miami Herald correspondent Bart Landeira

Under dictator Rafael Trujillo since 1930, the Dominican Republic has known nothing but brutality. Life to Trujillo means nothing. The stark evidence in support of the accusation was the genocidal atrocity known as the Parsley Massacre of 1937. Acting on Trujillo's orders, Dominican Army troops murdered 20,000 ethnic Haitians living within the border of the northwestern Dominican Republic frontier border with Haiti. To inflict greater terror, the Dominican military used machetes to hack the victims to death.

Since that time, the body count continues to rise. Rafael Trujillo came from lower middle class beginnings and turned to crime at an early age. A clever opportunist and sociopath, he fueled his rise to power through treachery and violence. After decades of unchallenged power promoting himself as the Dominican benefactor, Trujillo is arguably the most reviled homicidal dictator in Latin America.

Having never stood for election, Trujillo came to power in 1930 as the only candidate after terrorizing any opposition. Trujillo's rule is more akin to that of a medieval feudal lord. Everything belongs to him. People function to enrich him. It is difficult to assess the true extent of his wealth. However, Dominican public records make little attempt to conceal the endless listings of business and land ownerships of the Trujillo family. Bribes and kickbacks replaced by profits from seized holdings. The Trujillo family owns major percentages of every economic sector comprising the Dominican Republic gross national product.

That offers a brief background to the Trujillo regime. This article deals with the current pervasive climate of fear I witnessed during a recent trip to the county's capital, Ciudad Trujillo. Trujillo City, historically the former Santo Domingo. I went as a follow up to investigate the reported disappearance of a prominent anti-Trujillo dissident, Dr. Daniel Cabrera, a civil rights lawyer. Not only has Cabrera disappeared, but also his wife and two teenage children.

The story first came to light in an article published several weeks ago in the San Juan Newspaper El Mundo by reporter Gaspar Toussaint. Toussaint accused the Dominican regime as complicit in Cabrera's disappearance. An increasingly disturbing occurrence in the country. A spokesman for the Dominican Ministry of Justice made a public statement suggesting that Cabrera simply left the country by taking passage on a freighter. Toussaint alleges Dominican Military Intelligence, the SIM, is responsible for Cabrera's disappearance.

To anyone living in the Dominican Republic, the SIM is Trujillo's feared secret police. Disappearances of the type related to Cabrera are commonplace. Dominican newspapers never report such occurrences due to strict press censorship. In the case of Cabrera, the Justice Ministry only responded publically following the publication of the story in the Puerto Rican newspaper, subsequently disseminated by the international news wire services.

The El Mundo reporter Gaspar Toussaint is a recognized harsh critic of Rafael Trujillo. It is from Toussaint's reporting that those outside the Dominican Republic know something of how the police state operates there. Trujillo's enforcement arm is the SIM, the Servicio de Inteligencia Militar. They roam the streets of Ciudad Trujillo and other cities in black Volkswagens as a signal to the populace of their pervasive surveillance. With no meaningful criminal justice system, arrest by the SIM is the nightmare of every Dominican.

Coming to Ciudad Trujillo with the expectation of uncovering information regarding the disappearance of Daniel Cabrera yielded much more. My first issue was investigating the government's assertion that Cabrera left on a freighter named the *Princesa del Caribe* on August 28. The harbormaster's office confirmed the ship did sail from Ciudad Trujillo on that date. However, the ship's manifest listed no passengers. They also stated the small freighter had no accommodations for passengers.

I found Cabrera's law office locked. Inquiring at the next-door office in the same building provided my first glimpse of the widespread fear of the general populace. The staff of this adjacent business became visibly shaken when I asked questions. The same reaction repeated when visiting the Cabrera apartment building. Unlike the locked law office, the Cabrera apartment doorjamb was broken and the door open. Inside revealed destruction. An overturned kitchen table with spilled food swarming with flies and cockroaches as seen by my photograph indicates an unexpected departure by the family. A neighbor exiting her apartment appeared terrified by my presence and returned back inside locking her door.

I also witnessed another incident at a bar further illustrating the paranoia of the populace. Someone with too much to drink created a scene proclaiming his anguish over his brother's arrest by Trujillo's secret police. Friends quickly removed the man. The bartender cautioned me against asking questions.

Over decades in power, the Trujillo regime encouraged public denunciation, eventually making it an integral part of Dominican life. Easy for people to succumb to settling scores or furthering one's own interests at the expense of others. A social corrosive that breeds a culture of informers. While denunciation might lead to loss of job or societal stature for the subject, it meant far worse if the allegations were anti-government in nature.

That night, the Dominican culture of fear became personal for this reporter. A knock on the door at three o'clock in the morning. After asking who was at the door, the chilling reply came, "Security police." After dressing and opening the door, there was no one there. Only an envelope slipped under the door. Inside a sequence of photographic enlargements reprinted here. The most graphic being of three dead bodies lying on a concrete floor. The liquid pooling about the bodies clearly blood from fatal wounds to the neck. No accompanying explanation of the photographs was included. The captions are this reporter's own interpretation given the intent of the photographs as intimidation. The bodies obviously SIM murder victims. Note the unmarked black Volkswagen Beetle in one photo. The ubiquitous symbol of the SIM security police understood by all Dominicans. The hanging row of chains over a dark stained concrete floor surrounding a drain suggested a slaughterhouse. Is this how people disappear? Dismemberment with the human remains perhaps stuffed into the 55-gallon drums as seen in another photograph?

Ciudad Trujillo contains at least two notorious prisons. *La Nueve* and *La Cuarenta*. Places of unspeakable torture and murder. Previously published reports by survivors attest to the horrors inflicted in these places. By the number of missing persons associated in some way with anti-government behavior, it is likely the secret police employ other means of disposing bodies apart from the known prisons. I believe these photographs depict yet another form of spreading terror.

The origin of these photographs unmistakably delivered by the SIM. One hour after receiving the scare at my hotel room door, the night desk clerk telephoned. He informed me that my bill was ready for checkout as instructed. A taxi already waiting to take me to the airport. I of course gave no such instructions. A less than subtle warning by the SIM to leave the country. The obvious reason was asking too many questions about the disappearance of the Cabrera family. This avoided an international incident with an unexplained disappearance of an American journalist.

Little doubt remains as to the fate of Daniel Cabrera, his wife, and two children. It is also difficult to understand the United States government's indifference to Rafael Trujillo's brutal excesses. Yet the U.S. continues to support the Dominican regime economically and militarily as well as other dictatorships in Latin America. The same fear of a left wing revolutionary threat taking shape in Cuba undoubtedly compels Washington to continue on the same course.

Landeira disliked publishing the altered origins of the photographs. However, he was not about to admit in print even the self-defense killing of three Dominican secret police officers. Poetic justice to turn their deaths against them even if only he knows the truth.

* * * *

The violent experience brought back distressing memories of his wartime service. Recurring nightmares thought gone several years ago returned. As horrific as it was, he did not dwell on it. Nor did it consciously trouble him emotionally. He killed many times during the war. Most were just regular Wehrmacht German soldiers. The three SIM murderers were like the Nazi SS. Criminals deserving death.

Nonetheless, the incident did not diminish Landeira's resolve to continue investigative journalism. Looking to expose wrongdoing in places like the Dominican Republic and Cuba was inherently a dangerous profession. His wartime experiences beyond that of any correspondent during World War Two. The risks well understood.

Writing providing a truer sense of purpose than anything in his working life. The idea of becoming serious about writing fiction only encouraged by the events in the Dominican Republic. The trove of experiences of his life provided endless sources of compelling stories. Stories allowing him to explore the nature of serious subjects through fictional characters.

Investigating the darker side of Cuba from within Cuba required finding a way to circumvent censorship. Landeira had the means to burrow under the glamourous veneer of Havana through his father's suspect activities. Finding the means to conceal the source of his information as access to his father's secretive dealings might be a challenge. Even with that material, how could he avoid censorship in reporting material critical of the Batista regime without risking deportation?

While likely complicit in trafficking in illegal or at least unsavory financial enterprises, it pained him that his father had fallen in with organized criminals and corrupt Cuban officials. Their strained relationship now at a point of reconciliation made circumstances more troublesome. He accepted the fact he felt affection for his old man. Certainly felt a responsibility not to destroy his father no matter the questionable ethics of that work.

Part of honoring that responsibility was delivering on his commitment to oversee the rum business. At it only for a few weeks, he found it a welcoming diversion. The business seemed to run itself. He just looked after the numbers. The excellent staff managed with no interference from him. A reflection on the organizational skills of his Uncle Tomás.

Yet making little contribution ran counter to his character. That meant turning his focus on finding a suitable general manager. Not an easy task. Running the distillation business meant someone expert in making rum while possessing proven managerial skills. It seemed clear Landeira Grupo needed to lure someone from another Cuban rum producer.

The thought occurred to him of his uncle's mention of the owner of Montero Rum. Obviously, Montero knew how to make excellent rum. Must know something of running a business since he was third generation. Revisiting the acquisition attempt by Uncle Tomás appeared a better prospect than attempting to recruit from a large producer like Bacardi. At least Montero knew how to make excellent rum.

If Montero could take over management of a much larger combined enterprise was the question. The choice was his father's but he recognized his responsibility if making the recommendation. The larger question remained finding a reason that might entice Montero. At least his offer was more than simply an acquisition. Still it would take a skillful presentation of the benefits to entice Montero. What could motivate him to relinquish ownership of his family business? The first move obviously was to meet Augustin Montero and see if he was the right candidate before attempting to entice Montero to sell.

✳ ✳ ✳ ✳

The Montero distillery was only a half mile west of the Landeira distillery. Before arranging a meeting with Augustin Montero, he checked out the facility. Somewhat disappointing. Perhaps a third of the square footage of the two Landeira buildings. Older and a little shabby in need of painting. However, from this modest building Montero made extraordinary rum. Landeira thought how acquiring the Montero brand and Montero's knowhow might also be a marketing coup.

Landeira telephoned Augustin Montero early one morning. After introducing himself, Montero expressed his condolences for the passing of his friend Tomás. "I understood the funeral service was at the family estate in Camagüey but I was unable to attend."

Landeira said, "Understandable. Such a long distance from Havana. Uncle Tomás spoke highly of you. Introduced me to your very impressive rum, Señor Montero. Both of us in the same business and so close by, I thought we should meet. I am just temporally overseeing administration of Destilerias de Ron Landeira. Are you free for lunch today?"

"But of course."

"Excellent. I shall stop by before noon. Perhaps you can show me your distillery. Then I will treat you to a fine lunch, Se-ñor Montero. We shall make it a fine day."

Arriving at the Montero distillery office, a young man greet-ed him.

"Glad to meet you, Señor Landeira. I am Luis Montero. My father is expecting you."

After a warm greeting, Augustin Montero took Landeira into the distillery. Although unprepossessing from the outside, the interior was clean and well ordered. Cramped for space with the rows of wooden aging barrels, Landeira remarked, "Looks like you could use more warehouse space."

Montero nodded, "That has always been a struggle. Unfor-tunately no way to expand even if I had money to invest. We are a small producer. Our sales are steady but always a challenge to compete with larger producers like Bacardi or Landeira."

"Señor Montero, you do not compete with Bacardi, or even the less expensive Landeira rum. I am no expert like my Uncle Tomás however, I recognize the taste of outstanding rum. Landeira Reserve is *very* good rum but Montero rum is *excellent*. I am usually a Scotch drinker but I can appreciate the subtle dif-ferences."

"You are most kind, Señor Landeira."

"We have an excellent distilling master at Landeira, Gustavo Rodriguez. I am proud of our rum but it is Montero rum I order at a bar or restaurant when I can find it. Without giving away any trade secrets, what makes the difference between?"

Montero laughed. "There are no secrets. Just an endless number of factors that makes each rum distinct from another. No different from the Scotch you like. Each is distinct even if from the same location made with the same grain and water.

"The soil from which sugar cane or grain comes is another factor. The unique features of the still is yet another. Handcraft-ed, each still renders subtle differences to the raw distillate. The type of barrel used in the aging is particularly important. The art of blending different barrels produces the finished rum with the desired taste. Montero rum uses American bourbon whiskey barrels for the first maturation then a second maturation in sherry barrels years later.

"The secret is the talent of a master distiller. I know your Gustavo. We talk shop when we meet. We are more artists than craftsmen. What we do is like the way a painter uses brush strokes, the way he uses light and shadow. Like a painter, the finished product goes beyond the artist's expertise at his craft. The creation is part inspiration, part luck, and part magic. The magic is the part you cannot explain. Words cannot explain how all these different elements come together to create something of beauty."

Landeira smiled. "You are not only an artist at making rum but a poet. Looking forward to talking further over lunch. I will take you to my uncle's favorite restaurant."

After ordering cold beers, Landeira said, "I met your son when I arrived this morning. Is he involved in the business?"

"Like you, only temporarily. Luis was a year away from completing his legal studies when Batista closed the University. He now splits his time at the distillery and helping out at my daughter Emilia's law practice."

"Interesting. A family of lawyers. I too have a law degree in America. I was born in Florida. Chose not to follow my father in pursuing law as a career. Went to work instead for the American foreign service then became a journalist for the Miami Herald after the war. My father would like to see me join Landeira Grupo but I like the chase of pursuing news stories then shaping it into words."

Redirecting the conversation, Landeira said, "One of the problems with an old family-owned business as large as Landeira Grupo is the succession plan from one generation to the next. My father was one of three brothers that grew the family enterprise over the last thirty years. He now serves as the senior executive with the passing of Tomás and his older brother in poor health. My cousins now run the agricultural operations. Our management is spread too thin. The time has come to acquire new senior management strength from outside the family.

"Forgive my being direct, Señor Montero, you are a long way from old age, but who succeeds you when the time comes to step down?"

"Quite alright to ask. The truth is I do not know. The business is more than my livelihood. It is my heritage. My grandfather started making rum at our current location in 1880. After that my father. I took over before the war."

"Even if your children took over should something happen to you, they will not possess the *magic* for making Montero rum."

Montero nodded in agreement. "You are correct. I have the same problem as your family." The opening more than Landeira might have hoped. He took the opportunity to comment, "Your children would have little choice but to sell. No telling what might become of the fabled Montero rum."

"Yes. I worry about what will happen in my old age."

Landeira said, "Before today I did not know you. Only tasted your exceptional rum. But I recalled Uncle Tomás speaking fondly of you before he died. He said he even offered to buy Montero Rum some time ago. What I believe he actually meant was acquiring Augustin Montero. Without you, there is no way to sustain the making of Montero rum."

Montero nodded. "I liked Tomás but I was not prepared to Montero Rum."

"Circumstances are now different. Yet my uncle was correct. Let me be direct. It is my responsibility to find a suitable replacement to manage Landeira Rum. I have a better idea. Instead of Landeira Grupo acquiring Montero Rum, merge it while keeping it a separate operating unit. Preserve the distinct character and the magic of Montero Rum. To accomplish that, make Augustin Montero the general manager in charge of both Montero Rum and Landeira Rum."

Montero looked stunned. "That is quite an honor. A surprising offer. As I told Tomás when he offered to purchase us several years ago, I do not believe I am ready to sell."

"I certainly understand. Obviously I gave thought to this before coming here today. After meeting you, it however became clear that it resolves the same problem it seems for both our families. This is about family as much as about business.

"Let me explain further. My idea is to keep Montero Rum as a distinct brand. As you explained, the unique characteristics of the still construction become a critical factor in the distillation. You keep the same building but now Landeira has the capital to expand space. You continue to run it as a separate operation increasing production without compromising the brand. Of course, you now also manage Landeira Rum. Between you and Gustavo, you develop the next generation of master distillers. Both Landeira and Montero rums continue their long heritage, separate but complimentary. With Landeira capital, Montero Rum can increase production.

"Landeira Grupo makes a handsome offer to purchase Montero Rum and you receive a generous salary and bonus based on a percentage of profits. The numbers are all negotiable."

Montero smiled. "I am honored you place so much faith in my abilities."

Landeira held up his hand. "No need to give me an immediate reply. That is a lot to consider coming as a surprise. As I said, this is about family. You must of course discuss this with your wife and children. No rush. We can talk again. Now let's enjoy a good meal. I also know they serve Montero rum here."

Chapter 8

Despite the incident in the Dominican Republic, Landeira was committed to pursuing investigative journalism. What better place than Havana? A place of old world charm set in a tropical environment populated with a culture of warm and life-affirming people. For a journalist, a city with a broad cast of villains. A corrupt dictator. Secret police. A brutally repressive military beset by a growing leftist revolutionary insurgency. American mobsters erecting a gambling paradise out of reach of U.S. law enforcement.

The Miami Herald along with the New York Times already pushed the boundaries with articles about the origins of the growing threat of revolutionary opposition. While the Herald picked up stories from the wire services, Landeira explained his predicament to the managing editor. "I intend to focus my attention right now on the Mafia in Havana. Of interest to American readers. Although Mafia investment in the hotels and casinos is not news, the specifics are. Characters Americans recognize from the sustained interests generated by the Kefauver hearings."

"What about the political turmoil. A bloody dictatorship. An active insurgency," Fred Jansen said. He was managing editor of the Herald and an experienced reporter from the days of the newspaper's founding in 1946.

"First of all, the insurgency is not threatening Batista's hold on power. Fidel Castro is in exile in Mexico. His movement 26th of July has no effective footing beyond its origins in the rural sugarcane provinces of eastern Cuba. The other anti-government group is the Student Revolutionary Directorate. Former students of the University of Havana now closed and the DRE outlawed."

"Those stories still reach the wire services however," Jansen said.

"Sure, but lacking in substance. No details to engage the American reader. Not especially newsworthy, Fred."

"Reports of atrocities committed by Batista's military are newsworthy," Jansen interjected.

"At the risk of sounding callous, Fred, just more of the same political violence going on around the world. Just casualty numbers. Here's my deal, Carl. No reporter based in Cuba can report details of state-sponsored murder without running afoul of the regime's censorship. Without photographs and narrative accounts from the scene, it becomes no different than continual recurring accounts of violence in the world."

"I was not aware that journalists were at risk in Cuba," Jansen said.

"Not like Trujillo's Dominican Republic. Effective censorship however. Foreign journalists are just deported. Cuban journalists risk must worse treatment. Batista also has a secret police. "

"Speaking of secret police that was one helluva piece you put together on your experience in Ciudad Trujillo, Bart."

"My point exactly, Fred. Got myself deported from the DR. Lucky that was all. Batista's police are more subtle. I know the editors of several Cuban newspapers. Publishing something contrary to the regime's interest results in a telephone call from a censor at the Ministry of Propaganda. Imagine a government ministry identified for propaganda. Anything deemed critical of the regime becomes a target. The less than subtle instruction conveyed is to desist publishing anything further in that vain. The threat implicit. Once on their shit list, you thereafter come under intense scrutiny.

"Based in Havana, I must be careful to avoid getting kicked out of Cuba. I believe I can be freer going after the Mafia. Doubt they would go after me with physical violence. Bad for the gambling business. If I'm careful, I can indirectly suggest the corruption derived from the newfound glamour of Havana which is now outshining Las Vegas."

"Okay. I see your point. Does the prestige of your family provide any cover?"

Landeira appreciated the irony. Not only did it provide a measure of cover, but his father was likely up to his ears in official corruption.

"Don't know. Better I don't test how far I can go. However, I'm not forgetting the political side. Working a new source. Might provide useful material to probe the details of Batista's institutionalized corruption. I also believe the same source might have connections to the DRE revolutionaries. Will see where that goes. Anything particularly damaging to the Batista regime appearing in the Herald puts me under suspicion because I am your correspondent in Cuba."

"What about AP or UP wire material?"

"Can't do anything about that. Just make sure attribution clearly deflects away from me as the source. Do follow up pieces by staff reporters to my reporting by as you see fit. I can claim it is not my doing. I'll go as far as I can in my submissions but make up plausible alternative source attribution for anti-Batista material. If Batista objects to what the Herald prints, he will likely prohibit circulation in Cuba. What do we care? Our readership is Florida and the entire Caribbean. We can't avoid publishing negative material about assholes like Batista and Trujillo for the sake of circulation."

* * * *

The potential source was Dr. Mateo Pérez. Former professor of economics of the now shuttered Havana University. Landeira found his name while searching the archives of the Havana newspaper *Prensa Libre*. Cited in several articles since Batista assumed power in 1952, Pérez was a Batista critic carefully cloaked in financial technical jargon. Given his field of economics, his criticism focused on corruption of the Batista regime. It began immediately after Batista took up residence in the presidential palace. According to an early not so subtle quote attributed to Pérez, *"Fulgencio Batista has a long and infamous history in Cuban politics. With his unelected return to power his sights appear set on amassing personal wealth above any other objective."*

Pérez served as a close adviser to the Minister of Finance under former President Carlos Prío Socarrás, deposed by Batista's coup in 1952. He understood the structure of the Cuban government sufficient to observe Batista's personal machinations for enrichment. The Mafia was already entrenched in Havana in 1952. Pérez identified this as the primary means by which Batista could financially exploit his return to the presidency.

Pérez might be invaluable in pursuing Landeira's attack on the Mafia. Pérez argued that partnership with the American Mafia provided Batista the ability to solidify his power base. With Pérez's background knowledge, this could provide insights from which to quiz his father. No Mafioso's name appeared on legal documents. His father boasted of his setting up front companies for investors. All but admitted these probably included American organized crime figures. Pérez could provide targeted lines of inquiry to pose to his father.

Max Landeira was a tough bird. Good that they were rebuilding a relationship as father and son. That did not however extend to Bart condoning his father's architecting money laundering schemes for the Mafia, further corrupting Cuban institutions. His father's questionable past served as prologue to what Bart must do. No reason to expose his father but he felt no qualms about using him as a way to get confidential information on the Mafia and Batista. He would do his best to shield his father as the source.

If things turned out badly because of his journalistic crusade, Father could just retreat to Tampa until the regime changed. So could he for that matter. He assumed his father was careful to avoid breaking U.S. laws. Bart was indifferent to his extended Cuban family. Father sought to draw him in, yet he was still an outsider. He was born a Yanqui, in Cuba only by choice.

Of course, there remained the larger question of deceiving his father. Using him to further his own aims brought a twinge of guilt. The alternative? Dump everything, including a relationship with his father. Leave Cuba, and certainly not for Tampa. His rationale perhaps to appease his conscience that his father brought this on himself. Actively enabling criminal activity made you a criminal. No excuses. He father never had to take that path. In the end, he either accepts bringing this on himself, or choses to feel betrayed. Bart concluded he could live with his own actions and let circumstances play out.

✳ ✳ ✳ ✳

The Mafiosi involved in Havana were well known. The publicity went back as far as the meeting convened at the Hotel Nacional in 1946. What most people did not understand was the reason for the meeting. The commonly held opinion being a convenient venue close to the United States yet removed from FBI surveillance. The real reason was to lay the groundwork for developing Havana into a gambling mecca. Close enough geographically to be part of the United States yet out of reach of U.S. law enforcement. In a foreign country embracing gambling with a history of corruption since gaining independence fifty years ago. An assessable tropical paradise compared to the unattractive barren high-desert gambling venue of Las Vegas.

Therefore, Landeira needed to give these Mafiosi settled in Havana fresh treatment. Paint them as the purveyors of the dark side of glamorous Havana. Provide details of Mafia investment hidden behind front companies shielding identities. Landeira wanted names, amounts, which hotels, casinos, and nightclubs. Continue to play on the theme of money laundering. Mafia investment coming from illegal profits made in the United States. Those same details might reveal the conduits for money flow to President Batista.

How to accomplish such an ambitious plan was not yet clear. Finding knowledgeable sources willing to cooperate was a tall order. Just the activity of soliciting for sources presented a risk.

In a police state, repression could easily get out of hand. Being an American journalist from an important Cuban family might not be sufficient protection against Batista's National Police thugs. The more likely retribution of deportation defeated the entire objective of access to information.

Even if successful in uncovering damaging confidential material, how to publish anonymously remained the overriding dilemma. With his father as an unwitting source, the problem became more complicated. However, all that was premature. He needed first to uncover compelling material with news interest. Simply repeating allegations of Mafia investment as the catalyst for the Havana entertainment boom was not newsworthy. Having set a benchmark with his Dominican Republic story, about time he developed something on Cuba. Time to approach Professor Pérez.

The Havana telephone directory listed Pérez's telephone number and address. An upscale address in the Vedado district not far from his old apartment and a few blocks from his father's exclusive men's club. Makes sense since it is also close to the campus of the University of Havana. Yet still an expensive residence on the salary of a university professor now unemployed.

"Señor Pérez, my name is Bart Landeira. I am a correspondent for the Miami Herald newspaper. I wonder if I might meet with you to discuss a subject of mutual interest. Reading past newspaper articles, you are often quoted."

Pérez interrupted, "I have no interest in speaking to reporters."

Landeira ignored the response. "You have extensive knowledge about how Cuban financial institutions operate. How the Ministry of Finance functions. You are known as a critic of American organized crime investment to develop the Havana gambling industry."

"I am sorry. I cannot help you, Señor Landeira. Good day."

The call disconnected.

A good journalist learns to handle rejection. Before making another approach, he mailed Pérez copies of his Dominican Republic article and his earlier article on U.S. involvement in toppling the elected Guatemalan president in 1954. Pérez did not respond.

After a week, he staked out Pérez's apartment. From a newspaper photo, he recognized the tall, distinguished Pérez with his signature white hair from across the street. Pérez left his apartment building walking briskly, dressed impeccably in a light grey suit, white shirt, and tie. Looked as if ready to deliver a lecture at the university.

Landeira followed at a distance waiting to see where Pérez was headed. Surprisingly, he entered the *La Fraternidad de Cristóbal Colón*. His father's men's club where his father insisted on sponsoring Bart for membership. Hoping Pérez's destination perhaps a restaurant for lunch, this was even better.

Landeira allowed Pérez to check in first at the desk before making his approach. Entering the club's large lounge area, he asked a waiter, "I am looking for Dr. Pérez."

"Yes, Señor. Dr. Pérez is on the veranda."

Landeira spotted Pérez reading the Miami Herald Spanish addition, as a waiter brought him coffee.

"Excuse me Dr. Pérez, I did not expect to find you here," Landeira said.

Pérez looked up. "Excuse me. Should I know you?"

"Bart Landeira. I called you last week." Landeira extended his hand.

Pérez did not get up but at least took Landeira's hand. "Are you a member?"

"Yes. A new member."

"Are you related to Maximiliano Landeira?"

"Yes. He is my father."

"I do not wish to offend you but I thought I made it clear I have no interest in giving an interview to the press."

"I was not looking for an interview. More like a collaboration. I intend on doing a series of articles on American Mafia investment in Havana. You seem the most informed source."

Pérez folded the newspaper in his lap and looked at Landeira. "Is this some sort of joke?"

"Certainly not. Why would you suggest that?"

108

"Because you are Max Landeira's son. You do not need me. Your father knows more on that subject than I do. He is one of them."

Landeira knew what Pérez meant but the accusation still stung. It meant that he would have to find a way to distance himself from his father reputation.

"Might I sit down and explain, Dr. Pérez."

Not waiting for an answer, he sat down across from Pérez. "My father is the chief financial officer of Landeira Grupo. A large corporation involved in sugar, tobacco, rum, and cigars. He also maintains a law practice in Florida and Havana. I have been estranged from the family, including my father since before World War Two. After the war, I worked for the U.S. foreign service then became a journalist. I only came to Havana two years ago to continue working as a foreign correspondent for the Miami Herald. Perhaps you have read some of my reporting."

Pérez made no reply.

"I was born in the United States. I came to Havana to reconnect with my heritage and cease wandering around the world. I am also aware that my father's law practice consults on Cuban investment. He claims that no American organized crime figures are among his clients."

Pérez began to say something, but Landeira raised his hand. "Please let me finish. Either my father is lying or these mobsters have obscured their ownership trail and he chooses to turn a blind eye. I harbor no illusions about my father's activities.

"I have a U.S. law degree and know something about constructing legal entities whereby the true shareholders conceal their identities. The Mafia did not invent that practice."

"No. Clever lawyers like your father did," Pérez said. "Are you aware your father is the chief executive of a private Cuban bank?"

"Yes. Landeira Grupo is also the major shareholder. Another related business unit."

"More than that. A highly profitable enterprise by some estimates. Possibly more profitable than ever officially reported," Perez said.

"Obviously, you do not like my father?"

"More accurately, I despise what he represents. He is part of the cancer destroying Cuba. He is close to Batista and close to the Mafia. I cannot prove that, but those involved with Cuban economics understand where your father stands."

Not a surprise but still difficult to hear. Pérez describes his father as central figure in the corruption. His father describes himself as a business consultant constructing legal entities to facilitate investments. Bart suspicioned Pérez's accusation likely closer to the truth.

"I am not interested in protecting my father from bad publicity. He and I still have an arms-length relationship. As for official corruption, I must be cautious or risk censorship as a journalist. In my case that could mean deportation as a U.S. citizen. You read my story about my experience in the Dominican Republic I sent to you. This is not the United States where the law protects free speech objectionable to the government.

"I am a realist. Reporting from Cuba has strict limits. The Ministry of Propaganda censors any coverage sympathetic to the revolutionary insurgents. However, reporting on the Mafia in Havana still enjoys some latitude. That genie is out of the bottle. Until my reporting comes to close to exposing kickbacks to Batista, I believe the Mafia is fair game. The more I understand about how money flows to Batista, the better I can navigate how to avoid deportation from Cuba."

Pérez reflected for a moment taking a sip of his coffee. "Since Mafia investment is a frequent topic in the media given Havana's newfound celebrity status, what can I add?"

"Possibly details that can enlarge the story beyond the mystique of movie gangsters. It is still newsworthy to readers in the United States. I am looking to expose how the Mafia launders its profits from racketeering into this foreign mecca of decadent glamour. Counterpoint to the Hollywood celebrities and the rich and famous by showing the dark side of this tropical paradise."

Pérez said, "Did you follow me here today?"

Landeira nodded. "Yes. To try to convince you we share the same objective. I did not realize you were a member here. My reporting can benefit by your insights. Perhaps provide you with some satisfaction in protest to the repression of the Batista regime. While cautious, my research suggests you are critic of Batista.

"If I help you, Señor Landeira, I wish my name never mentioned. Bad enough I cannot continue my work at the university. I am Cuban. I intend to see Batista someday ousted. But I do not wish to witness his downfall from exile or prison."

"Does that mean you will assist me?"

"Conditionally, yes. How else can I exercise my protest?"

Landeira smiled. "Excellent. Will you join me for lunch? We can talk further."

* * * *

While working in his office at the distillery, one of the administration staff downstairs rang his telephone. "Señor Montero is here to see you."

"Please bring him to my office. Also bring us coffee."

"Good to see you," Landeira said. Please sit down." The young woman staffer brought them coffee on a tray with milk and sugar then left closing the office door.

Landeira waited for Montero to offer the reason for his visit. Based on Montero's initial reaction to his proposal, he was expecting him to politely decline. Gracious enough to convey his decision in person rather than by telephone.

"I have given much thought to your generous proposal, Señor Landeira. Discussed the matter at length with my wife and two children. A most difficult decision. My family has deferring opinions. My cautious answer, I would like to discuss the matter further. Much will depend on the details."

"Wonderful. That makes sense. What are the concerns of your family?"

"Well, my wife is concerned about how I will like taking on such a large responsibility."

"Do you have reservations about that?"

"Some. But I must think toward the future. I have many more working years. This seems the best opportunity for my life's work to live on. What is to become of Montero Rum when I become too old? I must embrace new challenges."

"What about your children?"

"My son dislikes the idea. Surprising how he ignores the question of what is to become of Montero Rum."

"Why surprising?"

"Because he has no interest in becoming involved in the business. Luis wants to get his law degree like his older sister. Bitter about the closing of the university. Unlike Emilia, his sights are set on politics. Yet he says only that things will somehow work out when I am old without offering any solutions."

"Considering we live under a dictatorship, what does he mean by entering politics?"

Montero reflected for a moment before answering, "Luis is an idealist. Concerned with social justice. Democracy. Not the dysfunctional Cuban brand of democracy. I worry that he might be too close to these student revolutionaries of the Directorio Revolucionario Estudiantil."

"What about your daughter Emilia? What are her thoughts about my offer?"

Montero smiled. "Emilia is smart, clever, and practical beyond her years. She understands your observation about what happens when I become too old. She points out I will eventually be forced to sell when too old to continue. Without me, Montero Rum dies."

"So she agrees to consider what I am offering?"

"Like I said, she is smart. She is also a tough lawyer. Says the devil is in the details. What is the offer? What does Landeira Grupo expect from me? Is my new job secure, or is this a ploy to buy me out at a lower price?"

Landeira smiled. Not in any way put off. Of course, there would be a tough negotiation over the offering price. Better to negotiate with a family member than some third party lawyer. "Good for her. All valid concerns. I assure you, Señor Montero, there are no ulterior motivations on the part of Landeira Grupo. I

112

am only temporary in my involvement as I explained to you. Landeira Grupo needs you far more than you need us. Not very good negotiating strategy on my part, but I am concerned about fairness. Both Landeira Rum and Montero Rum should live on. Combining the traditions of both is the best way to insure that.

"Before we negotiate the acquisition offering price and your salary, I want everyone to be assured this is a good deal for both parties. I suggest I meet with you and the family to answer questions. Once we agree on those important operational issues, I will approach my father who is the financial head of Landeira Grupo. His office is in Tampa, Florida. He will want to meet you of course. From there, we negotiate the money and the terms of the deal.

"I agreed to oversee Landeira Rum and look for a permanent management solution with the passing of my Uncle Tomás. I am convinced you are that solution, Señor Montero. My father delegated to me the task of finding a successor. He will follow my recommendation but he is the corporation's senior officer so he must agree to the deal."

"Before we go further, there are few legal prerequisites we need deal with. Things like confidentiality agreements, letter of intent, and reviewing financial records and other documents of Montero Rum. What is known as the buyer's due diligence. Will your daughter handle the legal affairs for you?"

"Oh yes. I trust Emilia's capabilities as a lawyer. Her specialty is business law. Expect her to be a tough negotiator."

"Excellent. Than you can trust she will argue for the best deal possible. I look forward to meeting her at the soonest. Please let me know if you wish me to meet with your family to answer questions."

"I believe a meeting with just me and Emilia will be sufficient."

"Very well. The sooner the better. I am at your service."

"Since we may soon be business partners, please call me Augustin."

"And please call me Bart. Short for Bartolo but only my mother called me Bartolo. This has been a rewarding day, Augustin. Rest assured my friend, we do this deal, and Montero Rum will continue as a brand. I will put that into the deal. The only difference is expanded marketing and distribution. You may have to increase production."

Perhaps he oversold his authority but he would not allow his father to overturn his agreement to terms of the deal. He knew his father. A domineering controlling arrogant personality. This was his son's deal, however. A perfect solution to Landeira Grupo's management problem. He would present his father a done deal in all respects, or walk away, including even running Landeira Rum temporarily. He would not allow the old man to manipulate the circumstances to get him to stay onboard indefinitely. His commitment fulfilled by finding this solution. If his father saw this as a way of manipulating their newfound relationship to bend matters to his liking, it would not work.

With that in mind, he would take negotiations further before involving his father. Meet with Montero and his daughter. Conclude everything pending a review of Montero's documents and then negotiating the financial details without consulting his father. Make Montero a specific offer. Make it a fait accompli subject only to his father's agreement, while leaving him no alternative.

* * * *

Two days later, Augustin returned to Bart's office at the distillery with his daughter Emilia.

Bart did not anticipate Emilia Montero to be the exceptionally attractive woman offering her hand. It was her eyes. The coloring giving them remarkable depth. Looking him straight on he felt self-conscious of his pronounced scar on his cheek compared to her face. A beautiful face yet the overwhelming effect conveyed intelligence. She was tall with long legs, further accentuated by heels. Her tailored business pantsuit amplified her figure and full breasts.

"I am Emilia Montero, Señor Landeira. A pleasure meeting you. Father speaks highly of you."

Slightly off balance Landeira said, "We have become friends. Please sit down." Turning to shake hands with her father, "Augustin, thank you for coming."

Landeira motioned them to a large round table, more suitable for this conversation than seated across his uncle's massive desk.

While a staffer brought a tray of coffee, Augustin looked around. "I always admired your Uncle Tomás' office."

Landeira smiled, "My uncle liked his creature comforts. Soon to be your office I hope. I am here only temporarily."

Emilia wanted to get right into discussing the deal. Reaching into her briefcase, she extracted several folders, placing them on the table.

She said, "I took the liberty of drafting confidentiality agreements and what I hope is a letter of intent acceptable to you. Of course, I defined certain issues I believe fundamental to my father's interests. I hope you don't feel I was being presumptuous."

Unexpected, but Augustin warned his daughter was tough.

He read the documents. Even the letter of intent she drafted was acceptable. Looking up he smiled at her. "These look to be in order. I also do not mind you taking the initiative. It will help to move things along. I have a license to practice law in the United States, but not in Cuba. I will defer to my father for executing the final documents for legal content should we come to agreement. He is licensed in both countries."

Emilia said, "Father said, your father has final say over doing this acquisition. Will he be participating in our negotiations?"

"No. He has left that to me. Let me digress and explain my role in this venture. Please pour yourself coffee while I explain the management of Landeira Grupo. It is important, Augustin, for you to understand and be comfortable with joining Landeira. You know much of this by our previous conversations. And of course you knew my uncle." Turning to Emilia, "I want your father to be comfortable in that he is not a Landeira. The truth of the matter is the Landeira bloodline is dwindling. Landeira Grupo must take on senior managers outside the family to sustain its business enterprises. Should have begun years ago. That lies at the heart of our interest in partnering with your father. The same concern he has for Montero Rum succeeding him."

Landeira gave her an unabridged overview of Landeira Grupo and those in the family involved in the businesses.

She replied, "Thank you, Señor Landeira. You will of course want to review my due diligence documentation before we discuss money. However, the larger issue is assurances of sustaining not only the Montero Rum identity, but also of my father's employment security.

"Regardless of your sincerity, as you said you are only temporary. Not even officially part of Landeira Grupo management. Only a stockholder. What assurances does my father have that once Landeira acquires Montero Rum they do not terminate my father? His employment just a tactic to buy Montero Rum?"

Augustin was aghast at his daughter's bluntness. "Emilia, there is no call for being rude. I must apologize, Bart."

"No need, Augustin. This is business. More than business, it affects your life's work. Your daughter is acting as your lawyer. Any lawyer would raise the question. After all it is the most critical concern in making your decision."

Turning toward Emilia, "Of course we are prepared to offer an employment contract to your father. Yet I see though that might not be enough. Everything centers on what your father created. The finest rum crafted by him representing his legacy. More art than business as he puts it."

Landeira stroked his chin while organizing an idea. "What about as part of the deal a clause stating your father shall retain all trademark rights to the name Montero Rum indefinitely? Remember, our interest is in acquiring the right to produce and market Montero rum. Landeira cannot replicate what your father accomplished by following a set of instructions. Therefore, the name carries the identity.

"We have a wonderful master distiller your father knows well. Gustavo makes excellent rum, just not outstanding like Montero rum."

Emilia was surprised at the offer and looked at her father.

Augustin said, "I told you, Dear, Bart wishes this to be attractive to us."

"Yes, I believe that is more than satisfactory," she said.

"Excellent. Perhaps you could draft the contractual language to encompass any additional thoughts."

"Very well. I have another question. I do not know how to frame this without it sounding rude as my father will undoubtedly feel. Your father will have the final say. Should we not be negotiating with him?"

"Good lord, Emilia," Augustin said.

"Emilia makes a good point, Augustin. A basic rule in negotiating is always to negotiate with the decision maker. I am offering a slightly different scenario for good reasons.

"My father is a brilliant lawyer and businessman. He would be a tough negotiator trying to get the best price and preferential terms. That is not what I am seeking. For this to work for Landeira Rum you must see it as an opportunity for you, Augustin. Landeira Rum needs not only a competent director, but Montero Rum represents a hidden marketing opportunity. Landeira has the resources to allow Montero to increase production. We have the marketing and distribution channels to make this a great business success.

"My father would see that but prefer it to remain a vague issue so as not to run up the acquisition price. I take the longer view of making this a sustaining success and to be a good move for your father."

"I am a journalist. Writing is what I do. Not a practicing lawyer or businessman. I simply am doing this as a favor to my father after the unexpected passing of my uncle. I assure you, if we come to terms, I will convince my father to accept my offering price and terms. He has little choice but to accept any agreement I make since I have no interest in pursuing other solutions for Landeira Rum management. Obviously, he must agree with my assessment that you are the right person to run Landeira Rum, Augustin. You will report to him not me."

Emilia nodded. "I do not believe I have any further questions, Señor Landeira. What is the next step?"

"I suggest setting a meeting with my father, Maximiliano. He splits his time between Havana and Tampa, Florida. Not only is he the chief financial officer of Landeira Grupo, but also maintains a business investment consulting practice separate from the company.

"However, there is no need to wait before diving into your financial documents. The real work is arriving at a purchase price. Also, not to overlook your compensation in your new role, Augustin. To be candid, I want to arrive at an agreed price that I can sell to my father as a done deal requiring only his approval."

He hoped Emilia Montero understand the unsubtle inference. He did not intend to allow his father to start arguing price and terms. Here is the deal, take it or find your own solution for managing Landeira Rum.

The prospect of negotiating with the attractive Emilia Montero a welcoming prospect. Been a very long time since a woman stirred his feelings. A few years younger probably in her early thirties. All he knew from Augustin was she was not married. Yet for someone with her looks, likely involved in a relationship.

"What do you think, Augustin? Still interested?"

Augustin smiled broadly. "Yes. Looking forward to meeting your father."

"And you, Señora Montero? Have I answered all your questions?"

For the first time since entering the office, she gave a warm smile. "Yes. You seem genuine about why you want my father to join Landeira. I may have specific questions at a later time, but you have been most convincing."

"Excellent. Once I review your documents, I shall call to arrange our next meeting. To avoid unwelcomed rumors circulating among Landeira or Montero employees, might it be better to meet elsewhere than here or your office, Augustin?"

Augustin said, "Yes. I do not want any of my employees becoming worried. We did not discuss them but I assumed they will all have jobs after becoming part of Landeira Rum?"

"Absolutely. This merger is not about cutting costs by eliminating employees. Montero Rum will continue to operate from your current facility. Part of the acquisition plan is to expand Montero rum production. For that, you need more warehouse aging space. Landeira has the capital to do that. So if anything, you may need more employees as you grow."

Emilia said, "May I suggest we meet at my law office. I have a small conference room."

Landeira replied, "Perfect. May I call you with any questions as I dig into the details?"

"Of course. Here is my business address and telephone number."

After they left his office, Landeira could think of little else than Emilia Montero.

Chapter 9

Landeira met his father at José Martí International Airport twelve miles southwest of central Havana. A beautiful sunny day just two weeks after New Year's 1957.

Bart was driving his new 1956 Buick convertible with the top up. Still cool in the morning but the skies were clear and the temperature expected to reach the high-seventies by afternoon. The reason people flocked to Cuba in the winter months. The climate, the gambling, and the anything-goes nightlife. Driving to Bart's new apartment in Old Havana, Max Landeira remarked, "You like it better here in this old quarter than the Vedado apartment?"

"Yes. Living in the Vedado is too artificial. Too many obnoxious Americans tourists. The Malecón overrun with them. Not why I came to Havana. Still keep my sailboat there though at a dock I rent in the Boca de la Chorrera. No recreational craft facilities on the western side of Havana harbor which otherwise is closer to where I live."

Bart's apartment was on the top floor of an older yet upscale apartment building with an interior courtyard accessed through a large door wide enough for his car. A balcony overlooked an interior courtyard. Reminiscent of Paris-style residential buildings. On the opposite exterior wall, his apartment windows overlooked a green area. A quiet comfortable residence with two bedrooms, office area, and large living area.

120

Used to staying at the Hotel Nacional, Max was impressed. "Not bad. So tell me about this Augustin Montero."

After giving the background, his father started firing questions. "I agree this Montero makes great rum. Better than ours. But can he run an operation of our size? You say his revenue is only twenty percent of ours."

"I think so. He's been running Montero Rum for thirty years. Profitable. Growth hampered by the size of his facility and lack of capital. Like our family history, he is adverse to debt, so his balance sheet is sound. In his fifties, he appears in good health. Enough working years ahead."

"Okay. So to hire him we must buy his business? How does that benefit us? Can't his expertise at rum making just transfer to our more modern distillery?"

Bart shook his head, "Part of making his exceptional rum is the stills. Tomás knew that when he offered to buy Montero years ago. Acquiring the Montero Rum brand and continuing production makes the deal financially attractive in addition to acquiring Augustin to address our management problem."

"What kind of profit does Montero Rum generate?"

"Something in the area of $90,000US annually at the current exchange rate."

Bart did not wish to get into details yet with his father. He knew his father would want to low-ball an offering price and jeopardize the deal.

"What about the value of the assets?"

"Father, let's not discuss financial details until you meet Montero. This is more about acquiring Augustin Montero. But I believe acquiring Montero Rum also offers addition business opportunities."

"Such as?"

"Montero rum could increase its sales by at least fifty percent with the right marketing. To increase production to support that growth requires purchasing the building next door to their distillery to move the aging barrels allowing for adding more stills."

"So you are suggesting keeping the current Montero facility?"

"Of course, Father. We cannot relocate the existing stills into our facility. It is also important to maintain production separate from Landeira rum."

"Why?"

"I have listened to Tomás, our master distiller Gustavo, and Augustin Montero all attempt to explain the art of making rum. And it is an art. Every part of the process contributes to the final product. I know something of how Scotch is made and rum is the same. Not only that, but we shall retain the Montero Rum branding. Good for marketing and I already made that part of the terms of purchase."

"Really?"

"Listen. First of all, it goes to satisfying Montero's sense of family heritage. From our standpoint, it becomes our signature premium brand. More identifiable with an already known brand name."

"Very well. When do we meet Señor Montero?"

"In an hour. We are having lunch at *Casa Maribel*, Tomás' favorite restaurant. Mine also. Only a short walk from here given such a beautiful day."

* * * *

Following a three-hour lunch, Max and Bart returned to the apartment.

"Very well, I agree. I like Montero. Seems to know business. No question about his skill at making rum. I like the idea of keeping separate operating facilities. Different cultures probably with the two different workforces. The Montero employees might feel lest threatened. Probably makes Gustavo more comfortable also. Montero speaks very highly of him, which is helpful.

"How do we proceed with negotiating a deal? Does Montero have a lawyer?"

"Yes. His daughter is an attorney. Business law. I have reviewed all the documents they provided. Everything is in good order. Just working on fixing on an offering price and the compensation package for Augustin."

"I can help with that," Max said.

"No. I rather you don't. I know you too well, Father. You feel the need to take charge. You will get mired down in minutiae looking for leverage to strike the best bargain. This deal will not happen if we haggle over money. This is not an asset buy nor an investment based on Montero's profitability. Earnings cannot solely dictate price. This is strategic. It is about acquiring Augustin Montero and his established brand of rum which we can exploit through our marketing and distribution."

"So you want to negotiate the deal without me?"

"Yes. The offer and the terms."

"What the hell has got into you? You admittedly know little about business. I make my living doing this sort of work."

"Not going to explain. That's just the way it is. I know how you operate. The Montero's are good people. The daughter is smart but not in your league negotiating something like this. Montero is selling his life's work. Three generations in the business. They deserve not only a fair deal, but a deal that preserves Augustin's heritage."

Bart was thinking with some resentment of his father's almost certain involvement with Mafia investment in Havana and by extension fueling Batista's corrupt regime.

"I will negotiate the deal, Father. Take it or leave it. If you agree to the deal I hand you, I agree to stay involved with Landeira Rum in a limited capacity. Assist Augustin in integrating into our company. Expanding the aging square footage for the Montero rum. I will also manage the marketing initiative of our new brand since that was my idea.

"However, if you want to take over negotiations, then I am done with any involvement effective immediately. Remember, Father, I am doing all this as a favor. I have no interest in running a business. I am not one of your employees."

Seeing Bart's resolve, Max backed down. If Bart remains in some way involved then there remains an opportunity to draw him further into the legal practice. A lucrative endeavor that might eventually prove a challenging alternative to journalism. Whatever price he must pay to buy Montero Rum was worth keeping his son in Havana.

Max held up his hands. "Very well. I will leave it to you. I want you to know how much I appreciate you taking on this project. I agree that Augustin represents a unique solution to the void left with the passing of Tomás."

Bart willed himself to tamp down his underlying angst with his father. The idea of his father's probable collaboration with organized crime always close to the surface. "Thank you, Father. I think I can wrap up all the details in two weeks."

Max responded, "Now with that business out of the way, will you join me for dinner this evening?"

* * * *

As usual, Max was staying at the Hotel Nacional. Dinner at the Club Parisién. Not Bart's favorite venue but at least they served excellent food and wine. Father was a creature of habit.

Over drinks, Max said, "I planned on being a week in Havana this trip. Longer if you need me to close the Montero deal. Thought I might introduce you to my Havana office staff. Besides a manager and accounting staff for Landeira Grupo and staff of the Landeira Servicios de Logistica division, I have two young Cuban lawyers and a small clerical staff for my law practice."

Ever tenacious, his father continued trying to entice him into joining his legal practice. Saw him finally bending with his agreeing to oversee Landeira Rum following the death of Tomás. Fulfilling his commitment to help now exploring a new opening. Not even subtle, but then Max Landeira was rarely subtle.

"I realize you have no interest in becoming involved with Landeira Grupo. Yet you should not rule out legal work. You could still be part of my law practice, perhaps take over the Havana office. The pay is excellent for even your part time services."

"Father, you don't seem to understand. I am a journalist. A Latin America correspondent for the Miami Herald. That is a full time job. I said I would help transitioning Augustin into Landeira Rum. That is as far as it goes. I have a full workload."

"Yes, I understand. Just want to show you what I do. I am getting up there in years. Sounds sentimental, but I would love to see my work carry beyond me in some way."

Bart could not help but feel empathy. Since coming to Havana, his father seemed desperate to reengage their strained relationship. Feeling his mortality or possibly concealing some terminal medical condition?

Regardless of these latent parental feelings, Bart still intended to pursue his father's involvement with the seamier side of the Batista regime and his partnership with the American Mafia. His father was close with these guys for too long not to be dirty. As a reporter, he could not shy away from pursuing the truth. The best he could do is give his father fair warning of his intentions.

"I understand your motivations, Father. Show me your investment handiwork of which you are so proud. However, I am giving you fair warning that I am going to investigate Mafia control of the Havana gaming and hospitality industry. Sin City not only for vice but Mafia money laundering undoubtedly fueling the corruption that keeps Batista afloat.

"I suspect organized crime figures are behind many of these front companies you created. You all but admitted they are a perfect shield for laundering money from illegal enterprises in the United States. Mafia involvement must be buried somewhere among the layers of shell companies and strawmen comprising your clients. Don't show me anything that you know will be compromising if it finds its way into print."

"You may be correct, at least in some circumstances. However, as I told you before, I do not vet companies, syndicates, or companies coming to me wanting to invest money in Cuba. Not my role to challenge the source of capital. May sound callous, but most financial transactions anywhere are the same. The people coming to me are attorneys or business executives representing various types of legal entities. I do not deal with individual investors."

"Do you have a problem with me investigating these companies you created to discover the individuals behind their covers?"

"No. If you discover anything newsworthy, publish it by all means. I appreciate you leaving my name out of it though. Negative publicity is harmful to perspective clientele. After all, I am just an attorney acting on behalf of clients. Even criminals are entitled to legal representation."

The type of self-serving bullshit that gives lawyers a bad name. Bart suspected his father did far more than represent clients. More a participating conspirator creating a means for the Mafia to launder money from operations in the United States while establishing a safe haven for a lucrative new profit center.

* * * *

Understanding his father's intentions, Bart nonetheless agreed to accompany him to the Havana corporate office. The door to the office suite read Landeira Grupo S.A. Oficina Corporativa and underneath, Consultoría Landeira.

While Bart offered no encouragement, his father took a different tact to illustrate his assertion of acting only as a neutral attorney. As an act of transparency, he agreed to identify the ownership names of casino investor entities he put together to explain the nature of his legal services.

Obviously, that would not directly reveal Mafia connections, but it could establish a starting point. Since these investors were legal entities, a paper trail existed somewhere. Perhaps a layered trail, but eventually it must lead back to an individual. If a U.S. corporation, LLC, or partnership, there was a record in the state where incorporated and a federal tax identification number. If the legal entity was Cuban, Dr. Pérez might be able to pierce the corporate secrecy.

With this in mind, Bart planned on pushing his father as far as possible. What did he know of the composition of these new investment entities? Place of incorporation, tax identification, etc. Father was one clever bastard. Confident that his work left no fingerprints linking him in documents to organized crime figures. No evidence of violating U.S. statutes. As for Cuban legal entities, probably of less concern. Knowing Bart's reaction, his father would never reveal anything implicating his direct knowledge of money flowing to President Batista.

Two days later, Max introduced Bart to the Havana corporate staff of Landeira Grupo and his legal staff. Located in an office building on Calle 23, or La Rampa, the street served as the main commercial street in Vedado not far from the Hotel Nacional. This professional office building also included several offices of local subsidiaries of well-known American companies.

Seated in his father's office, Max said, "Since you are interested in hotels and casinos, let me show you my contribution to the Havana investment boom. Already Havana outshines Las Vegas as the gambling mecca in the Americas. Let me start with Havana's signature nightclub venue, The Tropicana Hotel. You've been there of course?"

"Yes. Once. The showgirls are as beautiful and voluptuous as advertised. The lush tropical setting is extraordinary. Lots of loud Americans being obnoxious, including some celebrities. Place awash in money. Not exactly my kind of place."

"Well here are a couple of files related to the Tropicana. The venue began as a nightclub in 1939. A six-acre estate. Eventually owned by a guy named of Martin Fox. Cuban. A *guajiro*, a peasant. A showcase for Cuban talent. Made the place what it is today. Known for its exclusive Cuban ownership. Not exactly true. I set up two different Cuban companies for the express purpose of investing in the Tropicana. I did not represent either of them in any purchase transactions. However I believe both probably now have substantial ownership positions in the Tropicana."

Bart leafed through the pages of the first file titled Ybor Group Investments. The shareholders consisted of half a dozen different U.S. limited liability corporations. All with bland-sounding names. Incorporated in Florida or Louisiana. The other file titled Caribbean Investments consisted of a mix of U.S. and Cuban incorporated companies as shareholders.

"And you do not know the real people behind these front companies?"

"No. As I said, I just worked with attorneys. The signatories are all officers of these respective companies. I do not recognize any of them as organized criminal figures mentioned in the press."

"Yet you must have speculated as to who was really putting up the money."

"Look, Bart, let's not dance around the issue. Of course, I suspected the origin of some of the money to be from organized crime. Who else invests in big-time gambling venues? Even with tighter laws in the United States, law enforcement could not prevent organized crime making Las Vegas into the U.S. principal destination for casino gambling. Hotels, nightclubs, and restaurants are all necessary to attract Americans to come to the Havana casinos."

Bart replied sarcastically, "The marketing allure of gambling, sex, drugs, in a tropical setting close to mainland United States meshed perfectly with an ideal set of circumstances. A willing partner in Batista's eagerness to enrich himself. Located outside U.S. law enforcement jurisdiction yet geographically close enough to almost be part of the U.S."

His father responded, "Every successful commercial venture is about location. That is the attraction of Cuba. I deal largely with international investment, mostly in Cuba. Mostly American investment. That is why I base my office in Tampa. Closer to the client base.

"International investment functions on recognizing cross border opportunities. Part of those opportunities involves the political-economic-legal structure of the client's domicile and that of the investment jurisdiction. I deal in money without moralizing. Therefore, look into these investors. If you can find organized crime figures lurking in the background, publish their names. I never promised my clients absolute secrecy."

No question his father knew far more than willing to reveal. Max Landeira would never take on a client without knowing the identity of the individual investors. However, he was not about to go that far in openness. Better to hide behind the veneer of lawyer confidentiality even with his son.

"Here are some more files. These are incorporated in Cuba."

"Are all these companies created for investment?"

"Yes. Allows for a group of investors with differing levels of capital to participate in large-scale projects. Predominately investment hotels, casinos, and nightclubs that are collectively part of a booming market. Which specific projects I do not always know. Some investment companies probably invest in multiple projects. My work ended with the creation of these investment companies."

Bart chose against provoking an argument by pointing out that investing in Havana hotels and casinos, also served the purpose of laundering illegal profits to avoid U.S. taxes converting into legitimate investment. In a country with no government oversight, the Batista regime becomes a partner. The profits compelling even after factoring for the kickback expense.

The real newsworthy story was the consequential impact of Mafia investment in Havana gambling. Yet another corrosive imposed by the United States, it provided the means for Fulgencio Batista to enrich himself and fund his hold on power. To Cubans that meant corruption accompanied by state-sponsored violent oppression.

"Are the executives and board of directors of the hotels and casinos a matter of public record in Cuba?"

"Yes. The Ministry of Commerce licenses all business."

"Including these investment companies you created?"

"All legal entities doing business in Cuba."

"Can I get copies of these?"

Max expression turned downward. "Absolutely not. You should know that. Attorney client privilege. You can make notes about the stockholder names, but nothing more. That alone is an ethical stretch. I am only making it easier for you to research these companies and attempt to discover concealed Mafiosi. Tell you what, I will have one of the clerks type out the names of the companies while we enjoy lunch.

"I want to hear more about how you are getting along as a correspondent for the Miami Herald. I read your article about your trip to the Dominican Republic. Seems you got on the wrong side of those in power by asking uncomfortable questions. You need to be careful. Even here in Cuba."

Bart said, "Of course. Batista and Trujillo both run their countries through intimidation and corruption."

Max replied, "Batista is a strongman but he is necessary for Cuba. I know him. Trujillo is a violent anachronism in power far too long in a backward country."

Bart added, "The peasants in the cane fields in the eastern provinces of Cuba see Batista as a brutal dictator. He also has blood on his hands. Look at recent events."

"The Army is containing a growing revolutionary movement. A socialist, possibly communist threat infecting the rural peasantry. There you need to be very careful about what you write for the Herald. Avoid Cuban politics. There is no first amendment protection here."

"Of course, I would not want to fall victim to the Cuban National Police like I did with the Dominican SIM. Both are secret police without judicial oversight. Seems little difference."

"Come on, Bart, people in Havana are not snatched off the street as in Ciudad Trujillo.

"I hear otherwise. There are pervasive rumors about *the man in the white suit*, a colonel in the national police who roams Havana at night with his henchmen. People disappearing. Then of course, people disappear regularly in the Eastern Provinces. Turning up later as murdered with evidence of torture."

Max still arguing the government line, "Looking for criminals and revolutionaries. The Army's tactics may be crude but often necessary. People in our social strata have nothing to fear. Write about American organized crime invading Havana. That is an open secret. Articles appear regularly in American newspapers. Trust me about avoiding Cuban politics, Bart."

Max Landeira was a devious old fox. Well-practiced in the art of obfuscation and deceit. Bart knew that but not the full extent of his father's subterfuge. Max was still maneuvering using half-truths. Mafia investment in Havana hotels and casinos no longer seemed a part of his father's active business. He appearing more open on the subject therefore it must not jeopardize his interests.

Throwing the bone to his journalist son served his personal reasons. If Bart discovered and published the names of organized crime figures invested in Havana, it meant nothing. What he kept from his son and everyone else was the workings of Banco Crédito Industrial y Mercantil de Habana. Although Landeira Grupo owned the majority of shares, Max ran it as his personal financial institution.

The most lucrative services were creating mechanisms for managing the massive flow of American organized crime money funding investment in hotels and casinos. Cooperating Cuban banks took in the illegal cash thereby laundering the money as repayment against fictitious loans financing construction or acquisitions. The front company investors just a smoke and mirrors distraction to provide a false record for repaying non-existent loans. With Batista's participation, no fear of criminal exposure.

Banco Crédito Industrial y Mercantil de Habana and four other banks participated in Maximiliano Landeira's scheme and the means for channeling kickback money to Batista and key government officials. A lucrative profit stream for the banks in exchange for concealing the transactions as legitimate. The banks charged additional fees for secretly dispersing tens of millions of dollars into secret Swiss accounts. Batista understood a time would come when he must step down.

* * * *

In the final months of 1956 and January 1957, Cuban political turmoil took on new meaning. President Batista could no longer ignore revolutionary opposition as insignificant.

On Batista's orders, National Police assaulted the Haitian Embassy in Havana and seized Cuban dissidents seeking asylum there on October 29. An asylum seeker shot dead Rafael Salas, commander of the National Police during the confrontation while the police killed nine dissidents.

On November 30, Frank Pais a commander in Fidel Castro's M-26-7 revolutionary movement staged an uprising in the city of Santiago. Scheduled to coincide with Fidel Castro's landing by boat from Mexico with a small force of revolutionary guerrillas, it lasted four days. With little resistance from the Army's Moncada Garrison, the rebels took control of Santiago's downtown area. They attacked infrastructure, burning the maritime building and police station, cutting power lines, destroying railroad tracks and bridges.

With Fidel Castro's arrival in Cuba overdue, the Santiago uprising failed to ignite a widespread uprising among the population. The Army retook control and the rebels fled into the mountains.

Fidel Castro's return to Cuba was not only behind schedule but turned into disaster.

Castro sailed from Veracruz, Mexico with 82 rebels in a 60-foot diesel cabin cruiser named the *Granma*. A 1,200-mile voyage. The vessel was overloaded, poorly provisioned, and leaking. After seven days lost at sea, suffering hunger and seasickness, the vessel eventually landed in an inhospitable mangrove swamp on the south coast of Oriente Province. Staggering through the swamps, the rebels lost much of their weapons and gear. The Army pursued the beleaguered invaders into the Sierra Maestra Mountains for three days. Of the original 82 rebels, only 20 survived with the others killed or captured. The survivors, including Fidel Castro and the Argentine Marxist revolutionary Che Guevara, hide themselves in the mountains. A pathetic rabble, which only the idea of Cuban revolution kept barely alive.

Batista downplayed the event as proof that the security apparatus had the insurgency under control. Yet it remained a threat in the rural eastern provinces. He prematurely announced that Fidel Castro was among those killed.

Over several days during Christmas, the Army's Holguin Regiment under the command of the notorious Colonel Fermin Cowley, *the Jackal of Holguin*, engaged in a bloody orgy. They tortured and murdered 23 young revolutionaries after seizing them from their homes in Oriente Province. To maximize the terror effect, they dumped the badly abused bodies along highways or hung them from trees. The Cuban people name the massacre *Bloody Christmas*.

On January 2, the National Police arrested four youths in Santiago then turned them over to a paramilitary force known as the Los Tigres. Led by sadistic Rolando Masferrer, a Cuban senator and the founder of the Los Tigres, the bodies of the youths revealed brutal torture. One victim was fourteen.

Using these events as a pretext, on January 15, Batista proclaimed a state of siege in response to the guerrilla insurgency in eastern Cuba, imposing press censorship on any political reporting or policing activities.

Two days later, Castro's meager band of guerrillas sacked a small army outpost on the south coast. Although of no strategic significance, the attack resurrected the viability of the M-26-7 revolutionary movement by attracting new recruits. The international community took note. Revolution in Cuba remained a threat.

Chapter 10

Finished with the review of the financial status of Montero Rum, time came for Landeira to put together an offer. Fairly straight forward. While much smaller than Landeira Rum, Augustin Montero ran his business soundly. No long-term debt. He owned the building. Earnings were good. Most importantly, Augustin Montero resolved the management void at Landeira Rum. The marketing opportunities afforded with Landeira capital made the acquisition attractive. An asset based offer plus good will would not induce Montero to sell. Therefore, the only practical approach was making an offer based on a generous multiple of earnings.

As for Montero's compensation, that was easy. At least double the average of what he took as a salary the last five years based on the enlarged scope of responsibilities. Add a bonus based on Landeira Rum earnings. Should be an attractive package. Landeira felt an obligation to Montero to make this work since this was his idea. Once out of the picture, Montero worked for his father. Not sure how that might go. Father was a deal maker not a professional manager. While Montero's employment contract protected him, he still wanted to see Montero happy with his decision to sell.

He hoped Emilia Montero saw the offer as attractive. She remained an enigma. All he knew was she was not married. Married before? Children? Involved in a current relationship?

She awoke feelings thought buried from a long ago tragedy during World War Two. Like no other woman, Emilia Montero resurrected vivid memories of Chiara Ricci. The two women did not look alike, yet some unexplainable combination of characteristics registered within him the same profound emotional response.

From their first meeting, Emilia Montero dominated his thoughts. Since the war, Bart Landeira had passing affairs with several women. Nothing ever developed further. Emilia felt different.

His professional life moving about the globe made relationships difficult. In truth, he subconsciously avoided situations possibly leading to serious relationships. He enjoyed the company of women and sexual intimacy. Was there some latent barrier embedded in his psyche? It went beyond his ability to interpret with objectivity. The only possible course was to indulge his obsession over Emilia Montero and let it take its course At least he possessed a reason to continue seeing her if only for business reasons.

Two days later, he arrived at her law office. The meeting scheduled after telephoning her, he came prepared to present an offer.

"Will your father be joining us?" Bart asked.

"No. He relies on my business judgement. Said it best we both did not attempt to negotiate. I told him that negotiation was part of any such business deal. I believe Papa likes you and wishes to avoid any unpleasantness that might arise in a vigorous negotiation over money. I on the other hand will look at this in my professional capacity to get the best deal possible for the family."

Landeira nodded while offering a smile. "I understand perfectly. Your father is very personable and perceptive. That is why he will make a good fit to take over Landeira Rum. Good tactical managerial judgement to leave negotiations to the person with the skills."

"You mean I should not be reticent to advocate for the best deal," she said with a sly grin.

135

"Precisely. As it should be. I believe you will find my offer attractive. However, I will not be offended to hear any counter proposals.

"Before we begin, is your father still comfortable with going through with this? Provided of course the economics are attractive."

With a serious expression, Emilia said, "Yes. Still difficult emotionally for him to reconcile the feeling of giving up *his* business. His life's work. However, he understands the larger benefit. As he gets older, there will be an end of the family legacy. In this arrangement, he has the opportunity to pass on that legacy to others outside the family. My mother agrees."

"His legacy will live on, Emilia."

She nodded giving him a smile. "Luis is emotionally troubled by selling but objectively agrees with Papa's reasons. Luis has ambitions other than following in Papa's footsteps. I understand the business but making Montero rum is strictly Papa's domain."

Bart said, "Good. Keeping Montero Rum as a separate brand is good marketing strategy, yet it also preserves that heritage. I too am no expert on making rum, but I know continuing to produce from the current operation is vital for sustaining its distinctive character. Integrating distillation into the larger Landeira Rum operation would be a mistake.

"Here are the key elements of our offer. We do not approach this as an asset purchase but rather a strategic buy for the many reasons I previously outlined. Therefore, I based our offer on a multiple of the average annual earnings for the last five years. I suggest we structure the deal in U.S. dollars for its stability compared to Cuban currency. At the current exchange rate, earnings average $90,000 annually. We are prepared to offer $1,000,000 for the purchase of Montero Rum. A multiple of eleven times earnings."

Landeira could see a very slight indication of surprise cross her face. Reestablishing her composure, she said, "And that includes what?"

"Everything. The assets, the receivables, the payables. Assets include the real property, equipment, and inventory."

"What about my father's compensation?"

"More difficult to pin down a number based on what he draws currently since it is irregular. Looks to average close to $10,000 annually. His new responsibilities managing both distilleries warrant a significant greater salary. I propose a salary of $25,000.

"In addition, he will get an annual incentive bonus of two percent of pre-tax earnings of the Landeira Rum subsidiary."

Emilia nodded. "And this is codified in an employment contract?"

"Yes. In fact, I will leave it to you to draft the specific language. It should include a guaranteed minimum of at least three years employment and to run indefinitely thereafter, subject to termination by either party with six months' notice. As I promised earlier, you may include a clause that your father will retain the rights to the Montero Rum trademark indefinitely. That should provide him an even stronger assurance."

Emilia Montero let out a sigh. With a warm smile, she said, "A generous offer, Señor Landeira. I came here prepared to negotiate money. I had no specific numbers in mind. Wanted you to make the offer. I might try negotiating for more, yet that would run counter to the spirit of your more than fair offer. I believe you genuinely want my father to join Landeira Rum. I will therefore present your offer to my father without further negotiation. It is his decision however I will recommend he accepts your offer."

"Thank you, Señora Montero. If he agrees, please proceed to draft the necessary documents for my review before presenting to my father for signature. In the purchase agreement, include the bank of your choice and account number. Does Montero Rum use a Cuban bank?"

"Yes. Why?"

"With the amount of money involved I strongly suggest you use one of the three U.S. banks with branches in Havana. National City Bank of New York, First National Bank of Boston, or

Chase National Bank. Your deposits are insured by the U.S. government up to a limit. No repeat of people losing their savings like in 1929. U.S. banks are subject to strict banking regulations and government audit. Cuban banks operate under lax regulation with no deposit insurance. Since a million dollars exceeds the deposit insurance limit, you should spread funds among several U.S. banks after we close the deal. I will be glad to help you with that since I travel to Miami regularly."

"You have little faith in Cuban banks, yet your father is known to control a bank."

"I have no faith in the Batista regime to regulate anything fairly. Batista is in bed with American organized crime. I will soon be writing a series of articles for the Miami Herald about Mafia investment in Havana."

"Is that wise considering Batista's censorship of the press?"

"The censorship extends to coverage of the insurgency movement and the violent suppression efforts of the Army and National Police. The American Mafia in Havana is a subject already written about in American newspapers. Batista appears unthreatened and the U.S. government turns a blind eye. However, American readers are interested."

"Your family is among the prominent Cuban elite, yet you seem a critic of Batista."

"Far more than a critic. Fulgencio Batista is a corrupt dictator. A dictator with much blood on his hands. No different from Trujillo in the Dominican Republic. Did you perhaps read my piece in the Herald a couple of months ago about my experience in Ciudad Trujillo?"

She shook her head no.

"I went there to report on the disappearance of a Dominican dissident and his family. Asked too many uncomfortable questions. Got a late night visit from Trujillo's secret police and a trip to the airport. Fortunately, they only deported me. Not likely the fate suffered by the dissident and his family. I despise Batista no differently than Trujillo."

"Yet you choose to live in Havana."

"A complicated story. Being Cuban-American and living in Tampa, I visited extended family here several times each year before the war. The sugar holdings in Camagüey, the tobacco in Pinar del Rio. More the urban creature, my father preferred Havana. Then came World War Two. As it did for so many, life changed.

"Settling in Havana seemed a place to rebalance after leaving the U.S. foreign service. I love Cuba. Particularly Havana. The culture, the people, the history, the beauty. Regrettably, Cuba suffers from continually bad governance. Too much under the economic-political shadow of the United States. A virtual colony. As the Latin America correspondent for the Miami Herald, Havana is closer to my sources of material."

He paused realizing he might be making her feel uncomfortable. "Please excuse my rambling, Señora Montero."

"Not at all. Were you in the war?"

"Yes. Three difficult years, followed by government service in the early years of the Cold War in various postings throughout the world."

Sensing he did not wish to elaborate, she wondered if the deep scar on his cheek and the large star-like scar on his left hand were war wounds.

* * * *

Things moved quickly. Augustin Montero called Landeira the following day after presenting the offer. "I am overwhelmed by your generous offer and your confidence in my abilities to manage Landeira Rum. Emilia says the documents will be ready to present to you in a few days."

Emilia was an accomplished lawyer. The documents were in order with no changes required by Landeira. Two days later, Max Landeira returned to Havana. Together with Bart in the conference room of his law office, he reviewed the purchase agreement and employment contract in silence.

Sipping coffee, Bart observed his father. Max Landeira's face betrayed him. Looking up and removing his glasses, "This is far too much to pay for the business. I should have insisted on being part of the negotiations."

Bart expected this. Although resolving to control himself, he was not going to take any crap. Shaking his head, "No, that would have been a bad idea. You are thinking like an accountant. Worse yet, like an attorney. You totally miss the fundamental point of this. Montero must to be convinced to sell. This deal makes him a part of Landeira Grupo. Resolves the management void left by the passing of Tomás.

"And speaking of Tomás, he wanted to buy Montero Rum years ago. You are ignoring the marketing opportunities afforded by acquiring Montero Rum. Look at this financial projection I worked up."

Bart handed a folder to his father. "I anticipate we should increase profitability twofold in the first year by increased sales through our broader distribution channels. This increases to fourfold over the next couple of years through advanced marketing in the U.S. Following thereafter, revenues have the potential of steady increase as the brand gains an international reputation as the premier rum. This coupled with increased production starting immediately to keep pace. I project an expected five-year return on the total investment of more than thirty percent."

"Based on your rather aggressive revenue projections," Max commented sarcastically.

"This is no different than your entrepreneurial efforts during Prohibition to make Landeira Rum into what it is today. This is a strategic opportunity. A way to differentiate the Landeira brand. It also resolves an important management void with someone uniquely qualified. Rather than your bean-counter criticism, you should thank me for finding a solution to a difficult problem."

Realizing he had no option, Max nonetheless still pressed to gain some ground. "And you agree to stay involved to spearhead your grand marketing scheme to fulfill your aggressive projected ROI?"

"For a limited time. A consultant if you will. Not a long term employee of Landeira Grupo. Since this is my idea, I want both it and Augustin to succeed."

Max hesitated. Stalling for time looking to find an angle to negotiate for a lesser price.

Bart knew his father. "Well? Are you going to sign?"

"I suppose you will go through with your threat to dump any involvement in the business if I don't?"

"Jesus Christ!" Bart stood up. "No more negotiating. I am done as of this moment unless you sign. Does that answer your question?"

Max held up his hands. "Very well. Hold your temper and sit back down."

Max Landeira signed the stack of documents in a flourish then slid them over to Bart.

"How about dinner this evening?"

Irritated, Bart snapped back, "Not tonight. I am going to present the good news to Augustin and invite him to dinner. A celebratory dinner. Personal. No talk of business. Tomorrow I will introduce him to our employees as their new boss. I suggest you join us. Nine o'clock. Then you invite him to dinner. Get to know your new general manager. My recommendation, do not fuck it up, Father. You want Augustin to be enthusiastic. This is a bold move for him. Don't play the corporate executive from Tampa. If you want to run Landeira Grupo financial affairs from afar, let him manage Landeira Rum without interference."

Bart immediately telephoned Augustin Montero from a private office with the door closed. After delivering the goods news, "How about we celebrate tonight over dinner. Your whole family."

A jubilant Montero said, "Yes, of course. This is truly a special occasion. Let me call Emilia and Luis. Will your father be joining us?"

"Not tonight, but tomorrow I want to introduce you to the Landeira employees and he will join us. I suggested you and he discuss business over dinner tomorrow night. Tonight is for celebrating. Do you have a favorite restaurant?"

"Let me ask my wife after I tell her the news. Can I call you back?"

"Certainly. Here is the number for my father's law office. I look forward to this evening, Augustin."

A short time later Montero called back. "Alicia insists you have dinner at our house. She is a wonderful cook. Emilia and Luis will also join us. Considering the occasion, that will be more personal. Seven o'clock?"

"I agree. I will be there and bring the signed documents. Looking forward to seeing you, Augustin."

Landeira felt satisfied with events. His brief relationship with Uncle Tomás connected to rum led to engineering this acquisition. A warm sense of satisfaction. Everyone seemed a winner. He felt especially rewarded by what this meant for the Monteros.

The prospect of seeing Emilia in something other than a professional capacity stirred different feelings.

The evening proved a joyous event. The Monteros made him feel a close family friend. The younger son, Luis, initially opposed to the sale of the family business engaged Landeira with great interest. Outspokenly anti-Batista, his sister apparently conveyed Landeira's disapproval of Batista and Mafia investment in Havana. As a student with his studies interrupted by Batista's closing of the University of Havana, Landeira speculated if Luis Montero might even be involved with the revolutionary student movement the Directorio Revolucionario Estudiantil.

Seeing her younger brother monopolizing the conversation, Emilia said, "Luis, easy up on Señor Landeira. He is our guest not a witness to be subjected to cross examination."

"I do not mind at all, Señora Montero. I enjoy a lively discussion of matters of importance. I also share many of your brother's views."

The impetuous Luis, curious about Landeira, forged ahead, "Papa says you served in World War Two. Did you see combat?"

"Yes. In North Africa and Italy."

"Are those scars from the war?"

"Luis!" Emily exclaimed sharply, "That is rude. Apologize to Señor Landeira."

Although he rarely even acknowledged the origin of these prominent scars, he understood the natural curiosity of people.

"No need to apologize. I am not self-conscious. I received the wounds in Italy in 1944. A knife wound to my cheek. A bullet through my hand."

The scar ran close to four inches on his left cheek. While it marred his otherwise handsome features, it gave him a raffish appearance. A sense of mystery when considered along with the ugly spider-web scars on the back of his left hand left by the exit of a nine millimeter round at point-blank range. The wound inhibiting the normal function of two of his fingers.

Regardless of his words dismissing the intrusiveness of the question, his expression suggested something deeper. The circumstances far worse than evidenced by physical scars. The memory of that singular event never out of his thoughts. For years, the source of recurring nightmares. An enduring sense of profound loss.

Augustin sharply rebuked his son, "That is enough, Luis. Bart is our guest."

Alicia Montero stood up and grabbed her son roughly by the arm, "Come and help me serve dessert."

Emilia shot a withering look at her brother as he left the room with his mother then turned to Landeira with a softer look. "I apologize for my brother's adolescent social behavior, Señor Landeira."

Dinner was over with everyone consuming a good deal of Montero rum. Including Emilia. Throughout the evening Landeira saw a different side of her. The rum likely contributing to modifying what he felt was her unapproachable demeanor.

She looked at Landeira with an engaging smile, "You call Papa by his first name. You should therefore call me Emilia. Reserve Señora Montero for my mother."

"Thank you, Emilia. And please call me Bart."

The exchange stirred renewed excitement of getting closer to Emilia. In the many hours spent together finalizing the deal, she gave no indication of a relationship in her personal life. By an offhand comment by her father, he only knew she was not married. Such an attractive, intelligent woman must receive continual male attention. Just her nature to keep her personal life private.

* * * *

Mateo Pérez was astounded when Landeira presented the identities of five different investment front companies incorporated in Cuba by his father along with a list of U.S. incorporated companies. While no names of known American organized criminal associations stuck out, his father all but admitted Mafia money was behind these investor shell companies. Uncovering perhaps layers of cutouts to get to the source remained the challenge.

"How did you come by these?" Pérez asked as they gathered in the study of Pérez's home in the Vedado. Although a professor, Pérez came from another wealthy sugar family dynasty like Landeira. That and years in academia interacting with successive Cuban government administrations gave him a vast network of contacts.

"My father. A show of faith, a change of heart, or just a way of further trying to entice me to join his legal practice. No way to know. My father is both clever and devious. Claims he dealt only with attorneys representing theses investors. Did not know any names of individual investors involved, yet admits there is likely Mafia hidden in there."

"Does he know you are going to research these investors and publish what you find?"

"Yes. Claims he does not seem to care. Says that is not his problem. The real reason I believe is that he is no longer involved in setting up these front companies to channel Mafia money."

"If we can discover Mafia money in this, will it newsworthy?" Pérez asked.

"I think so. Everybody knows it is Mafia money financing the hotel and casino boom, but if we can explain the methods used for covering their tracks that will be of interest. For those investor shell companies incorporated in the United States, perhaps legal trouble for money laundering and tax evasion for the underlying individual investors. I will work that angle."

Pérez grinned as he continued to look over the pages of names. "Batista will not be happy with more press attention about American organized crime money flowing into Cuba. Might be common knowledge but he walks a fine line with the need to appease the U.S. government.

"My sources say there is significant disquiet in Washington about his excesses in attempting to crush the revolutionary movement. Castro's revolutionaries number so few but Batista's heavy-handed use of the Army and the National Police insure substantial support among the rural population for the revolutionaries."

"Anything that disturbs Batista is worthwhile. Where do you suggest we start?" Landeira said.

"I will proceed on investigating those Cuban legal entities. Do you have sources in the United States to research the U.S. incorporated companies?"

"The research staff of the Miami Herald a good starting point. Another thought occurred to me, Mateo. To further obscure the paper trail, the U.S. incorporated shell companies may be listed as investors in some of these Cuban companies."

Two weeks later, they pooled their progress. Landeira said, "I made good progress on Ybor Group Investments. It has Santo Traffacante's fingerprints all over it. Not surprising since he heads the Tampa Mafia family started by his father. Ybor City is actually a neighborhood in Tampa. Largely Cuban immigrants. Furthermore, my father was close to Traffacante Sr."

"What exactly did you find?" Pérez asked.

"Two of the investor firms consist of questionable shareholder groups. One is Cuban restaurants around Tampa. Another is a collection of rental apartment building owners. Neither group has sources of capital sufficient to invest in any Havana project. Since Trafficante controls the illegal bolita lotteries in the Tampa Bay area, he just recruited these characters to act as strawmen.

"Another group is actually a shell company formed as an investment vehicle for the New Orleans Dockworkers Union pension fund. New Orleans mob boss Carlos Marcello controls the union. Union pension funds are notoriously subject to corruption due to favorable U.S. laws and restricted oversight. Marcello can easily flow money through the pension fund and doctor the accounting records. How did you make out?"

"Similar results to what you found for those companies created in Cuba. One created for the musicians' guild. Another for the restauranteurs' association. Understandable since these people stand to benefit by investment in the hospitality and gambling business.

"There are many individuals actually identified as investors. Most of insufficient means to invest in projects of this scale but a few are well known. However, recognizing some of the names then digging deeper, I found a common connection. All of have some direct or indirect association to Meyer Lansky or Santo Traffacante.

"Among those better known Amadeo Barletta stands out. A colorful character with a long history in Cuba. Into everything. Hotels, casinos, banks, communications, with dozens of front companies. Since the war, running his version of a Cuban Mafia family. Barletta is Italian of Calabrian descent.

"Joe Stassi is the alleged representative for the American Mafia crime commission in Havana. Amleto Battisti is a well-established Uruguayan-Italian mobster and owner of the Sevilla-Biltmore Hotel since 1939. Known as a close associate of Santo Traffacante Jr. Another is Norman Rothman who runs the gambling at the San Souci for Traffacante. Several others.

"In every case, none of their names appear directly as investors. Not particularly difficult to identify because the investor names appear as people close to them. Wives or bodyguards mostly. This is Batista's Cuba so the attempt at concealment is only superficial."

Landeira remained silent for a moment deep in thought. "Must be more to this. Does the Mafia smuggle suitcases full of cash into Havana? Then what happens? Construction projects of this scope involve selecting contractors, awarding contracts, financing, and making progress payments. That does not happen by moving cash about. That means banks which must be central to the money laundering process."

Pérez nodded. "Of course. Did your father discuss the process for these investment companies actually financing projects?"

"No, he did not. In fact, he made a point of saying he was never involved in any of the actual financing deals. Said his work ended after forming the companies."

"I would venture to say he is lying," Pérez said.

Landeira nodded. "Undoubtedly. To complete this picture we need to trace the money trail all the way though. In addition to real estate sales, are there public records of construction contracts?"

Pérez smiled. "Yes. In all cases. Most of these development projects also involved public funds. You see, Batista was a founding partner in the Havana hotel and gambling boom. In exchange for licensing, Batista pledged Cuban public funds to match private investment dollar for dollar for development projects over a million dollars. A detailed public record therefore exists."

"And would that identify banks involved in financing the various projects?"

"Certainly."

"Can you access these records without raising suspicion?" Landeira said.

"I believe so. I know sources in the Finance Ministry. Many opposed to Batista's overt corruption are willing to throw sand in his machinery as their form of dissent."

"Good. We need to identify the banks. These investor fronts only serve to finance major projects by securing loans. Pledging likely fictitious collateral as security and actually funded by laundering Mafia money."

Pérez said, "Bank loan details are not public records."

"I understand. But identifying the participating banks gives us other threads to pursue."

Landeira knew without a doubt that one of those banks was his father's Banco Crédito Industrial y Mercantil de Habana. If true, he was not sure how he might use that information to his advantage.

Chapter 11

Fidel Castro's rebel activities with the landing of the yacht *Granma* and the Christmas massacre of 1956 resulted in President Batista censoring the New York Times and Miami Herald from reporting on rebel activities by prohibiting distribution of the popular American newspapers in Cuba.

Bart Landeira was cautious to keep his reporting on rebel activities narrowly to the facts, avoiding any editorializing. Anti-Batista news nonetheless flowed out of Cuba with the thriving American tourist trade. The wire services picked up news printed by the Miami Herald from sources within Florida's large Cuban expatriate population. It suggested to Landeira a possible way of circumventing Batista's censorship to reach American readers. For the time being, he would stick with probing American organized crime investment in Havana. With no censorship repercussions, Batista appeared to ignore the indirect implications of his association with the American Mafia.

New York Times reporter Herbert Mathews took a more direct approach. Toward the end of February, he smuggled into Cuba making his way with the aid of rebel sympathizers to Fidel Castro's stronghold in the Sierra Maestra Mountains of eastern Cuba. Although consisting only of small number of guerrillas, Fidel Castro was very much alive as attested by the pictorial display in the Times. A propaganda black eye for Batista after publically claiming Castro was among those killed in the disastrous invasion attempt in December of the previous year. Mathews' Times article highlighted to the world the inability of Batista to crush the anti-government revolutionaries.

The insider information provided by Bart Landeira's father provided a breakthrough in researching the trail of American organized crime investment in Havana. Knowing his father, Landeira reflected on the reason behind the sudden candor about his legal work. Not exactly a mea culpa confessing his participation in laundering Mafia money therefore no longer necessary to conceal this past shady activities. Use it to convince his son that whatever he did in the past from bootlegging to a vague admission of assisting in money laundering was history. Turning over a new leaf in his remaining years. Focused on developing a relationship with his son.

Within weeks, Landeira and Pérez uncovered sufficient evidence to point to specific Mob investment. More importantly, Pérez uncovered a vein of information that cast light on how the Mob inserted their illegal U.S. profits into the Cuban economy.

Pérez researched the new hotel and casino construction and ownership changes over the past several years. As Landeira suggested, the key turned out to be the banks involved in these projects.

Meeting in Pérez's study, Pérez said, "Thinking about the logistics, it now appears obvious that banking complicity is essential to the flow of money from illegal U.S. activities. How else could the Mafia insert such large sums of money into the financial system?"

Landeira said, "Yes, of course. These major purchases or construction projects must involve banks. The mobsters can bring cash into Havana but getting into legitimate circulation requires banking participation. That is the problem for the Mafia in the United States because of strict banking regulations and criminal statutes."

Perez responded, "Not a problem in Cuba if you know the right banks. Banks Batista uses to fund his corruption. You see, Mafia investment is just part of a larger partnership with everyone participating making a great deal of money. Batista's plans coincided with those of the Mafia, and Cuban banks saw the opportunity to join in."

Pérez handed a folder to Landeira. Inside a list of five banks. One name stood out. Banco Crédito Industrial y Mercantil de Habana. Max Landeira's bank.

"These banks all participated in financing recent purchases or construction of high-end hotels and casinos.

"Not surprising," Landeira said. "My father conveniently omitted his bank's involvement. Landeira Grupo owns sixty-percent of the stock. My father runs it as he pleases."

"The story becomes more interesting. One of my sources is a journalist like you. Covered financial news before his newspaper closed because of pressure from Batista's Ministry of Propaganda. We share the same feelings about Batista.

"When I asked him what he knew about this list of banks he asked what I was investigating? He seemed alarmed. Without mentioning your name, I said I was looking into the extent of American organized crime money coming into Havana from the United States to launder into investment.

"To my surprise, he broke down and wept. Obviously, I touched on something personally disturbing. He started by saying it involved Banco de Fomento Agricola e Industrial de Cuba and the Habana Hilton project currently under construction."

"Batista's personal project?" Landeira asked.

"Precisely. What disturbed my friend was the disappearance of another reporter from the same newspaper less than a year ago. An aggressive young investigative reporter. Before the reporter disappeared, he told my friend a story he uncovered. A story so explosive he even hesitated to take it to their managing editor. A warning you and I should heed considering what you intend to publish."

"Does your friend have a suspicion as to what happened?"

"Circumstances make that clear. The young reporter discovered the information from his girlfriend who learned the details from her brother."

"What circumstances?"

"Because the reporter and girlfriend disappeared. No bodies ever found but foul play clearly suspected."

"Who does your friend suspect?"

"The Mafia, probably using local contract killers. Perhaps even the National Police. After all, this is Batista's signature project."

"So tell me what this reporter discovered."

"The project budget is 24 million US dollars. Supposedly financed as an investment by Caja de Retiro y Asistencia Social de los Trabajadores Gastronomicos, the pension fund of the Cuban catering workers' union. That alone is absurd. The union has insufficient resources or the credit stature to fund a project of this size. That is where Banco de Fomento Agricola e Industrial de Cuba, BANFAIC, enters the picture. Advertised as the source for the financing, they actually serve the role as the banking front for both the Mafia and Batista.

"Okay, you have my attention. What did this reporter discover that cost him his life and that of his girlfriend?"

"The brother of the girlfriend was a mid-level manager at BANFAIC. Whatever his motivation, he confided in his sister and her boyfriend, the reporter, who was also his best friend."

"What happened to this BANFAIC guy?"

"Found dead several days later. His body found in an alley. Suffered terrible torture before death. Tongue cut out and his throat then cut to bleed to death. Photographs published in the newspapers. The message a clear warning to anyone else with knowledge of what is going on.

"The reporter explained scheme to my friend. The Mafia brings in cash to BANFAIC, which in turn extends a loan to the catering union. The loan is nothing more than a part of an elaborate paper trail. The Mafia money is the actual source of funds. Everyone benefits, except the people of Cuba. The Mafia launders a lot of cash while making a sound investment. The catering union gets a sizeable kickback for doing nothing. BANFAIC receives enormous commissions and fees for their service with no financial risk. Lastly, President Batista syphons off some unknown amount of money from public matching funds for large investments. His bribery covered by the Mafia."

Landeira asked, "Sonofabitch. Do you think this is what played out with other projects?"

Pérez shrugged. "Hard to say, but why not?"

Bart said, "Amazing work, Mateo. Let me see what you discovered about the other projects."

* * * *

Over the next week, Landeira secluded himself while assembling this story. Fortunately, his father was back in Tampa and out of his hair. Except for a brief visit with Augustin Montero to see how he was acclimating to his new role, shaping the story dominated his attention.

The visit proved more than just a courtesy. Augustin was doing nicely. The employees at Landeira Rum seemed happy and so did Augustin. Landeira saw in Augustin many of the same traits that drew him close to his Uncle Tomás. In this convivial mood, Landeira ventured to ask Augustin about Emilia.

"A personal question if I may ask, Augustin. It is about Emilia. To be honest, I am much taken by her. A strong, intelligent woman."

"And also beautiful," Augustin added with a broad grin. "I notice how you look at her, Bart. You want to know if there is a man in her life?"

Landeira nodded with a sheepish smile.

"No there is no one I know of. She never married but that was not for lack of opportunities. However, as a good father, I respect her privacy so I can say no more. If you are wondering if you should ask her to dinner though, I suggest you try. Emilia can be tough but she has made several complimentary comments when your name comes up, Bart. Good luck." Montero said with a broad grin and pat on Landeira's shoulder.

That encouragement only intensified fantasizing about Emilia. Discipline forced him to postpone asking her out until he completed drafting this article about the Mafia in Havana. The challenge to discover the truth hidden with considerable effort by this criminal cabal becoming obsessive in a fulfilling way. Investigative journalism could be addictive.

He had no illusions about the risks involved with publishing this incriminating material revealing not only Mafia methods but also implicating Batista. He did not take the Ciudad Trujillo experience lightly. Perhaps he craved the adrenalin rush. Was that why he voluntarily accepted assignment to the OSS during the war? Was working alone, surviving by your wits behind enemy lines more appealing than conventional soldiering?

None of that introspection mattered. It is whatever it is. For the first time since the end of the war, he felt a direction, a purpose, doing something of value. With all its problems, coming to Havana felt right. The side story of his uncle's passing and involvement with Augustin Montero created a personal attachment. The mysterious Emilia Montero stirred romantic prospects. Even experiencing the disappointment of his father's unsavory past was better than estrangement. Some sort of relationship might still evolve.

Finished with the draft, he reviewed it with Mateo Pérez. While Pérez never voiced concern over his personal safety, Landeira understood that publishing this article might put Pérez at personal risk due to their association.

Pérez carefully read the long article. Looking up he said, "An excellent piece. Well written. Enough detail to make it compelling to the average reader without undue complexity. One suggestion however."

"What is that, Mateo?"

"I recommend you remove the speculation about Batista skimming money from the project. Making the case for the implicit cooperation of Batista goes about as far as you dare without risk of censorship. Perhaps even deportation. Actually explaining the scheme indirectly implies his complicity with American organized crime."

Pérez of course was correct. Way too strong. Changes the story to an exposé of Batista rather than the safer public villains the American Mafia. Another Yanqui blight inflicted on Cuba.

154

Landeira nodded. "You are right, Mateo. I will rewrite that out. Maybe leave the impression that Batista is only the project sponsor, not directly involved in the financing."

Pérez said, "Too bad you are not free to go after Batista in the American Press. There are so many Cubans like me and my journalist friend willing to provide damaging material."

"That is always the problem for getting out the truth from within a police state. Look at my experience in the Dominican Republic. Trujillo's foremost critic is a reporter in San Juan, Puerto Rico. Relies on a network of sources to smuggle out damaging material on Trujillo's regime. Able to publish from outside the DR places him out of reach of Trujillo's secret police."

Making that observation to Pérez gave Landeira an idea. The substance of reporting on Cuba was far more than the Mafia making Havana a spectacular gambling venue. Once he published this planned series of Mafia pieces, he must find a way get to the real substantive news. Something similar to what Herbert Mathews of the New York Times accomplished by interviewing Fidel Castro in the mountains. That piece gave Castro's ragtag revolutionary movement new life while illustrating the inability of the Batista regime to stamp out what appears as an insignificant rural insurgency. Landeira needed to strike a forceful blow.

* * * *

After completing his work on the Mafia exposé, Landeira decided to first publish an introductory article. Since every detail of Mafia investment in Havana centered largely on two gangland figures, he would present a brief sketch of their backgrounds.

The American Mafia in Havana, Cuba
Miami Herald correspondent Bart Landeira

The most visible presence of American organized crime in Havana is Meyer Lansky and Santo Traffacante Jr. While maintaining low profiles, both are frequently seen in the Havana casinos as evidenced by these recent photographs. Not surprising since the spectacular creation of Havana as an international gambling venue of the rich and famous owes its success to these two figures.

The outcry in the United States of Havana becoming a haven for Mafia money has little effect on the government of Fulgencio Batista. For the simple reason that the Havana hospitality boom is an economic windfall. Undoubtedly, some portion of this windfall finds its way into the hands of government officials, greatly enhancing an existing culture of corruption.

Without attempting to provide a biography, I shall give the reader a brief sketch of the background of Meyer Lansky, the singular architect of the Havana success story.

Meyer Lansky

Unlike the majority of American organized crime transplanted by Sicilian immigrants, Lansky is Jewish. Born Meier Suchowlański in 1902 to Polish-Jewish parents in the city of Grodno in the Russian Empire, today Belarus. He emigrated to the Lower East Side of Manhattan, New York at the age of nine. Here Lansky became a lifelong friend of Charles "Lucky" Luciano and fell into a life of crime.

Like most mobsters, Lansky got his start as a young man in the bootlegging business in the early twenties after Prohibition became law. Partnering with his friend Benjamin "Bugsy" Siegel the diminutive Lansky ran the notoriously violent bootlegging gang known as the Bugs and Meyer Mob. In 1929, he joined with his friend Luciano in founding a national crime syndicate along with Chicago crime figure Johnny Torrio from Chicago and Frank Costello from New York.

With the repeal of Prohibition, the mathematically gifted Lansky turned his interests to gambling. Not the lottery numbers racket but casino games of chance. Lansky understood the profit potential by understanding the mathematical odds of wagering games and the structure allowing the "house" to hold a statistical advantage on any wager. By 1936, Lansky established casino gambling operations in Florida, New Orleans, and Havana. Locations with strong mob connections and corrupt law enforcement.

Following WWII, it was Lansky who promoted venturing into investment in Las Vegas. With Nevada permitting legal casino gambling, his first venture started with the Flamingo Hotel in the high desert backwater noted for its proximity to atomic bomb test sites. The point person became Lansky's longtime friend, Benjamin "Bugsy" Siegel. Unfortunately, the project suffered severe cost overruns. The Mafiosi backers accused the flamboyant Siegel with his movie star good looks of syphoning money to support his lavish life style. Rumor has it that it was Lansky who ultimately gave the final thumbs down on his friend's fate. Mob assassins shot Siegel dead in gangland style in Beverly Hills in 1947.

The Flamingo survived as the forerunner for other new hotels in Las Vegas. It became the most visible tribute to Meyer Lansky's skills in concealing organized crime money financing Las Vegas casino and hotel development. Circumventing running afoul of U.S. laws for tax fraud, money laundering, wire fraud, bank fraud, and conspiracy attested to Lansky's ingenuity when law enforcement knew the truth of the funding.

In 1940, Fulgencio Batista won election as president of Cuba. A newcomer with natural political instincts, Batista with only the rank of sergeant, rose to prominence in 1933 by instigating a military coup known as the Sargent's Revolt. Batista's political acumen quickly came to the forefront. A short-lived interim government gave way to the appointment of a president backed by University of Havana professors and student organizations. Batista immediately became chief of staff of the Army with the rank of colonel. The successful coup established the political power of the Cuban military effectively making Batista the power behind the civilian government.

It was during this time that Meyer Lansky realized the potential of becoming close to the real power in Cuban politics. Batista served as elected president to 1944. After leaving office, he moved to Daytona Beach, Florida. For Lansky, the war years offered few commercial prospects in Havana. However, Lansky was a strategic thinker. Although living in Daytona Beach, Florida, he understood Batista still exercised power through his stature with the Cuban military.

In 1946, Lansky organized a summit meeting at the Hotel Nacional in Havana consisting of representatives of all organized criminal elements in the United States. This included the Italian Mafia and the Jewish Syndicate. The keynote speaker was Lucky Luciano returned from exile in Italy, still regarded as the boss of bosses. The meeting intended to promote investment in Havana hotels and casinos by laundering illegal profits from every corner of the American underworld.

Lansky's preparation and long view paid off in 1952 when Batista running third in another bid for the presidency simply seized power in a bloodless coup backed by the Army. Batista and American organized crime joined in an unholy alliance to create the goldmine that is today Havana.

Santo Traffacante Jr. is a more prosaic figure compared to many of the more notorious Mafiosi bosses. He grew up in the shadow of his father, inheriting leadership of the Tampa Bay Mafia family following his father's death in 1954. Involved with illegal gambling in Tampa from an early age, he saw the profit potential of Havana without the constant threat of U.S. law enforcement. In 1955, he relocated to Havana to supervise aggressively investing in hotels, casinos, and nightclubs.

Santo Trafficante Jr.

Of all the mobsters involved in Havana, Trafficante is the most visible. His father, Sicilian-born Santo Sr. was a Mafiosi of the old school. In the rough and tumble era of Prohibition, Santo Sr. consolidated illegal gambling and bootlegging operations in Tampa by eliminating rivals. Cuba became the

158

principal conduit for running Prohibition liquor and narcotics. Santo Sr. forged one of the most powerful Sicilian Mafia families in the United States. Well respected, Santo Sr. had close ties to the Luciano and Lucchese Mafia families in New York.

With a history of involvement in gambling and the proximity of Cuba to Tampa, Santo Jr. saw the opportunity to make his own name by developing Havana as an accessible gambling mecca to rival Las Vegas. He began investing Tampa mob profits in Havana casinos and nightclubs, often run as separate businesses to the hotels where they were located. Trafficante owns interests in the most glamorous casinos in Havana. These include the Tropicana, San Souci, Habana Deauville, Capri, Comodoro, Sevilla Biltmore, Riviera, and Habana Hilton. Trafficante also controls the lucrative Havana entertainment business through his International Amusements Corporation that contracts all major entertainment bookings.

Whereas Meyer Lansky conceived and pioneered Havana in becoming the glamorous gambling venue in the Americas, Santo Trafficante Jr. turned Lansky's vision into reality. By widespread investment, Trafficante's example fostered a flood of Mafia investment from other American Mafia families. It is no understatement that Trafficante is the face of the American Mafia in Havana.

Chapter 12

Definitely, he crossed the Rubicon in his newfound relationship with his father who undoubtedly will feel betrayed. So be it. Bart felt a righteous indignation toward his father's continued obfuscation concerning his association with the Mafia. It was his father who volunteered the details of the front companies he created for the express Several days after publishing that first article introducing the Mafia in Havana by using the profiles of Meyer Lansky and Santo Trafficante Jr., the second article appeared in the Sunday Miami Herald. Landeira braced for the backlash.

purpose of investing in Havana. Claimed no specific knowledge that the actual investors were American Mafia. Even challenged Bart as a journalist to dig deeper stating he had no vested interest in protecting any of these clients.

However, this article implies his father's active participation by including Banco Crédito Industrial y Mercantil de Habana. His father made a point of claiming he had no involvement in the actual funding transactions of any projects. Avoided discussing the Bank as merely another method of Landeira Grupo integrating vertically by providing financial services for their core businesses. Bart now understood the real reason for founding Banco Crédito was to reap lucrative fees for laundering Mafia money and enabling Batista to shim a percentage.

160

Glamorous Havana or Gangster Haven?

Miami Herald correspondent Bart Landeira: The hospitality-gambling boom in Havana, Cuba fosters continual interest throughout the United States. It is now the favored gambling mecca for American tourists, rivaling Las Vegas. The origin of both locations attributed to investment of American organized crime. Imported with the flood of Italian immigrants during the early years of the 20th century, those from Sicily brought with them the Sicilian Mafia. Like a disease, the Mafia evolved as successor to the earlier Italian secret extortionist organization known as the Black Hand that came to the United States in the later decades of the 19th century.

From those early beginnings, the American Mafia transformed from localized criminal gangs plaguing impoverished urban immigrant neighborhoods into sophisticated organizations as a result of Prohibition. The new law enacted by constitutional amendment became the perfect illicit means for providing a product wanted by the entire population. Smuggling and distributing illegal alcohol overshadowed the profits from drugs, prostitution, extortion, or illegal gambling. Gambling amounted to the Italian lottery in large eastern cities known as the *numbers racket* and *bolita* in the Latin immigrant communities of Florida. Criminal enterprises targeting lower income populations. Venturing into games of chance in jurisdictions that legally allowed offered the ability for organized crime to expand its market. Coupled with luxury hotels, they could now attract customers from every economic stratum.

Legal casino gambling allowed the Mafia to come out of the shadows to operate legitimate businesses. The greater attraction inherent in casino gambling was the structured profit potential where the "house" enjoys a statistical advantage in games of chance. With transactions on a massive scale, statistical odds always return profits to the house. No need to cheat the gambling public. In fact, cheating becomes counterproductive. Large winners become good advertising. The actual reality, those winnings come from the losses of other gamblers not the house profit. Casino operators therefore self-police their operations to insure the gambling public gets fair treatment, albeit while wagering money when they have less than even odds of winning.

By definition, organized crime is a cash business. Inherently that becomes a problem for circumventing tax laws. Tax violation imprisoned Al Capone rather than complicity in countless murders. Legalized gambling allowed organized crime to venture into a legal enterprise with enormous profit potential. How then does the Mafia move millions of dollars in cash to finance large-scale development projects? Even in Cuba, financial transactions must convey the appearance of following conventional practices. Banks therefore become an essential part of the money chain. This reporter has discovered specific details of just how American organized crime transforms illegal cash profits into legitimate investment. The same complex subterfuge undoubtedly takes place in Las Vegas or anywhere the Mob operates. In the corrupt environment of Havana, it simply becomes easier to avoid the consequences of exposure.

Organized crime is a corrosive element to society. To operate, it must go to great lengths to conceal illegal profits. Corruption of law enforcement and even the courts becomes a natural byproduct. They do this by *laundering* money to obscure its origin and reintroduce that money back into the economy with its origin cleansed. The result, laundered money further corrupts society by contaminating otherwise legitimate enterprise.

This story exposes just how the process of money laundering takes place. Both Las Vegas and Havana profit from legalized gambling. What Havana offers is the ability to launder illegal profits gained from drugs, prostitution, extortion, and illegal gambling into capital for investment in lucrative legal enterprises. Unlike Las Vegas, Cuba is a lax regulatory country, with a government welcoming to investment regardless of the origin of the funds. Havana therefore avoids the intense scrutiny experienced by U.S. law enforcement. The Cuban government acts as a partner welcoming investment regardless of the origin of the money.

Havana is quickly overshadowing Las Vegas. Unlike the remote high desert location of Las Vegas, Havana is a charming old world city in an exotic tropical setting. Year-round warm weather and beaches. The anything goes atmosphere makes Havana the sin city of the western hemisphere. Celebrity entertainment, five-star hotels, gambling, drugs, and sex. Assessable from anywhere in the eastern United States.

While Cuba remains not only lax but also complicit in welcoming Mafia investment, its economic and political domination by the United States demands at least a modicum of discretion in the financial trail to deflect U.S. scrutiny since the majority of foreign investment is American. As in the United States, the names of known or suspected organized criminal figures do not appear on legal documents associated with Havana real estate development, ownership, or gambling licensing.

Even in the United States, everyone including law enforcement acknowledges organized crime investment exists in Las Vegas. Yet indictments against Mafia figures remain rare. While the circumstances are far more lax in Cuba, nonetheless the Mafia must still go to lengths to conceal its investment. Cuban political and economic ties with the U.S. make flaunting the Mafia presence unwise for fear of U.S. sanctions.

Here then are details recently discovered after extensive research providing a sense of the scope of America Mafia investment in Havana. There is good reason to believe this blueprint of front companies and strawmen is conceptually the way the Mafia infiltrates Las Vegas. The following examples are companies registered with the Cuban Ministry of Commerce. Among the officers and directors are no names recognizable as organized criminal figures. However, our research uncovered the true identities of the underlying investors to reveal their direct connection to organized criminal enterprises.

One such example is Ybor Group Investments consisting of legal entities with unfamiliar names. Yet their association with Tampa, Florida not surprisingly leads directly to the Trafficante Mafia Family. A restaurant association made up of small ethnic Cuban and Italian restaurants in the immigrant neighborhoods in the Tampa Bay. Santo Trafficante Jr. is of course one of the principal figures in Mafia investment in Havana. Another investor is New Orleans Dockworkers Union pension fund. The president of that organization is the brother-in-law of Carlos Marcello, Mafia boss of the New Orleans Mafia family.

A similar U.S. incorporated front company known as Caribbean Investments consists of investors leading indirectly back to Trafficante and known New York Mafia-associated businesses.

Ybor Group and Caribbean Investments are listed in purchase transactions and gambling licensing records associated with many of Havana's most prestigious casinos. These include the Tropicana, San Souci, Capri, Habana Deauville, Comodoro, and Sevilla Biltmore. Both these investment companies were created by prominent Cuban business attorney Maximiliano Landeira. Landeira maintains offices in Tampa, Florida and Havana and has a past relationship with the Tampa Mafia Trafficante family. Landeira is also president of Banco Crédito Industrial y Mercantil de Habana that serves as part of a consortium of banks financing the investments in the aforementioned properties.

Empresas del Vedado consists of predominantly Cuban investors. Names connected with various Cuban enterprises such as commercial construction and telecommunications. The common thread in their association with the hotel-casino boom. Opened in 1930, the iconic 500,000 square-foot ocean-front Hotel Nacional sold to a newly formed Cuban company, Corporacion International de Hoteles S.A. in 1955. To bring in other investors as well as Mafia partners, Meyer Lansky created the Cuban investment company of Empresas del Vedado. Empresas del Vedado is the largest shareholder with all its investors connected indirectly to Lansky. Although his name does not appear as managing director, Lansky runs Corporacion International de Hoteles. Banco Atlantico provided financing. The bank president, Italian-Cuban Amadeo Barletta is an established figure in Cuban business and finance circles and longtime associate of Lansky.

The Havana Hotel Nacional circa 1933

Although Jewish, Meyer Lansky is a high-ranking member of the "Commission", the umbrella board of directors' organization governing the confederation of all the U.S. Mafia families and the Jewish Syndicate. The pioneer in Havana gambling investment, Lansky is known as the "Mob's Accountant" for his proven entrepreneurial business acumen. Although a well-known organized crime figure, his name does not appear on ownership documents.

Everyone understands the new Riviera Hotel under construction is Lansky's personal project. The 21-floor $8 million dollar project on the Malecón overlooking the water is scheduled to open late this year. The project organized under the Riviera de Cuba S.A. corporation. Among its main investors is the aptly named Grupo Malecón consisting of several Las Vegas Mafia front men and hotel operators in Florida, all with close ties to Lansky. The Cuban state-run development bank, Banco de Desarrollo Económico y Social is listed as providing financing.

Numerous other examples exist, however the most striking example is the Habana Hilton just beginning construction. The elegant 600-room 25-floor $24 million dollar is to be President Fulgencio Batista's crown jewel. The project announced as an investment by Caja de Retiro y Asistencia Social de los Trabajadores Gastronomicos, the pension fund of the Cuban catering workers' union with matching public funds provided by the Cuban government. Financing the project is Banco de Fomento Agricola e Industrial de Cuba, BANFAIC.

President Fulgencio Batista with
model of the Habana Hilton in 1956

BANFAIC however is not the source of funding. The truth revealed by a courageous source provides for the first time details of how the American Mafia made their largest single in-

165

vestment in Havana. From various confidential sources, we corroborated how the money laundering-investment scheme works. Likely the blueprint for other Mafia investment in Havana. The scheme possible only with the active collusion of Cuban banks and a government encouraging investment regardless of its origin.

The scheme is simple. The Mafia brings in cash to BANFAIC, which then extends a loan to the catering union. The loan exists only on paper. Mafia cash from American unlawful enterprises is the actual source of funds. The Mafia therefore launders a great sum of cash into legitimate enterprise with an investment promising profitable returns. The catering union receives a sizeable kickback for cooperating. BANFAIC receives enormous commissions and fees for their service while incurring no financial risk.

We know these details because of insider information from a middle manager at BANFIAC by the name of Bernardo Calderon. Calderon actually handled the suitcases full of cash. He was also the person overseeing the Hilton project financial transactions for the BANFIAC.

Calderon appears to have confided what was going on at the Bank to his sister and her boyfriend, his best friend, a newspaper reporter. In turn, that reporter confided in someone else. We now know what actually goes on behind the public cover deception of the Habana Hilton project because that unnamed source provided the truth. That truth proving more than just a financial crime. In typical gangland fashion, the Mafia murdered those opposing them.

The wrong people learned of Bernardo Calderon's indiscretion. The condition of Calderon's dead body discovered weeks ago in Havana revealed he suffered horrific torture. In his final agony, the assailants cut out his tongue before murdering him by cutting his throat causing a slow death by loss of blood. An ace of spades playing card stuck in his hand. The Mob's signature warning to act as a deterrent to others. The reporter and his girlfriend, Calderon's sister, disappeared around the same time of Calderon's murder.

They undoubtedly suffered a similar fate since evidence suggests they did not leave their residence of their own accord. Their whereabouts remains unknown.

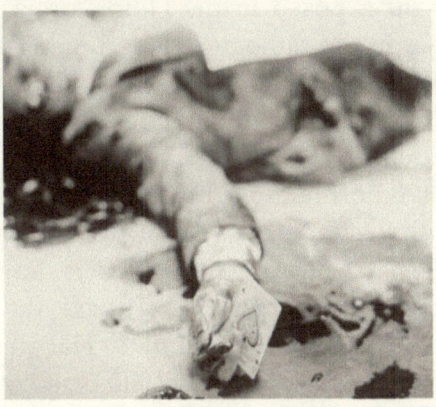

Body of Bernardo Calderon

Three people murdered because they divulged the Mafia scheme. This is the true face of the Mafia operating in Havana. These Mafiosi are more than businessmen operating gambling casinos out of five-star hotels in a tropical paradise. Among the glamour of Havana, the Mafia is still a collection of sociopaths willing to resort to violence to protect their illegal interests.

The exposé article earned a complimentary telegram from the managing editor of the Miami Herald. The following day, other major newspapers in the United States picked up the story from the news services. The New York Times and the Chicago Tribune put it on their front pages.

Swift backlash came from Landeira's father in a telephone call from Tampa.

"I cannot believe you would do this to your own father," Max Landeira angrily said.

"Don't play the victim, Father. It doesn't suit you."

"You betrayed a confidence."

"Really? How is that? You gave me the names of those shareholders in these investment front companies you created. You all but admitted the Mafia money was involved. Even challenged me to dig deeper. So where is the betrayal?"

His father sidestepped the question. "You cast me as a partner with Lansky and Trafficante. Implied I engaged in the same deception as you exposed in the Hilton project. Implied Banco Crédito engages in the same deceptive practices. Where did that come from? Not even sure I can believe what you wrote is true. You cite only confidential unnamed sources. Where is the corroborating evidence?"

"You're pissed off because I discovered your involvement in several casino investment deals. You told me you set up these front companies but never participated in any of the financial deals. You conveniently never discussed the involvement of Banco Crédito Industrial y Mercantil de Habana in the financing of the deals I cited in my reporting. The bank you run. Not likely you created it for the benefit of Landeira Grupo. Perhaps the scheme I made public about the Habana Hilton financing even originated with you."

"Listen to me," Max said in a quieter tone. "I may have done some things in the past which I am not proud of, but don't manufacture things of which you have no proof."

His father's response only made Bart angrier. Rather than deny anything, he sought to deflect and obfuscate. Acting the part of a defense attorney claiming the innocence of his client.

"The circumstantial evidence is overwhelming, Father. You grew up in Tampa. Went into bootlegging with Santo Trafficante Sr. You certainly know his son. These front companies you set up predominately all lead back to Santo Trafficante Jr. Your bank fronted many of Trafficante's casino investments. You spend considerable time in Havana. Trafficante is a familiar figure in the city. Add to that, you have close connections with Batista going back years. To think you are not up to your neck in laundering Mafia money by enabling their Havana investments strains the obvious logical conclusion."

A long silence ensued. "I neither wish to discuss my past legal work or continue arguing with you." His father sounded uncharacteristically deflated. "What I wish for is to find some common ground for us to have a relationship. I realize I press too hard. You are your own person. What you wrote hurt me. Yet I admire your investigative skills that produced what you wrote."

Pausing for a moment, his father continued. "A creative piece of work putting together the deal with Montero. All indications point to Augustin fitting well into managing Landeira Rum."

Still angry, Bart could only muster a sigh. Bart realized his father would never change. Abruptly changing tactics to achieve his aims. Somewhere deep down, Bart felt what might be a remnant of affection? More likely just some genetically encoded attachment to a parent. Little more to say. Should be clear to both of them that any relationship must be conditional and remain at a safe distance. No emotional rapprochement likely possible given their opposing ethical views. Neither of them could conceive of saying he understood the other. The best Bart could do was end the conversation on a neutral note.

"Yes. I check in with Augustin frequently. Need to start soon with developing a marketing plan for Montero Rum brand as I promised."

"Very good. I will be back in Havana in a couple of weeks. Let's get together," Max said in a calm voice as if their angry exchange had never taken place before disconnecting the call.

Bart just shook his head, saddened by the circumstances.

* * * *

Working up the nerve to ask Emilia Montero out, he telephoned her office. "Emilia, this is Bart Landeira."

"*Hola*, Bart. How are you?"

"Fine. Been busy working on a story that just came out in the Miami Herald."

"Yes, I read it. Quite a piece of bold reporting. Certainly will anger some bad characters."

"That was the intent. I went easy on the government. I hope enough to avoid a call from the Ministry of Propaganda by framing it as an attack on the Mafia. Had more material I could have used but wished to avoid deportation for violating censorship restrictions."

"I was surprised that you named your father as probably involved in the Mafia scheme. How did that go over?"

"Not well as you might image. He felt betrayed. Disingenuous since he is or was involved. He provided material related to his legal work setting up investment companies and acknowledged that the underlying investors probably included the Mafia. A complicated story. With your father now working for Landeira Grupo, I thought I should explain that those dealings that I exposed were outside my father's responsibilities as an executive of Landeira Grupo. None of that will affect your father's situation."

"Have you discussed this with my father?"

"Not yet, but I will on Monday. Had my own selfish reasons to explain to you first. Tomorrow I am going to take my sailboat out in the afternoon. Have not been on the water for weeks. Going to treat myself to a relaxing day. I would love for you to join me. Is that possible?"

An uncomfortable silence followed for several seconds before Emilia responded, "I have never been on a sailboat. Are you a good sailor?"

"At the risk of sounding boastful, a very good sailor. Since I was a kid growing up in Tampa. I will bring us lunch. The forecast promises to be a clear day with a good sailing breeze out of the west. I plan to sail east hugging the coast then tack our way back. Maybe three to four hours. It's a good size sailboat so we will not be tossed about with the expected small waves."

"Okay, Bart. It is Saturday and I have no plans. Sounds like an enjoyable day."

"Excellent. How about I pick you up at noon? I keep the boat in a slip near where the Malecón ends at the old Torreon de la Chorrera fortress."

"Very good. My home address is Number 301 San Martin. Apartment 208. Not far from my office. Telephone number is 51-6764."

"It will be a nice day but chilly out on the water this time of year. Dress accordingly."

He could not believe his good fortune. The rest of the day, he spent getting the boat ready. Fuel for the engine, a good cleaning, and provisions for lunch.

The next day before arriving at Emilia's apartment, he felt an excitement not experienced for a long time. Surprised by her acceptance, Emilia previously never showed any personal interest during their hours of interacting putting together the purchase deal for Montero Rum. Disconcerting because he thought himself reasonably good looking except for the scar on his cheek. She could not help but to recognize his attraction for her.

Knocking on her door promptly at noon he smiled as she opened the door. The first time seeing her in casual attire. Fashionable white slacks with wedge sandals accentuated her long legs. A tailored blue silk long-sleeve shirt did the same for her full breasts and narrow waist. Her long hair held in place by a matching blue scarf.

"You look stunning, Emilia."

"Thank you. Please come in while I gather my things."

She put on a broad-brimmed straw hat. Dark glasses gave her the look of a model in a fashion magazine. He replied silently with an expression of approval.

Picking up a beach bag, "I have a sweater in here since you said it could be chilly on the water."

Dressed in denim shirt, white slacks, and deck shoes, they presented a handsome couple.

"Then we are off for a wonderful day. I prepared the boat yesterday. Beer, soft drinks, and sandwiches in a basket in the trunk. A thermos of coffee if you prefer."

Stepping onto the boat, she remarked, "Bigger than I expected."

He was proud of the *Elegante Bellezza*, the Sleek Beauty. She looked good and performed like a thoroughbred under sail.

"Let me show you the galley. I'll stow the food away and put the drinks on ice. The toilet is right here next to the sink. Shower on the opposite side. Plenty of fresh water in a holding tank. Back here the bedroom. Good for running down the coast. Finding a secluded beach then anchoring on the leeward side in the protection of the barrier islands. Spending the night under the stars enjoying the solitude."

Emilia grinned at what that might suggest.

"I did not mean that the way it sounded. We are not going that far today." A bit flustered, "I seem to be making it worse."

"Not at all, Bart. I understand perfectly. You are proud of your beautiful boat."

Looking to extricate from his embarrassing comments, "So let's go topside and I will cast us off."

Still in the protected small bay of the mouth of the Almendares River as it emptied into the Gulf of Mexico, they motored past the 17th century Spanish fortress, the Torreon de la Chorrera. Once out into the Gulf, he cut the engine and raised the main and jib sails. The sea was relatively calm but running with three-foot waves. The boat took the wind, heeling the boat over gently.

Sitting on the bench near to Landeira behind the wheel, Emilia instinctively held onto the rails with both hands.

"Not to worry. She is just taking the wind. The keel prevents us from capsizing. Listen to the rush of water as she slices through the water."

Getting the feel for the rolling and the sensation of speed, she said, "Yes. A relaxing sensation. Something different from the distracting sound of an engine."

"I love the sounds of sailing. You can hear the straining of the sheets, that's what we call the ropes. An ancient art to harness the power of nature. Early on, I found it fascinating. Even in moderately heavy weather I feel enough control to enjoy the experience."

"I would rather avoid bad weather. Cannot imagine being out here in higher waves."

"No need to worry today. How about some coffee?"

"Sounds good."

He engaged the locking mechanism on the steering wheel pedestal to hold the rudder in its current position. As he got up to step down into the gallery. Emilia exclaimed, "Where are you going? What am I supposed to do? I can't steer the boat?"

Smiling, he said, "No need. I locked the rudder in position. I won't be long. Just relax."

She responded, "Tell you what. I will get the coffee. I need to put on my sweater anyway."

Several minutes later, she returned with two steaming mugs of coffee. "I don't think I would like being down below for any extended time. The rolling sensation is relaxing up here but below I can feel my stomach rebelling."

"Takes some getting used to. The first signs of seasickness. Confusion of the balance center in your middle ear and your eyes sending conflicting signals to your brain with the rhythmic movement."

"Well it is a fine day to be out in the open," she responded then segued into conversation of a more personal nature. "Father told me a little about your background. You were in World War Two?"

"Yes. A difficult three years."

"What did you do?"

"Served in combat all that time. First in North Africa then in the Italian theater."

"In the Army?"

He was not going to lie to her about his military service, but uncertain about how far to explain what he actually did. He never told anyone many details, including his family. Yet he felt the need to be more candid with Emilia.

"Yes. I joined the Army shortly after Pearl Harbor. After receiving my officer's commission, I volunteered for the OSS. The Office of Strategic Services."

"Are you familiar with the OSS?"

"No. What did they do?"

"Commandos and spies. We dropped behind enemy lines. Our mission was to disrupt the enemy. We worked closely with our British counterparts of the SOE. Winston Churchill's pronouncement of their mission to *set occupied Europe ablaze* also applied to the American OSS. We fought with partisan groups of occupied countries in Europe fighting against the Germans. Sabotage, assassination, reconnaissance."

"You worked in occupied territory held by the Germans?" She asked a bit surprised.

"Yes. I parachuted into Algeria in November of 1942. Eventually linked up with British SAS commandos. I speak Italian so I was helpful in interrogating Italian prisoners. At the start of the war, Italy fought as an ally of Germany.

From North Africa, I parachuted into Sicily ahead of Allied landings in 1943. Spent the rest of the war fighting up the Italian peninsula behind the German lines with Italian anti-Fascist partisans."

"Are those scars from the war?"

Landeira nodded. "The cheek scar from an SS dagger." Rubbing his cheek with the back of his fingers. "This from a bullet," holding out his hand then turning it over. "Through the palm and out the back."

"My god. How horrible. What happened?"

"Captured by Waffen SS along with three other partisans. You don't want to let yourself be captured by the Nazi SS. Out of uniform made me a spy, subject to execution. In my situation, I had no choice. Knocked unconscious by a tank shell exploding in a building where we were hiding."

She sensed he was retreating into himself recalling the horrific event, but she had to ask. "How did you escape?"

"Training. By the best trainer in the world when it came to close-quarter fighting. You repeat something often enough it can train your mind to override fear and get you out of trouble. He repeatedly taught us to recognize and seize every opportunity to prevail over your opponent. My captors made a mistake by providing that opportunity. Cost me these wounds but I managed to survive."

"I am sorry. That was not fair for me to ask something so personal."

"Not at all, Emilia. I've learned to live with the scars. Just have to be careful shaving. Two outside fingers on my left hand do not work quite right, but doesn't interfere with living."

"Well you still look handsome. Perhaps a little piratical with the scar adding an attractive air of mystery."

174

"Thank you, Emilia. Certainly better than wearing an eyepatch." Chuckling, he changed to a less uncomfortable subject. "So what do you think about sailing? Out here at sea gliding along with only the sound of the sails straining against the wind."

"Lovely. Peaceful. I admit I was a little uncomfortable when we left the protection of the bay into the open sea. Totally relaxed now since we got to talking. I see why you enjoy this."

"How about lunch then? Ham and cheese sandwiches. Assorted fruit."

"Sounds good. I'll go down and bring it up?" she said.

"Okay, but don't stay long enough to start feeling queasy. I'll take a beer, but there is Coke if you prefer."

After lunch and into their second beers, Emilia suddenly said, "Since I was rude enough to ask about your scars. I should reciprocate by offering something personal. No doubt you wondered why I am not in a relationship."

"That is your affair, Emilia. Just thrilled you accepted my invitation."

She smiled. "I am glad you did, Bart. I am flattered by the way you look at me. I have been reclusive for too long. I am truly enjoying myself today.

"I was engaged a few years ago. To an American naval officer. I was working at the time in the Foreign Ministry when I met him at a diplomatic function. He was serving as the assistant naval attaché at the U.S. Embassy. That was early in 1951. Robert died over Korea a year later flying an F-86 fighter."

Not responding with the meaningless comment *I am so sorry for your loss,* he just nodded his understanding with an empathetic expression.

"I always wanted to make my own way doing something interesting. Have a career. Children never seemed a part of my dreams. That made me different in Cuba's patriarchal society that considers women professionals as unusual. Being strong-willed, I am sure men think me a bitch. Easy enough to give that impression being a lawyer. After all, our business is arguing.

"Anyway, I had affairs along the way but none ever worked out."

Bart nodded. "I understand. In my case, I spent years wandering about the world working for the U.S. government and as a foreign newspaper correspondent. Absorbed in my work, made for only casual relationships with women looking for someone more conventional and stable."

Afraid these personal revelations might be making Emilia uncomfortable, Landeira abruptly announced, "Now back to immediate circumstances. Time to turn around. It will take longer to go back since we are heading into the wind."

"How do you against the wind without using the engine?"

"Ah. My opportunity to explain the physics behind sailing. The technique known as *tacking* is how you make progress against the wind direction. Seems counterintuitive but it works. We take a zigzag course by directing the boat allowing the wind to hit sails at an angle. The sails capture the wind by manipulating the tension on the sheets. All done in concert with steering of the rudder. The force of the captured wind pushes the boat forward even when coming at an angle to the boat. It is slower than running with the wind and the distance covered on the water is obviously greater since the course is an indirect zigzag."

They tacked their way back to the west over the next hour and a half. Talk turned to politics.

Emilia said, "By your newspaper articles, you don't like Batista. I also read the previous article about your experience in the Dominican Republic. Batista is no better than Trujillo."

"I could not agree more. Hard to write critical material considering his blanket censorship about publishing anything about the insurgency. I even had to be careful in my piece on exposing Mafia investment, by avoiding directly implicating Batista. Public funds Batista matches for investments over a million dollars do not go entirely toward funding the project. A sizeable portion goes to Batista personally. The shortfall is made up by Mafia laundered money from the United States."

Emilia said, "Yes, I see how you could not publish that without being thrown out of Cuba. Unfortunately, every Cuban government since independence from Spain suffered from corruption. In Batista, you have a dictator backed by a large military and secret police. The insurgency you speak of is more than Fidel Castro's 26 July Movement with his meager band of guerrillas in the Sierra Maestro Mountains. Right here in Havana the Student Revolutionary Directorate is very active. Especially after Batista closed the University."

Landeira replied, "Yes, I know. How do you see the difference between Castro's revolutionaries and the DRE?"

"Castro frightens me. A charismatic populist. An opportunistic fanatic. The background of all dictators. Batista also started out that way. Image a lowly sergeant able to organize a military coup d'état in 1933 then remain a political power over twenty years."

"How is the DRE different from Castro?"

She responded, "First of all, they have no single leader. Intellectuals looking to create a working democracy. Castro focuses on the rural peasantry in the agricultural sector. The most oppressed Cubans. All about land reform and economic opportunity. Laudable objectives, but what kind of government does he propose to deliver on those promises? The devil is in the details. Many fear Castro's extreme socialistic leanings. Possibly Marxist. His rhetoric appeals to his impoverished base but frightens the more educated. The DRE is dedicated to fundamental democratic principles to create socially responsible government. Many fear Castro as anti-democratic. An aspiring left wing dictator."

Surprised by her articulate political assessment, he said, "That is an astute political analysis."

With chagrin she said, "Sorry. Didn't mean to lecture. I took a degree in political science before going into law. That is how I ended up in the Foreign Ministry."

"You stated what many people feel. Including me. I worked in the state department for several years following World War Two. Saw first-hand my share of dictators and revolutionaries. The sad truth, most revolutions turn out badly. Hitler and Stalin are from opposite ideological extremes yet both created history's worst totalitarian regimes."

After considering pressing his good fortune further, he said, "Would you have dinner with me this evening? I am enjoying this day too much to have it end."

Equally enjoying herself with this interesting man, Emilia Montero did not hesitate. "I would like that too, Bart."

Chapter 13

Sitting in Mateo Pérez's study sipping coffee, Landeira launched into what he wanted to discuss. "About time I did something to earn my salary as a correspondent. Working on a piece I call *Weekend in Havana*. A tour of Havana nightlife from the glamorous to the debauched. What the well-heeled high rollers experience to the lesser tourist looking for drugs and sex. Good for one article spiced up with photos. Not likely though to make any more impact than telling the American reader how the Mafia launders money."

"No, Bart that was an important story. Especially for Cubans who read the Miami Herald."

"Okay. Guess I am being too critical. The real news about Cuba is not gambling but the political situation. The repression. The violence. Christ, Batista is killing people by the hundreds."

"Perhaps by the thousands," Pérez offered. "At least it will get to that level if the revolutionary insurgency becomes more threatening. Batista is a sociopath with a large army and secret police. Cuba might become no different than the Dominican Republic."

"My point exactly, Mateo. That is what I need to be reporting."

"You would already be doing that if not reporting under censorship. There are many reporters and editors in Cuba anxious to do the same. Many unemployed because their newspapers closed down. So how can you circumvent Batista's censorship?"

"That's what I came here to discuss. Got the idea by reading articles savaging Trujillo published by El Mundo, a San Juan, Puerto Rico newspaper. The reporter is Gaspar Toussaint. His material is good enough for the wire services to pick them up consistently.

"Toussaint is out of reach of Trujillo's secret police. Allows him to publish strong anti-Trujillo material, including photographs."

Pérez asked, "So how does he source his material?"

Landeira shrugged, "That I don't know. Has some sort of productive network willing to go to great risk. I witnessed first-hand just how dangerous the DR can be to dissidents. If I could develop a similar network in Cuba, I might be able to do something similar."

"So how do you publish the material since you are here?"

"I don't directly. I release it to Toussaint. Make up some fictitious anti-Batista group cited as the source. Toussaint publishes it first in San Juan then puts it out for the wire services."

Pérez looked at him quizzically. "A reporter giving up his material and staying secret? That is unusual. Sounds more like creating a spy network. What exactly did you do when you worked for the U.S. government?"

Landeira smiled. "Worked for the State Department. Not spying but doing confidential work that remains classified so I cannot be more specific. Although you are correct. It is a lot like gathering covert intelligence in a hostile political environment. Essentially investigative journalists operate very much the same as spies. Uncovering information others want kept secret."

"So how do we go about recruiting a network?"

"Works like a hierarchy. You already are my prime source. You know everyone. Among those you know are reliable sources. Like the reporter that passed on to you the real story behind the Habana Hilton deal we published. That Mafia exposé was your doing, Mateo. Each source has the potential of recruiting additional sources."

Pérez nodded as he absorbed Landeira's idea. "Yes. I see where you are going. The reporter who passed along how the Hilton scheme worked confided in someone else closely connected to me."

"You just mentioned there are many Cuban reporters willing to gather material damaging to Batista's dictatorship," Bart said. "There is the perfect network of committed sources if we can find a way to tap into it."

"This is about how the United States views Batista's regime," Perez said. "American corporations control Cuba's economy. U.S. aid props up his military enabling him to stay in power. Now this alliance with American organized crime. The hearts and minds needing change are the Americans not the Cubans who already despise Batista. The objective should be to make Batista an unacceptable alternative to a socialist revolution that the American government fears might become communist. All geopolitical issues are now viewed through the lens of the Cold War."

While Landeira felt compelled as a journalist to go after Batista, he knew the Eisenhower administration would continue to back authoritarian governments as a matter of policy. They seemed incapable of conceiving a middle ground. Beyond U.S. borders, U.S. foreign policy feared the democratic process. His CIA experiences confirmed that.

"Your idea is an ingenious subterfuge," Pérez said. He paused for several moments to consider the ramifications before proceeding. "Might be possible. Dangerous work for anyone caught. Hard to say if we can recruit enough of the right people. Can this San Juan reporter be trusted?"

"I need to determine that by meeting him in person. He has the right credentials though. According to my research, he is Haitian. As a teenager, he lived across the border in the Dominican Republic in 1937 when Trujillo massacred 20,000 Haitians living there. Lost his entire family. Managed to escape. Somehow made his way to Florida and earned a degree in journalism. Been with El Mundo in San Juan since 1942. A constant thorn in the side of Trujillo with the paper's large circulation in Spanish and English throughout the Caribbean."

Perez said, "I am anxious to do something. Your idea has possibilities. Let me discuss your proposal with someone I trust. Someone that has far more sources than I can muster. If he agrees to participate, so will I."

"I appreciate that, Mateo. For security, let's keep the details only between the three of us. I plan to meet with Toussaint the day after tomorrow. He is essential for security and deflecting attention away from me and therefore anyone associated with me. In the meantime, perhaps you can meet with your friend. Feel him out about joining us. If successful, we can institute a continual attack against Batista in the U.S. media where he is vulnerable.

"By the way, Toussaint will know only my name. No one else. There is a security measure in intelligence work known as a cutout. A break in the chain limits compromising the larger network. In fact, I will not fly from Havana to San Juan directly. I want no trail connecting me to Toussaint."

* * * *

Landeira telephoned Toussaint in advance and introduced himself. Toussaint recognized his name from the article Landeira published earlier in the Miami Herald. Landeira said he wanted to meet and discuss a joint project involving reporting on the Batista regime in Cuba.

Gaspar Toussaint was in his late-thirties. Small and slender in stature, he nonetheless presented a compelling presence. Immaculately dressed in pressed slacks with a crisply starch white shirt and carefully knotted tie, he stood apart from the other staff of the El Mundo newspaper. The only black man in the newsroom, Toussaint was also the news editor and the recognized star of the newspaper. An investigative journalist of considerable reputation throughout the Caribbean and Florida. For expatriate Dominicans and Haitians, the only reliable voice of both troubled countries occupying the Island of Hispaniola.

"I was impressed by your piece about your experience in Ciudad Trujillo. You realize you were fortunate to suffer only deportation," Toussaint said after introductions.

"I am well aware of that. Admittedly, I did not realize the extent of Trujillo's grip on the country. Especially underestimated the viciousness of his secret police. Before I get to the reason I came to see you, I must clarify something. Perhaps to illustrate the seriousness of what I wish to embark upon.

"My story recounting my experiences investigating the disappearance of Daniel Cabrera was true up to the ending. The SIM did not deport me. They detained me but I escaped."

Toussaint leaned forward looking intently at Landeira. "That is quite remarkable." The skepticism in his voice pronounced. "Never knew of anyone *escaping* the SIM."

Landeira sensed fear in Toussaint's eyes. Then came the sound of a drawer opening.

"Who sent you?"

"No one. I am what I said I was. The correspondent for the Miami Herald. No reason to feel threatened."

Toussaint held a revolver in his right hand, now resting it on the desk next to his typewriter and pointed at Landeira. "Please indulge my caution. Having survived two attempts on my life here in San Juan by the Dominican SIM makes me hyper-situationally aware. Trujillo has become so out of touch with reality he feels he can reach out to assassinate those opposing him even on foreign soil. Tell me then what really happened in Ciudad Trujillo."

"Three SIM agents took me from my hotel in the middle of the night. Told me I was being deported immediately. A matter of state security. Stuffed me in the back of one of their black VW Beetles. Passing the sign to the route to the airport, I realized that was not the destination.

"Knowing the reputation of Trujillo's secret police. My training kicked in. You see I served in the American OSS during World War Two. The Office of Strategic Services. I received commando training by the British in a secret camp in Ontario, Canada in 1942."

Toussaint said, "What kind of training?"

"British Special Operation Executive training since the American OSS was also meant to operate behind enemy lines. In my case, dropped in by parachute. Our mission was to disrupt the enemy. Sabotage, assassination, and reconnaissance. Field operatives, spies. Our training consisted of how to kill people quickly and efficiently. Armed or unarmed."

"Did you kill many in this way?"

"Yes. That is how those three SIM agents died. The ones in the photograph. Thought my article was poetic justice by portray them as victims in their own den of torture. No one slid that photograph under my hotel door. I took it. The film developed in the photo lab of the Miami Herald."

Landeira reached into his briefcase pausing as Toussaint raised the revolver.

"I didn't expect you would believe me without irrefutable proof. For obvious reasons, I did not intend to admit to killing three Dominican SIM agents in a newspaper. Therefore, I used the photo in the newspaper as a substitute for the hundreds of innocent victims. Perhaps you will understand the breach of journalistic ethics. You are the only one that knows the truth other than the SIM."

Landeira extracted an envelope and dumped the contents on Toussaint's desk.

Still holding the revolver, Toussaint spread out three close-up photographs of the faces of the dead agents. Grisly but the faces clearly recognizable when compared to their laminated identification photos also spread on the desk.

Toussaint was dumbfounded. Did Landeira kill these agents or was this some elaborate plot? Were the photographs doctored? Was he being unduly paranoid?

"If I am skeptical it is because your story strains credulity. The SIM are accomplished killers. To have overpowered three armed men then kill them sounds like something from a movie."

"Not when you look at all the circumstances. Fear consumes most secret police victims. In a climate of terror, the victim anticipates the prospect of torture or death. I am human and also experience fear. The difference is my repetitious wartime training taught me how to control fear and follow the training instinctively. Taught to look for the slightest opportunity to take aggressive action. Things overlooked to the untrained person facing dire circumstances. To the trained eye, the difference between living and dying. Reinforced repeatedly during my wartime experiences.

"The fellow that trained me taught combat skills to the Shanghai Municipal Police. Personally had over 600 physical confrontations in the line of duty against the viscous Tong gangs. He used various martial arts with the single objective to combine a defensive move with a disabling or killing assault. In his late fifties with most of us in our twenties, I never saw anyone best him in hand-to-hand combat even when practicing with real knives. He designed the British commando knife. In Camp X he was not training colonial police but preparing us to kill the enemy. Look him up. A British Royal Marine named William Fairbairn."

Having made his point, Landeira felt no need to expand on the graphic details of executing the disabled Dominican SIM agents with a knife.

Partly convinced, Toussaint said. "Quite the story. For the sake of discussion, let's say I believe you. What is it you want, Señor Landeira?"

Toussaint repositioned the revolver to his lap.

"To do what you do with regard to the Dominican Republic. Outside the grasp of Trujillo, you are the only voice of dissent by publishing accounts of his oppression. A remarkable achievement by whatever logistical means you use to smuggle information and photographs out of the DR. I want to do something similar regarding Cuba. Cannot do that alone since I am still putting together a network of sources and must remain in Havana. I also have the problem of avoiding identification as the source of material negative to Batista since I am the Latin American correspondent for the Miami Herald and based in Havana."

"How do you propose getting around that?" Toussaint said.

"By avoiding byline attribution. I propose to send you any inflammatory material. You will publish under your byline in El Mundo. Once available to the international news services, the Miami Herald republishes your stories citing the sources as API, UPI, or Reuters attributing them to you. As the Herald's Latin correspondent, I can arguably stay removed as being complicit."

"Batista also has a secret police. Are you sure you can deceive them?"

"Naturally a risk. You take those risks as an investigative journalist. For the present, I appear fixed on attacking the American Mafia. Maybe enough to deflect suspicion for directly attacking Batista. You read my articles?"

"Yes. You even mentioned the complicity of your father."

Landeira nodded. "I do not approve of my father's work. We are not on good terms. However, what I did not include in my article was damning evidence I possessed implicating Batista's participation. That would have violated his press censorship and got me deported or imprisoned. You see, Batista takes great amounts of money from the Mafia and from Cuban public funds. Another smoke and mirrors maneuver under the disguise of sham bank loans covered by Mafia money laundering. The meaningful story is Batista's repressive dictatorship. Mafia gambling investment is just a subset. To go after Batista I must be creative to publish."

"Very well. I will agree provisionally. Depends on the nature and the validity of what you send me. I will publish only what I feel appropriate to my own journalistic ethics. How do I explain the origin of the information?"

"I gave that some thought. I have friends that have informal networks of anti-Batista sources. Some of those sources undoubtedly will have ties to the two known insurgency movements. Fidel Castro's 26 July Movement and the Directorio Revolucionario Estudiantil. I personally have no connections directly with the revolutionists. I want these media attacks on Batista to reflect a broader view than those advocating revolution. Give the American reader a sense of disgust toward American corporations and the U.S. government propping up a corrupt murderer.

"My answer is creating another dissident organization. At least in name. I suggest citing unnamed sources associated with a new loosely organized opposition group called *Venganza de Martí*, Revenge of Martí. After the national hero of the last century, José Martí."

"What about these Dominican photographs and SIM identifications?"

"Keep them. I presented them only as a means of demonstrating my credibility. Perhaps we could discuss details about how to work this over lunch?"

****

Back in Havana, Landeira reported immediately to Pérez. "Toussaint is onboard. He is the real thing. Intelligent, determined. We talked at length, yet he never revealed how he secrets a continued flow of information out of the Dominican Republic. He understands what we are about. Now all we need to do is uncover damaging information on the Batista regime. He was impressed by a fellow journalist willing to give up attribution to see his material published."

"So how did you answer that, Bart?"

"Personal gratification doing something I deem important. More than just my investigative efforts. People like you and those that will provide information at great personal risk cannot receive credit for what they do. I am part of that."

Landeira chose not to delve into the psychological aspects of atonement for his years of work in the shadowy world of the CIA's Office of Policy Coordination. Practicing regime change in the cause of combating communist expansion by installing totalitarian dictatorships.

"I had long conversations with the good friend I spoke about. His name is Hector Vasquez. A journalist and former newspaper managing editor. For what it is worth under this blanket censorship, he is the president of the Cuban Newspaper Association. He sees possibilities in your plan of attack on Batista. At my suggestion, he is to meet us at the club this afternoon. With what we are about to initiate, we cannot be too cautious in our frequent meetings. The National Police have hundreds of *chivatos* in Havana willing to offer information for a price. Possibly even within the club. It provides the appearance as a logical place of social gathering for men of common interests."

"Good idea. Do you think between you and Vasquez you can muster enough sources to go after newsworthy information?"

"Hector believes so. Says there are many disgruntled reporters across Cuba willing to subvert the Batista regime. On that note, I have also been busy. Started a list of Batista's murderers to target for newspaper attacks. Hector and his reporters will populate their material with lessor known bad characters."

"Excellent. Looks like the Batista regime might be in for a rough time in the American press. Even though designed to impact public and government opinion in the United States, Batista cannot stop it from filtering back into Cuba regardless of censorship. He cannot regulate damaging information with the constant flow of American tourists and gamblers coming into Havana. Both Toussaint's El Mundo and the Miami Herald also publish Spanish language editions."

* * * *

There were few members at the club in the middle of the afternoon and Landeira found a table in the lounge well off to the side to insure privacy. A short time later, Pérez and Vasquez entered.

Vasquez was short and balding. Probably sixty yet even at a distance you could see his energy. As Pérez made introductions, Vasquez's eyes flashed with enthusiasm.

"Since we will be working closely, we should be on a first name basis. I am Bart."

"I agree. Call me Hector."

Once seated, Vasquez launched straight into discussion without preamble. "Mateo explained you have a scheme for publishing damaging material about the Batista regime. I looked into this Gaspar Toussaint. A colorful character. A forceful critic against Trujillo. His ability to interact with sources inside the Dominican Republic is impressive. How did you persuade him to do the same for us?"

"Once I convinced him I was not a Trujillo assassin or Batista propagandist, it took little persuasion. Assuming we send him legitimate fact-based material not editorializing anti-Batista rhetoric, he will publish what we provide. No journalist will forego access to newsworthy material."

"There are journalists all over Cuba ready to go after Batista," Vasquez said. "How do you propose to get material to San Juan?"

"I fly to Miami and simply mail it from there," Landeira said. "Since I work for the Miami Herald, frequent trips are normal. My concerns about security are at the source level. How can you be sure of the loyalty of your sources?"

Vasquez replied, "By relying only on those reporters and editors I know personally over time. Make no mistake, I understand the risks involved."

"Still, we must always be conscious of security. Even those unquestionably loyal can be forced to give up information under coercion. Batista's henchmen are not above threatening families and resorting to torture. Remain vigilant for even the slightest change in a source's behavior."

"We understand that, Bart," Pérez said. "Our targets will include sadists in the Army and National Police. We must also be prepared for repercussions."

"To be expected. Showing the violence inflicted by the regime will be the source of swaying American opinion. Photographs therefore are of particular importance. To be successful, we must make our readers viscerally experience a sense of what oppression looks like."

Vasquez nodded. "That could mean widespread indiscriminate retaliation. Just like what goes on in the east as the rural guard goes after Castro's guerrillas. Incapable of engaging with the guerrillas, they massacre civilians attempting to deter support through terrorism."

Landeira said, "In the process, they not only harden support for the revolutionaries but cannot help but intimidate a few that will offer them information. Either out of fear or for money. I spent the war working behind enemy lines with Italian partisans. Trusting the surrounding population was a constant security concern."

"How did you ensure your security?" Vasquez asked.

"By the implied threat of death to any informers. We do not have that ability. Our situation has more similarities to a spy ring. The interaction by you and Mateo with your sources is equivalent to running spies. I also worked for the U.S. Department of State so I know something of espionage networks.

"There are basic tradecraft methods to observe. Passing information is particularly sensitive. Make your meetings with sources part of the fabric of normal life. Like our meeting here. Never stand out. Never reveal the name of one source to another source.

"The best security for a source's control is to know the source intimately. Any behavior out of the ordinary is a warning signal. Imperfect and subjective, but your only way to sense if the source might be compromised. The next security measure may be more difficult in our situation. That is called cutouts, meaning if a source is compromised, the damage is limited."

Pérez said, "But we are not running networks in the sense you describe, Bart. Hector and I are using those we know and trust personally."

"Yes, I realize that. That is where my analogy does not fit our circumstances perfectly. However, Hector's reporter sources in particular will be using other people as their sources of information. That is the most likely place for something going wrong. These are experienced journalists, by nature tenacious in going after a story. Not always perhaps careful.

"The lines of our network will grow outward to include unknown numbers of sources as inquiries increase. Risk of exposure increases exponentially as our network expands. From the first publication, Batista's security forces will lash out indiscriminately searching for this new source of opposition. After all, if we are successful, our targets will continually read about themselves in American newspapers coming into Cuba in spite of Batista's censorship."

Pérez and Vasquez looked at each other with Vasquez saying, "Mateo and I understand what you are saying, Bart. I have been in the newspaper business all my life. We know full well the risks of going after important government figures in Cuba. We appreciate your valued counsel. However, to sit by and do nothing when presented with a way to resist oppression would be cowardice."

"I agree with Hector, Bart," Pérez said. "Now, let us move on to operational matters. I suggest we develop a list of target individuals or circumstances to optimize our efforts. With that in mind, I took the liberty to begin a list that will undoubtedly expand."

Pérez handed a copy each to Landeira and Vasquez.

"I broadly categorized according to government, Army, and National Police. Named individuals responsible for the worst of state-initiated violence. Others are associated in some manner of corruption. Feel free to offer suggestions."

Vasquez read the list, nodding in agreement since he was familiar with the names.

A newcomer to Cuba, Landeira was not as knowledgeable. "The names of these notorious Army commanders are recognizable but not the others. What makes them persons of interest, Mateo?"

"Corruption. Senior officials close to Batista. To rob the Cuban treasury indiscriminately, Batista needs critically placed accomplices. The others listed are officials necessary to keeping Batista in power. Supporting characters like those associated with the American Mafia."

Landeira said, "Let me suggest a two-pronged attack initially. The violence in the east by the Army and that psychopath Rolando Masferrer will invoke the most powerful impact on American readers. They read of glamourous Havana with American celebrity entertainers at high-end nightclubs. Yet the blood soaked brutality of the dictatorship in eastern Cuba seems more like political violence associated with places in South America, Asia, or Africa. That should be first on our agenda. Do you have reporters in the eastern provinces that you can trust, Hector?"

Vasquez nodded vigorously. "Several. Even for those with newspapers still publishing, they are prohibited from reporting anything concerning state-sponsored violence or rebel activity."

"What about photographers? Coverage of violence must have a visual component?"

"Yes. A couple of reporters I have in mind know how to use a camera."

"Excellent. No need to develop the film. Too dangerous. I can do that in Florida."

"Your second line of attack?" Pérez asked.

"Pursue the banks. More up your alley, Mateo. Perhaps Hector has reporters in Havana that might contribute. After all, it was a reporter that provided the breakthrough on the Habana Hilton scheme involving BANFAIC. Since we already exposed that can of snakes, what about going after the other banks cited in my article? Maybe even with complicity of the Cuban central bank? Furthermore, since I could not publish Batista's participation in skimming a large take from that project, he undoubtedly did the same with other projects. A good way to start drawing blood by inflicting wounds directly on El Presidente. Maybe make the Eisenhower administration squirm if syndicated columnists pick up the attack. "

"Yes of course," Pérez said. "As a member of the university faculty I have colleagues known to be sympathetic with the Directorio Revolucionario Estudiantil which might prove useful."

"Be cautious there, Mateo. Dissident organizations of idealistic students are notorious for infiltration by totalitarian regimes. Reveal nothing about your personal activities. The origin of anything useful must also be obscured to avoid leading back to any of us."

Chapter 14

It was over a week since that first date with Emilia Montero. She seemed genuinely interested. Enough to accept spending more time over dinner after the afternoon of sailing. Parting that evening, she gave him a kiss on the cheek. He might have hoped for more, but he realized he must go slowly. Surprised he even got this far given how he viewed her initial remoteness.

"Thank you, Bart. I enjoyed our day together. Let's do it again."

"No question about that, Emilia. A magnificent day. Went by too quickly. How about dinner next Saturday? I have a new article I just sent off to Miami. Would like to get your comments?"

"Yes. I would like that, Bart."

"What is your favorite restaurant?"

She bit her lip with an expression of serious thought. "Don't know that I have a favorite. I rarely go out to dinner."

"Personally, I avoid restaurants in the grand hotels. Too many tourists. What about *Casa Maribel* in Old Havana. Decidedly Cuban. Old world décor. Excellent food. A favorite of my Uncle Tomás. Your father knows it. They also serve Montero rum, so the drinks are superb."

With a broad smile, she said. "Sounds like my kind of place too."

Unexpectedly, she gave him another kiss on the cheek then touched his cheek before saying good night and quickly entering her apartment.

That departing gesture bearing the promise of much more amplified his anticipation of seeing her again.

The following Saturday he took special attention to look his best. Always a good dresser tonight felt special. Selecting a pale blue shirt with open collar, tropical weight grey slacks, cream-colored sport coat, with Italian loafers, he achieved the desired image. Looking trim and fit at age forty, and maybe even handsome. As long as he stood before the mirror in profile hiding the scar on his other cheek.

Ignoring the scar, except when taking care while shaving, he wondered how Emilia saw him. A foolish self-conscious concern. It obviously did not put her off. To the contrary, she went out of her way to reinforce her interest. Realizing he was acting like a love-struck teenager brought a self-conscious smile.

From the onset, the evening started off well. Emilia obviously took great pains to emphasize her beauty. Opening her apartment door, she figuratively took his breath away.

A knee-length cream-colored dress set off her dark skin tone the color of a perpetual suntan. But it was the plunging neckline augmented by a gold chain hanging down to her cleavage that drew attention.

"Oh my! Hard to find words to describe how wonderful you look, Emilia."

Giving him a kiss on the lips a welcomed shocker as she pulled him inside, "Please come in. I will be just a moment."

Stepping into the apartment, he closed the door and surveyed the pleasantly decorated apartment. A balcony with French doors looked out across the quiet street to other attractive buildings. Turning back to Emilia standing before a mirror on the wall checking her makeup, he could not help but smile at the vision of her shapely behind and bare legs with open-toed heels.

Arriving at the *Casa Maribel*, they took table in a quiet corner. After ordering drinks and making small talk, she asked, "You said you wanted to show me your latest article."

"Absolutely. I brought along a copy. Sent it off to Miami a couple of days ago. Wanted your opinion if I struck the right note. Consider the perspective of an American tourist knowing nothing about Cuba. Bear in mind my past attacks on American organized crime investment in Havana. Therefore, I intended a satirical description of a hedonistic weekend spent in Havana built around the allure of gambling spiced with experiencing entertainment prohibited in the United States. Not exactly a travel advertisement for coming to Havana."

Weekend in Havana
Miami Herald correspondent Bart Landeira

Americans typically come to Havana for the draw of gambling and glamourous entertainment. Unlike its mainland counterpart and rival as a city of sun and sin, Havana is a gloriously interesting city with a history predating the original American colonies. Meaning no disrespect to Las Vegas, all it has to offer is the lure of casino gambling. People making the trek from Southern California with its endless beaches arrive at a drab town with little vegetation and the uncompromising high desert climate. Brutally hot dry summers interrupted by short cold winters. Las Vegas only shines after dark with the neon lights of the casinos dominating the Strip and downtown. In the harsh sunlight of morning, she looks like a middle-aged woman without makeup with her hair in curlers.

My apologies to Las Vegas for my admitted bias as a Cuban-American. Yet no one coming to Havana can deny its tropical old world charm. Although the casinos fuel the tourism these last several years, they do not overwhelm Havana. Predominately located close along the Gulf of Mexico waterfront, the casinos do not cluster together and dominate the area as in Las Vegas.

Central Havana and Old Havana still retain their architectural charms from earlier times. Founded in the early 16th century by Spanish conquistadors, San Cristóbal de la Habana grew to the third largest city in the Americas. By the mid-18th century, larger than Boston or New York. Plagued by attacks by pirates, French corsairs, and later the British navy, iconic fortresses guard its north shore.

However, this is not a travel column or a chamber of commerce advertisement to induce visitors to Havana. As the title of this article suggests, it is about experiencing the new Havana over a long weekend. As such, it describes the attractions of fine hotels, expansive casinos, nightclubs with spectacular floorshows, often with name entertainers, and fine dining. A place geared to every economic class of tourist. A place unabashedly geared to a relaxed moral environment with respect to sex and drugs. A party town catering to every taste. It also offers itself to those looking for an exotic tropical getaway of sea, beaches, and charm. If that is your pleasure, stay longer than a weekend, avoid the neon lights, and mingle with the locals.

This reporter has previously written pieces unflattering to the Havana hotel-casino boom fueled by American organized crime investment. Be reassured, the gambler will get a fair shake at the gaming tables insofar as any casino game of choice always favors the house. The Mafia management makes enough profit without rigging the gaming tables. The prostitution and the drug availability are however homegrown Cuban enterprises. Female and male prostitution is legal in Cuba. This social acceptance breeds a wider exploitation of female sexuality in conventional entertainment such as the scantily clad women in the extravagant musical floorshows of the nightclubs.

Let's start our weekend by flying into José Martí International Airport 12 miles southwest of the center of Havana. Daily flights are available from Miami, Tampa, New Orleans, and Houston.

The taxi ride takes you through the rural outskirts of the city then through some of the poorest Havana neighborhoods before depositing you at your hotel. Likely one of the grand hotels located close to the water in the upscale district of Vedado or perhaps in the Central or Old Havana quarters of the city. Here are situated Havana's finest hotels. The Nacionale, Plaza, Sevilla Biltmore, Commodoro, Siboney, Presidente, Vedado, and St. John's. The newest luxury hotels Riviera, Habana Hilton, Deauville, and Capri are projected to open within the next 18 months. Checking into these five-star hotels prepare to tip generously. As the haunts of celebrities and high rollers, generous tips are necessary just to get noticed. A single dollar bill achieves nothing. Budget accordingly. Do not worry about using local currency. U.S. dollars are the preferred currency at every venue. Since these hotels all have casinos, you are likely to drop a good deal of money that subsidizes the reasonable cost of your accommodations making it good value compared with a comparable hotel in the United States.

We shall start our weekend booked at the iconic Hotel Nacionale. A room with a view over the waters of the Gulf of Mexico. However, we are here for the gambling not the beach. After dressing appropriately with coat and tie with wife or girlfriend in a suitable dress with heels, we go downstairs to enter the luxurious Casino Internacional in the hotel's new wing. In the evening, we might venture out to the Starlight Terrace Bar and perhaps take in a show at the Casino Parisién nightclub with its famous Dancing Waters fountain display. All these recent lavish accoutrements the result of investment by the "Mob's Accountant" Meyer Lansky.

After an afternoon at the gaming tables, our plans call for taking in a show at the famous Tropicana. Several miles from the center of Havana, the Tropicana is located on a former six-acre estate surrounded by lush tropical gardens. Nat King Cole is tonight's headline performer. As a matter of public record, the current owner of the Tropicana is Martin Fox. As this reporter however discovered, the largest investor is actually Santo Trafficante Jr., boss of the Tampa, Florida Mafia family. Likely, other Mafia investment is also involved given Trafficante's close ties with Sam Giancana in Chicago and the Bonanno crime family of New York but their names do not appear on licenses or public records.

No visit to Sin City is complete without sampling the extraordinary display of flesh at least voyeuristically. While all the showgirls at the best floorshows are selected for their voluptuousness and long legs, other venues go further. Displays of total nudity are commonplace with certain theater venues offering performances of live sex acts. If still standing with the exorbitant quantity of liquor consumed since arriving in Havana, you make a last stop at the notorious Shanghai Theater.

Located in the Barrio Chino, the Chinatown quarter, the former theater is capable of seating 500 hundred patrons with room for more in a balcony. Tonight, the popular dance team of Alfred López and Conchita Romero are doing their "apache dance" to a mambo rhythm. Alfred progressively strips off pieces of Conchita's clothing as they dance. Already a dance form suited to showing off the female form, they continue once she is completely naked.

If not by now too exhausted or drunk, you can stay for the main act. A parody of a play with a well-endowed male performing various sex acts with three gorgeous women.

The following morning, after a good breakfast with strong coffee to erase the hangover, you might take a stroll along the Malecón overlooking the endless stretch of beach before returning to the gambling tables. This time perhaps at the Sevilla Biltmore located not far in Old Havana on the Prado. While a venerable high-end hotel, a decidedly different environment. The Longchamps Restaurant inside the hotel sells cocaine and marijuana. Spend some time at the gaming tables of the hotel's Roof Garden Casino, a favorite haunt of both American and Cuban gangsters.

For those seeking to indulge in sexual activity, Havana offers every imaginable outlet. Female or male, heterosexual or homosexual. For every level of expenditure. By in large, free from any legal repercussions. Prostitution is a lucrative Cuban enterprise. At the upper end is a chain of brothels servicing the city's luxury hotels operated by a Spanish madam known as Doña Marina. Some claim the Casa Marina in Old Havana is the most luxurious brothel in The Western Hemisphere. El Templo de Marina is next door to the Sevilla Biltmore, and another on San Jose Street. On the opposite economic end of the sex trade are the brothels in the barrio of Colón. Here sex is cheap and quickly consummated on the street. For those truly addicted, a brothel called the Mambo located close to the airport accommodates the immediate needs of those arriving or departing.

Although the American Mafia largely funded the Havana hospitality boom, Havana is not dangerous city. You are safer here than in New York or Chicago. However, do not get out of line. A night in jail in Havana is as bad an experience as in Tijuana, Mexico. This is a police state. The tourist trade is economically too important to tolerate street crime or civil disturbance.

Nor is the Mafia totally responsible for the well-deserved label as Sin City. Havana has long embraced gambling of all types. Prostitution condoned as a natural element in society, with even an enlightened view toward how prostitutes are treated.

The weekend portrayed above is nothing more than a hedonistic excursion. It neither will afford a true appreciation for Havana, much less of Cuba in a broader sense. To experience a tropical environment separated from Florida by only a hundred miles of warm water, construct your own holiday. The warmth of the Cuban people and their celebration of life will be your reward.

Whatever your pleasure, enjoy your trip to this exotic extension to the United States. The Nobel Laureate novelist Ernest Hemingway fell in love with Cuba before World War Two and now makes his summer residence in a villa south of Havana. Hemingway's attachment to Cuba is the sea and the innate love of life embraced by the Cuban people, not the casinos or nightlife.

She looked up with a wry smile. "I see what you mean by satirical. A good travel advertisement for the hedonistic inclined American tourist. Reference to the Mafia only adds to the vicarious allure of forbidden pleasures. Speaking of the Mafia, any repercussions from government censorship over your previous articles?"

"Not yet. Looks like I guessed right. Since allegations of Mafia investment in Havana have been commonplace in the U.S. newspapers for some time, makes no sense for Batista to raise a stink now. Will only draw more attention to something that seems to have little impact on Batista's relations with the American government.

"Even with the public revelations of the Kefauver congressional hearings several years ago, the American public remains apathetic about organized crime. That it spreads to Havana becomes too remote to take notice. Americans are like that. My exposé revealing the mechanism of Mafia money laundering in Havana did not foster journalistic attacks on organized crime by other journalists or editorial columnists."

"So what can you write about that you feel is more newsworthy? You said the Ministry of Propaganda prohibits anything related to revolutionary activities."

"Now you see the problem for all journalists in Cuba. I know Cuban journalists chafing under Batista's censorship. Even having a government ministry titled *propaganda* is an obscenity. Best we can do is to introduce indirect references in our reporting. Most censors are too stupid to grasp subtleties, especially writing in English."

He withheld the urge to reveal his subversive conspiracy with Pérez and Vasquez but wanted to tell her he was still doing something. "Do you recall me describing how the Mafia disguised laundered money to finance the Habana Hilton project?"

"Yes. Remarkable how you uncovered that story. Certainly more than white-collar crime when it resulted in the deaths of three people for talking too much. You as much as accused the Mafia of those murders."

"I meant to. No question it was their doing. Or their Cuban associates. Probably not Batista's secret police."

"What do you mean?"

"Because I did not include certain details incriminating Batista. Details of how Batista skimmed large amounts of money from the influx of Mafia cash. Likely repeated in every other major project involving Mafia funding. I could not accuse Batista of personally benefiting from corruption without risking deportation, or maybe worse. Batista does not tolerate dissent.

"To report on Cuba, I need to remain in Havana close to a network of sources. Means searching for indirect ways to get important information published. Not sure how to go about that, but the real news is Cuban political turmoil amidst an oppressive dictatorship. Regrettably, propped up by American business interests and a shameful foreign policy. One based exclusively on U.S. interests and to hell with anyone else. Mafia investment in Havana is old news. Publishing details in the American press of how it works makes for interesting reading but does not appear to influence American foreign policy."

She nodded, her expression suggesting she understood that he chose not to be more specific. Even talking about opposition to the regime was dangerous. Not the kind of conversation suitable for this evening. Instead, she launched into commenting about how well her father was getting along in his new role. Enthusiastically engaged and by all indications, Landeira Rum continued functioning smoothly even with the acquisition of Montero Rum.

Bart offered, "Must be something about the rum business that shapes the character of men like your father and my Uncle Tomás."

Both steered clear of uncomfortable memories from their past and the remainder of the evening became full of laughter. Both obviously enjoying each other's company.

** ** ** **

They left the restaurant in a buoyant mood. Landeira cautioning himself to lower his expectations of what the rest of the night might hold when returning Emilia home.

A comfortably warm night even for early March. Being Saturday night, many people walked the street populated with eateries and bars. They began walking to Landeira's car parked not far down the street.

A sedan passed them then pulled to a screeching stop a short distance ahead of them in the middle of the street. Two men got out and the car drove away. The men slipped between the parked cars onto the sidewalk approaching from the opposite direction. Always aware of his surroundings, the sequence of those actions made Landeira uneasy.

As the two young men approached closer instead of looking at Emilia, both of them ignored her and stared intently at Landeira before averting their gaze. Their manner triggered alarm as they walked past on Landeira's left side.

Immediately after they walked past, Landeira felt a gun pressed into his back,

"Just keep walking," the man said.

From the corner of his eye, Landeira saw the other man grab Emilia's arm roughly.

Old training and experienced in dangerous situations, Landeira hesitated only momentarily after feeling the gun. A classic mistake of an assailant by getting too close to his victim.

Spinning to his left, Landeira enveloped the assailant's gun forearm with his left arm then thrust his knee hard into the man's groin while simultaneously delivering a blow under the chin with the heel of his hand. As the man slumped, the gun fell from his hand to the sidewalk.

The other man released Emilia and pulled a switchblade after seeing Landeira attack his colleague. Although facing the opened knife blade, Landeira immediately pressed his attack by taking a step directly toward the man.

Landeira's aggressive move startled the man who took a step backwards. Off balance, he swung the knife wildly catching Landeira's open sport coat snagging the blade in the fabric.

Disabling the man's arm with the same move as he applied to the gunman, Landeira drove his fist into the man's throat. Destruction of the larynx cartilages produced an audible sound.

Total time elapsed since feeling the gun was five seconds.

Emilia stepped back at the onset of the confrontation but never screamed.

Landeira picked up the revolver and knife and stood over the writhing gunman holding his groin and bleeding from the mouth.

The other man appeared in worse shape. Struggling for breath while choking, he repeatedly coughed blood from the mouth. Landeira gauged the man would likely die without immediate medical attention. He understood the extent of the damage he caused.

Although stoic without crying, Emilia began shaking. Landeira put his arm around her drawing her close. "You are going to be okay."

"I am so cold all of a sudden."

"A reaction to the adrenaline rush."

Taking off his sport coat, he wrapped it over her shoulders and continued to hold her tightly.

A small crowd gathered but most dispersed except for an elderly couple as a police officer arrived blowing a whistle and brandishing his service revolver. "What happen here?"

"Two armed men assaulted us," Landeira said. "Here are their weapons." He handed over the revolver and switchblade to the surprised officer.

The surprised officer rhetorically said, "You disarmed them and did this to them?"

"No choice. Self- defense. Could not allow harm to come to the lady."

Returning his revolver to his holster, the officer reasserted his authority. "Your papers."

Soon, two more officers arrive on scene at a run.

After conferring with each other, one officer entered the *Casa Maribel* to call in the incident.

Fifteen minutes later, a police armored van arrived. Out stepped a tall man with a thin mustache dressed in a white suit with black tie.

The police officers came to attention and saluted. The few gathered spectators quickly dispersed.

After conferring with the first uniformed police officer to arrive on the scene, the man in the white suit walked over to the wounded assailants lying on the sidewalk. The gunman remained conscious but his groaning suggested he was in a great deal of pain. The knife-wielding man was now silent with a growing pool of blood forming around his head on the sidewalk. The survey of the downed men pointedly unhurried by the man in the white suit.

Turning toward the uniformed officers, the official in the white suit said, "Handcuff these two criminals and call for an ambulance." Pointing to the conscious attacker. "Accompany the ambulance and report to me from the hospital if this one is able to talk."

All three officers replied, "*Si, Coronel.*"

Now standing in front of Landeira and Emilia, he said, "I am Police Colonel Esteban Ventura." Holding Landeira's U.S. passport and Cuban foreign identification card, and Emilia's Cuban identification, he said, "Tell me what happened."

Landeira knew Ventura's name. High on Mateo Pérez's target list of the worst of the regime's perpetrators of violence. Infamous for inflicting terror on the streets of Havana. Known as the *man in the white suit*, or *the killer of the fifth precinct*, snatched people off the street at night. Young men suspected of revolutionary activities simply disappeared. Those lucky enough to survive reported various degrees of maltreatment extending to severe forms of physical torture.

Landeira replied, "Soon after exiting the *Casa Maribel* after having dinner, two men came up behind us as we walked to my car. One put a gun in my back and said to keep walking."

"What else did he say?"

"I did not give him a chance to say more. He made a foolish mistake and I seized the opportunity to disarm him."

"What mistake did he make?"

"Got too close. Touched my back with the barrel of his revolver. I then knew his position."

Ventura looked at him intensely. Perhaps with a hint of malice. "Most remarkable. You then disarmed the other assailant threatening you with a knife. How were you able to disarm two armed men so easily?"

"Special training during the war. These assailants are nothing more than stupid thugs. They picked on a victim that knew something about self-defense."

"So it seems. You severely injured both attackers. Appears more than self-defense. What kind of training teaches you how to do this?"

"Commando training. How to kill the enemy quickly with your hands."

"Did you see combat in the war?"

"Yes."

"Is that where you received that scar on your cheek?"

"Yes. From a Nazi SS soldier with a knife."

"What happened?"

"I killed the Nazi."

Ventura turned to Emilia. "Were you harmed Señora Montero?"

"No."

"Señor Landeira is a well-known journalist for an American newspaper. How is it you know him?"

"My father and Señor Landeira's family are both in the rum business. That is where I met him."

Ventura nodded as he looked at her identification. Turning back to Landeira, "Why do you think these men attacked you, Señor Landeira?"

"I have no idea."

"Perhaps because of recent articles you published in the Miami Herald?"

"I have no way of knowing."

"Of course. You gave them no time before reacting violently." Pocketing their papers, Ventura announced, "Unfortunately, I must request both of you accompany me to the police station to make an official report. My apologies, Señora, I realize this has been a disturbing incident but I must follow procedure."

What followed was a gross indignity. The armored van was fitted in the rear with a holding cage with opposing benches. Filthy, it smelled of stale sweat and urine. Emilia gaged. Ventura could have made alternative arrangements to transport them, even allowing Landeira to drive his own car. Instead, Ventura wished to display his authority.

Fortunately, it was a brief ride to the notorious Fifth Precinct station on Belascoaín Street in Chinatown. Notorious as the place rumored where Ventura supervised torture. A place where people might disappear without record.

Soon they were seated in a brightly lit interrogation room smelling not much different from the police van. Colonel Ventura told Landeira to repeat what happened. A police officer sitting at a desk in the corner banged away at an old typewriter filling out the police report. Landeira held Emilia's hand throughout the ordeal hoping to ease her distress through this further indignity.

Periodically, Ventura interjected questions. "Now to the question I asked previously. Why do you believe these men confronted you, Señor Landeira?"

"I do not know."

"Your recent newspaper article making allegations surrounding the Habana Hilton project undoubtedly made you many enemies. No one cares about your American Mafia in Cuba. You alleged unnamed persons committed murder to cover up illegal activity. Implicated your own father. However, you went further by implying who might be guilty. A dangerous business, Señor Landeira. Have you received any threats?"

"No."

"Do you have any suspicions?"

"No"

Turning to Emilia, "Señora Montero, do you know of any reason why someone might wish to harm you or Señor Landeira? A jealous lover maybe?"

Emilia glared at Ventura and squeezed Landeira's hand.

"No. No one."

"You are an attorney. Perhaps a disgruntled client? She said, "No. I know of no one wishing to harm me."

After an hour with the uniformed officer struggling with the old typewriter, Ventura handed the typed report to Landeira to read and sign. Their statement of circumstances exceedingly brief considering Ventura's many questions. Full of typos it nonetheless substantially stated the facts. Landeira signed and pushed it across to Emilia and nodded for her to do the same.

Ventura said, "As you see, I categorize the incident as a failed robbery attempt. The perpetrators got what they deserved. One will survive. I understand the other probably will not. You are both free to go."

Landeira realized Ventura went through this whole process because he enjoyed the power of intimidation. He and Emilia did not fit the profile of his usual victims. Deprived of doing something far worse than just inflicting indignity, he still needed to exert authority. The arrogance of a notorious official of Batista's secret police acting in character.

Returned by a police car to the *Casa Maribel* to pick up his parked car, it was now approaching midnight. Pulling up to her building, Emilia broke down crying as the stress dissipated.

"My god, I was so terrified. Do you know that man's reputation?" She said through the tears.

"Yes. I know the name. I am so sorry, Emilia. My fault this happened tonight. My guess, whatever they intended to do was to warn me off investigating corruption. Could have been the Mafia using hired Cuban gangsters. Lots of money involved. Might even have been someone acting on behalf of Batista. Let me get you settled in your apartment. You're safe now."

Parking his car in front of her building, he helped her up the stairs with his arm around her waist while she leaned her head against his shoulder.

Fumbling in her handbag for the key, she dropped it on the floor in front of her apartment door. Still distraught, he could only lament the harm this might mean to their developing relationship.

Once inside she shed his jacket still draped around her shoulders. Looking at the torn fabric caused by the assailant's knife, she shook her head, tears running down her cheeks as if the evidence of the attack made the danger more tangible.

Surprisingly, she enveloped him in her arms. "Please don't leave, Bart. I don't want to be alone. I just need to make sense of what happened tonight."

"I understand, Emilia. I can't begin to tell you how much I regret subjecting you to something like that. No telling what might have happen to you."

"No, Bart. That is not what I mean. You must not blame yourself. You are a journalist. What you exposed about Mafia money behind the Havana gambling boom was courageous. What I meant was about us. I realize how little we know about each other, yet we both feel an attraction. Tonight I was having the best time I can ever remember."

She released her embrace and wiped the tears from her eyes. "I am too keyed up to sleep. How about I make us coffee?"

"I suggest a drink instead. We both need to get some sleep. Things will look better in the morning. I will bunk on the sofa. Not going to leave you after what you went through."

"What we both went through, Bart. It happened so fast. Still can't believe how you accomplished disarming those men. Tell me what went through your mind."

"Very well. Sit down. I will get us something to drink. You of course have Montero rum?"

She gave a short laugh. "In the cupboard to your right." Kicking off her shoes, she settled into the sofa and laid her head back.

Landeira brought over two generous glasses of rum and sat down next to her.

Taking a healthy gulp of rum, she let out a long sigh.

Landeira did the same.

Emilia looked at him with a warm smile that turned into a yawn. He noticed her eyelids fluttering trying to fend off sleep.

He stood up taking her hand, "Extreme fatigue is the final effect of coming down from an intense adrenaline rush. Come now and let me put you to bed."

She did not argue. Sitting down on the bed, she looked up at him. Her expression only intensified his urge to undress her and make love. Both felt it but he knew this was not the right moment. Fatigue was about to overcome him as well. Their first lovemaking must be under better circumstances.

"Change out of those clothes and get comfortable. Sleep is the best antidote. I will be just outside your door. We can talk in the morning."

He bent down and kissed her on the lips. "Sleep well." Then he left the bedroom closing the door softly before changing his mind.

Chapter 15

Landeira woke early with the sun streaming into the living room. He needed to use the toilet but decided to postpone as long as possible to avoid making noise and waking Emilia. The aroma of brewing coffee seemed like a better way to wake her than a toilet flushing.

Once the smell of coffee permeated the kitchen, he detected Emilia moving about behind the closed bedroom door. Time to relieve himself and run a comb through his hair.

Emerging from the bathroom in his stocking feet, Emilia stood in the kitchen reaching for coffee cups. Barefoot in a white terry robe with her long dark hair cascading about her shoulders, made his heart leap.

Turning toward him, she said, "My god, I must look a sight. Didn't even remove my makeup last night. Must have fallen asleep immediately after you tucked me in."

He smiled and said, "Regardless, you look beautiful."

She approached him giving him a quick kiss on the lips. "You are not a good liar but I like it anyway. Fix us coffee while I take care of business and make myself presentable. I like milk and sugar."

Sitting at the kitchen table, he felt good in spite of the traumatic events of yesterday. Last night both expressed their feelings. A developing romantic interest now the beginning of a real relationship. A wise call to postpone consummating that relationship. Circumstances already looked better this morning. If they could avoid dwelling on last night's catastrophe, they could make this a memorable day.

Emilia emerged from the bathroom. Even without makeup she looked attractive. The vision of her naked under the robe served to arouse him.

Walking over to the kitchen table without sitting down, she took a sip of coffee. Setting the cup down, she still made no move to sit. Instead, she stepped closer toward him. Bending down, she made no attempt at snugging her robe tightly about her.

She held his head with both hands as he looked straight ahead at her bare breasts revealed by her robe gapping open. Bending down, she kissed him long leaving no doubt about her intentions.

"We both wanted to make love last night. Glad we waited. "Care to join me in the shower?" As she backed away, he stood up and moved his hands inside the robe to her shoulders where he then slipped off her robe. Looking at her, he let out an audible sigh of pleasure.

In the shower, they both reveled in increasing arousal by the foreplay of washing each other. Emilia soaped his erection with slow strokes while Bart gently massaged her clitoris. Both deprived too long from experiencing sexual intimacy with a partner where they felt genuine affection. The foreplay in the shower achieved a state of heighten state of arousal by the time they moved to the bed.

That first taste of intimacy proved so intense, neither could prolong it as long as they wished, both climaxing in sustained simultaneous convulsions.

After remaining inside her for some time, he eventually extracted himself and rolled over. "That was exquisite, Emilia. Didn't want the sensation of being on the edge to end."

She rolled over with her breasts resting on his chest. "Me too. It could not have been better. We have the whole day and night together to enjoy each other again."

Kissing him she jumped out of bed. "Now I need my morning coffee."

Rising up on one elbow, he looked at her standing naked before putting on her robe.

Finding his underwear, pants, and shirt on the kitchen chair, he grinned at the domestic sight they represented.

Seated with their coffees, Emilia said, "I heard what you said to Ventura about your wartime training. I saw what happened. You destroyed those.... It was over in the blink of an eye."

"That is what happens in real life, not like the fight scenes in movies. In war, you kill the enemy or die. I was in the American OSS. Going behind enemy lines, they taught us how to kill efficiently. In every kind of circumstance."

"That was a long time ago."

"The training was so repetitious it became an unconscious response. Sorry you witnessed something that awful. The training has its base in judo. But in judo, you take down your opponent. In my type of fighting, you follow that initial defensive move with an offensive attack. My wartime job was to kill the enemy not to take prisoners.

She just nodded. "You told Ventura a Nazi inflicted that scar with a knife."

She left the implicit question of explaining further details up to him, not wishing to probe if he found the memory too painful.

Instinctively, he touched the scar with his fingertips. It was not the memory of the wound that was difficult to confront. He never told anyone the surrounding details of that terrible event. About to tell Emilia Montero after knowing her for only a brief time told him how much she mattered to him.

Removing his hand from his face, he held out the palm of his left hand then turned it over, tracing the larger scar on the back of the hand with the index finger of his right hand. "This happened at the same time. That is not the most disturbing part of the incident. Just a constant reminder."

She laid a hand on his left hand, fingering the spider web ridges of the scar. Regretting her curiosity, "I am sorry, Bart. That was insensitive to ask."

211

Covering her hand with his right hand, "No, Emilia. I want to tell you. About time I unburdened myself. Never told anyone before, not even my family.

"It was in the spring of 1944. I was working with a fellow OSS radio operator imbedded with an Italian partisan group. From behind the German Gothic defensive line bisecting the Italian peninsula in the hills 30 miles north of Florence. Our mission was reconnaissance of German preparations at positions around two strategic passes. By this time, Allied forces had pushed the Germans north after liberating Rome then threatening Florence by the spring of 1944.

"Working behind the front lines, a battalion of Waffen SS troops conducting search and destroy missions against Italian partisan groups surprised us the small village of Barberino di Mugello. Two German tanks sealed off the only road into the village.

"Because of the surrounding hills, I previously helped my radio operator string a makeshift antenna in the loft of a barn for better transmitting. Later, I guessed it might have been our radio transmission that led to discovery by the Germans using signal triangulation to locate our location.

"At any rate, one of the tanks fired a round into the barn. A good portion of the partisan group was trapped in a barn. A second round from the tank finished off all but four of us. The concussive shock of the blast rendered all of us unconscious.

"Captured and with our hands bound, the SS revived us with cold water. For a partisan or spy, capture meant certain death. Likely an unpleasant death following torture.

"The German SS forced us to kneel on the ground. One partisan was badly injured. Arm broken with the bone protruding from the skin and a lot of blood loss. There were four SS and a junior officer."

Landeira stopped with a distant look in his eyes.

"Bart, are you okay?" Emilia asked

He just nodded then resumed his narrative. "A large SS sergeant with a trench knife began working on the wounded partisan."

"What was he doing to him?"

Landeira shook his head. "No need to go into details. I can still hear the poor devil's screams. Hearing him say *Americano*, I realized he identified me trying to stop the torture."

"The German sergeant came over and stood in front of me. Saying something in German, two large soldiers picked me up by the arms. In fragmented Italian, the German wanted to know if I was American. When I did not answer, he said something to the soldiers who secured my arms by intertwining their arms in mine to hold me tightly." Landeira touched his face, "That's how I got this."

Emilia said nothing to avoid intruding on his describing of the disturbing memory.

"The sergeant extracted his SS dagger and threatened to cut my face. Said, if I did not answer his questions he would then do the same to the woman's face."

"Woman?"

"One of the partisans named Chiara Ricci. Of course, I did not answer his questions. He then proceeded slowly to give me this. Knowing I was about to die, I had nothing to lose. My training took over. The Germans made the mistake of tying our hands in front rather than behind. Not much advantage but enough.

"Difficult to even recall the specific details. Everything occurred in a matter of a couple of seconds. I disabled one soldier by stomping my heel into the instep of his boot giving me some mobility. Much like last night, I moved close into the sergeant, hammering his nose repeatedly with my elbow while twisting his wrist with my bound hands freeing his knife into my hand.

"With a soldier still holding one arm, I bent down and drove the knife into his groin from between my legs. Several knife thrusts to the neck quickly killed both the sergeant and the other soldier.

"My attention focused on the SS officer fumbling to remove his Lugar from its holster. My unexpected attack coming as a surprise, I charged straight for him. Stumbling backwards, he got off one shot. With my hands still bound the shot went high

213

but caught me in the palm of the left hand as I attempted to stab him with the knife."

She instinctively took his hand turning to see the wound. "Are there lasting effects or just the scars?"

"Cannot fully close my two outside fingers. The bullet smashed the bones. The uglier scar on the back of the hand is the exist wound. Not able to have proper surgery to repair things until the war ended a year later."

"But how did you get away. What happened to the officer after shooting you?"

"He died quickly after I sank the dagger into his throat. That should have been the fate of all of us except Chiara and the other partisan did their part. Attacking the two other confused soldiers, they managed to get hold of a submachinegun. Took out several other SS while covering our retreat. Still not sure how we accomplished that. Perhaps the SS thought it was other partisans rescuing us since they had taken us away from the larger encampment of SS to undergo interrogation and execution.

"The memory is fuzzy at this point. Looking at my destroyed left hand while still holding the German's dagger in my right hand is the only detail I can recall until we were well out of danger after traveling hours by foot in the hills."

"Chiara saved me. Tended the wounds and eventually got me to a local doctor several days later. Went through a bad time fighting through the pain with repeated alcohol irrigations of the wound by the country doctor to avoid infection."

"Sounds like you saved Chiara and the other partisan. What ever happened to her?"

A tear ran slowly down Landeira's cheek.

Emilia stood to cradle his head against her. They remained like that for several minutes.

"Were you in love with her?"

"Yes. My first real love. She died a few weeks later leading a raid while I was still recovering. Her death affected me for years afterwards. Maybe in ways I did not even realize at the time."

"I am so sorry for bringing it up."

"No, don't say that. Come here." After kissing her gently, he continued, "About time I got that out. Recalling that terrible time is not about to affect the rest of this special day, Emilia. How about you get dressed and we stop by my place so I can shave and get a change of clothes. I am already hungry after lovemaking. An excellent lunch is in order. After that, we shall let our natural desires take their course."

It turned out to be an extraordinary day. The violent confrontation the previous night and releasing the memory of Chiara Ricci curiously acted like a catharsis of his troubled past. Of course, it was all about Emilia Montero.

She also felt renewed meeting this enigmatic man. The chemistry overriding her well-constructed defenses. Both laughed knowing the reason why they ravenously attacked a hearty lunch.

Sated and enjoying daiquiris in a perfect setting overlooking Havana Harbor, she too unburdened her past.

"How did you know there was no man in my life when you asked me to go sailing?"

"I asked your father."

"What else did he tell you about me?"

"Very little other than you are very intelligent. He respects your privacy. However, I sensed he was encouraging me."

She smiled. "I am sure he was. He likes you very much, Bart. Papa is very perceptive. I suspect he thinks I scare men off. Which is probably true. I can be a bit of a bitch. I realize I carry a chip on my shoulder. Comes from the sense of superiority men seem to feel. I work in a male-dominated professional world. I am as talented as any man. No, that is not actually correct. I am *more talented* than most, admittedly making me professionally arrogant."

Landeira chuckled. "Perhaps that is why I am infatuated with you. You were not especially welcoming when we first met. Took it to be the circumstances and your concern for your father's wellbeing. However, from that first day, I could not get you out of my mind."

215

She stroked his hand. "Let me tell you about my past. From an early age, I wanted to do something with my life other than marry and raise a family. I watched those women in my life like my mother who led a good life, but I wanted a different life. To live my life as an individual, not through others. My good fortune to have parents that understood my ambitions in a culture that is not understanding of unconventional female aspirations. They provided the financial means and encouragement to pursue an education knowing I intended to pursue a professional career not marriage. Atypical to Cuban culture."

Bart interjected, "I saw that too growing up in Florida. There was never any talk of my sisters going to college. Don't even know if they had any such aspirations. Both are married with children but we are not close."

"That was my other issue. Never felt the desire for children. One of my aunts said to me that I was being selfish. I remember lashing out at her, calling her old world ignorant.

"I wanted to expand my horizons so I earned an undergraduate degree in international studies from Havana University. This was during World War Two. Foreign affairs seemed an uncertain career path. I then pursued a degree in law thinking it was complimentary while providing more opportunities.

"Graduated in 1946. With the war over, I obtained a position a year later in the Foreign Ministry of the Gau administration. At the same time, I took on managing the financial affairs of Montero Rum. With my English fluency, I also helped in making American and European distribution connections. Gave me practical experience in business.

"I spent a difficult year doing mundane work at the Ministry. Confronting the male dominated environment where all the other women held only clerical jobs was a constant challenge. Worse yet, I became romantically involved with my boss. A stupid move. When the relationship soured, it forced me to leave.

"In retrospect, a valuable learning experience. Joining a law firm, I proved to myself just how good I was. I was the only female attorney in the firm. After a couple of years, fed up with sharing my performance with less qualified male attorneys, I left to open my own law firm, taking a number of clients with me."

Landeira said, "Bet that felt good."

She nodded. "Very good. Anyway, you can see why I have some sharp edges."

Jokingly, he said, "I don't know about that. Seems like I found plenty of round, smooth contours."

She mouthed a kiss. Something more was on her mind or she might have pursued his sexual banter. "My last relationship ended in tragedy. I met an American naval officer in 1952 when he was serving as assistant U.S. naval attaché to Cuba. A fighter pilot. I recall him trying to explain the terror each time when landing on an aircraft carrier. Called up and sent to Korea was emotionally wrenching. Months later, I received a telegram from his best friend another fighter pilot. His plane shot down and officially declared missing in action."

He gripped her hand but said nothing. What can anyone say? Either the traumatic scars heal over or remain an open wound. How you adapt shapes the rest of your life.

She did not shed any tears recalling the memory. "Enough of our difficult histories. Let's not let put a damper on this special day. So now what do you suggest we do?"

"How about you give me your version of a guided tour of Havana. Since I came here I have only seen the city in snatches getting from one place to another. Show me what you like most of the city. The real Cuban Havana. Then we finish off the evening with dinner and wherever comes to mind."

* * * *

Within a few days, Landeira published the first-hand account of the violent confrontation in the Miami Herald. It gained prominent notoriety in Havana with its widely circulated Spanish edition. In contrast, Havana's foremost newspaper gave the story only a couple of paragraphs. Quoting Colonel Ventura, official reporting fell in line with the police version of the incident. *Police of Havana's Fifth Precinct prevented two thieves from robbing an American journalist. The police killed one assailant and wounded another now in custody awaiting trial.* Landeira's published version debunked the attempted robbery theory and added more detail.

With the help of Hector Vasquez, Landeira was able to expand on the backgrounds of the two assailants that the Cuban newspaper did not even identify by name. For good reason. Both were employed as security guards by the Sevilla Biltmore Hotel and Casino. Vasquez's sources also uncovered the extensive criminal backgrounds of the two men. As for how he escaped unharmed, Landeira provided no details, saying only that his wartime military training proved effective against incompetent street thugs. Unequivocally, Landeira claimed the confrontation was a warning by American organized criminal elements to cease his series of press attacks. A response to his recent publication of how illegal American Mafia money secretly finances the Havana hotel and casino boom.

Having killed one assailant, he chose not to contradict that part of the police version. Let the police claim credit for the death. However, he offered enough indirect information to leave the impression the man died in police custody. A careless move along with contradicting the notorious Ventura in print by claiming this was the work of organized crime rather than robbery. Embarking on a dangerous subversive press campaign against the regime, he pondered if he should avoid antagonizing someone like Colonel Ventura.

Correct about the origin of the assault as intimidation, Bart Landeira failed to appreciate the nuanced differences between the American Mafia comparative newcomers and the established Cuban underworld. For prominent Cuban criminal figures like the Italian-Cuban Amadeo Barletta and the Italian-Uruguayan Amleto Battisti, Havana was their domain. The American reporter was an unnatural threat. By exposing criminal complicity of their banks, it steered too close to upsetting long cultivated criminal enterprises integral to Cuban corruption. For the American Mafia, Landeira's attacks did not represent a serious threat. Under attack for years in the United States press, their situation in Havana remained secure given the partnership with President Batista.

Max Landeira also misread who was behind this. Hurt by learning of the incident by reading it in the Miami Herald, he called Bart from Tampa. Motivated by fatherly concern, Bart did not accept his father's criticism the same way.

"Are you suggesting I lay off the Mafia in my reporting? Are you feeling guilty for your years of cozying up with murders?"

"Christ, it's not fair to accuse me. I am just a business lawyer, not a mobster."

"No? How about a Mafia lawyer? Guys like you enable their criminal enterprises by keeping them out of jail."

"I told you that kind of work is all behind me. I am concerned about your safety. Havana is not the United States."

"I am a journalist. If I am doing my job, there are always risks. If I self-censor what I report than I am just a hack. Obviously, I can take care of myself. I chose not to provide full details in print to avoid venturing into prohibited areas of censorship."

He paused and his father also remained silent for several moments. Letting out a sigh, Bart broke the uncomfortable silence, "Thanks for your concern, Father. Take care of yourself."

Bart disconnected the call.

****

Max Landeira introduced Santo Trafficante Jr. to Havana in the 1930s. A close confidant of the Trafficante Mafia family from those bootlegging days when he worked closely with Trafficante Sr., it was a favor to the old man.

Max did not believe Trafficante was behind the move against Bart. Trafficante would first have tried to first pressure him to warn Bart against further attacks in the press. He did expect Trafficante to get the word around that it was bad for business to go after an American newspaper reporter. Santo Trafficante and Meyer Lansky held sway over American Mafia investment in Havana. Lansky was even less inclined to do something this rash. This was more the work of local Cuban mobsters affiliated with the American Mafia.

Max Landeira's call to Trafficante went sideways no different from his call to Bart. Max's combative style invited defensive response.

Trafficante already knew Barletta and Battisti were behind it. While stupid, Trafficante saw no particular harm had it been successful. Regardless what Landeira alleged in his newspaper without evidence, the perpetrators were Cuban thugs and the police classified it as a failed robbery attempt. Trafficante was in no mood to listen to an irate Max Landeira pressuring him.

In truth, he never liked Max Landeira. While Landeira did creative legal work, Max Landeira played on his long association with Trafficante's father. Arrogant and paternalistic, Santo Jr. began distancing himself from Max Landeira following the death of his father in 1954.

"Goddamn it Max, you think I am not already looking into this? Whoever ordered this is in deep shit. I don't need your lecturing. It will be taken care of."

"I need your assurance that nothing will happen to my son, Santo."

Trafficante replied, "I don't control Havana. Why should I make you a fucking promise? I suggest you talk with your son. Put the brakes on attacking us. Write about this bearded asshole Castro and his chicken shit revolution. Your son makes himself a target. Every week I read some shit he writes about Mafia investment in Havana. He even accuses you, Max. Makes a lot of enemies. Maybe even Batista's police. Does your son have a death wish?"

That touched a button with Max. "Listen, Santo. I've been around long enough to know how you people operate. I showed you the way to get into Havana. How to work the legal stuff to protect you in the U.S. and how to cover your ass in Cuba. Christ, I was the one who introduced you to Batista. Made you as important down there as Meyer Lansky. I know where the bodies are buried."

"What are you saying, Max? Sounds awfully close to a threat," Trafficante replied with his voice rising in anger.

"It is my only son, Santo. I just want to emphasize that I expect nothing unfortunate to happen to him."

Always resenting Max Landeira's arrogance as smarter than everyone, Trafficante was beyond angry and disconnected the call.

****

The week following the violent confrontation on Saturday followed by consummating his romance with Emilia Montero the next day, made for a surreal week. Other than the unpleasant telephone conversation with his father, spending time with Emilia dominated his thoughts. An enjoyable dinner with the entire Montero family. Although constraining outward displays of affection, obvious to Augustin and his wife Alicia they clearly enjoyed the company of each other. A joyous occasion since they also felt affection for Bart.

He recounted the conversation with his father to Emilia. While explaining the pattern of conversations with his father frequently degenerating into argument, she saw how that troubled him.

"You know, if you wish to change your relationship with your father, you have to change your behavior."

"Change how? Ignore his controlling nature? His paternalism? His arrogance?"

Emilia responded, "Of course not. Whether or not he will ever change is not something you can control. What you can control is how you manage the interaction."

"I understand what you are saying but I never seem able to steer clear of arguing. He infuriates me so easily then the arguing frustrates and upsets me further. For years I managed by avoiding him. Now we cannot avoid each other."

"You are smart and persuasive. Look at your relationship as something other than father and son. Take control and do not let him trap you into pushing your hot button. Quit reacting and start managing the situation."

She was of course right. An entrenched cycle of abrasion spanning years where his solution was avoidance. He felt saddened for all the lost opportunities.

Another glorious weekend with Emilia passed with nothing troubling to intrude. Their lovemaking intensifying. Like survivors from a long period of self-enforced abstinence. Their deepening emotional and intellectual bonding further affirming their love.

* * * *

Scheduled for an interview on Havana's Radio Reloj station about the attack the prior week, Landeira parked his car in the adjacent lot next to the Radiocentro CMQ Building. Located at the corner of Calle L and La Rampa in the Vedado sector, the art deco-styled building was only slightly more than two miles west of the presidential palace in Old Havana. On this Wednesday afternoon of March 13, 1957, both locations were about to take on significance.

As Landeira approached the front door to the building, three cars screeched to halt on the street in front of him. Three armed men jumped out of each car with the driver remaining and the car idling. Several men rushed by Landeira through the glass door. The others fanned out, looking down both streets with handguns at the ready.

Little more than twenty feet away, Landeira locked eyes with Luis Montero who then turned away. Within a minute came the sounds of gunfire from within the building. Those men standing watch outside became visibly anxious as minutes passed. Landeira cautiously extracted his Leica camera from a case on his belt and began snapping photographs.

Suddenly, the front door of the radio station burst open. Those assailants that entered only minutes earlier exited and began talking excitedly. Landeira was close enough to catch snatches of their talk. Something about Batista's assassination.

The chubby young man they addressed as José appeared to be the leader of whatever just transpired upstairs in the radio studio.

The assailants quickly jumped back into the cars as José shouted for everyone to leave.

Landeira ran to his car. A story was breaking before his eyes. Follow the two-tone Ford sedan that José jumped into making a U-turn to head south on Calle L. The maneuver gave Landeira sufficient time to pull out not far behind. In the distance, he could hear sirens.

One block after starting his chase, a police car pulled out from an intersecting side street and took up a position between Landeira and the speeding Ford. Seconds later, gunfire erupted between the Ford and the chasing police car. A block further, the Ford turned off Calle L unto a street with a slight hill and stopped.

Landeira slowed then pulled to the curb as he looked down the street surrounded by buildings of the University of Havana. The Ford stopped in the middle of the street with doors open and the police car stopped not far behind. An exchange of gunfire continued as several assailants ran away on foot. While the police officers took up the chase, Landeira rushed toward a body lying in the street. Moving closer, Landeira looked down on the bloodied body turned on its side into the lifeless eyes of the person he recognized as the one called José. He snapped what became an iconic photograph before making a hurried retreat before more police arrived.

As Landeira drove away, a broadcast bulletin came over the car radio. *Security forces successfully repelled an armed attack on the Presidential Palace. There are reports of many casualties among the attackers and presidential security forces. President Batista was unharmed.*

He must remain careful should his presence at the radio station prompt another interrogation by Colonel Ventura. Undoubtedly connected with whatever transpired in the assassination attempt on President Batista.

Chapter 16

Returning to his apartment, the radio began streaming continuous but fragmented reporting. The frequently repeated message, President Batista was alive and uninjured in a failed assassination attempt but details were inconsistent. The simultaneous attack on the Radio Reloj studio was the secondary target. A planned radio broadcast by the attackers never materialized. The reports spoke of dozens of police and attackers killed and wounded at the presidential palace. By all accounts, a sizeable force armed with military-type weapons attacked the palace.

Calling Emilia's office, her secretary said only she was not in the office. He left the message for her to call him immediately. No answer at her apartment number. Staying close to the telephone waiting to tell Emilia about her brother, he listened to the news broadcast for the next hour, jotting down the salient facts reported by the police and a spokesman for the President.

He wanted to call Mateo Pérez and Hector Vasquez to determine what they knew but hesitated since that might occupy his telephone for some time. He needed the line open until he spoke with Emilia. Concern raced through his mind. Was she perhaps involved in the same political activity as her younger brother? Did she know his whereabouts? Was she in danger?

It was two hours since the violent events when Emilia called. "You called? Is it about what happened this afternoon that is all over the news?"

"Yes. More than that though. I need to see you. Don't want to explain over the phone."

"What is going on, Bart? You are scaring me?"

"It's just very important but not something I want to discuss on the phone. Where are you?"

"At the office."

"Go to your apartment. I am leaving right now."

At her apartment, she gave him a quick kiss, before asking, "What is wrong?"

"It's about Luis."

"What about him?"

"I saw him today. I was at the Radiocentro building this afternoon. Out front when a dozen armed men stormed the place. Luis was among them. Holding a revolver only a few feet from where I stood. What is he into, Emilia?"

"Oh my god! I never knew they would do something like this."

"Who are *they*?"

"The Directorio Revolucionario Estudiantil. The DRE."

"The Catholic student splinter group opposing Batista?"

"Yes. Luis joined them a couple of years ago. His best friend, José Echeverría a fellow student, was one of the founding members."

"José? Short, stocky in his twenties? Baby face?"

Surprised, she said, "You know him?"

He shook his head, pursing his lips recalling the dead man he photographed. "No Emilia, but I am fairly certain he is the one I came across dead in the street at the University just a few blocks from the radio station. Luis spoke to him outside the radio station before leaving in another car. Come sit down. I'll tell you what happened."

"José is dead?"

"Killed by police in a gunfight. He seemed to be in charge so I followed his escape in my car."

"What about Luis?"

"I don't know. He left in a different car headed in another direction. Are you involved with the DRE, Emilia?"

225

She slumped forward. "Not actively. I just support their political aims. Social justice and economic independence from the United States. Opposed to everything Batista represents. Never thought they might resort to violence. As an outsider, José and Luis were careful to avoid such rhetoric in my presence."

"To what extent are you involved with the DRE?"

Turning defensive, she replied, "I am not involved with the Directorate. All I know are their political aims. The usual kind of activism of university students. Understandably, it became more strident after Batista closed the University. But Luis never gave any indication they were planning something as extreme as attempting to assassinate Batista."

"Luis will eventually make contact. Promise me you will let me know immediately. You must not get involved directly. Do not go to him. Tell me and I will do what I can to help. The police are reacting indiscriminately. As family, you might even be targeted. You must warn your parents. Warn them not to even reveal their knowledge of Luis' involvement with the DRE. Going forward, stick to your story of having no idea of his whereabouts, or certainly any knowledge of his participation in the DRE. Do not make up anything. It will only entrap you.

"Besides your brother and Echeverría, who else do you know in the DRE?"

She rigorously shook her head, "No one. In fact, I only met Echeverría briefly a couple of times. Luis was always careful."

* * * *

Days later, the full story came into focus with reporting in the Cuban press. A success for the president's security apparatus. With the total failure of the attack, the official line emphasized Batista's downplaying of any threat by revolutionary insurgents. Although unsuccessful in crushing Castro's 26 July Movement in the East, the guerrilla force remained comparatively small and inadequately armed. While a violent response from the Directorio Revolucionario Estudiantil came as a surprise, the government claimed that movement appeared now crushed.

The primary attack on the presidential palace involved an estimated 50 well-armed assailants. The assault on the radio station was intended to broadcast a message announcing the assassination of Batista with the hope of inciting widespread insurrection. Security guards disabled the transmission tower during the assault.

The assault on the palace was a total disaster for the insurgents. 30 died and the police arrested two wounded. Of the 100 palace guards protecting Batista, 20 died. The assailants reached the third floor but President Batista barricaded in his office slipped out through a back staircase. Although instigated by the DRE, surprisingly many of the attackers were not students. Many among the dead were in their thirties, forties, and even fifties, identified as members of the Partido Autentico political party with a history of opposition to Batista.

Five assailants in the radio station attack also died. Of the combined assault on both targets, only 16 assailants survived. Before his death, José Echeverría attempted to broadcast a statement from the radio station prematurely announcing the death of Batista as killed by the Revolutionary Directorate in the name of the Cuban Revolution.

To anyone well informed, the opposition to the dictatorship of Fulgencio Batista was much broader than a group of ragtag bearded guerrillas in the eastern mountains and a few militant students in Havana.

The attack on the Presidential Palace provoked immediate reprisals by the National Police seeking out remnants of the DRE. An indiscriminate response with police units acting on their own initiative. The incident used as justification to go after any suspected opposition regardless of organizational affiliation. This level of repressive violence by the regime was previously unknown in Havana. Incidents of mass killings occurred only in the rural areas of eastern Cuba, perpetrated by the Army. Few witnesses and censored reporting. In contrast, the citizens of Havana observed the violent excesses unleased by the National Police.

For weeks following March 13, the prior false sense of immunity Havana felt from the political violence plaguing rural Cuba vanished. A number of prominent opponents of the regime fell to police overreaction. Among those executed by police was a professor of law and economics at the University of Havana for alleged affiliation in the DRE. A colleague of Mateo Pérez Landeira learned, but Pérez apparently escaped targeting. Perhaps because Pérez stayed under the radar, preferring to conduct his opposition to Batista secretly with caution.

Landeira wisely decided not to publish a first-hand account of the attack on the radio station. Much less the source of the disturbing photograph of the bloody body of José Echeverría lying in the street that he mailed to Toussaint for release. A good call since Colonel Ventura was taking a leading role in going after suspected opposition. Landeira could not afford becoming linked suspiciously to another violent incident.

Fortunately, there were no indications the police were targeting Emilia or the Montero family. Unlike his friend José Echeverría, Luis Montero never occupied a leadership role in the DRE and his name perhaps overlooked by police intelligence.

It was three weeks later that the Monteros learned of Luis' whereabouts. It served to raise continued concern over his involvement in violent resistance to the Batista regime. Word came in the form of a note in the mail to Emilia's law office. The envelope marked personal read:

I am safe. Roughing it as a guerrilla in the Escambray Mountains. I joined the Second National Front commanded by Eloy Gutiérrez along with several others escaping Havana after what happened in March. Still very much fighting ahead to bring down Batista. Do not worry. Please comfort Mama and Papa for me. Love, Luis.

The message afforded the Monteros and Landeira some measure of relief. Whatever dangers Luis might face in the mountains, it was likely less risky than trying to remain in hiding in Havana with the police dragnet and informers on heightened alert.

The most striking example of police reprisal occurred at five-thirty in the afternoon of April 20. National Police banged on the door to apartment 201 at No.7 Humboldt Street. Led by Colonel Esteban Ventura, the police gunned down the four young DRE occupants with no attempt at making arrests. Outright murder. The victims all participants in the assaults on the Presidential Palace and the Radiocentro CMQ Building. Widely published graphic photographs added for effect with the implicit message warning of the intelligence reach of the National Police.

Emboldened by effectively removing the leadership of the DRE, Batista encouraged his National Police to continue a reign of terror toward anyone suspected of harboring opposition to his regime. Batista was intent on destroying all political opposition in Havana. Protecting the glamorous image of casino gambling for the American tourist trade was paramount. Protecting his source for amassing personal wealth. Havana must appear as just another American city, not as some Latin backwater in political turmoil. For the Cuban citizenry, Havana no longer seemed an oasis apart from the threats of revolutionary insurrection happening elsewhere in Cuba.

＊＊＊＊

"About time we put our media attack in motion," Landeira said to Mateo Pérez and Hector Vasquez meeting at the *La Fraternidad de Cristóbal Colón* men's club. Here the setting was perfect as a logical place for frequent social interaction. Seemingly semi-private yet by choosing off-hours, easy to sit comfortably well out of hearing from staff or other members.

The club's membership numbered among the prominent families in Havana. This translated into a strong conservative political bias which further meant support to varying degrees for the Batista regime. The club membership did not represent an overtly pro-Batista stance, but it provided sufficient cover as a conservative institution to divert attention from the police. Furthermore, since Landeira and Pérez were members, perfectly natural for them to be seen together frequently. Since Vasquez was not a member and given his prominence in Cuban journalism, they still must remain vigilant. Their attack campaign in the

American press with a suppressed Cuban press invited scrutiny for any journalists. What better sources than disaffected Cuban reporters laboring under censorship.

All three knew that Vasquez's network of reporters represented the weakest link susceptible to police counterintelligence efforts. In the world of intelligence agencies, the Cuban police were knuckle-draggers. However, what they lacked in operational expertise they made up for with indiscriminate use of torture to suspects.

Also as a foreign journalist, Landeira would naturally come under suspicion if the press campaign proved successful. Not the first time sticking his neck out. Yet not since the clarity of purpose experienced in World War Two did the risk seem justified.

Vasquez said, "I suggest we first go after the low hanging fruit. The most notorious of the butchers in the Army and the National Police."

"Yes. I concur," Pérez said. "At the top of that list should be Esteban Ventura, *the assassin in the white suit.* Not only featured in Bart's article about the run in with the Mafia thugs, but the chief murderer of the four DRE members at Humboldt 7."

Vasquez replied, "Certainly. Among the others, I nominate Rolando Masferrer, Colonel Fermin Cowley, and Colonel Alberto del Río. These are the chief murderers behind Batista's terror campaign to hold onto power. Lots of others but these guys are all poster-quality villains."

Pérez said, "Digging up material on these bastards will largely fall on your network of Cuban reporters. Does enough information exist to turn these murderers' lives inside out?"

Vasquez chuckled. "No question about that. These butchers leave a long trail of blood. No shortage of gruesome stories. My guess a lot of personally embarrassing information probably exists if people are willing to talk. What I can tell you is there are many reporters out there willing to go after them. No limit to the number of people wanting to seek revenge."

"I will contribute by setting my sights on the top officials benefiting by the corruption," Pérez said. "Particularly those necessary to facilitating the flow of money. Provide you names, my suspicions, and what I know of them. Perhaps I can even offer certain leads to pursue. Anything we can uncover to exploit by generating internal friction among Batista's corrupt conspiracy will be useful."

"Landeira said, "The United States is changing ambassadors. A businessman named Earl Smith is expected to be confirmed soon. Not a career diplomat. I will get an interview. Establish his views on Batista and the State Department's official position on the allegations of corruption and the increasing political violence. Of course, the U.S. Secretary of State remains John Foster Dulles. A twisted ultraconservative hawk and fanatical anticommunist. President Eisenhower allows Dulles to largely dictate U.S. foreign policy. Depending on how much damage we inflict on Batista in the American press, Smith might become a barometer of Washington's position."

Landeira saw John Dulles as the ultimate villain behind the CIA's regime change in Iran and Guatemala during his final years with the Agency. Although he railed against the operational incompetence of Frank Wisner, Landeira also blamed the complicity of the new CIA Director Allen Dulles, the younger brother of John Foster Dulles. In their self-serving logic, any right wing dictator was an acceptable alternative to any progressive government that inherently bred the risk of communism.

Landeira remained bitter toward American foreign policy and his personal guilt of participation. U.S. support for Batista existed for the same reasons. Not likely to change with the Dulles brothers in their current positions. Landeira's bitterness was a large part of pursuing this anti-Batista campaign.

Landeira ended the meeting with, "The sooner I can get something newsworthy the better to build on the climate created by the attempted Batista assassination and the violent police response."

* * * *

Hector Vasquez made good on Landeira's request for hard-hitting material. Several reporters provided a wealth of information on the infamous *man in the white suit*, Colonel Esteban Ventura. The portrayal of this monster coming on the heels of the murders he instigated at Humboldt Street made for an impressive opening salvo against the regime. Up to now, news of the regime's violence constituted only statistics. The occasional photographs appearing in print provided by the Army or National Police suited only to corroborate the government's narrative. By mid-1957, objective Cuban journalism did not exist under Batista's censorship.

The disaffected and often unemployed reporters in Vasquez's network already had a wealth of material gathered over the last couple of years. Testimonials from victims surviving torture directed by Colonel Ventura. Descriptions of the mutilated bodies by the families of those that did not survive. Graphic photographs. Several photographs even of Ventura's Fifth Precinct torture room. According to Vasquez, Ventura often took pictures of victims undergoing mistreatment. The origin of the leaked pictures probably a police officer disgusted with the barbarity.

Landeira drafted the article. Placing it in the false bottom of his suitcase, he flew to Miami where he mailed it to Toussaint. The Ministry of Propaganda long ago banned the San Juan newspaper El Mundo from Cuba because of its anti-totalitarian stance. To gauge the impact of Toussaint's articles, it was important to understand how widely his stories disseminated in major newspapers across the United States by the news services. This required reading follow up stories and editorials. Difficult to accomplish from a police state with distribution of American publications limited under strict censorship.

The answer was to employ a press clipping service in the United States. Such a service canvased major newspaper and periodicals for any publication related to a specific subject. To avoid associating his name, Landeira created his own shell company, Latin Affairs Consulting in Miami. The clipping service mailed accumulated material weekly to a Miami post office box.

On his periodic runs to Miami to mail new material to Toussaint, retrieve the clippings and smuggled them back into Havana. Follow up editorials by widely read syndicated columnists should provide the best barometer of the impact of their work. If the material began catching the attention of names like Theodore White, Joseph Alsop, Lowell Thomas, Walter Lippmann, and Edward R. Murrow that meant their efforts were reaching American readers and government officials.

Landeira's first story appeared in the San Juan El Mundo under Toussaint's byline.

Living in Fear in Batista's Cuba
El Mundo San Juan, PR, Gaspar Toussaint

It seems besieged Cuban dictator Fulgencio Batista has yet another active opposition movement growing out of his increasingly violent repression. In the rural eastern provinces, the revolutionary Fidel Castro leads a small guerrilla force, calling themselves the 26 July Movement, from inaccessible positions in the Sierra Maestra Mountains. Batista's large army has yet to crush these revolutionaries receiving support from the rural population. The success of the regime in decimating the leadership of the militant student organization the Directorio Revolucionario Estudiantil, also failed to crush entirely what was previously the urban revolutionary equivalent to Castro's M-26-7. Some remnants of the DRE fled Havana into the Escambray Mountains of central Cuba following their failed assassination attempt on President Batista. Reports indicate they are reorganizing as guerrillas under the banner of the Second National Front of Escambray.

A new opposition group now appears emerging using the name *Venganza de Martí,* or the Revenge of Martí. The name adopted from the 19th century Cuban national hero José Martí for his role in the liberation of Cuba from Spain. Unlike the M-26-7 and the DRE, this emerging group seeks to use the power of the press. Not by publishing damaging material toward the Batista regime within Cuba, which is impossible in a police state, but in the United States. *Venganza de Martí seeks* instead to influence the hearts and minds of Americans to pressure Washington to change their economic support toward Batista.

The United States dominates Cuba economically and supports Fulgencio Batista militarily as a U.S. puppet colony-state to insure no socialistic government intrudes into the Americas. Although the demagogue Senator Joseph McCarthy no longer has a voice in Washington, fear of communism still drives U.S. foreign policy. Therefore, the Eisenhower administration insures totalitarian regimes like that of Batista in Cuba and Trujillo in the Dominican Republic to remain in power. Violent repression of political opposition and crippling corruption become irrelevant. The vaunted values of America exist only within its borders but not as part of its foreign policy.

Venganza de Martí hopes to influence American public opinion. Cuban dependency on the United States might make Batista vulnerable. People read the effects of violence and injustice throughout the world each day in their newspapers. Largely explained in numbers killed, imprisoned, or made homeless. The sources of the political turmoil often incomprehensibly complex. Difficult for anyone to gain a true appreciation for events that go far beyond their own experiences. Americans do not experience state sponsored terror in the form of torture and murder. Yet that is what occurs daily in Batista's Cuba.

This article will attempt to convey some sense of the pervasive fear enveloping Cuba by revealing details of one of the state's most notorious assassins. His name is Lieutenant Colonel Esteban Ventura. National Police Commander of Havana's Fifth Precinct. Known as *the man in the white suit* by those in Havana he terrorizes. His hunting down of victims is far removed from the glamor of the Havana casinos and nightclubs.

Police Lt. Col. Esteban Ventura

From his early unremarkable career beginning as a soldier then later with the National Police, by 1949 he was only a second lieutenant. Recognizing an opportunity to further his ambitions, Ventura abruptly switched allegiance from those in the police command politically connected to the former administration when Fulgencio Batista engineered his coup in 1952. Setting out to differentiate himself, he manufactured conspiracies about his former associates. Aggressive persecution of those opposing the new Batista regime presented the best path to advancement. Batista's purge of the National Police left many vacancies. The acceptance of unrestrained violence also served to feed Ventura's proclivity for sadism. He turned to targeting the youth of Havana. For these victims without political influence, he manufactures conspiracies with impunity from any oversight. Simply declaring suspicion of revolutionary involvement for students, drug dealing, or common crimes for working class youths proves sufficient for arrest. Coerced false confessions denouncing others often the only means of escaping more extreme forms of torture. Terrorizing the mean streets of Havana satisfies Ventura's need for power.

From the onset of his blood soaked career, Ventura never dirtied his hands, or his immaculate white suits. The firsthand accounts cited here all confirm his voyeuristic approach to sadism.

Typically happening in the shadows, Colonel Ventura's latest outrage became very public. Following a failed attempt to assassinate President Batista in March of this year, the Cuban National Police went on an unrestrained rampage to destroy remnants the student Revolutionary Directorate responsible for the attack. Ventura turned to indiscriminate seizures of random citizens. Many taken to the Fifth Precinct station where he personally supervised interrogations under torture. Survivors' testimony claim their maltreatment continued even if they had no useful information. Some arrested solely for the purpose of spreading terror. All remarked on the calm demeanor of *the man in the white suit* as he directed their torment.

One middle-aged woman spoke of her hours-long ordeal. Stripped naked and tied to a chair for humiliation, she suffered repeated cigarette burns. A young man showed the deformed fingers of each hand broken individually. Another revealed massive bruising of his entire torso and arms from hours of beating by a stiff rubber hose. A long list of documented incidents exists, many accompanied by photographs too graphic for publication.

Through informers, police discovered four DRE leaders hiding in the heart of Havana weeks after the presidential palace attack. Ventura personally led the police raid on No. 7 Humboldt Street, not far from the popular seaside avenue the Malecón.

After surrounding the building, the police banged on the door to apartment 201 with the butts of their guns. Four leaders of the DRE inside attempted to escape. One managed to get to an adjacent apartment. The police entered that apartment and seized the young man. Marching him down the hall, Ventura nodded to an officer with a submachine gun who then killed Joe Westwood instantly.

The other three revolutionaries slipped through a vent into the apartment below. Not realizing the police already surrounded the building, they fled in different directions. A police officer repeatedly shot Juan Carbó trying to reach the elevator. Through a window, Fructuoso Rodriguez and José Machado jumped to the ground floor. Another officer with a machinegun killed both in a hail of bullets.

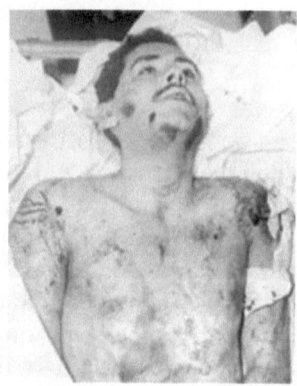

Body of Fructuoso Rodriguez

Colonel Ventura is just one of the many of President Batista's assassins. *Venganza de Martí* promises to provide the backgrounds of others that serve to maintain Fulgencio Batista in power through violence and terror. The oppression of the Cuban people through political violence is the real face of what should be a tropical paradise. The glamor of Havana gambling nightlife seen by the American tourist masks a country too long suffering a succession of corrupt governments since gaining independence as a colony of Spain over fifty years ago.

No matter how many celebrities entertain at the best Havana nightclubs, Cuba is anything but an inviting tropical paradise. The average Cuban lives in a climate of continual terror. Since Fulgencio Batista seized power in 1952, thousands have died from state sponsored murder. While Colonel Ventura seizes selective victims off the streets of Havana, the Cuban Army deals wholesale murder in rural eastern Cuba with repeated military incursions to eradicate revolutionaries and active supporters.

Two weeks later came evidence of that first effort by Landeira and his conspirators. At a Havana newsstand, Hector Vasquez was the first to see the article in print in the Washington Post and the Saturday Evening Post. They would have to wait until Landeira made the trip to Miami to retrieve the clippings before assessing the scope of U.S.-wide newspaper interest. Just as well the Miami Herald remained banned in Cuba. Colonel Ventura might not appreciate the nuance of the byline identifying Toussaint as the reporter rather than Landeira as the Miami Herald correspondent based in Havana.

* * * *

As Landeira entered his apartment late one evening with Emilia Montero, the telephone was ringing as he unlocked the door.

"*Hola?*"

"Bart, is that you? This is Isabel."

"Isabel? Good to hear from you." Cupping the handset, he said to Emilia, "My sister."

"I have been trying to reach you all day. I have some distressing news. Father is dead."

"Dead? What happened?"

"A terrible accident. Happened last night. I received a call from the Tampa police early this morning. A car struck him as he left a restaurant last night. Hit and run according to the police. They found a stolen car abandoned a few blocks away. They say it was the car that struck Father. I guess they have ways of telling that."

Through tears, Isabel said. "Marta and her husband arrived in Tampa this afternoon. We need to make funeral arrange-ments. Can you come to Tampa, Bart? We feel overwhelmed with so much to do."

"Of course. I will get the first flight out in the morning and take a taxi to your house."

Chapter 17

Before leaving for the airport early the following morning, Landeira called his cousin Rafael. "Sorry for calling so early. I have some bad news. Your Uncle Max is dead." After explaining what little he knew, "I am catching a plane to Tampa leaving in an hour. I will call you later when I know more. Break the news carefully to your father. He will take it hard and I worry about his bad heart. Let the rest of the family know. I will see what my sisters want but I believe my father would want to be buried in the family cemetery in Camagüey."

"I should not ask at a time like this but the family could use your help with the business, Bart. Other than our sugarcane operations, your father ran everything else since my father's health deteriorated over the last few years. We all appreciate what you did after the death of Uncle Tomás."

"I understand, Rafael. I will do what I can. I will call the Havana office later today. We do not want them passing the news to the outside world until we prepare a public statement. I realize the extent of my father's leadership in the financial aspects of running Landeira Grupo. I will keep involved until we stabilize the situation, Rafael. On your end, reassure the family and the senior managers. I will call Augustin Montero."

* * * *

Arriving in Tampa and before joining his sisters, Landeira met with the Tampa police detective handling the case of his father's death now categorized as manslaughter. After offering condolences, the detective surprised him by asking, "Did your father have any enemies?"

The honest answer was *undoubtedly*, however Landeira said, "Why would you ask that? I thought this was a hit and run manslaughter investigation."

"For the moment it is. However, something unusual came up just this morning. Your father's office was burglarized. Are you familiar with your father's law practice?"

"Yes. I also have a law license but currently I am a foreign correspondent for the Miami Herald based in Havana. I worked with my father here before the war. His area of specialty was corporate law and business consulting."

"Mind accompanying me to visit his office? See if you can add anything."

Inside the office, Bart had a stirring of long ago memories. It became clear the burglary targeted the many locked file cabinets. Most showed signs of locks broken away with a tool. Landeira had no way of knowing what if any files might be missing. Yet it became clear the burglar discovered something of interest in one particular file now entirely empty. The only indication of the file cabinet contents was a drawer number. Bart knew his father's secretary kept a master ledger cataloguing the contents of each file drawer.

The burglar apparently did not know this accounting for most of the files vandalized. Bart recalled the location of the secretary's desk. "Have you contacted any of my father's staff?"

"Not yet. It is Sunday and we do not know the names and addresses of his employees. We secured the scene and plan to be here first thing tomorrow morning when they arrive to work."

"This is the secretary's desk. Years ago she kept a ledger identifying every file and its location."

The detective tried the desk. Locked.

Landeira said, "Look underneath the coffee kiosk. There should be a spare set of keys hanging on a hook toward the back."

Opening the desk drawer, the detective found the ledger. Finding the page for the emptied file cabinet, the detective scanned the list then handed the ledger to Landeira.

"Any of these file names mean anything to you?"

The list included Ybor Group Investments and Caribbean Investments among others previously identified by his father. Front companies created by his father for Santo Trafficante Jr. and associates of the American Mafia.

"No, but I know nothing of my father's business dealings."

The detective nodded and set the ledger on the desk. Landeira guessed the detective never read his article in the Miami Herald attacking the Mafia and Santo Trafficante specifically. "I will wait to interview the staff tomorrow. Too much a coincidence. Someone in a stolen car killed your father and his office burglarized in the same night. A cop doesn't believe in coincidences. I will let you know if we come up with anything."

The conflicted emotions of the loss of his father affected Bart Landeira more than he wished to admit. For their decades of discord, Max was not a bad father. In spite of being overbearing, he loved his children, especially his only son. Never mistreated them. Hard to define, but Maximiliano Landeira could best be described as a complex man, often difficult in his personal relationships.

Their years of estrangement only solidified Bart's critical views. Since leaving the CIA and coming to Havana, some sort of rapprochement seemed possible. That went sour as Max guardedly revealed his legal dealings in Cuba while Bart sensed he was being less than entirely candid. Now he simply felt the visceral pain left by a father's death.

Having only a distant relationship with both sisters, the outpouring of grief with his immediate family only exacerbated his conflicting feelings. His way of coping turned to taking charge of the situation. All three siblings agreed internment should be in the family plot in Camagüey unless a will turned up stating something different. Bart left his sisters to deal with matters in Tampa. He would manage the funeral arrangements from Cuba.

He made his escape by staying at a hotel near the airport that night. He talked to Emilia for an hour as he sipped Scotch in his hotel room. Among their conversation, he realized a measure of guilt intruded into the mix of emotions. An unspecific guilt of not doing more to build a relationship with his father's advancing age. Critical of his father attempting to rationalize his shady past. Insensitive to his father clumsy but desperate reaching out to his son. Now an added guilt that his attack on the Mafia in the press may have had something to do with his father's death. His death obviously not an accident.

"I think the Mafia may have killed my father. Santo Trafficante perhaps specifically."

"What? Why do you suspect that?" Emilia asked.

After reciting all the details, she said, "Pretty thin evidence to draw that conclusion. Did you tell the police of your suspicion?"

"No. Like you said no evidence. With the clout Trafficante has in Tampa, the police would never pursue an investigation. If it was Trafficante, the perpetrator was some low-level soldier in the Tampa mob. No one in the Mafia ever talks unless they have a death wish."

"When will you be back?"

"Tomorrow morning."

"Good, I will pick you up at the airport. How are you holding up?"

"Okay I guess. Given our strained relationship, his death is more difficult than I expected."

Before his plane took off, he placed a call to the Landeira Grupo accounting manager at the Havana office. Told him about the death of Max Landeira. None of the employees must talk about this to anyone until he arrived at the office sometime later today.

Uncertain what he was going to say, he felt an obligation to help as he promised his cousin. How far that extended he did not know. Life in Havana was becoming increasing more complicated.

Emilia was at the airport to meet him with an embrace and kisses. Once in her car, he said, "I need to stop at the Havana office. I told my cousin Rafael I would try to help out by temporarily taking over managing financial affairs of Landeira Grupo. I could use your help. Pay you well as a consultant."

"Of course I will help," she said.

The stop at the Havana office was unpleasant but brief. Having visited previously with his father, his announcement that he was taking over accepted as natural by the staff. His instructions were not to discuss his father's death should anyone call with questions. Refer them to me. He would return tomorrow afternoon for briefings on Landeira Grupo accounting operations and the logistics operations of Landeira Servicios de Logistica, as well as the law practice of Landeira Servicios Juridicos. He assured all the employees that business should continue as usual.

Even stepping in on a temporary basis involved vastly broader commitments to the family business. His father's death represented a much greater leadership void than that of his Uncle Tomás. The five-member board of directors now had two vacancies. Uncle Enrique as chairman was also in declining health.

Banco Crédito Industrial y Mercantil de Habana was an entirely different matter. Landeira Grupo owned sixty percent of the shares with his father as president. Not part of Landeira Grupo. All Landeira Grupo could do was press for a special board meeting to name a new president. Considering the bank was complicit in Mafia money laundering and undoubtedly bribery, he must suggest a way to liquidate their holdings in the bank. That might prove awkward. Did Uncle Enrique and his cousin Rafael know what his father was up to with the Bank?

The funeral for Max Landeira was a subdued affair compared with that of Tomás a year earlier. Only Augustin Montero made the journey with Bart and Emilia from Havana. Max may have had many business associates, but apparently no friends. From Tampa, only Bart's sisters and their husbands attended. Bart coordinated the arrangements. The logistics division made the arrangement for flying the body to Camagüey.

Following interment at the family estate, Bart huddled with Uncle Enrique, Aunt Marta, and cousin Rafael. Max's death thrust Landeira Grupo into crisis. Enrique's health appeared deteriorated since Bart saw him only a year ago. Bart's paternal Aunt Marta was at the meeting only because of her position as a member of the board of directors. Holding that position because she was a major stockholder. Rafael already had far too much on his plate to take on anything more. He also had no experience with the organizational and financial complexities of Landeira Grupo. The family let Max pursue his own agenda since the family business prospered under his financial leadership.

They all looked to Bart for help. Impressed by his acquisition of Montero Rum and bringing in Augustin Montero, they ascribed to him more business expertise than deserved. Simply having a law degree did not qualify him for standing in for his father.

While feeling empathy for their plight, his extended family was alien to his life. He was an outsider. Other than his deceased Uncle Tomás, he harbored no strong attachments. They however viewed him as the son of the brilliant Max Landeira. Bart was blood family meaning everything.

They tried to entice him to join the board, but he declined. "I am a journalist not a businessman. I will try to help as I did after the passing of Tomás. I have an understanding of the legal aspects of a corporation like Landeira Grupo so I can at least hold things together until you find a permanent solution. I am not that solution. Now is the time to look outside the family, starting with a chief financial officer. I will do what I can to start that process."

Settling on his appointment as temporary chief financial officer and corporate counsel with a generous salary was as far as he was willing to go.

* * * *

Something else weighed on Landeira's mind beyond the family's problems. Since being in Camagüey a year ago, the tension in rural eastern Cuba was now palpable. Evident from the moment he stepped off the plane. The airport was an armed camp protected by a sizeable number of Cuban Army soldiers. Frustrated with the inability to crush Castro's M-26-7 insurgency, the Army began escalating their reign of terror against the populace, centering their efforts in Oriente Province a hundred miles to the east.

On May 19, a yacht named *Carinthia* left Florida's Biscayne Bay headed for Cuba. The vessel carried 27 armed revolutionaries financed by former Cuban President Carlos Prio deposed by Batista's coup in 1952. The foolish plan called for linking up with Castro's M-26-7 forces in the mountains in the south. It remains unclear how the Army discovered the plot, but it is clear what resulted. The Holguin Regiment commanded by Colonel Fermin Cowley pounced on the revolutionaries shortly following their landing on the northern coast of Oriente Province. Over the next several days, the disoriented revolutionaries unfamiliar with the terrain, fell prey to Cuban Army patrols. Crowley ordered the murders of all 27 revolutionaries making no attempt to detain those captured. A repeat of the grisly massacre months earlier during Christmas also perpetrated by Crowley, *the Jackal of Holguin.*

On May 28, Fidel Castro launched the first major attack of his meager revolutionary force against an Army garrison in Uvero, a village on the southern coast. The rebels killed 14 and wounded 19, while suffering 15 causalities of their own. Castro's force melted back into the inaccessible Sierra Maestra Mountains out of reach of counter measures by the Cuban Army. A strategically meaningless engagement but it served to bolster the viability of Castro's revolutionary movement, essential for sustaining support of his guerrilla force.

While the Cuban revolutionary insurgency remained fragmented and seemingly ineffective against Batista's security forces, it survived the reactionary terror efforts of the regime. Yet it remained difficult to see Fidel Castro's guerrillas ever reaching a level of presenting a serious military threat.

Renewed violent encounters would inevitably lead to greater atrocities. The typical approach of security forces in a totalitarian state. Knowing something of insurgencies, Landeira recognized the underlying problem faced by Batista. Regardless of the superior size of the Cuban Army, it proved incapable of subjugating rural Cuba. Although well-equipped by the United States, the average Cuban soldier was poorly paid, poorly trained, and poorly led. The geographic area was too vast while affording refuge in inaccessible mountains. A sympathetic population provided logistical and intelligence support for the insurgency. Batista's state-sponsored terror only hardened popular resistance.

With these intractable opposing forces, violence inevitably increased. Impossible to predict how that might play out. The foreign press reported the Cuban political violence death toll in the thousands. Would cosmopolitan Havana survive as an isolated island within the larger island of Cuba, or eventually descend into the same violence?

Landeira hoped Vasquez's network could produce newsworthy material on the increasing government initiated violence in Oriente. This was the compelling news of Cuba. Under Cuban censorship, the American press could provide only fragmentary coverage from restricted access to Cuban sources. The only photographs available those provided by the government serving their propaganda narrative. Landeira needed graphic photographs and first-hand accounts for another article attributed to Venganza de Martí.

* * * *

Following their return to Havana, Landeira returned to the Havana corporate office to clarify his new role as chief financial officer of Landeira Grupo.

To the attorneys in his father's separate law practice, he said that he was also a lawyer with a license to practice in the United States but not yet accredited to practice in Cuba. For the time being, they should conduct business as usual for current clients.

Their salaries would continue. He left the question of the practice remaining open vague. While having no interest in running a law practice, he wanted time to interrogate them about what they knew of his father's work in Cuba. Mostly he wanted to look at the files privately. With files stolen from the Tampa office, what might exist here?

After furnished with a set of office keys, one of the lawyers handed him a separate key. "This is the key to your father's private office."

From his only prior visit, he remembered the office as elegantly furnished. Expensive hardwood paneling with bookshelves. Several leather chairs for visitors. A massive desk with matching lateral file cabinets. Paintings of Cuban landscapes. A bar. A private toilet.

Sitting in his father's chair brought an unsettling feeling. Irrespective of their strained relationship, the impact of losing him to murder left him angry. Regardless becoming involved with violent criminals and corrupt Cuban officials, what prompted his murder? Did Bart's actions possibly contribute to his father's death?

The desk was locked. The key given to him only opened the office door. He discovered the file drawers also locked. The file keys probably located inside the locked desk. Easy enough to force the desk open with a screwdriver. Something for after hours with no one else around.

He finished the day with the Landeira accounting staff briefing him on procedures and a review of current financial statements. Much of the information lost on him with no practical experience of corporate finance. Only limited exposure for the year after law school in his father's practice was over fifteen years ago. Nonetheless, anticipation of what he might find in his father's private files dominated his thoughts.

That evening, he waited in his car outside the office building for everyone to leave. The office suite located on the second floor was locked confirming all the staff left for the day. Passing a cleaning woman in the hallway, he smiled pleasantly and made of point of saying something so an unfamiliar face would not alarm her as he unlocked the double doors. "I am new here. Need to work for a couple of hours. Did not realize everyone in the office left already. Feel free to come in and do your cleaning."

From his briefcase, he extracted a large screwdriver. Easy enough to force open drawers if not sensitive to damaging the wood. The drawers all well organized, but he found no keys for the files. Perhaps just another layer of security, he began feeling on the underside of each of the desk drawers. Sure enough, he found several keys held by a magnet screwed into the bottom of one drawer.

He began going through the files. Several files registered immediate interest. All labeled Banco Crédito Industrial y Mercantil de Habana. He knew the bank was at the center of his father's criminal complicity with the Mafia and Batista's corruption. Might these records confirm the same role played by his father's bank in laundering Mafia money as that played out by BANFAIC in the financing of the Habana Hilton? Was he the originator of the scheme?

Other files of interest included names of hotels, casinos, and names Landeira recognized as important figures in the Batista government. The discovery of the files needed thorough study to be able to piece together into a clear picture of his father's activities. He dreaded discovering new details of his father's criminal conduct. Difficult to understand why his father chose such a path. To learn the details required the assistance of Mateo Pérez and Hector Vasquez to make sense of the material.

Also needing to back away from delving into his father's past, he left it to Pérez and Vasquez to examine the secret files without him for a week. He needed some distance from the chain of recent events. Delving into his father's past added another difficult emotional element. Pérez and Vasquez possessed greater expertise. They were also Habaneros professionally experienced in understanding Cuban affairs.

Many of the documents consisted of his father's handwritten notes. Understandable given the likely sensitivity. Not something to expose to a secretary for typing. He did not relish handling such personal reminders.

Instead, he took the opportunity to spend more time with Emilia. Even time spent reviewing financial statements with her and the Landeira Grupo staff had a sense of normalcy. Another sailing outing. Emilia more comfortable and actually trying her hand at the wheel. Still early summer before the brutal heat slowing the pace of life in Cuba.

After a week, he met with Pérez and Vasquez at the *La Fraternidad de Cristóbal Colón* men's club. Greatly animated, Vasquez said. "Your father was not only complicit in the laundering of Mafia money and funding Batista's corruption, he appears to be the chief architect of the scheme. The files on Banco Crédito Industrial y Mercantil de Habana explain the same scheme used in Trafficante's hotel and casino investments as used by BANFAIC in the Habana Hilton deal. Yet dated much earlier. It also describes in the detail various mechanisms for flowing kickback money to Batista. "

Pérez offered, "Unfortunately, you cannot use such specific material in your anonymous articles sent to Toussaint without exposing yourself as the likely source."

Landeira nodded. "Just as well. I prefer to let my father rest in peace."

Vasquez offered, "However, the file on Trafficante and certain Batista government officials might be a different matter. If we can add enough material from other sources, we can integrate your father's contribution into the larger narrative without pointing back to you."

Pérez said, "I have a suggestion, Bart. To distance yourself even further, consider taking a leave of absence from the Herald. No more bylines. You cannot do meaningful reporting from here anyway under censorship."

Vasquez added, "Yes. A good idea. Also, close down the law office. Payoff the staff and turn over the client base and all the client files to them. Obviously not your father's secret files. Become a Cuban businessman. An executive of a Cuban corporation from a prominent Cuban family. Becomes a perfect cover for a covert campaign in the American press.

"Some of your father's notes on Trafficante are very specific," Pérez said. "I am no lawyer and certainly not conversant with U.S. law, but it could be legally incriminating to Trafficante. The Mafia came to Havana where they operate freely without the shadow of the American FBI. It might have something to do with his murder. Isn't that the way the Mafia insures witnesses do not testify against them?"

"Yes it is. Was the information that incriminating?"

Pérez replied, "You are the American lawyer, but there seems to be things pointing to evading taxes and possibly violation of U.S. banking regulations. Aren't those the reasons your father setup these American front companies to conceal the actual source of investment funds? Under corrupt Cuban bureaucracy with the president as a partner, less need to go to such elaborate lengths of concealment in Cuba."

"Something else seems apparent through your father's notes on Trafficante," Vasquez said. "They span many years. I am very familiar with the history of the Mafia in Havana. His more recently dated notes confirm indicators that Santo Trafficante is consolidating his control of Havana Mafia operations. Meyer Lansky continues to stay out of the spotlight. Not so with Trafficante."

Chapter 18

Landeira finished a new article centered on the murders of the revolutionaries from the *Carinthia* yacht in Oriente by the Army's Holguin Regiment commanded by Colonel Fermin Cowley. While the incident of the ill-conceived *Carinthia* mission and the aftermath made good media propaganda for the Batista regime, it was yet another example of the government's brutality in Oriente Province.

The actual body count of the violent conflict raging in eastern Cuba remained unknown. Censorship denied in any Cuban print or broadcast media to independently report on matters related to the insurgency. From anecdotal accounts unrecorded deaths mounted continually. A one-sided war with few casualties among the Cuban Army. The majority of victims were just civilians with no direct involvement with the guerilla insurgency. Whether suspected of supporting rebel activity or simply a means of inflicting terror among became irrelevant.

The longer the conflict continues with no successful strategy chasing an unseen enemy, government security forces became increasing frustrated. Not only commanders like Colonel Cowley, but soldiers of all ranks under their command. Brutality becoming commonplace with acts of horrific sadism more frequent. Landeira's personal experiences fighting with Italian partisans against the Waffen SS bore out the same pattern of behavior.

Landeira therefore structured the next piece making Colonel Cowley and the vicious leader of the paramilitary Los Tigres, Rolando Masferrer the most recognizable figures of Batista's reign of terror in eastern Cuba. Vasquez produced exceptionally strong material on the Carinthia Massacre with impressive graphic photos. Antidotal material produced by his reporters on Cowley and Masferrer provided grisly examples of their depravity. The objective intended to jar the American reader from the welcoming tourist view presented of Havana. Display the irony of a greater Cuba immersed in a growing civil war seen in juxtaposition to the glamorous tropical gambling playground.

Following posting the article to Toussaint by mail from Miami, Landeira chose the opportunity to meet with the managing director of the Miami Herald. Citing the death of his father and family obligations to the Cuban family businesses, he requested an indefinite leave of absence from full-time reporting. He would file the occasional story from Cuba when possible but travel to other Latin American countries was currently not possible.

Landeira also added, "The other reality is the inability to publish newsworthy material under Batista's censorship for anyone reporting from within Cuba. Herbert Matthews' Castro interview in the mountains in February was a one-off."

Returning to Havana, he suggested to Emilia a long weekend sail down the coast to the barrier islands of the Archipiélago de Sábana on Cuba's northern shore. Unpopulated islands with pristine beaches. A natural barrier against bad weather in the waterway between the islands and the mainland. An isolated getaway in paradise sleeping on the sailboat with the nights cooled by the ocean. A perfect respite. An opportunity for uninterrupted intimacy.

Emilia loved the idea since becoming comfortable with the heeling over of the sailboat as it filled the sails with wind propelling it forward. He assured her at night they would anchor in calm water of a cove protected by the prevailing winds on the leeward side of the islands. About a hundred miles to the east. A day's sailing one-way with a good wind.

****

The weather turned warm and the sea was running with modest swells with a ten-knot wind out of the northwest. Perfect conditions to make the run down the coast. As they exited the shelter of the protected small bay into the Caribbean, the *Elegante Bellezza* took hold of the wind like a thoroughbred leaving the gate.

"This is a beautiful day," she said. "I'm glad you suggested we get away."

Seated next to him behind the wheel, she leaned over and kissed him.

As the sun turned warmer, Emilia shed her terrycloth beach jacket. She wore a two-piece white swimsuit and sandals with floppy hat and sunglasses. He took in her body with a smile. "You look like a movie star. Put on a lot of sun lotion. Easy to get burned with the sun reflecting off the water."

He watched her oil her exposed skin with pleasure.

"You too. I'll do it. Just pay attention to your driving."

He enjoyed her touching his arms and face.

"Thank you," he said. How about some coffee? There is a thermos down below and coffee mugs."

Settled into the rhythm of sailing enjoying their coffee, he brought up the subject of his father. Considering her strong bond with her father, she must find his contentious relationship difficult to understand. As it was for him. Impossible to explain the clash of two strong-willed people to someone coming from an entirely different experience. Max Landeira was not necessarily a bad father. Just a bad pairing with the equally difficult personality of his only son.

"You never asked why I implicated my father in the Miami Herald article I wrote about Mafia investment in Havana?"

She shrugged. "I knew you were not on the best of terms. As a journalist, you uncovered information that also involved your father. You did not directly accuse him of wrongdoing. However your journalistic integrity dictated you could not cover it up."

"He was dirty, Emilia. Money laundering and bribery. I suspected that for some time. He angered me by rationalizing what he did as nothing more than typical legal work. Lied about his active involvement using his bank. Using the bank as he did represented direct participation in criminal activity. Ever wonder why I went after the Mafia so aggressively?"

"I assumed your sense of outrage that they were using profits from criminal activities in the United States to corrupt Cuba?"

"That too. If you looked at my reporting, you can see I went after Santo Trafficante with particular vengeance. That was partly personal.

"I grew up in Tampa, Florida. Tampa not only has a large Cuban immigrant community, but also a large Italian community. Specifically Sicilian ancestry. I had a lot of Italian friends from an early age. That is how I learned Italian. Easy enough because of the similarity of words with Spanish. At the time, I did not understand my father's association with Italians. In fact, I only learned that after my Uncle Tomás revealed the story of our success in the rum business.

"My uncle related how my father increased business during Prohibition by supplying the organized crime family of Santo Trafficante Sr. with rum. Trafficante controlled Tampa bootlegging and gambling throughout the prohibition era. I recall my Italian schoolmates pointing to kids of the Mafiosi. The Trafficante Mob invoked fear in the Italian community. The son of the mob boss, Santo Jr. was a few years older so I did not know him back then.

"I also never knew of my father's involvement in bootlegging at the time. Tampa was a *wet* city during Prohibition. A corrupt city. Police and judges on the take. Everybody drank. Even us teenagers. Only later did I realize the business of illegal alcohol during Prohibition created the modern day Mafia. Perverting civil society by the accompanying corruption.

"Coming to Havana as a journalist, the open secret of the Mafia laundering their dirty money offshore by transforming Havana into a gambling mecca seemed fair game. Exposed to the scope of today's organized crime in congressional hearings several years ago, the American public sees them for what they are. Unable to report on Cuban political violence because of censorship, I instead went after the Mafia.

"I confronted my father. He sidestepped by saying he only created companies for the purpose of investing in Cuba. Claims he worked only with attorneys, not knowing the actual source of funds. Acknowledged that Mafia figures may have been involved. Showed me a list of shareholder names in these companies he created. I took that information and dug deeper. Father knew I would likely pursue the matter but didn't seem to care. Until I uncovered the involvement of Banco Crédito Industrial y Mercantil de Habana. Max Landeira's own bank. Seems my father created the means for laundering Mafia money into Havana investment and paying Batista his share in bribery.

"Now I know how my father died. Just not why."

"What are you talking about, Bart?"

"The Mafia killed him."

"What?"

"On the night he died, his Tampa office was burglarized. I met with the local police. Files stolen. From a secretary's list, the stolen files involved those front companies my father created for Santo Trafficante Jr. Then in his private files in his Havana office, I discovered information suggesting some rift between him and Trafficante."

"Why would they want to kill him? Weren't they partners of sorts?"

"That I do not know. It bothers me though to think I might have had something to do with his death because of what I published."

She stroked his cheek with the backs of her fingers. "No reason to think that. The Mafia receives bad press in the American newspapers all the time. If it was their doing, it was something else your father did."

"I don't know. That attack on us outside *Casa Maribel* was clearly the doing of the Mafia. They are murders. Vicious thugs that don't always act rationally."

255

To change the subject, he said, "What's done is done. Just wanted you to know. Although my father consorted with criminals, that was apart from his involvement with Landeira Grupo. Landeira is a solid company having nothing to do with my father's legal consulting practice. Your father is secure in a legitimate corporation.

"Anyway, that is why I agreed to help with managing the corporation's financial affairs until we find a permanent solution. I care for you, Emilia. It is important that you feel good about your father joining Landeira. I have an obligation to him and your family to see the business continues to prosper.

Emilia replied, "Thank you. I will do all I can to help you. My father is happy with his expanded role. So sorry for all the pain you feel about your father. You are a good man. Another reason I love you."

A full day of sailing passed quickly as they talked all day. Emilia felt comfortable enough to take the helm and keep on course as he went below and made them lunch with cold beers.

They arrived at their destination at dusk passing into the Bahia de Cardenas, well protected by the barrier islands. A short time later, he located a secluded anchorage in a small cove of the irregular shoreline of uninhabited Cayo Cruz del Padre.

Bart said. "We have steaks for tonight. Tomorrow, freshly caught fresh is on the menu. What do you say to a drink?"

"How about a swim first. I feel sticky with all the sun oil."

"Good idea."

She looked around. No other boats, no lights. "Are we totally alone out here?"

"Yep."

"Then I do not need a swim suit."

Bart grinned. "No you don't."

She gave him a teasing expression as she undid her swimsuit top. She knew the sight of her breasts aroused him.

While she wiggled out of the lower half of her swimsuit, he shed his shirt and pulled down his swim trunks. His full erection prompted her to say, "Keep that for after our swim."

The swim was short. More rubbing and groping of each other's bodies. Climbing back onboard, they immediately went below and toweled off before climbing into the bed.

The next day was clear with few clouds. However, later in the afternoon, Bart checked the U.S. Coast Guard's marine shortwave band for the weather. Not good news. A weather front was forecast to begin moving west before turning north on a typical track up the west coast of Florida. By the afternoon of the following day, they could see winds exceeding 25 knots. Categorized as a tropical depression, not yet tropical storm strength, but enough that he did not want to be out with Emilia under those conditions.

Instead of spending the second night in this secluded bay, he decided to get a head start back to Havana by sailing to the port of Matanza a couple of hours west. Matanza had a small harbor where they could anchor. He would check the weather early in the morning before attempting the run to Havana 90 miles further west. If the weather did not cooperate, they could wait it out in Matanza.

After dinner in town, they spent a quiet night on the anchored sailboat. The next morning before dawn, he checked the marine weather band again. Nothing had changed. They should be able to get ahead of the wind, especially if the storm track turned north to go across Key West as forecast. Still a day's sailing but at least they were running with the wind.

A couple of hours later, the wind began to pick up gradually. Landeira's barometer indicated a drop in pressure soon after leaving Matanza. Still no change however from the prior marine forecast. Two hours later, the forecast changed dramatically.

Several storm cells located 50 miles south-southwest of the Bahamas have consolidated raising wind speeds gusting over 40 knots. Upgraded now to a tropical storm, the cell is moving in a westerly direction at 15 knots. The storm is expected to make a turn north sometime in the next few hours to directly make landfall at Key West. Wind advisories for small vessels within 30 miles of the north coast of Cuba from eastern Cuba to Havana indicating seas forecast with 2 to 3 meter swells with the possibility of shortening dominant wave periods.

Shit! The *Elegante Bellezza* could handle those kinds of seas but it would be a hell of ride even for him. It would terrify Emilia. It was now a matter of timing. What level of wind would they see before reaching Havana? Too many variables to calculate. The map showed no sheltered anchorages until they reached the small fishing fleet harbor of Cojímar east of Havana harbor. That was still hours away.

To Emilia he said, "Weather conditions are turning worse. The marine weather forecast just changed significantly. Good that we got a head start by spending the night in Matanza."

"Are we in danger?"

"No. Not at all. This boat can handle conditions like this. We are going to experience larger waves but I don't want you to worry. I've sailed all my life. Been in worse weather in smaller boats. Going to keep all the sails up to make the fastest time possible to try outrunning the storm. If luck is with us, the storm will to turn to the north which will give us some relief if we can get further to the west."

Luck was not with them. The barometric pressure continued to drop. The marine band reported the storm strengthening. Winds upgraded to over 50 knots. They began getting the first bands of rain.

"In the closet next to the stairs there is foul weather gear. You'll feel better up here with me where you can see what is going on but it is going to get very wet."

She did as instructed without uttering a word. Before donning the water repellant hooded parkas, he handed her a life vest. She sat down close to him.

In a cabinet below the seat, he extracted two webbed canvas military belts. "Put this around your waist. Just another safety precaution."

"What is this for?"

"To secure you to the boat. In case a wave catches the boat wrong it insures you cannot be washed overboard."

"Oh god! Is it going to get that bad?"

He secured her by attaching a short clip line to the safety belt as well as his own. "All this is just precaution. Unfortunately, I expect the weather it to get worse. We will be okay though. I can handle this and so can the boat."

His assurances may have helped but she remained terrified.

The situation did get worse. Although confident, the situation called on all his seamanship skills to battle the elements. Not alarmed, sailing in intense weather was nevertheless a high anxiety experience.

Checking his chronometer and pitometer gauge to measure their now with a fluctuating surface speed as the vessel rose and descended the mounting wave troughs, he was looking for landmarks or navigation beacons. Estimating their position within a couple of miles was the best he could do. Soon he visually identified a navigation beacon of what should be the inlet to Cojímar harbor. Ahead of him was a fishing yacht battling the high seas.

If correct, it was possibly another hour to reach his slip west of Havana harbor. He was not about to put Emilia through anymore of this. Without checking the radio weather again, he suspected the heavier weather meant the storm continued strengthening or did not make the turn north as forecasted. Whatever the reason, he misjudged and should have stayed the night in Matanza. Overconfidence killed a lot of sailors. This was a good blow and for someone unexperienced on the water like Emilia, pure terror. He felt terrible for unnecessarily putting her through this ordeal.

As they made the turn into the shelter of the harbor, he dropped the jib and started the engine. following the fishing yacht. No other vessels foolish enough to be on the water in this kind of storm.

Rain began coming down at a savage rate.

Once inside the protection of the small Cojímar harbor she looked at him. "Never a dull moment being around you, Bart Landeira. Do you always flirt with danger?"

Although she was making light of this and the incident of the attack weeks earlier for his sake, he felt like a real shit for putting her through this.

Shaking his head, "I am so sorry. My mistake. Should know better. Weather is unpredictable no matter what meteorologists forecast. Should have played it safe and spent the night in Matanza. Can you forgive me?"

"Of course I forgive you," kissing him on the lips. With a grin she added, "You rarely play things safe do you?"

* * * *

As they motored slowly into Cojímar, Landeira began searching for a place to tie his boat to a dock or anchor. All available space seemed taken with all the fishing fleet in port riding out the storm. As Landeira pulled closer to the fishing yacht he followed into harbor, a closer look revealed a beautiful boat. A distinctive black hull with red mahogany decking. The transom stenciled *Pilar, Key West*.

The *Pilar* docked at what seemed the only remaining slip in the harbor. From the back, a large man with a white beard waved his arm. Seemed to be beckoning Landeira toward the *Pilar*.

Landeira motored slowly coming alongside the transom of the *Pilar*. A small Cuban of indeterminate age jumped down from the higher deck of the motor launch onto the bow of the *Elegante Bellezza*. Holding a line in his hand, he secured the sailboat to the *Pilar*. Another Cuban threw him a second line and he then walked toward the stern without holding on to anything as the sailboat rocked in the swells. Reaching the stern well, he made the sailboat fast with the second line secured to a cleat then turned toward Landeira and Emilia.

Removing his beat-up straw hat revealed a rough-hewed sun-weathered face of someone part of the sea. Grinning broadly revealed a couple of missing teeth. In Spanish he said, "Señor Hemingway said to tie your boat to the stern of his. I am Gregorio Fuentes."

"*Gracias*, Señor Fuentes. I am Bartolo Landeira and this is Emilia Montero. Did you say the bearded gentlemen's name is Hemingway?"

260

"Si. Ernesto. The great writer. Papa wishes you to come aboard. Wants to meet this fine sailor that wrestled mother nature to a draw is what Papa said."

Looking over to Emilia, "Our day becomes even more interesting. You know who Ernest Hemingway is?"

"Of course I do. Everyone in Havana knows the great Nobel laureate novelist lives here. I read many of his books."

After shedding their foul weather gear and changing into regular clothing below deck, they immerged and made their way to board the *Pilar*. Hemingway dropped a ladder over the stern allowing them to step up over the transom into the *Pilar*. Landeira steadied Emilia from below while Hemingway reached down taking a firm hold of her wrist.

As Landeira swung his leg over, Hemingway was already engaging with Emilia protected from the rain under the yacht's cabin roof. Dressed in a faded denim work shirt, shorts, and sandals, Hemingway kissed her hand in European style. To Landeira, he appeared older up close in person than in magazine photos.

Turning to Landeira, Hemingway gripped his hand and placed his left hand on Landeira's shoulder. "That was some sailing. Don't mind admitting that I was becoming uncomfortable, but here you are in a sailboat still taking the wind to make the fastest headway. Carlos and Gregorio said we should stay close in case you got into trouble. We throttled back to keep an eye on you before entering the harbor."

"I appreciate that Mr. Hemingway."

"Call me Ernest. And you are?"

"Bart Landeira. That is Emilia Montero."

"Well, I tell you, you did not seem to need our help. You've been in bad weather before under sail?"

"Oh yes. Most of the time being foolish or careless. Today was bad judgement."

"What did Emilia think?"

Bart rolled his eyes, "I think she was terrified. I dock the *Elegante Bellezza* in the inlet near the Torreón de la Chorrera. Maybe an hour's sailing from here in this weather. I wasn't going to make another mistake and have her endure more of this blow."

"Nonetheless, impressive seamanship, Bart. I can tell you that Carlos and Gregorio were not having any fun out there once the wind came up, and they have lived on the water all their lives. My fault also for staying out longer than we should have fishing for marlin. They know the sea and don't need weather forecasts to read a storm on the horizon or feel the drop in pressure. We are going to a bar close by so I can make amends to my friends for my own foolishness. Celebrate our good fortune with liquor and a good meal. Will you and Emilia join us?"

Turning to Emilia, she said, "Yes, I would like that. I could use a couple of drinks right now."

Drinks turned into more than a couple.

Carlos Gutierrez and Gregorio Fuentes were former fishing boat captains now in the employ of Hemingway. Clearly more than hired help. When they talked about marlin fishing, it was among friends and equals. Hemingway just as happy to listen to the fishing wisdom of these two old salts.

Landeira watched as Emilia found ways of contributing to their fishing talk with insightful questions. He could see the reciprocated affection of Carlos and Gregorio to this beautiful educated Cuban woman treating them as equals with respect for what they knew.

As for Hemingway, he fell under her spell. Likely, a combination of her strong willed personality combined with a worldliness and undoubtedly her exceptional looks. Hemingway liked women, especially smart women.

After dinner next door, they returned to the same bar where they resumed drinking. Landeira sensed Hemingway liked the working class atmosphere of Cojímar because no one fawned over his celebrity status. Fishing for marlin for many years, he earned a reputation as an accomplished fisherman not some dilettante rich American.

Somewhere in the flow of conversation, Hemingway asked Landeira, "Were you in the war?"

"Yes. From the beginning."

"What branch?"

"The American Army, but mostly the Office of Strategic Services. The OSS."

Hemingway looked surprised. "God lord. My oldest son Jack was in the OSS. Where did you serve?"

"North Africa then Italy."

"Jack parachuted into France more than once. Captured in the Vosges in 1944 he spent a terrible six months in a German POW camp. Lost 70 pounds. Did you get those scars in the war?"

Landeira nodded. Seeing Hemingway was slightly drunk, "Perhaps another time we can share war stories, Ernest. Right now, I see Emilia is exhausted and I'm not far behind. Can I leave my boat tied up to yours until I return in the morning?"

Slurring his words slightly, Hemingway said, "Carlos is going to stay on the Pilar tonight. We are taking it out again tomorrow and he needs to get us resupplied. It is entirely safe here. Gregorio will drive us all home tonight."

On the way to Emilia's in Hemingway's Buick, Hemingway turned to Landeira and Emilia in the backseat, "This has been a helluva great day even if I didn't catch a marlin. What about coming out to my place next weekend and spending the night. A big place with guesthouse and swimming pool surrounded by lush gardens south of the city. A great place to work and enjoy life. My wife Mary will love having both of you?"

Landeira looked over at Emilia. She gave a subtle expression with her eyes signifying okay.

"We'd love to, Ernest."

"Excellent!" He handed Landeira a card with the address and telephone number for Finca Vigía.

Chapter 19

Emilia recovered from the sailing ordeal with no ill feelings towards Landeira despite his repeated apologies for underestimating the unpredictability of the weather. The following weekend, they took up Hemingway on his invitation for a weekend at his villa.

Mary Welsh Hemingway was Hemingway's fourth wife, married ten years ago. An attractive woman, her diminutive stature made more pronounced when standing next to Hemingway's large six-foot frame. A former war correspondent, she met Hemingway in London during the war. Prior to the war, Welsh worked as a reporter for the *Chicago Daily News* and later for the London *Daily Express*.

Purchased by his third wife in 1940, Mary was proud of what she did to make Finca Vigía the perfect place for Ernest to write. A brightly decorated airy place, bustling with staff. She explained that Ernest's generosity spread to offering more locals employment than needed. Asked about the workshop tower at the front of the property, Mary said, "I had that built for Papa as a secluded place to work. However, he prefers to write in his bedroom. The tower is now largely the domain for our many cats. But Finca Vigía has been good for Papa's work. Here he wrote *The Old Man and the Sea*, and *Across the River and into the Trees*."

Ernest insisted on showing Landeira and Emilia about the estate while Mary assisted their cook with preparing lunch. A true tropical paradise with tennis court and swimming pool maintained by a crew of landscape workers. A former one-car garage converted into a guesthouse. Coming to the swimming pool. Hemingway pointed. "Ava Gardner once swam here in the nude."

Emilia raised an eyebrow. Hemingway made no effort to conceal his appreciation of attractive women. Emilia was certainly that, along with a sharp mind.

Mary served lunch outside in a shaded veranda. Cuban chicken soup followed by Cuban-style paella. Served with a good French Sancerre.

Following lunch with two bottles of wine, talk naturally turned to journalism and politics Ernest said, "We read your articles in the Miami Herald. Outstanding investigative journalism in your campaign of going after the Mafia. Especially intrigued with your first person account of the confrontation with those armed men. Claimed it was the Mafia's doing. If correct, how did you manage to get out of that? You were vague on details in the newspaper. How did one of the assailants die?"

Landeira looked over at Emilia. She nodded with an expression of *go ahead*.

"I killed him."

Both Hemingways looked startled by Landeira's blunt pronouncement.

"Your account and even the official police version suggested he died at the hands of the police," Ernest said.

"Thought it better to avoid explaining what actually happened and openly contradict Colonel Esteban's version."

"Sonofabitch. You put down two armed men with your bare hands and killed one? How did you accomplish that?"

"OSS training. Muscle memory honed from endless repetition."

Ernest replied skeptically, "My son Jack described receiving rigorous hand-to-hand combat training. Never went into specific details. Yet taking out two armed assailants still seems a remarkable feat."

"Not for someone well trained against incompetent thugs. At some other time I will show you some of the techniques they taught us and how this confrontation went down."

Mary said, "And you believe it was the Mafia who did this?"

Landeira nodded. "Hired muscle. Local Cuban criminals. Probably intended as intimidation."

"Did they say anything to you?" Ernest asked.

"Didn't give them the chance. I wasn't about to let them lead Emilia and me away at gunpoint. When the guy pressed his gun in my back, I seized the opportunity and counterattacked immediately."

Ernest nodded with a grim expression of approval.

"You have seen your share of combat, Ernest. There is no such thing as giving the enemy a chance. OSS training teaches you to look for an opportunity then act aggressively. The objective is to kill or incapacitate, not merely to defend."

Mary let out a deep sigh. "I thought it fearless going after the Mafia in the press from here in Havana. Although you deftly skirted the obvious fact that Batista is in bed with the American Mafia, that experience proves you are playing a dangerous game."

"As a journalist yourself, Mary, you know the obsession when going after a story. Like a moth, it's about gauging how close you can get to the flame," Landeira said.

Turning the conversation to politics, Emilia asked the Hemingways, "You have made your home in Cuba for many years. How do you feel about the Batista regime?"

Ernest answered, "The political violence is troubling. Corruption unfortunately is a fact of Cuban political life. The prior governments of Grau and Prio were also notoriously corrupt. However, I cannot change any of that. I live here because I love the people, Cuban culture, and the sea. The best I can do is to avoid all contact with anyone political."

"What do you think about the revolutionary movements? Fidel Castro's M-26-7 and the Revolutionary Directorate," Emilia asked.

Ernest replied, "I embrace their idealism for a better Cuba. I also don't harbor the common fears of socialistic movements necessarily becoming communist. These movements profess basic human rights. Yet if they were to take power, they might also become totalitarian. That is the most common outcome. I therefore remain, neutral on the subject."

Landeira thought that was weasel language coming from Ernest Hemingway. For someone that fought against Fascism in Spain then covered the war in Europe against the Nazis, remarkable how he could choose to live under Batista's dictatorship. He liked Hemingway but found it difficult to reconcile his political apathy. On the other hand, as an international celebrity, he could not live as he did in Cuba if seen as favoring any political position. Hemingway's avoidance of government figures, or making public comments made practical sense. Just because Landeira chose to oppose Batista by covert action did not give him a platform to moralize.

Emilia was quick to put forth her own view. "Cubans are not idealists. People anywhere denied basic human rights simply want to live a decent life. Food, security, a future for their children. I am Cuban. Even those like me living in Havana cannot appreciate the extent of Batista's oppression. Cuban security forces murder people daily in the rural areas of the eastern part of the island. I can identify with the aspirations of revolutionists like Fidel Castro and the Revolutionary Directorate. Obviously left leaning politically, they are at heart Cuban nationalists. Batista is not a nationalist, just a greedy power-obsessed dictator. I see myself as a Cuban nationalist. I am optimistic someday of seeing Cuba governed by a functioning democracy.

"The Cuban press cannot write about Batista's pursuit of violent means to suppress opposition because of censorship. Batista is careful not to tarnish the glamorous image of Havana. Bad for gambling tourist business."

Ernest said, "Well said, Emilia." Turning to Landeira, "What do you say, Bart? By the way, please don't publish any of my comments. I make it a point of avoiding interviews, and certainly not commenting on politics. I have enough enemies already."

Landeira smiled. "No fear there, Ernest. This is just talk among friends. I agree with Emilia. Batista is a corrupt vicious pig. No different from Trujillo who everyone condemns as a murderer. I got a taste of that when I went there to research a piece on a missing dissident. Got myself deported. Had I not been American, might have suffered far worse.

"That is the underlying problem. America controls the economy of Cuba. An American colony really. Like any colonial power, America props up Batista as it does Trujillo. Funds Batista's military and secret police. My angst is with the Eisenhower administration. I left government service to take up journalism because I disagreed with U.S. foreign policy around the world."

"What did you do in the government?" Ernest asked.

"Classified work for the State Department. Still bound by secrecy. I can tell you generally I was involved in regime change. Putting American puppets in power under the pretext of preventing countries going communist."

"What countries?" Mary asked.

"Unfortunately those are details I cannot divulge. Suffice it say that is why I resigned."

Landeira avoided identifying being a CIA field operative for its shadowy connotation. Still bound under the National Security Act, claiming he worked for the State Department implied a cloak of respectability.

Ernest said, "Yet you still chose to make your home in Cuba."

"True. For much the same reasons you do. I was born in The United States but I am as much Cuban as American. Spent summers growing up at the family sugar cane estate in Camagüey. Covering Latin America for the Miami Herald, Havana seemed more interesting than living in Miami.

"My situation became more complicated following the death of an uncle then my father. My father maintained his position as chief financial officer for the family's collection of businesses in Cuba for the last twenty years. Following their deaths, I felt an obligation to help out with the management void in the Landeira enterprises."

Emilia easily held her own in the conversations given her broad worldviews and her surprising familiarity with American foreign policy. As to American involvement in Cuba, she did not attempt to conceal her critical opinions.

The afternoon passed by quickly. Emilia and Landeira chose a swim in the pool to offer a break in the conversation and to avoid further drinking as late afternoon approached. The rumors about Hemingway's drinking proved to be no exaggeration.

It turned out Emilia was better read on Hemingway's novels than Landeira. Enough for her to ask Hemingway insightful questions about his personal experiences contributing to various novels.

"Bart brings to my mind your character Colonel Cantwell in *Across the River and into the Trees*. Listening to his stories of World War Two in Italy and the wound on his hand," Emilia said.

She did not add and *the death of Bart's first love*. Nor did she add the rumored salacious stories about Hemingway's infatuation with Adriana Ivancich. A flirtatious teenager when they met in 1948 at a duck shooting party outside of Venice clearly became the basis of the novel. Like Hemingway, the damaged fifty-year-old protagonist and eighteen-year-old Contessa Renata the love interest character with duck hunting forming the story's backdrop. Bart's wartime reality and the dark tone of Hemingway's novel both Shakespearean tragedies.

"I thought the same thing last week when we first met. Bart is a true warrior. Knows the worst of war. He spent years in Italy with an obvious fondness for the culture and people. Italy entered my blood at an early age. Spain and Cuba came later. Bart is a journalist and so was I for twenty-five years."

"Did you pattern your Cantwell character on anyone?" Emilia asked.

"More a composite embellished with imagination," Hemingway said.

"Some say there is much of you revealed in the character," Emilia said.

Hemingway flashed his famous engaging grin, "Well if so, I hope I come to a better end than Colonel Cantwell. Wish I'd met Bart at the end of the war. Could have created a helluva protagonist out of his exploits. Exaggerated whatever it was he did after the war that he says is still classified. Perhaps made his character a Cold War spy."

Mary prepared a wonderful dinner of sea bass that evening on the veranda. More wine and too much liquor. Slightly drunk by the time they retired to the guesthouse, Landeira and Emilia both remarked about enjoying a full day of endlessly stimulating conversation. Once you got past the idea you were talking to a living literary icon, Ernest Hemingway was engaging. While opinionated, he genuinely listened to those he respected. A raconteur with a wealth of captivating personal stories populated with famous people and interesting locations.

Making their goodbyes the next morning after breakfast, both Hemingway's embraced each of them. The Hemingways were leaving Cuba to spend the summer months in Sun Valley Idaho. Embracing their newfound friendship, the foursome pledged to get together on their return to Cuba.

* * * *

As promised to his fellow conspirators, Landeira arranged an interview with the new U.S. Ambassador Earl Smith. His objective to get some idea of Washington's view toward Cuba. What does the U.S. administration make of the current political situation in Cuba? What are Smith's specific views? Do Landeira's attacks on the Mafia provoke any action within the U.S. government? What about the graphic accounts of violent repressive measures of Cuban security forces appearing regularly in the international news?

According to the Miami Herald's research department, Smith was a former Wall Street investment broker. His only government experience was with the War Production Board in the early months of World War Two before joining the army. With no diplomatic experience, nor fluency in Spanish, a seemingly unusual choice. However, considering his overtly pro-Batista predecessor it might suggest a shifting of the Eisenhower administration's faithful support of Batista.

Because of the overwhelming influence of the United States on Cuba, a syndicated editorial recently made the cynical statement that the second most influential person in Havana to the Cuban president was the U.S. ambassador. Cuba's status as a defacto U.S. colony obvious by any metric made the statement more than mere hyperbole.

The new CIA head-of-station Walter Peterson briefed Smith on Landeira's background. "Mr. Landeira has a most unusual background, Mr. Ambassador. U.S. citizen. Holds a law degree. He is ex-CIA. Stayed in U.S. intelligence after three years in the field as an OSS field operative during World War Two. Multiple decorations. Rank of major. Served in Italy working with Italian partisans after Italy changed sides in 1943. He remained in fieldwork with the CIA as part of the covert operations wing of the Office of Policy Coordination.

"Quit abruptly while involved with a classified operation in Guatemala in 1954. Never gave a reason other than making anti-dotal comments about American foreign policy favoring dictators. Landeira refused any exit interviews telling his superiors to go to hell.

"Landeira is a long-time correspondent for the Miami Herald. Part of his cover with the CIA. Currently involved with the management of his family's Cuban enterprises after the deaths of his father and uncle. Most recently, he published a series of articles exposing details of American organized crime investment in Havana. Probably doesn't play well with Batista since he and his cronies are obviously on the take."

Smith agreed to the interview after briefed on the Landeira's background. Cuban-American with U.S. citizenship with business interests in Cuba. Part of an influential old landholding Cuban family. According to Peterson, Landeira's recently deceased father was a well-connected lawyer with ties to American Mafia investment in the Havana hotel and gambling industry. Yet the son is a vocal critic in the press. The contradictions made Landeira someone of interest.

Landeira showed up at the U.S. Embassy overlooking the Gulf of Mexico on the Malecón. The seven-story concrete and glass modern-brutalist style building built in 1953. Emphasizing the construction materials with minimalist functionality, it was just plain ugly. All the more so when contrasted with the old world architectural elegance of Havana and the new elegant five-star hotels.

The seventh floor corner office of the ambassador however held a spectacular view of the water. Ushered into the office, Smith came around from behind his desk to shake Landeira's hand. Smith then introduced a younger man, "This is Walter Peterson. Walter is second secretary for political affairs. Like me, also new to Havana. However, unlike me, Walter is fluent in Spanish."

After exchanging pleasantries, Landeira launched into his questions. "As you know, I have written extensively on American organized crime investment in hotels and casinos in Havana. How does the Administration view the laundering of criminal profits in a recipient country of so much U.S. foreign aid?"

Smith responded, "Unfortunately, your allegations are correct, there is little we can do in Cuba other than lodge protests."

"With the political and economic clout of the United States, it would appear easy enough to exert meaningful pressure," Landeira responded.

"More complicated than that I believe. To be credible, still requires evidence to make a forceful case. Money laundering is a problem to prosecute in the United States. Certainly troubling that it might represent significant investment in the Cuban hospitality industry, but the political situation here is of larger concern to Washington."

Diplomatic non-speak to avoid an inconvenient truth by pivoting to another subject. "Let me ask you something, Mr. Landeira, what is your read on Cuban political turmoil? I sense you are no fan of President Batista."

Landeira said, "Batista is a despot. He has no support other than those profiting by his corruption. Political opposition is the understood norm throughout most of the population. The only distinction is whether passive or active.

"The violent repression of the security forces following a failed assassination attempt drove the urban opposition of the Revolutionary Directorate into the Escambray Mountains. Fidel Castro's M-26-7 rural revolutionary guerrillas are now firmly ensconced in the Sierra Maestra Mountains. Batista's forces are unable to dislodge them principally because of widespread support among the general population. Therefore, Batista resorts to terror. Tries to conceal the excesses of state sponsored violence by press censorship. That is no longer working. The rise of a new opposition force using the name Venganza de Martí is finding ways of smuggling news and photographs out of Cuba into the American press."

Peterson asked, "Yes, I have seen those articles. In your view does Castro's revolutionary movement present a serious threat to the Batista government?"

"Depends on your definition of threat," Landeira said. "Castro is waging a guerrilla war. That requires the active support of the population. Their hearts and minds. A source of new recruits. Food. Intelligence. Castro does not need significant military victories to keep his movement alive. The government's inability to crush him increases his stature."

"Is Castro a Marxist?" Peterson asked.

Landeira shook his head. "I have no idea. That is the problem with U.S. foreign policy. Any movement pressing for social equality or human rights raises the fear of communism. Things like land reform become a red flag for socialism. Washington makes no distinction between socialism and communism. Hence support always favors right wing totalitarianism."

Smith spoke up. "For a reporter you sound like an intellectual. What do you then see as the political outcome for Cuba?"

Landeira answered, "I would not attempt to make any predictions. In the case of Cuba, that may rest largely with Washington. In many respects, Cuba functions as a U.S. colony. The United States continues to prop up Rafael Trujillo's reign as dictator of the Dominican Republic for the last twenty-five years. Batista can only last if sustained by U.S. support."

Smith said. "Seems as if I have been interviewing you, Mr. Landeira. The United States government does not speak with one voice. I am new to Cuba. I prefer to speak my own mind. Not probably the best qualifications for a diplomatic posting but here I am.

"In the couple of weeks I have been in Cuba, I sense that Havana is another world compared to the vast rural areas of the island. I was astounded to learn that the length of the island was over 700 miles. Several of my staff suggested I get out of Havana to understand the full scope of Cuba."

Landeira seized on the opportunity to expand his relationship with Smith. No telling when he might need help if he continued with his subversive activity. "Let me make you an offer, Mr. Ambassador. With the death of my father, I have taken on temporary duties with our family's corporation Landeira Grupo. Our sugar operations are located in the Province of Camagüey. I must make a visit there at the end of the month. My uncle and cousin represent Landeira senior management. As part of the growers association, I could arrange for an opportunity for you to meet important members of the group. An informal exchange of views. I suspect their collective views on Cuban politics, U.S. foreign policy, and any other subject will likely be different from mine. Although I am Cuban, like you, Mr. Ambassador, I am relatively new to Cuba."

"An interesting offer, Mr. Landeira. How do you travel there?"

"By plane. It's 350 miles from Havana."

Smith looked at Peterson who nodded, then said, "Let me check my schedule. I am booked with endless social commitments, but your suggestion sounds intriguing. Is this an area under threat from the insurgents?"

"Not as yet. For now Castro's M-26-7 guerrillas are operating further east in the province of Oriente."

Before leaving, Landeira and Smith settled on a departure date of Monday morning 29 July from Havana to the city of Camagüey. Landeira offered to meet Smith and Peterson upon their arrival and drive them to the family estate for the growers' meeting in the afternoon. He and Emilia would fly in on Saturday to conduct a financial review of Landeira Grupo with his Uncle Enrique and cousin Rafael.

* * * *

The family was most gracious toward Emilia and to Bart for filling the void left by his father. Landeira Rum was doing well under the management of Augustin Montero. Overall, the corporation continued to do well. Bart made it clear that he retained Emilia's law firm to assist him in his financial management role. He sidestepped any discussion about his father's law firm staff in Havana. Independent from Landeira Grupo, he dismissed the staff, wanting nothing connected to his father's sordid past associations to remain.

Along with financial consulting, he would outsource corporate legal work Emilia's law practice. Bart left the impression that Emilia was here in a professional capacity. Both agreed it better to avoid bringing up their romantic relationship.

He convinced the Board to liquidate their holdings in Banco Crédito Industrial y Mercantil de Habana. Avoiding knowledge of the bank's participation in Mafia money laundering, he simply said that without his father as bank president, it represented yet another management vacancy and an uncertain stockholding investment risk. It was not their core business. Without stating his actual reason, he intended to make a new relationship with an American branch bank.

The meeting with Ambassador Smith would take place in the great room of the family's estate house reminiscent of a great

275

antebellum plantation house of the American South. Smith and Peterson would spend the night at the estate. Six other large sugarcane landowners would join them for lunch followed by discussions throughout the afternoon. The meeting advertised as an opportunity for sharing views regarding the current Cuban political crisis with the U.S. ambassador. Landeira was curious as to the political position of these prominent agrarian businessmen toward the Batista regime, some already feeling the effects of insurgency-related violence. All understood the influence the U.S. ambassador.

* * * *

The meeting of the sugarcane growers and Ambassador Smith went much as Landeira expected. The growers, including his uncle and cousin held a common resentment for Fidel Castro's populist rebellion. While Landeira saw the abject poverty of workers in the cane fields and sugar mills, they saw a threat to their way of life.

However, they collectively criticized the Cuban security forces methods to put down the insurrectionists. The unrestrained violent reign of terror was counterproductive. The campaign inflicted on the general population only served to deepen support for the rebels. Furthermore, the Cuban Army was incompetent. Even with military aid from the United States, they proved incapable of eliminating a rebel force of only a few hundred. All voiced the fact that hatred for Fulgencio Batista was so pervasive that the situation could only worsen as long as he remained in power.

For Landeira, a powerful message to the U.S. ambassador. Equally important, Landeira now had the ear of someone with vast power in Cuba. A relationship with the American ambassador complimented his press campaign efforts meant to influence American public opinion.

Over the hours of the informal gathering, Walter Peterson spent considerable time with Landeira. He appeared particularly interested in Landeira's views on how Fidel Castro was able to make international news while representing such an insignificantly tangible threat to the Batista government.

Landeira knew full well the reason. The same kind of tactics waged by the CIA.

"Propaganda. Castro is brilliant at public relations. So good, that following imprisonment for his first act of rebellion, he convinced Batista to release him into exile with the general amnesty. Then the masterful stroke of the Matthews interview for the New York Times back in February.

"Intuitively, Castro understands the essence of guerrilla warfare. Cultivating support among the rural population contrasts sharply with the terror tactics of Cuban security forces. Castro's rebels not only do not steal to sustain themselves as guerrillas, but contribute to public welfare where possible. Security forces rampage in frustration by seizing suspected rebel sympathizers then subjecting them to torture or murder. Castro's propaganda reinforced by his treatment toward the population is better than Batista's. Everyone loves the underdog in a contest with a bully. Internationally, Castro is a freedom fighter confronting a murderous dictator. David versus Goliath."

Peterson said, "What's your best guess as to how this will play out, Mr. Landeira?"

"Eventually, the United States must dump Batista. His dictatorship is not sustainable. The question will be what comes next? The United States will likely back some new puppet under the fig leaf of democratic elections. Another corrupt Cuban government consistent with Cuban history since we kicked out the Spanish."

"For an American, you have a low opinion of our foreign policy," Peterson said.

Landeira glared at him. "Why shouldn't I? Since World War Two, the U.S. government fucked up a lot of countries for its own self-interest. It sees everything through a lens of the threat of communism."

The following morning while having breakfast on the veranda, one of the servants whispered in Rafael's ear. He stood up and said, "Please excuse me, I must take a telephone call."

Minutes later, he came back to the table. Gentlemen, that was Francisco Ortega you met yesterday that called. He flew back to Santiago early this morning. He reports the entire city is shutdown from a general strike. Seems the police killed the fugitive rebel leader Frank Pais just this morning."

Instead of returning to Havana, Landeira announced he was flying instead to Santiago to cover the situation as a journalist. He persuaded Smith and Peterson to accompany him.

Emilia insisted on joining them. At Camagüey Airport, commercial flights to Santiago were cancelled. Smith however was determined to take advantage of the opportunity to access the face of the Cuban rebellion first hand. Invoking his status provided the ability to hire an available cargo aircraft.

Landeira used his press credentials to hire a Santiago taxi for the day. The driver clearly a supporter of the rebels eager to provide Landeira opportunities for photographs.

Spontaneous street demonstrations broke out overwhelming any attempt by the police to do anything except to guard police barracks and government offices. Not some small town backwater in rural Cuba, Santiago was the second largest city in Cuba located on the southern coast. With a population close to 200,000, the outpouring of anti-Batista expression made a strong impression on Smith and Peterson. Smith's predecessor consistently debunked the viability of Fidel Castro's insurgency. This was evidence of Landeira's claim that Castro was winning the propaganda war and sustaining widespread support.

Landeira shot rolls of film. Before leaving the airport, he placed a call to Hector Vasquez to contact his journalistic assets in Santiago to discover the circumstances leading to this massive repudiation of Batista. Only four months since the failed attack on the presidential palace by the Revolutionary Directorate, this could elevate the situation in Cuba to a broader insurgency resembling civil war.

Already informed of the Santiago situation, Vasquez told him his sources were actively working the developing story. "Rumors are circulating about a massive turnout for Pais' funeral. A popular charismatic young man of only twenty-three, his murder touched a collective public nerve. If the Army responds aggressively, this could result in something much larger."

Chapter 20

The massive general strike in Santiago pointed to widespread support of the revolutionary 26 July Movement. It further reflected Batista's failed campaign to crush the rebellion. The resources of the police and Army proved inadequate to wrest control from the spontaneous response of the general population.

Several days later, a much greater demonstration of the impotence of the security forces unfolded. 200,000 people turned out for the funeral of Frank Pais. In a further expression of defiance of the Batista regime, they buried Pais in the olive green uniform with the red and black armband of the 26 July Movement.

Landeira filed a story in the Miami Herald consisting largely of his photographs of the general strike. He made a point of describing his reason for being in Santiago following attending a conference in Camagüey with the new U.S. Ambassador Earl Smith. *On receiving the news of the general strike in Santiago, Ambassador Smith insisted on seeing the demonstration first-hand.* He meant the article to provide some cover for his breach of censorship by publishing news related to political events involving the insurgency. It further signified his relationship with the powerful U.S. ambassador that might add a degree of protection should that become necessary if caught crosswise with the regime.

Huddled with Pérez and Landeira, Vasquez reviewed the article he drafted for sending to Toussaint under the byline of Venganza de Martí. Using photographs of the banded funeral provided visual evidence of the esteem felt for Frank Pais, and by extension Castro's revolutionary movement. The amazing reporting work by Vasquez's sources provided the real impact to the reader. Unlike the reports of mass casualties resulting from Cuban Army excesses with the names becoming lost as statistics, Vasquez captured the visceral impact for the reader by personalizing the murder of Frank Pais. The Venganza de Martí piece went far beyond Landeira's piece in the Miami Herald that covered only the general strike. The El Mundo piece described not only the funeral but provided a detailed description of the execution-style murder of Pais.

The background to the murder of Frank Pais started eight months earlier. Preparing for the arrival of Fidel Castro from Mexico, Pais organized a general uprising in Santiago. Already a hotbed of support for the revolution, the uprising was to coincide with Castro's band of eighty guerrilla fighters arriving from Mexico aboard the yacht *Granma*. The combined events intended to ignite a wider uprising in Oriente Province. The poorly planned operation fell into disaster with Castro and only twenty others narrowly escaping into the Sierra Maestra Mountains with the others killed or captured.

The uprising in Santiago lasted four days but without the revolution's spiritual leader Fidel Castro, it too fell apart. Police detained Pais and other leaders of the Santiago uprising. The police charged Pais along with survivors of the Granma expedition. Illustrative of Pais popularity amidst large popular protests, the local court miraculously acquitted him two months later.

Pais continued his subversive activities. Just a month before his death, police killed his younger brother forcing Pais into hiding.

Vasquez's Venganza de Martí article picks up at this point.

On the morning of July 30, Frank Pais and Raúl Pujol discovered the safe house where they spent the night surrounded by police. Information from sources within M-26-7 claim Pais was warned that the location might not be secure. Once in that location, Pais and Pujol mistakenly decided to stay just the one night.

Warning came too late in the early hours of the following morning of a police raid in progress. Thinking they could escape the apartment building, Pais and Pujol attempted to walk away hoping to reach a waiting getaway car before recognized. A police informant immediately pointed them out.

According to witnesses, the notorious Santiago Police Colonel José Salas commanded the raid. The police handcuffed Pais and Pujol then bundled them into waiting police cars and drove away. The destination was not the closest police barracks. Other sources came forward to report in graphic detail the fate of both men.

Three police cars entered the short one block-long Santiago street of Callejón del Muro. Stopping in the middle of the street, police officers pulled Pais and Pujol out of the vehicles. Colonel Salas ordered his officers to force them to their knees in the street. Unholstering his revolver, he pulled back the hammer shooting Pujol first in the back of the head. After saying something, he then executed Pais in the same manner.

Leaving the bodies in the street as a means of communicating terror, the police even provided the opportunity to take pictures of the bodies. We have reprinted the disturbing photographs here.

Consistent with the failure of the Batista's security forces to crush the rebellion, what followed is further evidence of Batista's failure to subjugate the general population.

Locals spirited the bodies away to prepare them for burial. A priest gave a requiem mass for Pais and Pujol in a small church heavily secured by armed M-26-7 members and supporters. According to multiple sources, the police knew of the planned internment in Santa Ifigenia Cemetery only a mile and a half from the scene of their murders. However, the scope of support suggested any further policing action might ignite widespread rebellion. One large enough possibly beyond the Army's ability to contain without additional massive troop deployment. Therefore, internment proceeded with a noticeable lack of any police or Army presence.

"Outstanding, Hector," Landeira said. "Extraordinary journalism. Indicative of the level of hatred toward Batista with so many willing to talk in spite the Army's reign of terror. Does this outpouring of resistance to Batista suggest Castro could be a real threat?"

Pérez shrugged. "Hard to see him able to recruit enough fighters to make a difference. How does he train them? How does he arm them? Seems unlikely. Castro's greatest ally is the misbehavior of the security forces leadership. Difficult now for Batista to retreat from such brutal tactics without appearing weak. How could he possibly switch gears and embark on a campaign to win over the hearts and minds of the population after inflicting such bloodshed? Yet it is still difficult to conceive that Castro can prevail militarily against the sheer weight of Cuban security forces. A more likely scenario is a military coup against Batista."

Vasquez replied, "By whom? He holds power by making essential subordinates wealthy. Including the Army leadership. He has been controlling Cuban politics for so long there is no political opposition with a national following. Castro is the closest thing. A bearded revolutionary hardly endearing to the powerful elements in Cuban society."

"A more plausible demise of Batista could come about from the United States," Landeira said. "They made Batista, they can destroy him. They could strangle Cuba economically. Make travel difficult from the United States to squeeze off gambling tourism. Cease subsidizing the Cuban military. It is all about money. Turn it off and Batista is finished. The problem is what comes after Batista."

"Removing Batista holds little promise for a better future," Pérez said. "Cuba has neither the history nor the institutions to develop a stable democratic government."

Landeira said, "The one given however is that Batista must go. Viewed through the lens of Havana, the Cuban political situation becomes distorted. Witnessing the general strike in Santiago was an eye opener. Hector's description of the murder of

Frank Pais is a perfect example of Batista's terror campaign. We cannot control what comes after Batista.

"I got an impression of the new U.S. ambassador. Not a seasoned diplomat he is more direct Not sure that is meaningful but maybe he is more than just a mouthpiece for the State Department. Too early to predict if he represents a change in U.S. foreign policy toward Batista, but he is not a Batista apologist like his predecessor. Witnessing the Santiago general strike made clear to him the depth of popular hatred for Batista. Ample evidence of widespread support for Fidel Castro. Now it is more difficult for Washington to dismiss the threat of the revolutionary movement."

Pérez asked, "What transpired at the meeting with the sugarcane producers?"

"Surprisingly, they condemned both Batista and Castro. Obviously fearful of the economic demands of Castro, they voiced their opposition to Batista's violent efforts in rural Cuba. Only making the situation worse. They collectively voiced their lack of confidence in the ability of Cuban security forces to ever crush the Castro rebellion."

Pérez said, "You know Washington better than we do, Bart. Does our campaign have any chance of influencing United States foreign policy toward Cuba?"

"I don't know, Mateo. The best we can do is to continue targeting American readers. If there is enough press coverage of the right kind, those in Congress will take note. Washington listens to the influential syndicated columnists like reading tealeaves. That is why photographs are so important. Provocative graphic images sell."

"What are you suggesting, Bart?" Vasquez said.

"Nothing essentially different, but perhaps more tightly focused. The graphic material your reporters are uncovering about security forces' violence in Oriente should remain our mainstay. Those secret records I discovered in my father's files presenting leads for exposing Batista's vast corruption might now carry some weight by making the Batista regime's use of murder and torture for financial gain. It serves nothing more than to provide motive for the regime's violent oppression that remains the theme.

"I doubt if those articles I write about Mafia investment in Havana have much impact on the American reader. That is only about money. White-collar crime. Out of context, Batista's corruption viewed no differently. However, if we portray Batista as a blood soaked dictator using his military to stay in power to amass a fortune, he becomes a violent criminal rather than a political figure. Enough American readers with strong opinions might influence Washington.

"Dead bodies and innocent bloodshed stir outrage among Americans. Not coverage of clashes between the Army and Castro's guerrillas. Details and photos of murders like that of Pais. We focus on reporting crimes against humanity. Evidence like that presented at Nuremberg. Especially graphic photographs. That will also have the most effect on Americans and therefore Washington policy."

Pérez offered, "Instead of waiting for more opportunities to photograph the victims, we should publish profiles of the principal faces of the regime's violence to provide background instead of just names."

Vasquez replied, "Army commanders like Colonels Fermin Crowley, Alberto del Río, and this José Salas that murdered Pais. That psychopath Rolando Masferrer and his squad of vigilante murders."

Pérez said, "I would add Mariano Faget, Chief the BRAC, the Bureau for the Repression of Communist Activities. Also Irenaldo Garcia, Chief of Military Intelligence, the SIM. In addition, his father, the General Garcia head of the national police. Publish profiles like what Bart wrote on Colonel Ventura."

Landeira nodded in agreement. "There you have it. Batista's henchmen. The men behind the massacres. Murderers, torturers. Make them the face of Batista's oppression. Then paint them with photographs of their bloody handiwork."

Addressing Vasquez, Landeira turned the discussion toward security. "Ramping this up by making it personal with our enemy, we are kicking the hornet's nest. These are the guys commanding in the field. Batista may condone the overall tactics, but these are the individuals responsible for murdering and torturing people as they see fit. Like the Nazi Gestapo. Our campaign to paint them as monsters will likely provoke indiscriminate reprisals.

"The security forces are bound to detain sources that feed information to your network of reporters, Hector. Any reporters, especially those in Oriente Province, are themselves going to be targets. How many are sending you information directly?"

"A few."

"How do they communicate the material to you?"

"Like any reporter, they type up their stories."

"Come on, Hector, this is important. How do they get the material to you?"

Vasquez replied, "What I think in spy craft is called a dead drop."

"What do you mean?"

"The typed sheets I share with you are posted by my contacts. Disguised as magazines and mailed to different post office boxes under fictitious female names. They insert the typed contraband material among the magazine pages. My contacts receive the magazines by subscription from the publisher and reuse the original mailing envelope with the designated post box address. Unless examined closely, it appears as coming from the publisher."

"Okay. So you have these reporters sending material to this location?"

"Not exactly. When you talked about security before we started this, I listened. You said I needed to have cutouts. Only a couple of people I know very well actually send me material to different post boxes. I trust them implicitly. Cuban newspaper managing editors. Two with newspapers still publishing, the other now closed. They have certain trusted reporters who in turn run their own sources."

"Huh. Not bad, Hector. Actually pretty good. Still too many people can connect you to the Venganza de Martí articles. Going to be hard to insulate you totally since it is your network producing most of the substantive material."

Vasquez said, "Lots of good reporters and people willing to take risks. Batista and his henchmen are universally hated. I am risking no more than they are."

Landeira responded, "Unfortunately, informers exist. The more likely threat though is the person threatened with torture or death giving up information in exchange for survival. Eventually they may get to one of your direct contacts by starting with detaining someone on the lower end of the information chain then applying pressure."

"I do not see a way to avoid at least those few direct contacts knowing my identity. What do you suggest, Bart?"

The thought came to Landeira to replicate what Toussaint did. Report from outside the Dominican Republic and now Cuba. Vasquez should take a vacation. Manage his network from outside Cuba.

"You should take an extended vacation, Hector."

Vasquez raised his eyebrows in a questioning expression.

Landeira explained. "Do your work from outside Cuba. Out of reach of the police. Like Toussaint."

Vasquez shook his head rigorously. "I cannot do that. My wife would never agree to separation from our grown children and grandchildren. I also cannot expect those reporters doing the most dangerous work to continue risking their lives while I am safely out of reach in Florida. Doing business from outside Cuba means coordinating with my contacts by international calling. Too risky for government eavesdropping. They mail me their material but I must still communicate with them by telephone with questions. I am the managing editor of this clandestine publication we call Venganza de Martí. I therefore cannot leave Cuba."

Landeira nodded. "I understand, Hector. I cannot suggest any better arrangement then you constructed. This is risky business with no way for absolute protection."

* * * *

Going after Batista's notorious henchmen and providing an outlet to publish motivated many in Vasquez's network of reporters. For those operating in the East victimizing the peasantry in recurring reprisal operations, volumes of documented testimony already existed in reporters' notes and photographs. Victims, families, witnesses, priests finding their only means of defying the dictator's terror by telling their stories. Even under censorship, bearing witness to someone documenting the horrific violence was an act of rebellion. Someday the truth might become public. That someday was now.

The first candidate for exposure in the foreign press was Rolando Masferrer. Neither army nor police, Masferrer was the founder of a vigilante paramilitary organization comprised of death squads. As if Batista needed yet another means of inflicting state sponsored murder and torture, Masferrer's Los Tigres proved to be the most sadistically degenerate.

A lawyer, congressman, newspaper publisher, political extremist and ardent supporter of President Batista, Masferrer developed a niche role for his fanatical followers. In addition to supporting Army and police actions, Los Tigres served a unique offensive role. The Army repeatedly proved unable to inflict damage on Fidel Castro's guerrillas operating from the Sierra Maestra Mountains. Comprised of fighters familiar with Castro's area of operations, Los Tigres engaged in the same small-unit hit and run tactics as the M-26-7 rebels. Although not inflicting significant casualties on the rebel guerillas, their search and destroy forays into the mountains produced another element of terror for rebel sympathizers.

The article produced under the Venganza de Martí byline revealed an embarrassing background for Masferrer. As a member of the Cuban Communist Party, he fought with the Abraham Lincoln Brigade against the Fascists in the Spanish Civil War in the late 1930s. Later in the war, he indulged his proclivity for violence by acting as an enforcer for the International Brigades. In Cuba in the 1940s, he resumed his violent career participating in bloody factional political deputes. Opportunistic violence drove Masferrer rather than political ideology.

Archival photographs resurrected from newspaper files added graphic evidence of his murderous past. Included were photographs taken by a priest of the bodies of four youths tortured and murdered by Los Tigres in Santiago earlier in the year.

A portrait of Colonel Fermin Cowley, commander of the Cuban Army's Holguin Regiment, immediately followed the article featuring Masferrer. Known as the *Jackal of Holguin*, Cowley earned the name as the perpetrator of some of the most notorious massacres in Oriente Province.

Cowley's notoriety began with the pursuit of Fidel Castro's ill-fated landing aboard the yacht *Granma* with his 80 revolutionaries arriving from Mexico. Many of those captured suffered summary execution on Cowley's orders. The murders and public displays of the mutilated bodies of suspected revolutionaries a month later became known as *Bloody Christmas*. Cowley followed the same tactic by murdering the revolutionaries landing on the yacht *Carinthia* arriving from Florida in the spring of this year.

A third article comprising a trilogy of the massacres in the heart of the rural civil war in eastern Cuba came out a week later. This featured another Army commander with the pejorative label of the *Jackal of the East*, Colonel Alberto del Río commanding the 1st Regiment. Del Rio's hatred for Fidel Castro began years earlier as the commander of the Army's Moncada Barracks in Santiago. On 26 July 1953, Fidel Castro attacked the barracks with a group of rebels arriving in automobiles. Although killing 18 and wounding 28 soldiers and police, Castro's attack floundered then collapsed into total disaster. Outnumbered by the Cuban Army and suffering 20 casualties, the remaining attacking force fled in disarray.

In reprisal, Del Rio ordered the execution of 18 captured wounded rebels detained in the civil hospital. The corpses then strewn about the garrison grounds to simulate combat deaths. The Army murdered a further 34 fleeing rebels over the next three days.

Fidel Castro was among those captured soon after. Tried and sentenced to prison, Batista made the mistake of releasing him under an amnesty in 1955, sending him into exile in Mexico. Castro returned in yet another poorly organized disaster of the *Granma* yacht invasion in December of 1956. Born of that first attack on the Santiago army barracks was the *Movimiento 26 Julio,* or M-26-7, and the cementing of Fidel Castro as the recognized face of the Cuban insurrection.

* * * *

With these recent articles appearing in the San Juan El Mundo, Mateo Pérez offered the idea of purchasing large numbers of copies. "Given the increasing incidents of violent repression by Batista's security forces, we should find a way of distributing as many copies as possible within Cuba. These articles on Batista's killers present another means of provocation."

Vasquez slapped his forehead. "I have been so focused on producing the stories for American readership I ignored the propaganda value here in Cuba. Under Batista's censorship, contraband copies will be passed from person to person. Does El Mundo publish a Spanish language addition, Bart?"

"Yes, of course," Landeira replied. "Any ideas how to go about that?"

After several moments of thought, Vasquez said, "What about sending copies to all the newsstands and other places selling newspapers?"

Pérez said, "How do we do that?"

"Mail them," Vasquez responded. "I can produce the addresses from all the major Cuban newspapers distribution lists."

Landeira said, "I can arrange with Toussaint to increase the print runs of his Spanish edition. Landeira Grupo will pay for the subscriptions and the postage through a shell company I use for hiding the clipping service."

Pérez said, "It will not take long for the government to realize what is going on and seize the newspapers as they arrive from Puerto Rico."

"But it will take them some time before they catch on," Landeira said. "I might even be able to work a deal with the Miami Herald to temporarily distribute El Mundo by individual mailings using the Herald's Cuban distribution list. Now you have mailings coming in from Florida as well. It will drive Cuban Customs and the Ministry of Propaganda crazy."

Landeira worked out the arrangement by telephoning Toussaint on his next trip to Miami.

* * * *

More than driving the Ministry of Propaganda crazy, once reports reached President Batista, he flew into a rage. Immediately calling a meeting of senior security officers to his office, Batista said, "This group calling themselves Venganza de Martí has gone too far. Bringing these newspapers into Cuba from Puerto Rico circumventing censorship restrictions calls for stronger measures. Up to now, this group only targeted the American audience. Who is suspected behind this press campaign?"

Present were the minister of defense, chief of staff of the army, chief of the national police, head of police intelligence, and chief of military intelligence.

The most junior officer of the group was Lieutenant Colonel Irenaldo Garcia, Chief of the Servicio de Inteligencia Militar, SIM. Seated next to his father Brigadier General Pilar Garcia, Chief of the National Police, the younger Garcia's operational area was Eastern Cuba. "I believe Colonel Romero agrees with me, that the source of the material used in the Puerto Rican newspaper must originate primarily from Cuban reporters. At least in the areas where the insurgents are operating militarily."

"Why?" Batista asked.

"The gathering of so much material is the work of professionals. Anyone other than reporters asking questions would become obvious to our informers. Then the photographs. Few people have cameras, and fewer still have the ability to develop film secretly. Reporters and newspaper editors represent a kind of intellectual class among the peasantry. People look to them as a means of voicing dissent much like priests."

'So what do you suggest, Colonel, round up all reporters?" Batista asked sarcastically.

"No, Sir. Too much backlash, including international condemnation. Local reporters represent a network of sources. Like cockroaches, too many to stamp out. These articles appearing under the byline Venganza de Martí suggest some central organizing body inside Cuba. They are the adversary.

"We start by targeting reporters known for their anti-government views. All we need is to squeeze the right ones hard enough for them to give up the person in the next chain of their conspiracy. No different from interrogations looking for members in the revolutionary movement. The difference, we knew who to go after and they cannot escape in the mountains."

Batista turned to Colonel Romero, head of police intelligence, "Do you agree with Colonel Garcia's assessment?"

"Yes, Mr. President. We have discussed it at length since these articles began appearing in the American press. I propose setting up a joint army and national police task force to pool information. The Army has a greater intelligence presence in the rural areas and the National Police strongest in the urban centers."

After further discussion, Batista adjourned the meeting. "I would like Colonels Romero and Garcia to remain behind. There is another matter I need to discuss."

With the door closed and the officers reseated, Batista said, "Proceed with your plan of rooting out these conspirators. However, I wish to pursue a parallel mission. Without the cooperation of this Puerto Rican journalist, it would be more difficult for those behind this press campaign to get the material published regularly. He is essential to this press conspiracy.

"Since the first article attributed to this Venganza de Martí appeared, I called friends in Florida asking about this Gaspar Toussaint. Interestingly, they said he has waged a press campaign against Rafael Trujillo for decades. Apparently, he has a network of sources within the Dominican Republic providing detailed material. Sounds similar to what we are facing. Discover everything you can about Toussaint. Is this a propaganda campaign by Castro or others? Someone is organizing this from within Cuba as you point out, Colonel Garcia."

Chapter 21

Toward the end of summer, the Cuban Army embarked on a mission to target this new group of dissidents believed to be newspaper reporters. Those personally featured in the Puerto Rican newspaper articles resorted to aggressive means in pursuit of the source of this new act of rebellion.

Hector Vasquez's idea to distribute Spanish language edition copies of Toussaint's articles in Cuban through the mail proved a masterful stroke. As anticipated, the copies of El Mundo spread underground like a wildfire throughout both the rural and urban populations. Everyone soon knew the faces of Masferrer, Crowley, Del Rio, Salas, and Ventura.

With Eastern Cuba the active theater of the war against Fidel Castro's M-26-7 guerrillas, the Cuban Army launched a renewed round of sweeps. Lists of suspected rebel sympathizers now including anyone associated with newspapers. Even those owning cameras or those places offering film-processing services became targets for intensive interrogation.

Assisting the operation, Colonel Garcia of the SIM setup headquarters in Santiago. Field commanders had orders to deliver any seriously incriminated suspects to Garcia. The term *suspect* meant far more than someone suspected of anti-government sympathies given that could mean almost anyone. For the sadistic predispositions of those like Masferrer and Crowley, a person became a suspect after physically induced questioning produced incriminating information. To the extent that resorted to more extreme forms of torture was a function of the interrogator's situational inclinations. A suspect therefore became someone already sufficiently determined as possessing further information.

In this process, the Army detained virtually every active or former reporter in Oriente Province. The uneven process produced only fragmented results after a couple of weeks. A lot of innocent reporters suffered terribly with nothing of value to reveal while sustaining continued physical abuse from frustrated interrogators. The same tactics as deployed throughout 1957 often targeted whole families in an attempt to root out rebel supporters.

Hector Vasquez took to heart the admonitions of Bart Landeira when assembling his network of subversive journalists. Although Vasquez restricted direct contact to only a few individuals, he knew many of the reporters by reputation doing the work. All vetted by others he trusted for their journalist abilities and commitment to resisting the Batista regime in the only way they knew.

Against the vast resources of the police state, going after President Batista was a deadly undertaking. Censorship prohibited any reporting of the carnage related to government actions against the insurgency. Although no verifiable estimate existed, Batista's death toll ran into the many thousands. Some placed the figure well over 10,000 since seizing power in 1952. No matter how careful, those reporters uncovering material used in the articles published by Toussaint did so under extraordinary risk.

Two reporters actively involved fell into the hands of aggressive interrogators. One from Santiago, the other from Holguin. Both elevated to priority status after searches of their homes revealed camera equipment and makeshift darkrooms for developing the film.

Delivered to Colonel Garcia, both were already in severe physical shape. The torturers sufficiently expert at their craft by pushing their victims to breaking just short of causing death. Both men ultimately revealed they provided information on

Colonel Crowley and Rolando Masferrer. Both confessed to delivering the information to known members of Castro's M-26-7.

The retired former managing editor of a prominent Santiago newspaper suggested that story should they find themselves compromised and suffering physical abuse. Not the best alternative by admitting to helping the rebels, but perhaps a way to mitigate larger complicity by claiming it was done threat by the M-26-7. Prison better than a bullet. Now with both facing renewed interrogation by Colonel Garcia, the same unverifiable story sounded rehearsed.

Already in poor physical condition, the first application of another round of intense abuse quickly proved too much for both victims. They gave up the same name as the recipient of the anti-government material appearing in the foreign newspaper articles. Few victims can resist breaking under a practiced torturer. At some point, lying to the interrogator does not stop the torment. Usually making matters worse since it requires fabricating subsequent supporting lies, impossible to sound convincing and keep lies straight while suffering extreme agony.

The police arrested the named accomplice living alone in Santiago. A widower in his sixties. A longtime professional acquaintance of Hector Vasquez, Manuel Serrano was a crusading journalist for forty years. He gained a professional reputation as a formidable critic to prior corrupt Cuban administrations. Starting with Fulgencio Batista's first term as elected president in 1940, followed by Ramón Grau then Carlos Prio deposed by Batista's assumption of power in his 1952 coup.

In all those years, Serrano successfully navigated the dangerous waters while continually publishing embarrassing material. Receiving his share of death threats, those earlier years bore little resemblance to Batista's elevation of corruption to new levels by partnering with American organized crime. During the last several years of Batista's illegitimate presidency, violent suppression of political dissent overshadowed corruption. The Cuban Army destroyed the printing presses of Serrano's newspaper a year ago putting him out of work.

As other journalists making their work an ethical crusade to confront those like Batista, Serrano searched for an outlet from which to resume opposition. Hector Vasquez offered such a means. The work took on the dangers of spy ring. Yet it allowed for unrestrained journalistic attack on the criminal regime created by Fulgencio Batista. For the few months of his involvement, Serrano came alive. This was important work. Not just publishing the truth, but also striking a blow for the victimized Cuban people.

As in all police states, the knock on the door came in the early hours of the morning before dawn. The time of day when the victim was most vulnerable. While thinking himself prepared should that knock on the door come by keeping a loaded revolver on the nightstand next to the bed, it proved useless.

Allowed to dress, police officers handcuffed him and hustled him out of the apartment to a waiting police van. Colonel Garcia and two of his SIM agents then made a thorough search of the residence.

Serrano avoided keeping anything directly linking him to subversive activities. He violated that discipline by keeping a copy handed to him of Toussaint's latest Venganza de Martí article. Serrano himself had written this piece. Seeing his own published words of dissent validated his sense of purpose.

The usual process involved reading the material his sources sent to him disguised in various forms. He then repackaged the material sending it off to the name and post box address provided by Vasquez. For this particular article, Serrano could not resist going beyond simply acting as an intermediary. Mindful of the danger of possessing this information, he reverted to the discipline of an editor to meet a deadline by writing the story in one night. The reason for violating security protocol by keeping this outlawed copy of El Mundo was personal.

Not practiced in the tradecraft of espionage, Serrano's address book included the names of the two reporters that gave up his name under torture. The book yielded a wealth of other names that now set off targeted seizures. Indiscriminate, security forces were only interested in wringing out every scrap of information. Those listed and found to be reporters suffered terrible maltreatment. Others eventually confessed to providing Serrano anti-government information.

As for Manuel Serrano, his ordeal began in a dank cellar room of the Santiago police barracks. The room was located along a subterranean corridor of cells of the 19th century military building. A former dungeon now serving the same purpose. Little changed in over a hundred years except for electric lighting.

Serrano knew he was in for a bad time. Seated in a badly stained wooden chair with his wrists handcuffed behind the chair back, he looked down at the stains on the stone floor. A pervasive smell of urine and fear hung in the air. A single light bulb illuminated the center of the room casting shadows in the corners. A table stood off to the side displaying various tools of torture. The effect intended to intensify the victim's fear. His heart began racing.

Serrano held no illusions about his fate. Tell them what they wanted and someone else would die. For him, perhaps a quick death by a bullet. He was therefore already dead. Simply a matter of how much he could endure to preserve his integrity.

Yet he held a secret. Hypertension and a serious heart condition required regular use of nitroglycerin pills to alleviate attacks of angina pain. For a man of sixty-five, he otherwise appeared lean and fit with a full head of grey hair. Reconciled to his fate, he resolved to endure whatever maltreatment they had in store and hope that his underlying infirmities would provide a merciful death.

Although it took over an hour of increasingly more violent abuse from a rubber truncheon, he eventually succumbed to a massive coronary. At the end, Manuel Serrano never revealed the name of Hector Vasquez.

Colonel Garcia berated the torturer for allowing the prisoner to die prematurely. He was already sure of someone else higher up involved in the press conspiracy. Several photographs in Serrano's apartment revealed the image of the same man. A place for Garcia to start although he had hoped to gain much more incriminating information from Serrano. If this person in the photographs was someone of prominence, he needed convincing evidence.

* * * *

Colonel Garcia flew back to Havana. He immediately went to his father's office in the executive office building. As the head of the Cuban National Police, Brigadier General Pilar Garcia like all senior police officials came from the Cuban military. With the onset of insurrectionist violence, Army intelligence and the National Police worked in close cooperation.

"I made a breakthrough in this new movement called Venganza de Martí. I have two reporters from Oriente in custody. Both know the material they were passing on ended up in the foreign press. Others made similar confessions. Another in the conspiracy chain unexpectedly died while undergoing interrogation. Regrettably, he revealed nothing of value before dying due to a heart condition. However, from his home I retrieved his address book and these photographs."

The younger Garcia slid the address book and stack of photographs across his father's desk.

He continued briefing his father. Pointing to the man appearing in each of the four photographs, "I am interested in the identity of this man. Do you recognize him?"

His father said, "Oh yes. His name is Hector Vasquez. Former president of the Cuban Newspaper Association. Resigned in protest after the President imposed censorship."

"So he is an opponent of the government?"

"Perhaps, although not publically known as such. How is he connected to this Venganza de Martí group?" General Garcia asked.

"That is to be determined. I believe he might be the next link in the chain of information gathered by anti-government newspaper reporters. Possibly a high-ranking leader."

General Garcia said, "You found no other evidence implicating Vasquez other than these photographs found at the home of this Serrano?"

"Only a copy of El Mundo with the latest article by this reporter Toussaint. Although Serrano died before giving up any information, there is no question about his involvement. There are certainly others higher up. Most likely operating from Havana making Vasquez a prime suspect."

The senior Garcia responded, "Is it not possible that Serrano simply sent the material to this reporter in San Juan?"

"Possible, but this series of articles involves a wider group," the younger Garcia said although knowing he had no evidence to back that up. "Vasquez was a personal friend and a prominent figure in the Cuban newspaper business. Even if not directly involved, Vasquez must know what Serrano was doing."

Thumbing through Serrano's address book, the younger Garcia found Vasquez listed. Pointing to the listing with two telephone numbers. "Vasquez lives in Havana. He must have connections with those in the American press. Puerto Rico is part of the United States."

The senior Garcia's expression reflected skepticism.

"I am suggesting arresting everyone listed in this address book, Father."

The General looked through the address book. "Perhaps that is going a bit too far, Irenaldo. There are many influential people listed here. Some maybe even close to the President. We need to be selective. I only know Vasquez by name, but nothing about his politics."

"What about arresting Vasquez? For these newspaper articles to appear repeatedly in the Puerto Rican newspaper suggests the involvement of someone with connections to the international press. Someone like Vasquez."

"Very well. There is some basis for cause. We must however proceed with caution. I will assign that task to Colonel Ventura of the Fifth Precinct. I believe you must know Ventura's reputation for obtaining confessions."

The younger Garcia grinned. "Of course. He is very thorough. What about others listed among Vasquez's contacts?"

"Premature for making arrests yet. Some of these journalists might even be supporters of the President. For the time being, see what we can learn from Vasquez. Regardless, I will inform the President of your excellent work. At the least, you established the source of the anti-government material originating with dissident reporters."

****

Later that day, General Garcia summoned Esteban Ventura to his office. "I want you to arrest Hector Vasquez. He is suspected of complicity in these anti-government articles appearing in the American press."

Garcia preceded by explaining the background of his son's success in Oriente with at least several of those involved in this anti-government press campaign in the United States.

"My son is convinced of Vasquez's involvement. As you can see, no credible evidence exists. Therefore, you must avoid physical abuse in your interrogations. We need something more than his personal association with this Serrano fellow. Vasquez is widely respected. Not publically known as an anti-government critic. While these articles in the American press infuriate President Batista, they do not impact our war with the revolutionaries. Even smuggled copies of the Puerto Rican newspaper only serve to spread fear for supporting of the rebels. Am I making myself understood, Colonel?"

"Yes, Sir. However, without leverage, a suspect has no reason for giving up information," Ventura said.

"I understand, Colonel. Do what is necessary to apply *leverage* as you say. What I do not want is Vasquez a bloodied mess. If he has important connections in the American press, I expect to avoid any embarrassing photographs making Vasquez into an international issue with the Americans. Within that constraint, find out what Vasquez knows about this group Venganza de Martí."

"Yes, Sir."

Colonel Ventura and a team of police arrested Hector Vasquez that night. Again in the early morning hours. A terrifying experience for anyone in a police state, but coming as no surprise for Vasquez given what he was doing. Much worse however for Vasquez's wife. He kept what he was doing a secret to avoid worrying her.

Although not arrested with her husband, the parting was wrenchingly devastating. Vasquez had no idea if he would be returning. In front of the wife, Colonel Ventura openly threatened Vasquez with subjecting his wife to interrogation should he prove uncooperative.

Again, a thorough search of the residence followed. Taking heed to observe Landeira's covert tradecraft precautions, Vasquez never left anything incriminating at home. Trusted relatives with keys to the post office boxes under false female names picked up the material forwarded by his sources. Vasquez then brought the collected material to the office of another family member running a fruit and vegetable distribution business. It was here that Vasquez composed the articles on an old typewriter before handing them over to Landeira.

Denied the use of physical abuse by General Garcia placed Ventura at a disadvantage. Nonetheless, applying indirect physical stress accompanied by intense physiological abuse was a terrible ordeal. While Vasquez did not suffer from a critical underlying medical condition like his friend Manuel Serrano, he was still in his sixties.

Mateo Pérez was the first to learn of his friend's arrest. Immediately he called Landeira who rushed to Pérez's house in the middle of the night.

"Are we next, Bart?" Pérez asked.

"Hard to say. Unless this is a police fishing expedition because of Hector's position in Cuban journalism, they may have taken him because someone in his network gave up his name. In which case we should not be implicated except by our association with Hector as personal friends."

"But this pig Ventura will torture Hector until he reveals our names," Pérez said. "What the hell do I tell Yolanda is the reason you came knocking on the door in the middle of the night. Christ, I thought it was the police."

"Stay calm, Mateo. Not the time to panic. Tell Yolanda a half-truth. The police arrested Hector because he is a prominent Cuban journalist and must know something about these anti-government articles appearing in the American press. You and she go and stay with Hector's wife until we know more. Hector is not about to reveal our names."

Landeira knew that was not necessarily true regardless of Vasquez's resolve. Everyone has a breaking point under torture well before lasting long enough for the body to give out.

"The best defense is often to counterattack. I believe I established a relationship with U.S. Ambassador Smith by arranging that trip to Camagüey then accompanied him to Santiago following the Pais murder. I will lobby him to make the case to Batista that going after Cuban journalists accused of feeding information on human rights violations to the American press will only further damage Batista's standing with the United States. I will find out if Smith really is the second most powerful person in Cuban. See if he has sufficient *cojones* to act independently without first consulting Washington."

Ambassador Smith agreed to see Landeira that afternoon after Landeira explained the circumstances and the urgency behind his request.

****

Speaking to Peterson after taking Landeira's call Smith said. "The United States made Batista now we're stuck with a Frankenstein monster. What's this flap involving the Cuban journalist about?"

"Our source within the National Police says it likely is about Hector Vasquez. Respected former president of the Cuban Newspaper Association. These foreign articles appearing in the San Juan El Mundo newspaper got under Batista's skin. Overreacted. Worse than that, Vasquez is currently in the custody of a notorious police commander. A known murderer and torturer. If something happens to Vasquez, it could spark a real anti-Batista backlash in the international press."

"Your suggestion, Walter?"

"Listen to what Landeira has to say. If the Cuban police have no evidence against Vasquez, pressure Batista to order his release to avoid damage to his standing with the U.S. administration. Perhaps as a quid pro quo, Landeira might become a cooperating source."

"What value do you see in Landeira cooperating with us?" Smith asked.

"He is both American and Cuban. Made Havana his home after leaving government service. With the death of his father, he became more involved with the family enterprises. Obviously hates Batista. My guess however is he does not likely favor a coup by a left-leaning charismatic popular figure like Fidel Castro. Yet Batista is so unpopular his dictatorship is unsustainable. Perhaps the Administration will soon come to that conclusion. We must be prepared with alternatives. Bart Landeira might prove helpful as a source into Cuban business and intellectual circles. A window in how the political winds are blowing."

Smith said, "And if this Vasquez fellow is behind these anti-government newspaper articles?"

Peterson shrugged. "Irrelevant. Batista needs to get a grip on his sadistic henchmen. These massacres and excesses of torture and disappearances only provoke increased revolutionary sentiment. He already demonstrates his inability to crush the rebels with his large army. His campaign of terror is a knee-jerk reaction. Counterproductive.

"There is also another possibility, Sir. Landeira is also an American journalist. He might actually be involved in this anonymous press campaign targeting the regime."

"If he is, does that change anything?" Smith said.

"Not really," Peterson said.

* * * *

That afternoon, Landeira presented his argument for Smith to intercede for the release of Vasquez. "Hector Vasquez is a close personal friend. We connected because of our common professional careers as journalists. I doubt seriously that Vasquez is involved in this foreign press campaign under the anonymous byline Venganza de Martí, in English, Revenge of Martí, after the celebrated 19th century Cuban patriot. Vasquez is however a devoted nationalist seeking a return to Cuban democracy."

Landeira handed Smith a newspaper clipping of the El Mundo article featuring Colonel Esteban Ventura. "Regardless, this press campaign exposes the gross human rights abuses of specific Cuban security officials. Individuals like Lieutenant Colonel Esteban Ventura of the National Police. This group serves to expose state-sponsored atrocities through the press as a means of protest against the Batista regime. It is directed to the American public because of the extensive American involvement in Cuban affairs. This is about human rights abuses with the hope of bringing pressure to bear on Batista by influencing U.S. economic support."

Smith scanned the newspaper article on Ventura while listening to Landeira.

"Hector Vasquez is now being held by a murderous psychopath at the Fifth Precinct police barracks. The subject of one of those newspaper articles. No telling what maltreatment Vasquez is undergoing as we speak."

"Very well, Mr. Landeira, I will request an immediate meeting with President Batista. Press him about what evidence exists against your friend Vasquez. I cannot promise any results but I will communicate the United States' official denunciation of the Cuban government targeting journalists for articles appearing in the American press. Cuban censorship is reprehensible enough. The United States takes seriously the freedom of the press. That is also reflected in its foreign policy."

* * * *

It was early evening when General Garcia telephoned Colonel Ventura. Called out of the latest interrogation session with Hector Vasquez, Ventura listened with evident displeasure at receiving new orders.

"Has Vasquez provided any information, Colonel?" Garcia asked.

"Nothing, Sir. Continues to claim knowing nothing about the origin of these articles in the foreign press. Been at it continually for fifteen hours. Restricted to applying only psychological pressure makes our work more difficult."

"What is Vasquez's condition?"

"Ventura responded, "Exhausted. Otherwise, no visible marks as you ordered. I believe the ordeal may have reached a point that threatening to bring in his wife to undergo the same treatment might bring results."

"No," Garcia said declaratively. "The President just telephoned me. Release Vasquez immediately. Return him to his home."

"The President? How was it he even knew we detained Vasquez?"

"I do not know. He simply said he had an unpleasant discussion with the American Ambassador demanding Vasquez's release. Just do as ordered, Colonel."

Chapter 22

After a couple days recovery for Hector Vasquez, Landeira reconvened a meeting at the club with him and Pérez.

Vasquez explained what happened after consulting with certain sources. "The police detained two reporters in Oriente. That was several days ago. No word on what happened to them. Others also reported missing. I think it is obvious someone gave up my associate Manuel Serrano who died under torture during interrogation. I know these reporters. They worked for Serrano. They would not give up Serrano without physical coercion. Probably murdered.

"The undertaker attending to Serrano's body told me it revealed massive bruising. Manuel had a serious heart condition and high blood pressure. The undertaker said the cause of death was likely a heart attack.

"Manuel apparently never revealed anything before he died. That is why I did not receive the same treatment. Afraid of the backlash without anything concrete after you got to the American ambassador I imagine, Bart. Good you did. Even without suffering intense physical torture like Manuel, it was a terrible ordeal. So now what do we do?"

"Continue of course, however with changes. First thing, Hector, shutdown your pipeline with those in direct contact with you. Not sure just how to reorganize our efforts, but you need to get out of the loop. This is still your network but we need those reporters doing the dangerous work to get their material directly out of Cuba. We need to run this the same way Toussaint runs his sources in the Dominican Republic.

"With you under suspicion, Mateo and I also come under scrutiny. Colonel Ventura now presents an even larger danger. It wasn't Ambassador Smith's intervention that constrained Ventura from resorting to physical abuse. From the onset, Ventura never laid a hand on you. Not his style. Someone higher up told him to proceed with caution. My guess you have too many connections in the foreign press. When Ventura discovers I lobbied the American ambassador that will further aggravate him. He now harbors resentment toward both of us, Hector. We cannot count on the American ambassador to get us out of jail again."

Pérez said, "What about each of these reporters sending their material to some designated location in Miami? Instead of you couriering the articles to Miami written by you and Hector, what about just having the raw material go directly from the field to Toussaint. Let Toussaint write the copy for publication citing Venganza de Martí as the source."

Landeira nodded his understanding. "Why not? Same thing Toussaint does for the Dominican material he receives for going after Trujillo. I like that. The method for getting it out of Cuba from so many different sources is still a problem.

"Is there a way to discretely make contact with your sources and present a new procedure for filing their material?"

"I think so. What do you have in mind?" Vasquez asked.

"I meet with Toussaint. Explain the situation here," Landeira said. "He has some way of receiving material from his sources in the Dominican Republic. Perhaps we can adopt the same means for material coming out of Cuba. At the least, I can work with Toussaint to construct the Cuban pipeline without our direct involvement. It narrows the risk to each source and their individual activities. Now that it is functioning we decentralize."

* * * *

Ernest and Mary Hemingway returned to Havana in October from summering in Idaho. After settling into Finca Vigia, Ernest telephoned Landeira.

"Ever been marlin fishing, Bart?"

"No. Spent a lot of time sailing but never large game fishing."

"Care to join me Thursday? Emilia is welcome too. Still a good time for hunting blue marlin. Gregorio is getting the *Pilar* ready."

"Sure, Ernest. Sounds interesting," Landeira said. "Let me ask Emilia."

Emilia took the phone. "Welcome back, Ernest. We look forward to seeing you and Mary. I think I will pass though on the fishing. Prefer to stick to sailing closer to shore given my last experience."

"I understand, Emilia. Will see you another time soon."

Bart took the phone and Hemingway said, "We'll leave early at six in the morning from the dock in Cojímar, Bart. Takes a couple of hours to get out to the best hunting grounds."

A different experience for Landeira. While occasionally fishing as a boy in the Gulf of Mexico while living in Tampa, it was never for game fish such as the large blue marlin. For Ernest Hemingway it represented something more than sport. On the same order as Hemingway's publicized big game safaris in Africa, only this involved the sea. As they motored out to the fishing area selected by Gregorio Fuentes, Hemingway talked of his attraction to the sea.

"Ever since I settled in Key West, Florida with my second wife Pauline in 1928, the sea became a large part of my life. A source of wonder, beauty, and adventure, always with the hint of danger. Did a lot of writing in Key West. That experience became part of the reason for moving to Cuba. For Cuban fishermen like Gregorio and Carlos, the water is their life."

"I understand the feeling," Landeira said. "For me it is a personal relationship with nature. I enjoy using my sailing skills as mastery of the profound forces of nature. Always mindful of the danger if not vigilante."

Hemingway nodded. "Perhaps the allure of the blue marlin is for the same reason. The contest between my skills pitted against a great force of nature. A majestic apex predator. Ever seen a marlin up close?"

"No."

"A magnificent beast with its spear-like snout and large dorsal fin. Females are four times the weight of males frequently running 800 to 1000 pounds. Eight to twelve feet from tail to the tip of snout. Two-tone coloring. Top half is blue-black with a silvery-white belly. Sometimes called Cuban black marlins. Landing one takes skill and patience. Hook a marlin and it is a contest between man and nature like no other. Even my hunts in Africa don't compare."

Hemingway then discoursed on basic fishing techniques. The overriding element of the contest to landing the monster successfully was the delicate process of avoiding breaking the line during the exhausting physical contest. A contest Hemingway relished. The interplay of manipulating the force on the line, letting it play out reducing pull when the fish breaches or runs, and reeling in while the marlin rests before resuming the fight.

Landeira was both apprehensive and not especially keen to engage in a protracted wrestling match with a big fish.

"Certainly a different challenge than sailing, Ernest. Football versus tennis."

As they reached the hunting ground, Gregorio hooked baitfish on each of the two fishing rods secured in saddles. Hemingway took the steering wheel as *Pilar* motored eastward at an appropriate trolling speed.

Hemingway told Landeira to follow Gregorio's instructions should the line suddenly began paying out signaling a strike. Then get into the chair. Securely bolted to the deck, the wooden chair had a leather seat belt to secure you against the strain on the fishing rod. An adjustable extension for your feet allowed for maximum leverage when pulling against the force exerted by an animal four times your weight.

Intimidating to the novice, Landeira said, "If we get a strike, you take it, Ernest. I can learn better from watching you."

They argued back and forth. After another couple of hours after no strikes. Hemingway said, "Some days it is like this. But a gorgeous day to be on the sea."

"That it is. With a good lunch and interesting company," Landeira responded.

Soon after this exchange, the fishing reel began to sing as line fed out at a furious rate signaling a solid strike. With no time for further debate, Landeira maneuvered Hemingway into the chair as Gregorio took over the helm to maneuver *Pilar* for the ensuing contest.

As the great fish left the water for the first time after feeling the hook set firmly into its mouth, Hemingway said, "Sonofabitch! Look at that, Bart! Look at the size of that beauty."

Over an hour later, Gregorio throttled down *Pilar* to idle then he came aft. Grabbing two gaffs and handing one to Landeira, he said, "Get a firm hold into the gills. Watch out for the sharp snout when she twists about."

Gregorio set a gaff into the marlin alongside Landeira's then deftly dropped a looped line over the long spear-like snout down to its larger diameter base. Pulling the slack cinched the line tight. After making the end of the line fast to a cleat, he said to Hemingway, "Alright, Papa, she is secure."

Hemingway unfastened himself and set the fishing rod into the stand then grabbed Gregorio's gaff. With design forethought, *Pilar* was fitted with a roller spanning the width of the stern facilitating hauling large fish into the boat. It still required the muscle of three men.

"What do you think, Gregorio?"

"Over 700 pounds maybe closer to 800, Papa. A beautiful fish."

Much backslapping and sharing of more beer followed.

The remainder of the afternoon passed by without another strike. Hemingway apologized but only half-heartedly, instead reveling in the day's success of a prize catch. Landeira just as happy to enjoy the sea and the beer without the physical combat.

To celebrate, Hemingway insisted they go to his favorite watering hole the El Floridita Bar on the other side of Havana harbor in Old Havana.

* * * *

Immediately on entering the El Floridita came a greeting from one of the bartenders, *Hola, Papa. Como estas¿* Ernest Hemingway was a regular. It was here they invented the daiquiri for their celebrity customer.

Without asking, two patrons sitting on the curved end of the bar vacated after shaking Hemingway's hand. The regulars knew this was Papa's favorite spot. It afforded a location from which to fend off autograph intruders. Along with Gregorio, Landeira shielded Hemingway sitting at the very end of the bar.

Without asking, the bartender kept them supplied with tapas and endless daiquiris. Hemingway was enjoying himself immensely. Back in his beloved Cuba and a perfect day of successful fishing. Now enjoying the company of his newest friend, Bart Landeira.

Talk soon turned to war. Unlike Hemingway sharing wartime adventures with other famous correspondents, Landeira was an uncommon warrior. Someone repeatedly experiencing combat at close quarters. Having survived three years behind enemy lines engaged in sabotage and killing made Landeira a warrior from an earlier era.

After several daiquiris, Hemingway asked how he came by scars on his cheek and hand. Perhaps loosened by the alcohol, Landeira chose to relate the details of the event where he received the wounds. Perhaps because Hemingway possessed an uncommon skill for shaping extreme human emotions into credible characters. Perhaps because he liked Hemingway or maybe enthralled by Hemingway's literary skills, he recounted the story of that day in great detail. Hemingway listened with rapt attention.

"Emilia said you reminded her of my character Colonel Cantwell in *Across the River and into the Trees*. She is wrong. You

312

are nothing like Cantwell. He was hardened by life but resigned to fate. You however feel you hold fate in your own hands.

"As you may know, I am an aficionado of Spanish bull-fighting. I have spent considerable time in trying to understand what I consider to be a noble art form. Complete with elaborate tradition and ceremony. More in common with ballet or Japanese Kabuki than something like boxing or fencing. In my early novel *The Sun Also Rises,* I patterned my character Pedro Romero on the great bullfighter Cayetano Ordóñez. I even published a study of the pageantry of bullfighting in 1932 titled *Death in the Afternoon.*

"You remind me of a great bullfighter, Bart. Particularly two of the greats I have been privileged to call close friends. Antonio Ordóñez, Cayetano's son, and Luis Miguel Dominguín. Antonio and Luis gave me a deep understanding of the essence of bull-fighting short of experiencing it personally. Your exploits a similar uncommon union of skills and courage."

"I do not willingly put myself in harm's way like they do," Landeira said.

"You did by joining the OSS. Not only going to fight but then doing so from behind enemy lines. Few could have done what you did for years and survived. Like a matador, you repeatedly faced death armed only with your wits and skills."

"My skills at killing men?"

"An enemy bent on killing you. Not unlike the Spanish fighting bull. A 1200-pound aggressive beast with lethal horns."

Landeira shook his head. "The bullfighter chooses the dangerous contest."

"However, once training in the killing arts began, you understood the nature of the undertaking and excelled. Like the matador working the bull, you are confident in your skills to avoid injury and death. I realize the analogy is imperfect but I can see behind the execution of such skills to the nature of such a man."

Hemingway paused for several moments. "I have searched all my life for that indefinable essence behind living a life while contesting with danger. Covering wars and killing large animals does not measure up against what individuals like you and the great matadors possess. Look at what happened when those two thugs threatened you and Emilia. You did not hesitate before killing them. Christ, you should have been awarded their ears like in the bullring."

Hemingway emptied his glass and motioned the bartender for another drink.

Landeira said nothing. He did not agree with Hemingway's comparison. It perhaps revealed more about the demons driving Hemingway's overtly macho pursuit of life. Perhaps illustrative of the intellectual struggle for someone exceptionally gifted in objectively portraying profound human behavior in his fiction writing.

"You should pursue writing fiction, Bart. God knows you have a wealth of material from which to draw on. You are a writer by profession. I read some of your articles on the Mafia. *Weekend in Havana* showed a literary flare.

"I started out as a journalist. Still think of myself as one. After the First World War, I found the draw of fiction more compelling than reporting on events. In fiction you can explore the real substance of events through the behavior of your characters."

Changing the subject, Landeira said, "What are you working on now, Ernest?"

Animated and more than a little drunk, Hemingway responded, "Reaching back to those roots when I thought I could write meaningful fiction. Those glorious years of struggle in the twenties spent in Paris. Just last year when I was at the Hotel Ritz, Charles Ritz informed me they found an old steamer trunk of mine in the basement storage. Been there since 1930. In the chaos of covering wars and traveling, living in different places, I lost track of the trunk.

"Inside I rediscovered dozens of notebooks thought lost. Ideas and observations. As a compulsive taker of notes, the scribblings cover everything imaginable. Struggling to find my voice and gain recognition during my early years in Paris. With a wealth of material, I am beginning work on assembling a memoir of that special time in my life. The Working title is *A Moveable Feast.*"

A day of introspection for Landeira. While not agreeing with the comparison to bullfighters, Hemingway rightfully identified a trait he never could quite articulate. Certainly not a death wish, nor even the intoxication of adrenalin highs. At least he did not think so. Yet why join the OSS rather than taking a commission in the conventional military?

He became highly proficient in close-quarter combat because he discovered a natural affinity for translating technique into practice. Yet was it something more profound? This was about the ability to kill people in innumerable ways. Human combat in its most primal form. A decision not bred out of patriotic fervor or hatred. Hemingway's analogy spoke to a comparison with the bullfighter's repeated contest with death. Did Hemingway detect something in him that gravitated to danger? Something perhaps Hemingway identified in his own psyche. Something too complex to explain by a label.

* * * *

On November 23, in the city of Holguin in Oriente province, revenge visited one of Batista's notorious murderers. Seven commandos of Castro's M-26-7 tracked Army Colonel Fermin Crowley, *the Jackal of Holguin,* to the commercial offices of Cuban Air Company. The Army commander responsible for the torture and murder of 23 members of M-26-7 a year earlier, and the murder of 18 others from the *Carinthia* yacht landing in May of this year.

With Crowley's car parked outside with the driver behind the wheel, a lone gunman entered the office. Identifying Crowley among several civilians in the office, Crowley died from multiple gunshot wounds fired from close range.

Adding increased credibility to the anonymous Venganza de Martí, a reporter accompanied the M-26-7 assassins on the mission. He captured Crowley's automobile on film parked in front of the building before the police arrived on scene. The enterprising reporter somehow later managed access to Crowley's bullet-ridden body at the hospital morgue providing graphic photographs.

One of Vasquez's numerous sources, the reporter's background story accompanied by the photographs found their way into another published article by Gaspar Toussaint. The first direct transmission to Toussaint from Cuba using Landeira's new arrangement. Toussaint took the opportunity to editorialize about the Cuban revolutionary movement gaining ground. The regime proving incapable of destroying the rebels. This assassination thus providing contrasting evidence of the rebels increasing capabilities.

* * * *

In contrast to the heightened political violence, the Mafia continued to be bullish on continued investment in Havana. Havana represented too important a source of legitimate revenue while providing the perfect vehicle for laundering illegal U.S. profits beyond the reach of U.S. law enforcement. Sufficiently important to Mafia interests and the Cuban economy so as to transcend Batista's presidency. Whoever replaced Batista would either welcome the lucrative partnership with the Mafia, or find it economically impossible to severe the connection without harm to the Cuban economy.

With limited success in participating in Havana, the New York Mafia families simply forced their way in by developing some casinos in early 1957. Convinced of the inevitability of war between the five New York Mafia families, Meyer Lansky began taking steps to protect Havana from the fallout of the internecine New York conflict.

With his strategic vision, in 1956, Lansky envisioned establishing a Havana syndicate that would eventually pass to the direction of Santo Trafficante Jr., already a leading figure based in Havana. Forming alliances with organized criminal elements in Chicago, Las Vegas, and Los Angeles, Lansky began building a semi-autonomous Havana syndicate. Mobsters like Sam

Giancana from Chicago took a large investment position in Havana. A form of corporatization of the Mafia excluding the New York families.

Lansky embarked on a mission to negotiate alliances with many mid-level Mafiosi relocating to Havana seeking expanded opportunities out of reach of U.S. law enforcement. Lansky also created an influential network of select U.S. businessmen with strong political ties in Washington.

Owned by Santo Trafficante Jr., the newly constructed Hotel Capri in downtown Havana became the pleasure haven for Hollywood celebrities connected to the Mafia. These included Frank Sinatra, Tony Martin, Donald O'Connor, and George Raft. Charles "The Blade" Tourine managed the nightclub. Nicholas "Fat Butcher" de Constanzo, a feared six foot seven gangland enforcer, ran the casino. George Raft became the casino celebrity greeter.

When war erupted in New York over the spoils of Cuba, it was quick and violent. The most spectacular casualty was Albert Anastasia. Among his other nicknames, *the Mad Hatter* best described Anastasia for his unstable violent nature of resolving every problem by murder. In October, two gunmen shot Anastasia dead while seated in a barber chair on 7th Avenue in midtown Manhattan. With the level of violence culminated in Anastasia's death, the five New York Mafia families had little choice but to convene a nationwide summit meeting.

While the November meeting in rural southern New York resulted in disaster by drawing unwanted attention from U.S. federal law enforcement, for the emerging Cuban Mafia syndicate, it clarified a new status of leadership control. Santo Trafficante Jr. and Joe Sileci now represented all Cuban Mafia operations. Almost everything previously run by Cubans now subordinated to the implanted U.S. Mafiosi.

Buoyed by the consolidation of Cuban enterprises with the New York families no longer representing a threat, a grand new project moved toward construction. The Monte Carlo de La Habana was to be a massive 656-room resort-like hotel on the water. A large casino geared to high rolling tourists, a cabaret

nightclub, a golf course, a large pier, and docks with interior canals for accommodating various sized yachts. At a projected cost
of 20 million U.S. dollars, the state-run development bank, Banco
de Desarrollo Económico y Social announced it was providing
financing. The same bank used to finance Lansky's Riviera Hotel. However, funding actually followed the same Mafia money-
laundering scheme revealed in Landeira's earlier exposé in the
Miami Herald.

Chapter 23

In spite of the personal turmoil since coming to Havana, the holiday season of Christmas 1957 was the happiest in memory for Bart Landeira. Largely because of falling in love with Emilia Montero. Along with Emilia, he acquired the close relationship of her father and mother. Augustin and Alicia becoming like family. For Landeira, a new experience. Although Cuba's political turmoil continued to worsen, his subversive resistance as a matter of conscience provided a sense of purpose. Some measure of atonement for assisting in establishing dictatorships like that of Batista. This is why journalism matters.

With a lightened work schedule at Landeira Grupo and Emilia's law practice, they enjoyed quality time together. Their lovemaking devoted to pleasuring the other created a deepening physical bond. They talked of their future together.

The first week of the new year, a letter arrived from Emilia's brother Luis.

Dearest Mother and Father,

I am well. Cannot say where I am specifically since we move camp frequently. With most of the leadership of the DRE killed. Those of us that fled Havana into the mountains are now part of a new revolutionary movement called the Second National Front of Escambray. We will continue to wage war on the criminal regime of Batista in the urban and rural areas of central Cuba. We call for the restoration of the 1940 constitution and return to democracy. We joined with those fighting in eastern Cuba under the banner of the 26 July Movement. Batista is unable to defeat the revolution. The Cuban Army is not equipped to fight our well-supported guerrillas that can attack and retreat back into the mountains. Our second front will increase the pressure on Batista.

I believe I have acquitted myself as a man and a patriot in my limited combat experience. I now command a squad. Healthy and fit. Hardened by the rough outdoor life. A bit scruffy with my beard and unable to bathe regularly. Yet we have enough to eat. We are led by a brilliant commander, Eloy Gutiérrez. I knew his brother Carlos who died in the attack on the Presidential Palace last March.

Do not worry for my safety. What a man does in life is more important than a long life under oppression. Give my love to Emilia.

Your loving son, Luis

Emilia read the letter to Landeira. Enclosed was a photograph. Dressed in combat fatigues holding a rifle. Sporting a scraggly beard, his youthful face made him look like a teenager playing soldier. Emilia wept.

Landeira spent that night at Emilia's apartment. The following morning was Sunday. Although not an observant Catholic, she said she wished to go to mass this morning. Would he come with her?

After the church service, they went to lunch. Suddenly she said, "I feel responsible for Luis' revolutionary ideas. While he was still in high school, I would talk about politics. That was during the Prio administration just before Batista returned to power in his coup in 1952.

"Prio was unable to curtail corruption or solve Cuba's growing economic problems. Easy for Luis to become attracted to radical solutions. The underlying problem of course is social injustice and land reform. As an agrarian economy, the relationship of those working the land in extreme poverty remains an intractable problem.

"I also assigned blame on the United States for much of Cuba's problems. Luis even accused me of being hypocritical since I counsel American clients on Cuban investment. Maybe I am by rationalizing there is little alternative to American investment under current circumstances."

Landeira responded, "You are correct. To change the economic dominance of the Cuban economy by the United States requires many different things to happen. The United States must remove support for Batista as a prerequisite for any progress."

"How will that ever happen?" Emilia said. "Hard to image Fidel Castro ever coming to power."

"Perhaps. However, Batista has been unable to eliminate his small band of guerrillas even with his thousands of troops and modern weapons. Batista's problem continues to worsen."

Emilia added, "There is something troubling about Fidel Castro. He sounds like a fanatic. One with a messianic complex. A history of unrealistic failed attacks on the Cuban Army.

Sounds like the making of another dictator should he ever replace Batista. Do you think that is even possible, Bart?"

"Hard to say. Best estimates place his guerrilla forces at only a couple of hundred. This Second Front of which Luis is part of cannot be very large. All Castro has going for him is the mountains to hide in and widespread support from the population. I don't think much of Castro either. However, there is no one of national prominence likely to replace Batista. He firmly controls the Cuban military. Created a government operating as a criminal enterprise, no different from his Mafia partners. Batista's oppression fuels Castro's popularity."

"Like most Cubans, I feel incapable of even seeing what the future brings," she said. "I worry about what will happen to any of us. To Luis. To my mother and father. Your family's business. To you and I."

Her distress prompted him to reveal his clandestine activities. Being close to him put her in danger once before. What he was doing might be far worse.

"Emilia, there is something I must tell you. Something so secret you cannot reveal it even to your mother and father."

She looked at him with an expression of alarm.

"I have been secretly working against President Batista. Are you aware of the press campaign waging against Batista in the American press?"

"No."

"What about the banned Puerto Rican newspaper El Mundo circulating around Havana."

"Yes. One of my staff showed me a copy. Portrayed that monster Colonel Ventura. Some new anti-Batista group taking credit."

"They are called Venganza de Martí. However, they are not a new dissident group. Just a fabrication of my making. I wrote that piece on Ventura. I work with a couple of close associates who feel equally committed to opposing Batista and the help of the cooperative journalist in San Juan. We are the resistance group along with a network of Cuban reporters risking their lives to get the truth published."

"Do you believe what you are doing might help topple Batista?"

"Depends if it influences Cuban related U.S. foreign policy The real reason is because I am a journalist and Cuban. I can't report on Batista's repression from within without risking deportation. Cannot expose details of Batista's corruption in my stories about Mafia investment. Therefore, this is the only way of circumventing Batista's censorship. I have come to love Cuba. Falling in love with you only makes it more so. Batista is a murdering pig. Your brother is acting on his principles. This is my way of doing the same. I cannot live here and remain detached from Batista's repression like Hemingway does."

She embraced him. "I am not surprised. It is in your nature. When my father told me about your interest in buying Montero Rum, I immediately placed you as a probable supporter of Batista given your family. As I came to know you that view quickly changed. Then the way you attacked the Mafia suggested you also despised the Batista regime for partnering with them."

He nodded and touched her cheek. "The next piece appearing in the San Juan El Mundo turns attention on Batista directly. Takes some time for banned copies of the publication to make the rounds underground in Cuba. Rather than exposing the brutality of his henchmen, this piece shows how he is robbing Cuba for personal gain. No way to tell how much but it must be in the many millions of dollars. We are now turning our full attention on President Batista. Maybe if we publish graphic details and photos of blood and death caused by bastard's reign of terror continually in the American media, it might insight outrage among Americans."

Emilia said, "You don't need to tell me how you smuggle these stories and photographs out of Cuba, but are you in any danger?"

"I don't know. I am an American citizen, part of a prominent Cuban family. Yet the police just arrested one of my associates under suspicion of involvement for publishing these damaging exposés in the American press. I used my influence with Ambassador Smith to pressure Batista directly for his release.

"My associate went through a terrible time in the custody of Colonel Ventura. Fortunately, he did not suffer physical torture but it was still a terrible experience. Ventura's constraint probably due to a lack of incriminating evidence and my friend's standing as a prominent figure in the Cuban press. Nonetheless, Ventura must resent the interference. That makes the second time I have come within Colonel Ventura's orbit.

"I am concerned about you because of your connection to me. Circumstances for Batista continue to worsen. He remains in power only because he controls the Cuban military and a secret police. That power base comes from U.S. economic aid. Increasing pressure might make Batista unstable. Murderers like Ventura might be turned against anyone even remotely suspected of subversion."

"These stories may provoke Batista to do just that before they influence U.S. policy," she said.

He shrugged his shoulders. "Quite possibly. Just something we must do. For me some atonement for past involvement with the United States installing right wing dictatorships around the world. Disguised as confronting communism, the reality something more self-serving. American imperialism comes in the form of creating quasi-colonies to extend its political reach. As a consequence, the populations of these countries suffer injustice and poverty under the yoke of corrupt totalitarian regimes."

Emilia could sense the pain in Landeira's voice. "At the time you did not feel that way or you would not have participated. I know you."

"It was a confused time. The world turned upside down after World War Two. I drifted into peacetime intelligence work following the disbanding of the wartime OSS. Did not want to return to the United States like every other soldier and resume an interrupted career practicing law with my father.

"From the beginning, the Cold War held none of the clarity of purpose as did World War Two. Although equal to the threat presented by Hitler and Nazi Germany, we never confronted Stalin and the Soviet Union directly. Even now, the United States wages indirect war in proxy conflicts in a contest between the two superpowers. In so doing, the United States has lost its moral compass. After working in Italy and then Egypt, I understood there was something wrong with our interference in the affairs of other countries solely for our own purposes. Then came Iraq followed by Guatemala. Took me nine years to realize the immorality of what I was doing so I left."

"Quit beating yourself up over the past. It was not as clear cut during that time as it is in retrospect."

Landeira smiled and nodded.

"Can Batista last?" Emilia said.

"That probably depends on the United States government. Without U.S. military aid to support the Cuban Army, difficult to see how he holds onto power."

She responded, "If he leaves or is removed, what do you see in store for Cuba?"

"Chaos. Possibly an expanded civil war between the revolutionary Fidel Castro and the Cuban Army. That of course assumes some general or group of senior officers takes charge. Having no success in crushing the revolutionaries, war might rage for some time in the East. Hard to predict what that might mean for Havana."

* * * *

Hector Vasquez drafted the next article for Toussaint to publish in El Mundo. Given the nature of the personal attack on President Batista and the prohibited circulation within Cuba, this publication might prove more provocative. Simultaneous with the article's wide dissemination through the wire services, the new infiltration arrangement brought the Spanish language edition of El Mundo into Cuba. As the only source of uncensored attacks on the Batista regime, the story attacking Batista directly spread throughout Cuba. Cuban customs could not stem the tide. People shared the contraband copies in a linear chain with trusted friends. The story spread throughout Cuba faster than had El Mundo been available on the newsstands.

With Vasquez's network of dissident Cuban reporters now sending material to postbox addresses in the United States, subsequently forwarded to Toussaint in San Juan, Batista was in for a rough ride in the American press. Toussaint's initial article set the tone.

Batista - The Criminal Dictator of Cuba
El Mundo San Juan, PR, Gaspar Toussaint

There have been many articles previously published about American organized crime investment in Havana. The mechanism for laundering profits from illegal operations in the United States with the complicity of Cuban banks previously exposed in detail. A new Cuban dissident organization known as the *Venganza de Martí,* the Vengeance of Martí, adopting the name of the great Cuban patriot, has repeatedly provided this reporter with a flow of damning information and graphic photographs of the brutal Cuban dictatorship of Fulgencio Batista. Whereas revolutionaries such as the 26 July Movement headed by Fidel Castro continue a military guerrilla insurgency, *Venganza de Martí* seeks to attack the Batista regime through the power of the uncensored press.

This article seeks to expose the true nature of President Batista. He is neither a Cuban statesman nor a trusted ally of the United States. Apart from his record of using his military and secret police to torture and murder thousands of Cuban citizens, Fulgencio Batista is robbing Cuba in order to amass personal wealth. The majority of funding for that corruption comes from partnering with the American Mafia. Batista provides safe haven from U.S. law enforcement and the opportunity to create an international casino gaming center a hundred miles from the U.S. mainland. All this funded by profits from U.S. criminal enterprises. Investment in Havana therefore serves the dual function of laundering unlawfully earned money into legitimate foreign businesses. For these unique services, Batista amasses great personal wealth from Mafia bribery while looting the Cuban treasury. The following describes the process for channeling money directly to the Cuban President.

The latest Mafia investment project overshadows all previous hotel-casino projects in Havana. Not only in scope but also by the mobsters less concerned about concealing their identities. Contrary to Mafia tradition of avoiding publicity, the Monte Carlo de la Habana project puckishly flaunts its presence and boasts its connections to famous American entertainment celebrities.

The following details come from various sources intimate with the project. This is the nature of *Venganza de Martí's* opposition to the Batista regime. Changing hearts and minds by presenting the truth. Although this reporter is not privy to their organizational structure, the material produced illustrates a broad infiltration into all corners of government activities. A barometer of the universal hatred for Batista. The following uncovered details behind the Monte Carlo de la Habana scheduled to begin construction this summer in Havana illustrate the underlying economic reason fueling Batista's reign of terror to hold onto power.

The Monte Carlo will rival the Habana Hilton with a planned 656 rooms. Located on the beachfront, there will be a marina with internal canals, berths for large yachts, a golf course, and landing pad for helicopters. The casino, nightclub, cocktail lounge, and five-star restaurant round out the array of amenities. The first all-encompassing resort in Havana.

The official announcement indicates the state-run development bank, Banco de Desarrollo Económico y Social, will provide financing. The same Cuban bank supposedly financing the Riviera Hotel, the Jewish mobster Meyer Lansky's project. The bank a creation by presidential decree for the sole purpose of diverting the flow of capital for concealment and personal enrichment for President Batista. Like that previous project, the bank plays a pivotal role in the scheme. It launders Mafia unlawful U.S. profits into legitimate investment under the pretext of loan repayments by American Mafia front companies. It further affords a mechanism for Batista to collect massive kickbacks disguised as fictitious expenses. The development bank puts up very little money. Ninety percent of the funds come from the Mafia in the form of cash laundered clean through bank transactions. The Cuban state appears to hold a significant ownership position equivalent to that of the private investors. However, that is not the case as revealed by confidential documents. The state's ownership position only requires the resort operators to pay a modest annual operating fee for licensing. Publically, Batista touts the broader economic benefits from the resort, but there is no direct participation in operating profits by the state. The profits belong to the Mafia. Line items of nonexistent operating expenses disguise the kickbacks to Batista.

In this shell game of financial subterfuge, the big winner is Fulgencio Batista. His personal initial take estimated at as much as twenty-five percent of project costs does not include a sustaining percentage of operating income disguised as the Cuban state's share of income. The source of Batista's wealth therefore comes from criminal activities in the United States, or from diverting funds from the Cuban treasury. For the Mafia and its affiliated investors, Batista's graft is simply the cost of doing business in Havana. The bribery partly offset by preferential tax exemptions. No matter the perspective, the corruption serves to bring violent repression to every corner of Cuban society.

Confidential sources identify many of those aforementioned affiliated investors. The Mob created a management company to run this new resort, La Compañía Hotelera de Monte Carlo. Among the board of directors is "Chairman of The Board" Frank Sinatra, singer and actor Tony Martin, actor and dancer Donald O'Connor, and new York restauranteur and entertainment producer William Miller. Another proposed director is Walter Kirschner, a close adviser to former President Roosevelt and someone with a close personal relationship with President Eisenhower. Having served as a U.S. envoy to Vatican City, Kirschner also enjoys close connections with the Vatican Curia. From President Batista's standpoint as a Mob-affiliated partner, the Monte Carlo brings together the influence of Hollywood celebrities, influential American businessmen, with direct lines to the White House and the Holy See.

The Monte Carlo is only illustrative of a vast conspiracy between American organized crime, Cuban banks, and President Batista. In all cases, suitcases full of cash arrive at one of many participating banks by curriers from the United States. The bank issues loans to finance construction or purchases for American organized crime front companies. The Mafia cash deposits serve to satisfy fictitious loan repayment. The bank takes a large commission and obscures the kickbacks to Batista. In the Monte Carlo project, Batista's kickback may be as large as 25% of the budget. Those kickbacks are booked as various expenses paid out to nonexistent business entities controlled by Batista to accounts at Banco de Desarrollo Económico y Social, BANDES.

Batista created BANDES by degree to act as his personal piggybank. That is widely known within the Cuban financial community. *Venganza de Martí* sources provided documentation of private Batista accounts and records of subsequent transfers of the funds to Swiss accounts. Known for its absolute depositor secrecy, moving money out of Cuban into the Swiss banking system represents more than prima facie evidence of Batista's systemic looting of the Cuban treasury.

Previous reporting by others identified the collusion between the banks and the American Mafia. Missing was identifying President Batista's participation equivalent to that of a full partner acting on his own behalf. Very little in the transformation of Havana into the premier gambling tourist destination of the Americas benefits the Cuban people. Batista's position as an autocratic head of state ruling by degree was essential for bringing largescale Mafia investment to Havana. Providing a legal safe haven with preferential tax treatment with no regulatory oversight makes for a perfect environment. For Cuban banks to cooperate in the money laundering subterfuge also requires the Cuban central bank to turn a blind eye. In Batista's dictatorship, everything is possible and permissible if it lines El Presidente's pockets.

From the political perspective, Fulgencio Batista cannot remain in power indefinitely. Universally despised by the Cuban people, he cannot honor his vague pledge to hold elections. To prevail as a candidate will require an entirely fraudulent election. His only base of support is the Cuban Army. Funded by United States foreign aid. Beset by a revolutionary insurgency, the Army remains incapable of crushing only several hundred guerrillas operating out of the eastern mountains. What the future holds for Cuba is uncertainty. Its governance history since independence is not encouraging. Free people of the world should weep for Cuba as yet another failed embryonic democratic state stunted at birth.

* * * *

The early months of 1958 proved unsettling for Batista. A rebel radio station began twice-daily broadcasts from the security of the Sierra Maestra Mountains. Initiated by Che Guevara, *Radio Rebelde* grew from Guevarra's first-hand experience of the successful CIA clandestine radio station used in the overthrow of the Arbenz government in Guatemala in 1954.

At the same time, Raúl Castro took a modest number of the guerrillas into northern Oriente Province to open a new front in the Sierra Cristal Mountains. Fidel Castro's larger force remained entrenched in the inaccessible Sierra Maestra Mountains in the south. The splinter group from the former Revolutionary Directorate now began guerrilla operations as the Second Front in the Escambray Mountains located in central Cuba. While still comparatively few in military strength, the rebel units began regularly venturing out of their mountain sanctuaries to attack Cuban Army outposts.

Then in an unexpected surprise move, the United States suspended weapons sales to Cuba. U.S. Ambassador Smith delivered the news to Batista personally. The explanation given was lack of Batista's progress in putting down the rebellion worsening after sixteen months. With all the U.S. aid money expended on bolstering the Cuban military, it was proving incapable of suppressing a small group of poorly armed insurgents. Smith added that recent press reports of atrocities committed by Cuban security forces in his terror campaign were proving counterproductive and turning many in the administration against his government.

The meeting with Ambassador Smith followed within a week of the direct attack on Batista in the Puerto Rican newspaper attributed to the Venganza de Martí group. The damaging information not only published in the United States but now appearing widely throughout Cuba in spite of censorship. The group appeared to have sources infiltrated everywhere. Did their press attacks have something to do with the U.S. withdrawal of military support?

Batista flew into an uncharacteristic rage. Like a cornered animal, he needed to lash out and stem the downward spiral. Disrupting this press attack in the American media alienating the U.S. administration became foremost on his agenda. The larger intractable problem remained in finding the means to destroy the charismatic Fidel Castro representing the unifying figure in the revolutionary insurrection.

Days later Batista convened a meeting. Present in his office were Colonel Romero, Chief of Intelligence for the National Police, Lieutenant Colonel Irenaldo Garcia, Chief of the Servicio de Inteligencia Militar, and Lieutenant Colonel Ventura of the National Police in Havana.

Having ordered Romero and Garcia, to bring intelligence on the Puerto Rican reporter, Batista turned to Romero, "What do we know about this Gaspar Toussaint, Colonel?"

"Born 1920 to Haitian parents. Escaped the great massacre of Haitians living in western Dominica in 1937. Lost his entire family. Fled to Florida. Earned a university degree in journalism. Reporting for the San Juan El Mundo newspaper since 1942. Currently managing editor. Known for his continual newspaper attacks on President Trujillo. Two unsuccessful attempts made on his life, presumably ordered by Trujillo."

"How does he receive his information?" Batista asked.

Romero shook his head. "That is not entirely known. I had a conversation with my counterpart in the Dominican Republic. They have arrested individuals over the years that confessed to providing Toussaint information using the mail. However, it may be more elaborate than that."

Colonel Garcia added, "I also contacted the head of the Dominican Servicio de Inteligencia Militar. They are frustrated after years of not being able to dismantle his network of sources."

"Who are those sources?" Batista asked.

"The Dominican SIM believes a broad network of journalists, activists, and the Catholic clergy. Because of the inability to cut off the flow of damaging information leaving the country, they believe Catholic priests provide the main conduit to Toussaint. Catholicism enjoys special official privilege in the Dominican Republic because of strong support among the population. However, many in the clergy denounce Trujillo."

Batista asked, "Is it possible that Catholic priests in Cuba are involved?"

Garcia said, "My opinion is probably not. What we discovered that led to the series of arrests suggest Toussaint's sources are Cuban reporters."

Romero added, "I agree. By the nature of the articles, it is likely that journalists in Cuba are providing the material appearing in Toussaint's column. Colonel Ventura believes that the president of the Cuban Newspaper Association, Hector Vasquez is involved. Unfortunately, American interference forced his premature release before interrogation could produce results."

Batista looked at Ventura, "Do you agree, Colonel?"

"Yes, Sir. Vasquez is the principal suspect controlling this group called Venganza de Martí. He knew the reporters and the newspaper editor implicated in the plotting. Vasquez knows every journalist in Cuba. Highly respected. Furthermore, Vasquez is a close associate of Bartolo Landeira, the person that convinced the U.S. ambassador to intervene to free Vasquez. I know Landeira from a previous encounter. A journalist for an American newspaper also puts him under suspicion. Something is also not right about him."

"What do you mean?" Batista asked.

"He is an American citizen. From a prominent Cuban family. Suddenly arrives in Cuba and becomes involved with the Landeira family enterprises. Then that incident where he disarmed two men attempting to rob him. Killed one and badly injured the other without using a weapon. Suggests some sort of military training."

"Interesting. I knew his father for many years. A brilliant lawyer," Batista said digesting Ventura's comments.

"Yes, Sir. However, Landeira has written newspaper articles critical of American investment in Havana hotels and casinos."

"I am aware of that. He repeatedly attacks our American investor friends as being associated with organized crime. What is your point, Colonel?"

"Precisely that, Sir. Those press attacks on the American businessmen indirectly attack your presidency because of your public connection to developing the Havana tourist industry. He is careful not to criticize you, but by attacking your important development projects, he demonstrates his opposition."

"You believe Landeira and Vasquez are conspirators?" Batista asked.

Ventura replied, "Yes, Sir. Since ordered to release Vasquez from custody, we are following Landeira and Vasquez around the clock. They meet frequently at an exclusive men's club in Vedado. Sources within the club inform me of the presence of a third person. An economics professor from Havana University. Well respected in the Cuban financial community. Sources suggest he might have ties to members of the disbanded Revolutionary Directorate following closure of the university."

Romero asked, "Are you suggesting these three might be behind this media campaign in the American press?"

Ventura responded, "Yes. I am sure of Vasquez's complicity. The other two only add to my certainty. Landeira understands the workings of the American press. Puerto Rico is American. He travels frequently to Miami. As for Pérez's possible contribution, these articles contain explicit details about money and banking. Pérez might even be the direct conduit of confidential insider financial information given his reputation and wide range of connections."

Batista interrupted, "Colonel Ventura's comments raise many unanswered questions about Landeira. Colonel Romero, as head of police intelligence, we need to know more about Landeira's background. What did he do during the war and the following years before coming to Havana? Do you have sources in the United States with the ability to obtain that kind of information?"

"Yes, Sir, I believe so. I will get on it immediately," Romero said.

Batista sat through further discussion nodding his head slightly as if in agreement, eventually saying, "I have heard enough, gentlemen. Now is the time to act. I wish this troublesome reporter in San Juan silenced. Permanently. He is critical to these inflammatory stories smuggled into Cuba appearing in print. Remove him and we disrupt the activities of this Venganza de Martí.

"After that, perhaps we shall move more aggressively against Cuban journalists. How many reporters can there be? A couple of hundred? Should be easy enough to purge the dissidents and curtail any opposition from the rest through intimidation. Let the American ambassador lodge a complaint. What else can they do since they cut off weapons sales?"

This was a reversal of his previous orders following U.S. pressure to release Hector Vasquez from custody. Pressuring security commanders with a contradictory policy to increase pressure on Cuban journalists yet acting with constraint to avoid the appearance of an all-out crackdown to avoid international condemnation.

"Now to removing this Puerto Rican reporter. I believe you are the man for the job, Colonel Ventura. You have a free hand. Cost is no object. The one requirement is there cannot be any suspicion this is a Cuban operation. Fortunately, we have President Trujillo to thank for setting a precedent of going after this reporter. His killing must be explainable as the work of the Dominican SIM. Can you accomplish that?"

"Yes, Señor Presidente." After pausing to gather his thoughts while piecing together a basic outline of a plan, "I have a trusted sergeant in my precinct. A Dominican. He grew up in San Juan among the large Dominican immigrant population. He can recruit an assassination team made up of ethnic Dominicans from the local criminal element. Should not be difficult for the right amount of money. My sergeant can pass as an agent of the Dominican SIM. Once the reporter is dead, the trail leads back to Trujillo."

Batista smiled. "Very good, Colonel. Move quickly. Keep Colonel Romero informed of your progress."

Batista chose Ventura for the risky mission because Ventura was accustomed to operating in an urban environment. Fluent in English, he was a natural-born killer with a personal reason to silence this reporter. Batista could plausibly disavow any knowledge claiming it was a personal vendetta by a rogue police officer should Cuban involvement become an issue.

Chapter 24

Landeira was in the Havana office of Landeira Grupo sitting at his father's old desk when his secretary announced a visitor. To his surprise, the visitor was Walter Peterson from the U.S. Embassy.

"Ambassador Smith sends his regards. I trust your friend Mr. Vasquez is recovered from his ordeal with the police."

"Yes. Fortunately, he did not suffer the physical torture as so many others detained by Colonel Ventura. His arrest was a stupid reaction over the bad publicity Batista is receiving in the American press. My guess is that detaining Vasquez was a clumsy fishing expedition with orders for Ventura to avoid resorting to visible torture."

"Glad we could help. Washington asked me to discuss something highly confidential with you, Mr. Landeira."

"Washington? Who in Washington?"

"Let me be candid. My position as diplomatic political officer is just a cover. I am the Havana head-of-station for the CIA. Director Dulles asked that I contact you."

Defensively, Landeira responded, "For what purpose?"

"To act in an advisory capacity. As a former CIA officer you could be invaluable given your unique situation in Havana."

Landeira responded, "What makes my situation unique?"

"You are ethnically Cuban. An American citizen living in Havana. An executive with your family's business enterprises.

336

As a correspondent for the Miami Herald, you are conversant with the political environment in Cuba. I also believe you are romantically involved with a Cuban lawyer."

Angrily, Landeira shot back, "Not sure I appreciate the CIA's intrusion into my personal life, Peterson. Get to the point."

"Your political position is not clear other than by all appearances you are no fan of President Batista. You consistently attack American organized crime investment in Havana while avoiding censorship by directly accusing Batista of corruption. Your girlfriend's brother formerly associated with the DRE rumored to be with the rebels in the Escambray Mountains. From your background, I doubt you are a fan of the rebel leader Fidel Castro."

"Then where do you think I stand?"

"I don't know. I would rather you tell me. However, as a Cuban invested in your adopted country, I believe you would like to see a functional democratic Cuban government. Batista obviously cannot last much longer."

"Christ. You people never change. This fucking administration thinks they can shape the character of every small country to suit American interests. America doesn't give a shit about things like social justice or human rights outside its borders. That's why I left the CIA."

"Regardless your opinion of the current administration's motives, the United States remains the only influence capable of promoting something better than a Batista or a possible Marxist regime."

"Of course, the feared specter of the communist bogeyman. The choice always between the two undemocratic alternatives. You think Castro is a Marxist because he speaks of land reform. Cuba will never see social justice unless circumstances for agricultural workers improve. Land ownership lies at the heart of the problem. My extended family is a major sugarcane producer therefore part of the problem. The current economic system must change for Cuba to ever embrace democracy."

Peterson responded, "Whether Fidel Castro is himself a committed communist is debatable. Yet one of his closest lieutenants, the Argentine doctor Guevara is a known Marxist. Notwithstanding Castro's politics, Washington believes a government formed by these fragmented revolutionaries led by a charismatic popular figure will be a disaster. A disaster for both the United States and the Cuban people."

"What is it Director Dulles thinks I can do?"

"You are well-connected among many influential Cubans. Both Washington and the Cuban people would like to see something better than another totalitarian regime like Batista or a repressive leftist regime. At present, no one stands out as a possible democratic successor to Batista. Washington is looking for alternatives."

"The find the idea of working for the CIA as a source repugnant. Besides that, the problem is far more complex than finding a replacement for Batista. The United States maintains Cuba as a pseudo-colony since its liberation. U.S. corporations control every sector of the Cuban economy. Reforming those entrenched practices may be impossible, certainly problematic. Then you have a vast Cuban military. Incapable of effectively crushing this insurgency in spite of their superior resources. They will not willingly relinquish their power enjoyed under Batista. Dismantling the security apparatus of a police state becomes another formidable obstacle."

"Irrespective of your personal feelings, I believe you wish the best for Cuba. We are not looking for you to act as source in the conventional sense of the meaning. Yet if another alternative exists in the form of someone that you believe might be an acceptable successor, don't you have an obligation to promote that possibility?"

Landeira did not respond.

Peterson continued, "Let me share a piece of highly confidential information to fortify the reason for approaching you. There is no longer speculation about forcing Batista stepping down, at least from the office of the President of the United States."

Peterson's candid revelation startled Landeira.

"When we ceased arms shipments to Cuba, Batista was forcefully informed that he must call for elections this year as required by the 1940 Cuban constitution. He is waffling but a date will soon be announced."

Landeira shook his head. "Batista knows he cannot win under any circumstances if he runs for election. Unless the election is heavily rigged."

"True. Therefore, he will be backing a candidate of his choice. The current prime minister Andrés Rivero. As a known supporter of Batista, Rivero also has little chance of winning unless Batista rigs the election. Rivero's candidacy becomes a concession to the United States. Batista will of course never leave power willingly. Following the term of his first presidency in 1944, he remained a powerful force in Cuban politics after looting the Cuban treasury. Even while living in the United States for the next eight years he managed to cultivate strong support among the Cuban military. That power base sufficient to orchestrate his bloodless coup in 1952. Should Rivero win, he will be in Batista's pocket. The present governing situation will remain intact. Civil war will continue."

"So you are looking for someone that could win the popular vote," Landeira said. "A little late in the game for that."

"Perhaps. Our intelligence suggests a couple of other candidates might run. One is former president Ramón Grau. But he lacks any popular following. Rivero will have the backing of conservative factions supportive of Batista, including large landowners and certain businessmen. Our sources also state that Castro will boycott the elections, possibly to the extent of threatening those going to the polls. A compromise candidate acceptable to the rebels might stand an outside chance."

Landeira could hardly believe the CIA considered such a hail Mary idea had any possibility of success. Then again, he reflected on all those ill-conceived operations experienced during his tenure with the CIA. Insular thinking by deskbound cowboys with little experience in practical circumstances.

Landeira shook his head. "That has no possibility of success. Even if you found this individual, there is no time to promote him effectively for an election this year."

"You are probably right. However, we need to pursue all options. The way things are progressing, Cuba is in for continuing bad times unless an electable alternative can be found."

Landeira knew of no such alternative. The current situation will play out to some form of political crisis, insuring and unpredictable future. The United States recognizing its loss of control was desperately casting about to salvage something from the disaster of Batista.

"Tell Director Dulles there is no white knight to save Cuba. If I knew of such a person, I would gladly offer an opinion," Landeira said.

Peterson just nodded. The discussion at an end. He understood that his assignment to contact Landeira was too little too late. "Thank you for hearing me out, Mr. Landeira. I trust you will keep what I told you in the strictest confidence. Contact me if you have anything of interest to share."

As Peterson left, two men in civilian clothes sat in a car across the street. Holding a camera with a telephoto lens, one man snapped a series of photographs. Hours later, photo enlargements spread over the desk of the head of police intelligence Colonel Romero.

* * * *

Ventura approached his Dominican sergeant to describe the mission to assassinate Gaspar Toussaint. A man with a sadistic streak to match his own, Sergeant Miguel Torres killed many times before following Ventura's orders. The adventure of leaving the country on a special assignment for El Presidente, with a bonus of $2000 only added to his motivation.

A handsome man in his mid-thirties, Torres consuming vice was violence. Like Ventura, he worked in civilian clothes and liked to dress well.

"You leave tomorrow for San Juan. Flying to Miami then changing planes to San Juan to obscure your destination," Ventura said. "Here are photographs of your target Gaspar Toussaint and the address of the newspaper office and his apartment.

340

From now on, you are from the Dominican Republic. Here is a Dominican passport. It will get you through U.S. Customs with no problem. Even shows an entry stamp into Cuba. Here is a forged identification as an agent of the Dominican Servicio de Inteligencia Militar. Good enough to convince those you are hiring. Inside this envelope is $15,000. Enough cash for hiring the assassination team and expenses. Can you find trustworthy Dominican killers in San Juan, Sergeant?"

"Should be easy enough for this much money. Give me a week, Sir. I need to observe the target's habits and plan the hit before hiring any locals. Best to keep it to as few as possible. That should not be a problem after spreading some money around. Better though if I go armed. It will give me credibility when I pose as an agent of the Dominican SIM. I also need to supervise the hit. In fact, why not just let me do it?"

"We are not sure what security precautions Toussaint takes. After previous failed attempts on his life, we must assume he carries a gun. He will avoid high-risk circumstances where we can catch him alone. An assassination team provides more options. Any arrests or casualties points to the Dominican Republic rather than Cuba. You provide the assurance that the job gets done."

Torres asked, "How can I get a gun past U.S. Customs?"

Ventura expected Torres to go to Puerto Rico armed. "Already taken care of. Go to the Cuban consulate. There is a package waiting for you under the name on the Dominican passport. Inside is a 9mm with several clips of ammunition and a holster.

"Keep me informed of progress daily by telephone. Always use the name on the Dominican passport. Very few people know of the mission. No telling who might be listening in on international telephone calls. Therefore, make no direct references. Toussaint is the *objective*. The recruited assassination team is the *resources*. Once you devise a plan with everything in place, I will join you in San Juan to run through your plan on location."

Three days later, Colonel Romero called Ventura to come to his office. "Certain alarming information just came to light on Landeira. You previously said something was not right about him," Romero said. "You were correct. During World War Two Landeira was an officer in the U.S. Army serving with the Office of Strategic Services. The American spy organization. He saw action in North Africa and Italy. Worked behind the lines with Italian partisans fighting the Germans. He disarmed those two attackers using his commando training. Yet of much greater interest is what he did after the war. Seems that Landeira continued working in intelligence as a field operative for the United States Central Intelligence Agency.

"We observed the local CIA chief in Havana visiting Landeira just days ago. Explains his influence with the U.S. ambassador. Perhaps Señor Landeira is still associated with the American CIA?"

Romero's revelations stunned Ventura. "That could mean this negative press campaign disguised as a new insurgency group Venganza de Martí might actually be a CIA operation. Another U.S. pressure tactic like cutting off arms shipments to Cuba. Does this change the mission to kill the San Juan reporter?"

Romero replied, "No. General Garcia says the President wants the reporter killed. The real issue is about crushing Castro's M-26-7 guerrillas. If the Army can find the means to accomplish that, the U.S. administration will continue U.S.-Cuban relations as before. Human rights no longer become an awkward issue in the American press if the Army can back away from mass killings in the rural areas."

General Garcia and Colonel Romero knew of plans for a major offensive against Castro's stronghold in the Sierra Maestra Mountains scheduled in a couple of months. If successful, Batista could retain his hold on power.

The fact that Landeira was meeting with the senior Havana CIA agent made little difference to Ventura for killing the San Juan reporter. However, it was important intelligence to bolster his case for going after Landeira and Vasquez once he removed the San Juan reporter. Convinced of their involvement in this Venganza de Martí press campaign, their arrests would provide personal satisfaction.

****

The assassination mission moved forward according to plan. Making contact with a San Juan Dominican criminal gang, Torres negotiated the hit on Gaspar Toussaint. The exceptional $10,000 fee convinced the local gang leader it was a high profile killing, adding credence for its sanctioning by the Dominican SIM as Torres claimed. Once Colonel Ventura arrived, Torres laid out the plan in his hotel room.

"I followed Toussaint from early morning to nightfall for four days. He moves about very little. Mostly between his office and apartment using his own car. Always leaves the office before dark. Parks his car on the busy street in front of the newspaper building."

"Where do you make the hit?" Ventura asked.

"At Toussaint's apartment building. Less people, less traffic. My two hired locals will park a car in front of his apartment building. They fake a car problem. Because Toussaint is wary because of past attacks, they fake a flat tire. When Toussaint arrives, the two guys have the wheel removed. Toussaint less likely to sense a trap from a disabled car missing a wheel. It is a stolen car. Abandoned after shooting Toussaint."

"Then what happens?"

"Depending on where Toussaint parks, he must walk either toward my team or past them to reach the front door of his building. They pull guns and take Toussaint if possible. I am across the street in another car. We take him somewhere quiet and put a bullet in his head."

"If Toussaint is armed then what?"

"If he pulls a gun, the locals shoot him on the spot. They have killed before."

"If these two recruits fail to capture Toussaint or kill him on the spot, what is your backup plan?"

"As Toussaint drives up, I cross the street at a distance so as not to alarm him. I will be in position as backup to complete the job should the locals fail."

Ventura nodded with an expression of approval. "Very good, Sergeant. When do you do this?"

"I suggest the day after tomorrow as Toussaint leaves the office. Enough time to get my team ready and show you the locations."

Ventura could not suggest any better plan. His preference for using a larger force as in Havana was not practical for a foreign mission in San Juan, Puerto Rico. Torres dry run convinced him the plan was simple and solid.

On the appointed day, Ventura left for the airport. He would wait for Torres to report on the success of the operation. From there they would purchase tickets for an evening flight to Miami. If Torres does not show up at the airport, Ventura quietly leaves with no record of his presence in Puerto Rico.

Gaspar Toussaint left his office at five o'clock in the afternoon. As usual, his revolver tucked in the waistband of his trousers, concealed by his jacket. Yet as usual emerging from the newspaper building, his right hand grasped the revolver handle as he surveyed the street.

He always parked his car in plain view from his office window. It was not possible to rig a bomb to the car without him seeing suspicious activity. The previous assassination attempts occurred many years ago. Both times from gunfire. The last time wounding him by a single bullet from a handgun. Both attacks by a lone gunman approaching him. Therefore, his fear was more a car bombing or a sniper with a scoped rifle from a distance. Difficult to guard against such eventualities.

His recent participation publishing inflammatory material targeting the Cuban regime of the dictator Batista heightened his awareness. Fulgencio Batista might be every bit a threat as Rafael Trujillo. Landeira's funding of large overruns of El Mundo's Spanish language edition for these articles attacking Batista added to Toussaint's high profile. With mailings to hundreds of subscribers in Cuba circumventing censorship, Landeira's campaign went well beyond attacks in the American press. Toussaint understood the subversive effects of circulating prohibited material in a police state.

Toussaint got into his car and pulled away headed for home using an alternate route from the prior day. Arriving at his apartment building, he surveyed his parking options. Always preferring a spot closest to the front door, today offered typical options. He decided on a spot a short distance from a disabled car jacked up with two men changing a tire. Likely just a normal occurrence, but anything out of the ordinary merited careful attention. The possibility of a car rigged with a bomb came to mind since his apartment faced to the street.

He parked and locked his car. Two other parked cars separated his from the car with the flat tire. The men looked busy having just removed the left rear tire. As Toussaint made his way on the sidewalk approaching the adjoining sidewalk leading to his building's front door, the trunk of the disabled vehicle opened. Thinking it was to retrieve the spare tire, Toussaint nonetheless placed his right hand on his revolver.

As Toussaint got closer, one man walked out from the rear of the disabled car stepping onto the sidewalk. From the corner of his eye, Toussaint saw the second man move around the front of the car. Both men then withdrew handguns now pointed in his direction. Immediately, he drew his Colt .38 police revolver.

After his last wounding years ago, Toussaint not only went armed but periodically spent time at a local firing range to maintain his skills. Hitting a target even at close range with a handgun is notoriously difficult without training and practice. More difficult yet with a target shooting back at you. Regular practice gave him a measure of confidence.

Seeing their target armed, both assailants immediately fired on Toussaint. Toussaint fired at almost at the same instant recognizing what was about to happen. One assailant dropped to one knee after Toussaint's shot hit him in the upper chest. Two shots struck Toussaint in the abdomen. Staggering from his wounds, Toussaint continued firing hitting the wounded attacker closest to him in the forehead killing him instantly. Firing continued from the other man as Toussaint crumpled to the ground struck by another round to his abdomen and another to his thigh.

The uninjured assailant looked at the unconscious bleeding Toussaint. The target appeared dead or at least mortally wounded. A quick check of his partner with a bullet hole in his forehead left no doubt as to his condition.

As instructed, the man began running across the street toward the waiting Manuel Torres standing next to the getaway car. Breathlessly, the shooter said to Torres, "*El reportero esta muerto o moribundo. Disparado cuatro veces. Mi compañero esta muerto.*"

Torres nodded. With several people now visible on the street, Torres chose not to expose himself by personally verifying the man's report. Observing the exchange of gunfire from this close would have to be sufficient.

Torres drove away with the surviving gunman. Paying him for the successful mission, the gunman also served the purpose of corroborating this as a Dominican SIM assassination. Common criminals cannot resist talking too much.

* * * *

Picking up a copy of the Washington Post from a newsstand close to the Landeira Group office, Landeira turned sick to his stomach seeing the title of a short column on page one.

Newspaper Reporter in San Juan Gunned Down
Associated Press International

Yesterday gunmen shot dead the noted reporter Gaspar Toussaint in front of his home San Juan, Puerto Rico as he arrived from his office. Toussaint was pronounced dead at the hospital from four gunshot wounds after transport by ambulance. Having previously survived two earlier assassination attempts years ago, Toussaint always carried a handgun. In this attack, he was able to kill one assailant found at the scene. Witnesses report two assailants and possibly more since reporting the surviving assailant left in a waiting car.

The article went on to offer the usual information about the stolen car used as a ruse for the assailants to wait for Toussaint in front of his home. The dead assailant was a member of a local Dominican gang in San Juan with a violent criminal record association.

Over the years, Toussaint made a reputation for his hard-hitting newspaper reporting on the violence and repression in the Dominican Republic governed by the dictator Rafael Trujillo. Of Haitian ancestry, Toussaint was the only member of his immediate family to escape what became known as the Parsley Massacre while living at the time just over the border in the Dominican Republic. The genocidal outrage of the butchering by machete of as many as 20,000 Haitians by the Dominican Army occurred in 1937 on orders from the dictator Rafael Trujillo.

Toussaint fled to the United States, becoming educated and for over the last twenty years published remarkably graphic material and photographs of Trujillo's oppression. Two previous failed assassination attempts on Toussaint's life are generally attributed to Trujillo's secret police. Although those occurred many years ago, the Trujillo regime remains a prime suspect in Toussaint's murder. Toussaint never ceased his attacks on Trujillo through a network of sources in the Dominican Republic.

Over the past several months, Toussaint devoted many columns to a new target, Cuban dictator Fulgencio Batista. The Batista regime is facing an intractable insurgency for the last sixteen months mostly in the form of rebel guerrillas ensconced in the mountainous terrain of eastern Cuba. A group calling themselves *Venganza de Martí,* in English, the Revenge of Martí consistently provided Toussaint with inflammatory material exposing the tyranny and violence of the Batista regime.

Landeira contacted Vasquez and Pérez to meet for lunch at the club. Careful to avoid saying anything incriminating on the telephone, Toussaint's murder made evident their precarious security situation. Even within the confines of the *La Fraternidad de Cristóbal Colón* they must remain cautious.

Landeira showed them the Miami Herald article reporting Toussaint's murder.

Vasquez exclaimed, "We must attend his funeral."

347

Pérez responded, "We cannot do that, Hector. Both you and Bart must be under police suspicion after what happened to you. Possibly both of you are under surveillance."

"Mateo is right, Hector," Landeira said. "This might be a Cuban operation, not Trujillo. Using local Dominican criminals perhaps a way of claiming deniability. We struck a nerve with Batista. He may feel emboldened enough to come after us. With the United States suspending arms sales, Batista might be willing to ignore U.S. diplomatic pressure. Convincing the U.S. ambassador to pressure for your release might not work again."

"We cannot just fold up our operation," Vasquez responded vehemently. "We have a whole army of reporters out there willing to risk their lives in opposition to Batista."

"I agree, Hector. The problem is our exposed situation while located here in Havana," Landeira said. "We can easily reach other American journalists to publish our material, but not as long as we stay in Cuba."

"What if one of us relocates to the United States and replaces the role Toussaint played?" Pérez said.

Landeira said, "That only works if all three of us leave Cuba. Each of us has personal reasons for making that an unacceptable sacrifice."

Both Pérez and Vasquez appeared to agree by their silence. Discussion then ensued for possible alternatives. Everything returned to the underlying problem, if the press attacks continued in the American press, all three remained at risk from Batista's police. Landeira's scheme sealed their collective fate.

* * * *

President Batista scored a minor success in silencing the negative press campaign however, the rebellion showed no sign of abating. After Raúl Castro opened a new front in northern Oriente Province only a couple of months earlier, he took the unprecedented tactic of kidnapping foreign nationals.

On June 26, Raúl Castro kidnapped ten American and two Canadian employees of the American owned Moa Bay Mining

Company on the northern coast of Oriente Province. The following day, his guerrillas took 24 U.S. naval personnel on leave from Guantanamo Bay Naval Base hostage. While it may have angering Washington, it provided a propaganda benefit to the revolutionary movement after an earlier failure in calling for a general strike failed to materialize.

In the weeks following the kidnappings, Raúl Castro released all the hostages with the captives issuing statements to newspaper reporters of the excellent treatment afforded by their captors. Many likened their experience to an unexpected vacation.

It also served to ground Cuban Air Force bombing operations of Fidel Castro's main body of guerrillas secluded in the Sierra Maestra Maintains in the south. The enhanced prestige of continual international press coverage of the Cuban rebellion increased recruitment to the rebel armed forces.

Notwithstanding these setbacks, Batista saw disabling the damaging press campaign by killing the San Juan reporter as a victory. Now he must focus on the larger objective to put an end to this rebellion. That meant destroying the unifying figure of the revolution Fidel Castro. He would take personal charge of the planning. Confident he could devise an operation where up to now the general staff had failed.

Chapter 25

In May 1958, President Batista began planning his grand offensive to crush Fidel Castro's 26 July Movement revolutionaries. Command of *Operation Verano*, operation Summer, was given to General Eulogio Cantillo, Chief of Staff of the Cuban Armed Forces.

Cantillo wanted to use a force of 24 battalions representing 20,000 men in the offensive. His strategy was to surround the Sierra Maestra Mountains creating a blockade to eliminate weapons going to the rebels while preventing any escape. A force of about 12,000 men would then attack from the north, supported by military aircraft for spotting as well as bombing and strafing. The mountains came down to the Caribbean in the south and to the west making for a natural barrier. Surrounding Castro's mountain stronghold was therefore feasible with a sufficiently sized force.

On paper, seemingly a plan of overkill even considering the Cuban military's over-assessment of rebel strength. Given the successes of the M-26-7 guerrillas in widespread attacks throughout Oriente Province, they estimated Castro's forces between 1,000 and 2,000 veteran guerrillas. The actual number was closer to 300.

However, ignored in the planning were basic shortcomings of the Cuban Army's combat readiness. Although provided with good weaponry through U.S. arms sales, Cuban soldiers were poorly paid. With little money allocated for training, what training existed focused on conventional warfare tactics. The Cuban Army had no experience in asymmetrical warfare with guerrillas attacking targets of opportunity then retreated into impenetrable terrain. Few Army units were combat ready. Lack of training extended equally to the entire officer corps.

The nature of the war experienced from the perspective of the Cuban Army soldier was constant fear of sniper attack in an alien environment offering concealment of the enemy. Even airborne assets offered little value given the inability to penetrate dense mountain foliage.

Yet another factor played against military success of the Cuban military offensive. President Batista's interference. He possessed no formal military training and attained only the rank of sergeant when he instigated the Sergeants' Revolt in 1933. Immediately elevated to Cuban Army Chief of Staff following the successful coup, Batista turned to politics. Nothing in his background qualified him to manage tactical aspects of a large-scale military operation.

Ignoring the reality that remaining in power required continuing U.S. foreign aid which rested with crushing the revolutionary movement, Batista arbitrarily reduced the size of the operational forces. He authorized using only 14 battalions or 12,000 soldiers for Operation Verano. Of that number, 7,000 were new recruits with essentially no training.

Batista then meddled further by dividing operational command. For some inexplicable reason, Batista inserted himself into the detail planning by appointing newly promoted Brigadier General Alberto Del Río into a position commanding certain aspects of the operation. As former commander of the 1st Regimiento of Del Rio earned the sobriquet *Jackal of the East* for his acts of violent repression. The counterproductive move speculated as politically motivated. A possibility given Batista's tenuous hold on power now rested solely on continued support of the military leadership.

Regardless of the shortcomings of the Cuban Army, the offensive represented the greatest threat to date against Castro's revolutionary movement.

Impossible for the Cuban Army to conceal deployment of so many troops, the civilian population continuously provided the rebels with good intelligence. This allowed advance preparation to lay land mines and construct defensive positions along major routes likely to be used by the Cuban Army.

The first attack occurred with an attack by the Cuban Army starting from the east just north of the city of Santiago. It illustrated the level of tactical proficiency of Castro's small guerrilla force and the inferior fighting capability of the Cuban forces.

Small arms fire forced a spearhead of Cuban armored cars off the road into a minefield. Disabled, a rebel ambush led by Che Guevara followed. Chaos ensued among the Cuban soldiers. During the disorganized retreat, the Cuban Army suffered 86 casualties against only three rebels wounded.

Two weeks later, the situation worsened for Cuban forces while further revealed their fighting inadequacies. Landing a battalion at the mouth of the La Plata River, the Army's objective was to move north and surround Castro's mountain stronghold at Turquino Peak.

The poorly led Cuban soldiers numbering close to 900 consisted mostly of raw recruits. The rebels made first contact with an ambush. The dense undergrowth quickly separated many Cuban soldiers from their units. The assault lost all continuity. With the rebels in entrenched positions and the Cubans able to maneuver, the soldiers looked for cover instead of pressing the fight. The rebels soon surrounded the Cubans after inflicting heavy causalities. Radio messages from the beleaguered Cuban battalion prompted landing a second battalion on the beach to come to the rescue by advancing north. This move failed before it ever got underway. A small rebel force contained the Cuban rescue force on the beach.

Strategically positioned rebels stopped a third Cuban battalion sent along the coast well short of relieving the entrapped troops to the north. A couple of hundred better-trained rebel guerrillas commanding the terrain therefore blunted the Cuban offensive of 2,500 attacking troops. Trapped in the hills, the initial battalion to engage the rebels eventually suffered 40 killed, 30 wounded, and 240 taken prisoner. Rebel losses again numbered only three.

All Cuba and much of the world knew of the rebel success against the overwhelming strength of the Cuban forces through the daily broadcasts of M-26-7's Radio Rebelde. Batista could do nothing to counter the bad news with his discredited state-controlled radio propaganda.

* * * *

On orders from Director Dulles, recent events prompted Havana CIA station chief Walter Peterson to contact Landeira again. This time more cautiously. With the murder of the San Juan reporter publishing damaging material to the Batista regime, Peterson recognized the possible connection to Landeira. With his lobbying of Ambassador Smith for release of the Cuban journalist Vasquez from police custody, it might suggest Landeira's involvement with the anti-Batista press campaign. Best not to potentially incriminate Landeira further with the Cuban police by his presence.

Instead of showing up at Landeira's business office, he would make contact somewhere out of sight should the police be watching Landeira.

Landeira discovered a note slipped under his apartment door in the middle of the night.

Need to meet secretly with you. A matter of urgency. Making assumption you might be under surveillance by National Police given events in San Juan. Of vital interest affecting the evolving Cuban political situation. Suggest you arrange lunch with members of your staff the day after tomorrow at the Hotel Nacional restaurant as cover. A waiter will come to your table saying there is a telephone call for you. Excuse yourself and meet me in the men's restroom. I am acting on orders from very high up. WP.

Fuck. That was all he needed. Contact with the CIA only adding to his uncertain status with the regime. More likely, the CIA wanted his participation in some desperate U.S. scheme to salvage a mess partly of America's creation. However, as a journalist, he could not pass up the opportunity to gain insight into U.S. intensions. The reversals of Batista's summer military offensive possibly causing Washington to reevaluate Batista's longevity. The prospect for a general election resolving anything seemed more uncertain.

At lunch with three of his administrative staff after ordering a round of drinks, the maître d' approached announcing there was a call for him on the house phone. Excusing himself, he entered the restroom. No one else was in the restroom when Peterson said from one of the stalls, "I will remain concealed. Cough if someone enters than appear acting normal until we are alone. I shall be brief. Director Dulles asks if you might act as an intermediary to Fidel Castro?"

"Are you serious?"

"Very."

"Why approach me for this?"

"Because you know the ropes. You can be credible as an impartial intermediary. Both Cuban and American with no history of backing Batista. Your newspaper articles attacking Mafia investment in Havana support that. Logistically you can travel closer to Castro with reason to visit your family's estate in Camagüey. Still outside the current war zone, but easier to arrange clandestine contact with Castro."

"What message do you wish to convey to Castro?"

"Continued denial of weapons and military support to Batista. Allowing Castro to continue weapons smuggling activities without U.S. interference. Possibly offering financial support in exchange for certain assurances should his revolutionary movement topple Batista. Details are negotiable."

Landeira said. "Sounds like Washington laying off bets in order to break even? Tell me something. What happens to the Cuban military? They certainly will not fall in behind this bearded fanatic that has made them look incompetent. Isn't a military coup the more obvious scenario? With or without U.S. interference? Retrench by consolidating into large garrisons with their superior troop strength and armor. Give up the troublesome provinces east of Camagüey. Continue to promote the gambling tourist industry and steal Cuba blind. An altered form of the status quo. Even the current U.S. administration might be content with that."

Someone entered the restroom. They resumed the conversation minutes later once alone.

Peterson said, "There are few with the rank of colonel or above with the ability or ambition to seize power. The smartest one is General Cantillo, but he is also proving incapable. However, a military takeover remains an option."

Landeira replied sarcastically, "Ruled by a corrupt military junta in the pocket of the United States also means that Cuba continues under corrupt totalitarian rule. No chance for democracy. Things have gone too far for the United States to dictate an outcome. Washington only makes matters worse. Impossible to predict how Cuba's future will evolve. Likely not for the better. Do not contact me again, Peterson."

Landeira left the restroom. Minutes later, Walter Peterson left.

The man that entered the restroom interrupting Landeira and Peterson's conversation stood at a public telephone outside the restroom. "Peterson met with someone lunching at the hotel with three other men." From the party on the other end of the line came orders to follow the man Peterson met with.

The man was a police officer working for Colonel Romero assigned to following Walter Peterson. The clandestine meeting went unnoticed to one of Colonel Ventura's officers following Landeira. Expecting Peterson was experienced enough to insure he was not followed, Landeira was unaware of the new danger caused by Peterson's flawed tradecraft.

* * * *

With victory already achieved against General Cantillo's offensive in the Sierra Maestra Mountains, Fidel Castro made yet another flawed military decision to consolidate his gains. The Cuban third battalion sent into the offensive bottled up on the coast road began to retreat. Castro sent a column of guerrillas to ambush the retreating Cubans. After killing 30 Cuban soldiers, the guerrillas came under counterattack. Castro responded by bringing another guerrilla column to join the attack on the retreating Cubans. The ambush backfired on Castro's forces as additional Cuban forces unexpectedly advanced to enter the battle.

Cantillo thinking he now held the advantage, called in additional forces amounting to 1,500 troops from nearby towns. Leading another column of guerrillas, Che Guevara intercepted these new Cuban forces. Although uneven in numbers, fighting raged for a week with little movement from either side. By this time, Castro suffered 70 casualties. Perhaps a third of his Sierra Maestra forces. Worse yet, he was surrounded.

Ever the talker, Castro requested a cease-fire with General Cantillo. He even offered to negotiate an end to the war. Inexplicably, Cantillo accepted. Castro's delaying tactic worked. Within a week, all of Castro's remaining guerrillas slipped through the Cuban Army corridor using the advantage of terrain familiarity at night.

The failure of the massive Operation Verano offensive confirmed the Cuban Army's complete lack of effectivity as a fighting force. The point not lost on military and intelligence officials in the Eisenhower administration.

Added bad news for Batista came from reports of attacks against Cuban Army garrisons from the rebel Second Front of Escambray operating in central Cuba. The military situation was quickly deteriorating for Batista.

The opening of a new insurgency front based in the central Cuban highlands of the Escambray Mountains also brought bad news for the Montero family. They received a hand written message penned by the commander of the Second Front. *With regret, I must inform you of the death of your son Luis. He died bravely in combat fighting for Cuba. Eloy Gutiérrez, Commander.*

356

The news devastated the Montero family. Made all the worse that Luis Montero was buried in an unmarked grave in some remote location. Only an enlarged photograph represented his memory at the requiem mass.

Among the large crowd of mourners, an individual stood at the back of the church. An undercover police officer from Lieutenant Colonel Ventura's command assigned surveillance duty on Bart Landeira. The revelation that the deceased revolutionary was the brother of Landeira's girlfriend would add yet another incriminating element to Ventura's case against Landeira.

* * * *

Ventura received congratulations from President Batista via a telephone call for the successful mission in San Juan after returning to Havana. Batista however made no mention of authorizing Ventura to go after those he claimed were behind the Venganza de Martí conspiracy.

Harboring personal animosity toward Hector Vasquez and Bartolo Landeira for the attack in the press, Ventura was not about to back away from seeking revenge. With new information about Landeira's collusion with the CIA and ties to revolutionaries, he could make a powerful case for taking action against Landeira. With Landeira removed, he could manufacture a case for going after Vasquez.

Ventura presented his plan to move against Landeira to his boss Brigadier General Garcia, head of the National Police and Colonel Romero, head of police intelligence.

"Landeira is the suspected ringleader of the American press campaign against the government. He is likely behind recruiting the reporter Toussaint as the means for publishing anonymously. Frequently makes trips from Havana to Miami. Clearly working for the CIA. With the suspension of U.S. arms sales to Cuba, the CIA might be actively working against President Batista. Venganza de Martí appears to be a CIA operation."

Ventura was careful to avoid stating the obvious reason for eroding U.S. support of Batista. The dramatic failure of Operation Verano made clear his inability to crush the strengthening rebellion by military means.

"We now discover Landeira has direct ties to the revolutionaries."

"What are you suggesting, Colonel Ventura?" General Garcia asked.

"Eliminate Landeira, Vasquez, and their coconspirator Professor Pérez. Remove the ringleaders of Venganza de Martí. Then clamp down on all journalists in Cuba as the President suggested previously."

Garcia responded, "That will anger the American government."

"Perhaps. Yet what can they do? They are no longer supplying us weapons. It will demonstrate that President Batista still holds power."

General Garcia agreed with Ventura's suggested actions but for entirely different reasons. President Batista was acting erratic. A man running out of options. Garcia's son Lieutenant Colonel Irenaldo Garcia, chief of military intelligence, shared insights of Batista's failing support among the general staff. The failure of the massive summer offensive further damaging the already strained relationship with the United States evidenced by U.S. increasing pressure to hold elections. Batista's options for holding power diminishing. Ventura might be correct that the CIA was behind the negative press campaign.

The younger Garcia confided to his father rumors circulating among the military general staff. Criticism over the mismanagement of Operation Verano. Blame attributed to either Chief of Staff Cantillo or Batista's meddling in the planning. Rumors speculating about Cantillo's loyalty to Batista by agreeing to a cease-fire rather than crushing Castro's force. Batista's inexplicable decision to withhold requested forces compounded by splitting operational command.

Circumstances raised the specter of a military coup. However, according to Garcia's son, no senior military officer appeared to possess enough support to contemplate such action. Every senior military officer including Garcia appeared tied to Batista's fate.

For General Garcia, pursuing the actions suggested by his subordinate Ventura might have effects better left not discussed with anyone, even his own son. Ventura's plan to go after the journalists would give the unstable Batista something concrete to focus on. It would also enhance the stature of the National Police. In the wake of repeated failures of the military, perhaps signaling a shift in power favorable to Garcia.

Thinking further ahead, Garcia planned privately suggesting a bold strategy for Batista to salvage power. Strategically cede the eastern half of the island to the revolutionaries. The western half of Cuba does not have the inaccessible mountainous regions essential for the guerrilla insurgency. Forced to operate on the plains the Cuban military can use its numerical strength to confront the revolutionaries in conventional warfare including the advantage of aircraft. The crown jewel of Havana remaining firmly fortified in the center of the western half of Cuba. A divided nation like Korea and Vietnam. Western Cuba controlled as a police state like East Germany. These precedents might convince Batista to pursue a similar solution. The Cuban National Police turned into an all-powerful security force on the order of the East German Stasi.

"How do you propose eliminating Landeira, given his connection with the CIA?"

"Indirectly of course," Ventura said. "The Americans would see his arrest as a direct confrontation. Instead, we shall blame it on the revolutionaries."

Garcia and Romero look at him questionably.

"A kidnapping. We kidnap his girlfriend. Demand a large ransom. After all, Landeira is an important businessman with a large corporation. Raúl Castro recently set the precedent for kidnapping.

"The kidnapping is discovered by the police. Landeira, the woman, and the kidnappers all killed as the police rescue attempt goes badly. The perpetrators subsequently identified as members of Castro's M-26-7 revolutionary movement."

"Who are these expendable kidnappers?" Romero asked.

"Local criminals. Recruited by my man who engineered the assassination on the reporter. To the criminals, he is a rogue police officer looking to score a large sum of money. An alternative explanation is a Mafia hit. Landeira previously accused the Mafia for a personal attack as intimidation to cease his newspaper attacks. With all those involved dead we control the narrative."

After discussing details further, Garcia said, "And what about Landeira's other conspirators?"

Ventura shrugged his shoulders and said, "Arrested and disappear. Then we go after Cuban journalists. Expel foreign journalists. A total crackdown. We control the radio and newspapers?"

"What about the rebel broadcasts?"

"Outside of our control. Their broadcasts are about the civil war. Leftist propaganda for consumption by illiterate rural peasants. The government controls the information important to the urban population centers."

Garcia said. "A creative solution to the subversive press campaign. I will recommend your plan to the President. You will hear from me, Colonel Ventura."

Chapter 26

Within days, General Garcia met with President Batista. He described a scenario of U.S. subversion as a direct attack on Batista by using Landeira's background and his suspected CIA activity portrayed as a product of police intelligence efforts. Batista flew into a rage. The past weeks proving a rollercoaster of unrelenting setbacks. The emotional satisfaction of the San Juan assassination erased by the larger disaster of the failed military offensive. The realization that he has no workable plan for defeating the insurgency led to the unsettling truth that failing to do so means he cannot maintain his hold on power.

With the failed Summer Offensive and the escape of Fidel Castro, the military situation worsened further. Commanding separate rebel formations, Che Guevara and Camilo Cienfuegos left Oriente Province moving west to attack Army garrisons in Camagüey Province.

Having set the tone, Garcia launched into his drastic scenario about holding onto power by ceding rural eastern Cuba to the revolutionaries and dividing the country.

Despondent, Batista seemed receptive to any possible solution to remain in power. Over the next two hours, Garcia laid out an impressive, although questionable scenario for sustaining Batista's dictatorship.

With Batista energized by the prospects, Garcia pressed forward his idea. Since seizing on the idea of partitioning Cuba,

Garcia added further nuisances. "Cuba has always been a divided country. Rural and urban. East and west. Drawing a defensible boundary at the western border of Camagüey Province leaves the sugar industry to the rural peasantry and the revolutionaries. Let them wrestle with dealing with the social problems of producing sugar. Let them contend with the problem of the United States offering a fair price for sugar.

"The government firmly holds the western half of the country and the crown jewel of Havana. We continue to exploit the profitable gambling and tourist trade. Havana is already a modern Western city. We grow Havana further. Perhaps offering preferential financial services. A tax haven for wealthy Americans and corporations similar to what is happening in the Cayman Islands and Bermuda. We develop specifically designed Cuban laws to compete."

"Very interesting, General," Batista said. Garcia's idea meant tacitly admitting defeat that carried unknown repercussions. As a risk taker the idea was however intriguing. "Such a bold move will take much further thought. The United States remains the wild card. Impossible to anticipate how they might react."

"Of course, Sir. However, there is no need to announce your intentions should you move in that direction. It means simply redeploying the Army in eastward. Consolidating into a defensive line of large defensible garrisons. Force the rebels to engaging our forces only in conventional warfare. Lacking in numbers of fighters with no heavy weapons places them at disadvantage. This relieves the Army from attempting to dislodge the rebels from the mountains. Let the military situation play with the rebels forced on the offensive while the Army occupies the strongest defensive position with superior numbers and weapons."

"Very well, General. We shall talk further." Garcia's idea was not only radical but went counter to Batista's instincts. Yet with no other apparent solution, it merited consideration.

In a calmer frame of mind, it was easier to turn his attention to something more immediate. Batista continued, "Now to the matter involving this troublesome American. Proceed with

Colonel Ventura's plan. Let him finish what he started in San Juan.

"The Americans will never acknowledge Landeira as working for the CIA. At the moment, I am very unhappy with the Americans. Let this send them a message. You may therefore proceed with utmost caution. No different from the San Juan mission, nothing must lead back to official Cuban involvement. Both you and I will disavow Colonel Ventura's actions should anything go wrong."

The ambitious General Garcia was pleased with his performance. He felt no particular loyalty to Batista but his future rested on Batista remaining in power. Should a scenario unfold along the lines he suggested to Batista, it would place him at the pinnacle of power. In a position to greatly improve his financial circumstances. Possibly positioning him to even succeeding Batista should circumstances evolve favorably. As head of a powerful secret police with expanded powers, he could reshape the use of security forces to avoid Batista's failed policies.

* * * *

Given the green light, Ventura set about refining details for the kidnapping and assassination of Landeira from the broad outline presented to General Garcia and Colonel Romero. The personal gratification of eliminating Landeira and Vasquez was only part of his enthusiasm. Garcia explained that Batista also agreed to the broader crackdown on Cuban journalists after eliminating the CIA spy Landeira. That wider endeavor appealed to Ventura's obsessive inclination for exercising power through intimidation. Of the many psychopaths within the Cuban military and National Police, few embraced the sheer enjoyment of inflicting terror and violence to the extent exhibited by Ventura.

As with any plan, it was the details that dictated success. To implement the killing of Landeira, Ventura turned again to his valued subordinate Miguel Torres. A similar assignment to that of the Toussaint killing in San Juan by recruiting participants from Havana criminal elements under the subterfuge of participating in a kidnapping for ransom.

"I have a new assignment for you, Sergeant. This one will pay you handsomely. Ten times the bonus of the job in Puerto Rico. Can you find three men to do a kidnapping?"

Torres looked at his boss with a smile. "That should be easy enough."

"This is not to be known as an official police operation. Those you recruit must think this is simply an opportunity to make a lot of money. The kidnapping blamed on revolutionaries. The victim is the girlfriend of an executive of a large corporation. An important Cuban family with a lot of money."

"What happens after they pay the ransom?"

"Everyone involved must be killed. The woman, the executive, and those you hire. They die in a failed police raid that you supervise. You collect the money and make sure there are no witnesses. An unfortunate outcome after the police receive an anonymous tip and the kidnappers react violently when the police arrive. The kidnapping blamed on Castro's M-26-7 revolutionaries. A way to get money to finance their rebellion."

"How is the missing money explained?" Torres asked.

"What money? Explained as an attempt not to pay the kidnappers. Details become unknown with everyone dead. You will be there when the executive delivers the ransom. His name is Bartolo Landeira. Do you recall the American who took down those two thugs sent by the Mafia earlier this year?"

"Of course. He killed one and sent the other to the hospital. A dangerous *hijo de puta*."

"That he is. Trained as commando in the war. It will account for his attempt to rescue the woman. Never let him get close though. Kill him immediately since he might act unpredictably. He is the target. Involved in sending material to the San Juan reporter. Landeira and his friends are this Venganza de Martí group. The President wants them stamped out. Landeira is also working for American intelligence so we must disguise his death in this way. That is absolutely important, Sergeant."

"I understand, Sir. What if Landeira goes to the police and reports the kidnapping?"

"He will not risk harm coming to his girlfriend. Here is a picture of her."

Torres smiled as he looked at the photograph of Emilia Montero.

"See what I mean. Landeira also has access to the $100,000 ransom as the financial executive of Landeira Grupo. Why risk losing her when it is not even his money?"

Torres looked up in surprise after Ventura mentioned the ransom amount.

"That is right, Sergeant, $100,000. $20,000 of which is yours if you pull this off."

Torres nodded enthusiastically. "What is the plan?"

"Once you hire these kidnappers, find a location for Landeira to deliver the money in exchange for the return of the woman. Somewhere here in the city where we can stage the police raid in advance while remaining hidden until Landeira arrives with the money and you give the signal for the police to close in."

"We also need someplace to keep the woman hidden for a couple of days," Torres added. "How many kidnappers?"

Ventura answered, "Three I should think since you will be with them until Landeira comes to make the exchange."

Miguel Torres knew the mean neighborhoods of Havana. The cheap brothels, the drug dealers, the poorest sectors populated mostly by local Cubans. Few tourists ventured here other than occasional groups of sailors in port. Torres knew it well because he grew up here.

He turned to a career in the police as an alternative to a life of crime. Observing police corruption even at the lowest level paid better while providing a sanctioned outlet for his violent tendencies.

Since Batista seized power in 1952, the National Police increasingly turned into an instrument directed against political opposition to his regime. Torres intellect and instincts fit perfectly into those of the secret police. No longer working in uniform gave him elevated status. He could indulge his habit of dressing well while carrying a concealed handgun under his shirt and enjoying respect from the fear generated as an agent of the feared National Police.

Ventura recognized Torres skills and mentored him along with Ventura's own rise within the police. Ventura's infamous reputation for taking people off the street to suffer torture or death required equally violently inclined subordinates like Torres.

Torres asked, "Where do we grab the woman?"

"That is to be determined. Essential that it happens quietly without any witnesses. Along with recruiting your kidnappers, your job is to scout the woman's habits the same as in San Juan. Tell me how you will pull this off after studying the problem, Sergeant."

The abduction was critical to the plan's success. If witnessed, police might be alerted. No one other than General Garcia and Colonel Romero knew of the assassination plot. Secrecy was essential for plausible deniability to deflect suspicion from Landeira's CIA connection.

* * * *

Sergeant Torres began the task of finding three reliable criminals. That was a job for trolling the right places at night and buying drinks. He knew of someone that occasionally worked as an enforcer in the Cuban criminal environment. If Torres determined him reliable for this operation, he might know others. He devoted the daytime hours to observing the habits of the woman.

On the first night, Torres found the guy he was looking for after asking around at several bars in the rough Cayo Hueso district east of Central Havana. Flashing his badge in the third bar, the intimidated bartender gestured with his head toward a table in the corner.

Torres approached saying to one of the three men at the table, "Been looking for you, Pablo."

The man looked up with his expression turning to fear as he recognized Torres.

"Tell your friends to leave," Torres said raising his untucked shirt to reveal a holstered pistol on his hip.

The two men abruptly left and Torres sat down.

"Relax Pablo. I am not here to give you trouble. Actually, I want to offer you an opportunity to make a lot of money. Let me buy you another drink."

Torres interrogated Pablo about his recent activities explained as working mostly for people Torres recognized as connected to the Cuban underworld. Satisfied he found the right man, Pablo enthusiastically agreed after Torres explained the job as the kidnapping of a girlfriend of a wealthy Cuban with his cut being $5,000.

"I need two others for the job, Pablo. *Hombres con experiencia. No pendejos.* What about the two that just left?"

"How much for them?" Pablo asked

"$2,500 each."

Pablo shook his head, "For that much money, I know two brothers better suited for this. Worked with them before."

"Good. Here is a thousand dollars good faith money for you. Tell these guys to say nothing to anyone. Everyone gets paid after we pull this off. I will meet you here on Friday night same time. Bring your amigos. I trust these are the right guys for the job. Do not disappoint me, Pablo."

"Are we working for someone?" Pablo asked.

Torres clamped his hand on Pablo's forearm spilling his beer. "Don't be stupid by asking questions, Pablo. But just so you understand to keep your mouth shut, I will tell you this is not a police operation. Certain powerful Americans want to send a strong message to the woman's lover. Do a good job and there may be future work for you. These people are scarier than I am. Do not fuck up, Pablo."

Giving out that information was Ventura's suggestion. Expecting the hired kidnappers might be indiscreet, it would serve imply the American Mafia while instilling fear to keep their mouths shut.

Torres spent the next three days watching Emilia Montero. The first day she drove to the office at eight o'clock in the morning. A long boring day for Torres broken only for the hour she left the office for lunch nearby then returning to her apartment in a good neighborhood late in the afternoon. The same routine the second day. The third day started the same except the woman drove instead to another apartment that evening. Torres stayed until well into the night. The woman never left. Returning early the next morning, Torres observed her leaving then followed as she drove to her office.

This other apartment was a well-maintained good neighborhood in Old Havana but not a quarter like the Vedado where he would expect her wealthy boyfriend to live. Perhaps she was screwing another man on the side. Maybe just visiting a woman friend or relative. It did not matter. Torres already made up his mind about how to seize her.

Torres met Pablo and the brothers making up his kidnapping team at the bar. Sitting down, Torres said to the two brothers, "Did Pablo explain what this is about?"

Both answered yes starring at Torres with respect and a measure of fear. They knew Torres reputation on the street as Colonel Ventura's hit man.

"Your names?"

The older brother answered Santos, the younger brother Ramon.

"Do all of you have guns?"

All three men nodded.

"Show me," Torres said.

All three lifted their shirts to reveal the grips of large caliber handguns.

"Can you provide a car for the job? A four-door sedan? Clean, not stolen?"

Pablo said, "I can arrange that. What happens once we snatch the woman?

"We keep her someplace secure for a few days while the boyfriend gets the ransom money together. An apartment. One with two bedrooms, a kitchen, and toilet. A building with a back entrance shielded from view. Got any suggestions?" Torres said.

"I can find a place," Pablo said.

The older of the two brothers Santos asked, "How do we take the woman?"

"In the morning, she drives to her office. We follow. Pablo you drive. Following her very closely, somewhere along the way you bump her car hard from behind. Once she stops get out of the car and make as if examining for damage. Whether she gets out of the car or remains behind the wheel approach her and stick a gun in her face."

"Take her back to the sedan quickly. Put these handcuffs on her and sit her in the back seat." Torres handed Pablo the handcuffs under the table then slid him the keys. "Does one of you carry a knife?"

The younger brother Ramon produced a switchblade and flicked it open.

"Handcuffed her and put in the back seat. Then put the knife close to her face. The threat of cutting the face is terrifying to any woman. Your brother drives her car out of the street and parks it close by. We then take her to the apartment. Make sure to stock the apartment with enough food and beer for all of us for a couple of days.

Pablo asked, "What if she does not stop?"

"Christ, Pablo, do I need to explain everything?" Torres said. "If she does not stop along the way giving you the opportunity to fake the accident, grab her when she parks at her office. She parks at an adjacent parking lot. Create a minor accident first by hitting her car there. Understood?"

"Okay. When do we do this?" Pablo asked.

"In a few days," Torres replied. "We do a trial run then make sure she spends that night alone in her own apartment. You join me at sunrise the next morning. I will be waiting outside her building."

Santos asked, "When do we get paid."

Torres glared at him. "When the ransom is paid, I pay you on the spot. Like I warned Pablo, keep your mouths shut. Nothing must go wrong. Follow the plan. No fuck ups. I do not tolerate excuses. You do not want me as an enemy."

* * * *

Torres reported developments to Colonel Ventura and outlined the plan for kidnapping Emilia Montero.

"Good work, Sergeant," Ventura said as they sat in his office. "Are these three reliable?"

"They will follow orders. The plan is simple enough. I will do a trial run the day before with them."

Ventura nodded. "Who do they think is behind this?"

"I gave them the impression the American Mafia."

"Once this is done, it will not matter. You will see that everyone dies in the police raid, Sergeant."

"What about the location for Landeira to deliver the money?"

"I have a couple of ideas. I believe the Cerro district offers the best options. A poor area with many closed businesses. I will select a couple of suitable locations tomorrow."

"Good. The following day you can show me. If I agree on a location, then we schedule the kidnapping for Wednesday morning."

Chapter 27

Emilia left her apartment as usual at eight o'clock for the short drive to her law office. As she pulled away from the curb, a man standing on the sidewalk smoking a cigarette jumped into a sedan parked close by.

"That is the woman," Torres said to Pablo as he got into the passenger seat.

Both cars proceeded at a slow speed for several blocks before Emilia braked at a stop sign.

"Now, Pablo. Hit her hard enough to startle her."

Pablo hit her bumper enough to push her car a couple of feet forward. Once stopped, he and the younger brother Ramon got out and walked toward her car. They stopped at the rear of her car as if examining for damage.

After a couple of moments, Emilia joined them. Angrily gesturing with he hands, "What the hell were you doing?"

Pablo reached under his shirt and pulled out his revolver. Sticking it in her face, he grabbed her arm. "Come with me. This is a kidnapping. Do not make a sound or I will hurt you badly. You will not be harmed if your boyfriend pays a ransom."

Screaming unlikely helpful with nobody visible on the street, she remained silent.

Ramon grabbed her other arm. With Pablo, they pushed her toward their car. Ramon extracted the handcuffs secured them on her wrists then pushed her into the backseat. Emilia's eyes widened in fear when Ramon flicked open the switchblade.

"Do not make trouble or I will cut you," Ramon said getting in beside her.

Santos got into Emilia's car and drove it to a perpendicular street followed by Pablo in the sedan. Finding a parking lot with many cars, he locked the car taking her purse and briefcase.

Miguel Torres placed a telephone call to Landeira's apartment. Getting no answer, he tried the Landeira Grupo office. Without giving his name, saying it was a personal matter, the receptionist put him through to Landeira.

"Who is this?" Landeira said.

"Your worst nightmare. We have your girlfriend Emilia Montero. If you want her back in good condition, you need to buy her back. The price is $100,000US. Nothing larger than fifty-dollar bills. I will call in two days with instructions for making the exchange. Do not be stupid and call the police."

Torres disconnected the call.

Landeira experienced terrible news before but nothing approaching the impact of this. He called her apartment. No answer. Her office said she never called or showed up this morning. He drove to her apartment and let himself in with his key. Nothing out of place. Bed made. No sign of a struggle. Coffee cup in the sink. Cold coffee in the coffee pot.

Returning to his apartment he sat by the window trying to process the shock. It took several minutes before he could turn his mind to the problem. What if this was not about money? Kidnappings were uncommon in Havana. Possibly related to the press attacks or by his association with Hector Vasquez? If that was the case, that meant the police were behind this. However, with Toussaint dead, why bother? Mafia retaliation? Yet why now? He had published nothing attacking the Mafia since beginning the clandestine Venganza de Martí campaign. Yet possibly the Mafia for something related to his father.

If it was to get at him, why not just gun him down like Gaspar Toussaint. That train of thought brought the realization that Toussaint's murder might be the work of Batista. Landeira's gut said Batista not Trujillo. If it was to get at him, then it could only mean the regime wanted plausible deniability for killing an American with influence with the U.S. Ambassador. What about the visit by Walter Peterson? Did the regime think he was working with the CIA? Batista was unquestionably out of favor with the Eisenhower administration. Had his secret police simply overreacted?

Was he important enough for them to disguise his murder as a common criminal matter? Then again, maybe it was just an individual that wanted him out of the way. Killed in a manner explainable like a kidnapping gone wrong?

Other than a Mafioso like Trafficante, the only person coming to mind was Colonel Ventura. That would mean Ventura must be sure of his involvement in the press campaign. Possible since Ventura may remain convinced of Vasquez's involvement. Did not seem logical but Cuba was disintegrating rapidly and circumstances might not follow logic.

Of course, it might be nothing more than local criminals looking for a big score. Not to over-think this, but a risky move if it was locals since kidnapping would be counterproductive to Mafia's interests in enticing high-rollers to Havana. Locals going off the reservation would fear Mafia retribution.

This internal debate went on for an hour before Landeira decided on a course of action. Not yet thoroughly thought out but with immediate steps he could begin taking immediately. Gathering the money first on the list. Easy enough given Landeira Grupo's credit stature, but a highly unusual request for this amount of cash. Without divulging any reason, he pressured the local president of Landeira Grupo's new American branch bank in a telephone call. Let the bank think that he might be planning to leave the country given the current political turmoil.

Now thinking clearer, his course of action remained the same regardless who might be behind this. Either this was to kill him or a legitimate kidnapping for ransom. If these were ordinary criminals then killing him and Emilia was the likely outcome to eliminate witnesses. Therefore, this must result in confrontation. One with poor odds for success. Emilia's survival the singular objective. If the National Police were behind this then difficult to see how they might survive.

If they somehow prevailed, escaping Cuba became the next hurdle. A real problem if the secret police was behind this. One problem at a time. Preparing to attack an unknown number of enemies at a location of their choosing was almost impossible. All he could do was make preparations affording flexibility to adapt to fluid circumstances. That meant finding a way to conceal a weapon and seizing the offensive given only the broadest imaginable situation as a starting point.

This enemy might expect him to arrive armed but withholding any initial threat for fear of risking harm to Emilia. At some point, they should allow him to get close enough to determine he is unarmed. How could he conceal a weapon from view and still be able to access it quickly? However, they could simply shoot him when he arrived. No way to guard against that.

The overriding decision to assault the kidnappers at the first opportunity stood as the essential factor if he was to have any chance of saving Emilia. Major Fairbairn schooled his trainees to seize any opportunity by attacking the enemy without over-thinking. Too many variables always existed. Rely on instinctive responses bred of repetitive training.

At the least, he would strap on his ankle holster to carry his backup Walther PPK .380 ACP. Impossible though to access quickly. Good at close range, but not as the primary weapon to bring to a gunfight. With weapons pointed at him, the bad guys held an overwhelming advantage. Survival meant accuracy and knockdown power. To stand any chance, that meant his .45 Browning M1911 semi-automatic service pistol. During the war, he was a crack shot with the weapon but that was years ago. Yet how could he conceal something nine inches long weighing two and a half pounds?

The answer must lay with the bag used to carry the money. Find a bag with the means for concealing the Browning yet allowing for its quick access. Assume the bad guys would expect him to demonstrate he was unarmed as he approached. Walking toward them offered probably the only opportunity to surprise them. That meant creating a way to cause that to happen prior to the exchange of money for Emilia.

Walking through that in his mind, success seemed out of reach. Killing several armed kidnappers and surviving impossible unless he could create some advantage. If there was a squad of police with orders to shoot, there was no chance. He put that out of his mind.

What he needed was a diversion. Something to give him an edge. Seemingly impossible to plan without knowing the location for the exchange. No opportunity to make a reconnaissance run.

The only diversion possible therefore was something related to his car. Rig it for explosion? With what explosive and how to control the detonation?

His wartime training provided extensive demolitions knowledge but always with military grade explosives. He understood something of improvised explosives but even that seemed out of reach in Havana. Ammonium nitrate fertilizer and fuel oil mixture was the most commonly known. Hard to find in urban Havana. Remote detonation presented another problem. He had neither the time nor the ability to construct some complex detonator for an improvised explosive.

The simplest idea was igniting the car's fuel tank. A fire certainly a diversion but nothing spectacular. If he could add an explosion, much more dramatic. But gasoline does not explode it just burns. Explosion occurs only when the gasoline mixes with oxygen. So igniting the fuel tank might not produce much of an explosion.

Taking that thought further, what about using the gasoline fire to generate a secondary explosion? The source of which could be propane tanks in the trunk. His Buick should be able to hold a number of 20-pound propane tanks. Rigging them to a common valve that he opens just before he exits the car releases the propane gas. Mixing with oxygen from the air inside the car it becomes a potent explosive source.

The method of detonation becomes the problem. Perhaps devising a way for the car's fuel tank to drain the gasoline out under the car is the answer. Igniting the gasoline using a road flare could then provide a delayed detonation of the releasing propane gas within the car. The trick becomes timing and dropping the lit flare under the car such that it provides enough time to walk clear before the gasoline ignites. No way to calculate the violence of the propane explosion or how long for ignition after starting the gasoline fire. He risked dying in the explosion if he did not get it right.

By nightfall that first day, he felt emotionally and physically exhausted worrying about Emilia. What was happening to her? He needed to eat something and sleep if he was to function for the next forty-eight hours. Tomorrow he expected the money to be ready. Also needed to rig the Buick tomorrow. Get that behind him to concentrate on refining his plan.

He harbored no illusions about their probable fate. Even so, there was no rethinking his attack strategy. Paying the ransom expecting their release was never an option. Trusting the enemy to honor a bargain always a flawed strategy. Regardless who was behind this, logic dictated the perpetrators most likely intended killing him and Emilia.

That first night yielded only a couple of hours of fitful interrupted sleep after sketching out how to booby-trap his car. The same disciplined planning he used for wartime demolition missions. However, here in Havana the challenge was cobbling together from readily available materials. He had no access to military grade munitions, dynamite, blasting caps, quantities of gunpowder, or even fertilizer.

He dedicated the next morning to purchasing the necessary items, the afternoon for assembling the hardware inside the trunk of his Buick. If this was a police trap, he must also assume he was under surveillance. For that matter even if this was a Mafia operation or just enterprising criminals, they too might be watching his movements.

The items he needed should be available at a hardware store. However, he could not risk the perpetrators observing him filling his trunk with propane tanks and jerry cans, or even visiting a hardware store under the circumstances. He must play the part of someone victimized by the kidnapping of his woman.

After some thought, the solution became simple. He drove to the corporate office stopping first to fill the car's gas tank. At the filling station, he convinced a garage mechanic to drill a one-inch hole in the floor of the Buick's trunk without explaining the reason. For anyone watching, the car pulling into a garage service bay was undergoing some minor repair.

Entering the office building he immediately left by a rear entrance. Having earlier confirmed by telephone the availability of all the required items, he took a taxi to the hardware store. His bill of materials included four 20-pound propane tanks, four 5-gallon jerry cans, assorted pipefittings for rigging the propane tanks, hoses, and fittings for rigging the jerry cans, two 90-degree shutoff valves, a box of road flares, and some hand tools. He arranged delivery to his apartment that afternoon. returning to the office, for anyone surveilling him, he never left. Driving home, he stopped and filled the jerry cans with gasoline.

The parking arrangement inside the inner courtyard of his apartment building allowed assembling the hardware in the Buick's trunk without observation by anyone watching from the street. Accomplishing the mechanical work to rig the car did not take particular skill or special tools. Hooking up the propane tanks to a manifold constructed from hoses and pipefittings allowed activating a single valve to release the volatile propane gas inside the car. A similar arrangement allowed releasing the gasoline from the jerry cans through a pipe penetrating through the hole drilled in the trunk. He sealed the pipe with a rubber gasket to prevent premature ignition of the propane filling the Buick's interior.

His plan called for stopping his car as close as possible to the exchange point. Adapting to circumstances at the time of the exchange, he opens the trunk. Under the disguise of retrieving the duffle bag with the ransom money, he opens both the propane release valve and the gasoline release valve. The gasoline begins emptying under the car, the propane filling the interior of the Buick.

The propane ignition meant as a delayed secondary explosion made more violent by the anticipated rupture of the Buick's gas tank spreading another fifteen gallons of burning gasoline. He needed some indeterminate amount of time to get outside the blast radius.

Before closing the trunk and extracting the duffle bag with the money and his .45 Browning pistol inside, he ignites the road flare and drops it underneath the car positioned to provide time to walk away before the flare ignites the spreading pool of gasoline.

Timing of setting off the diversion sequence was the delicate factor for achieving maximum effect and getting clear of the explosion. Shielded from view behind the car, the sequence of events started when activating a road flare.

Extracting the .45 from the bag holding the cash while facing one or more armed kidnappers made timing of the gasoline fire critical as a diversion to give him an edge for drawing first blood. The propane gas explosion intended as a last-ditch secondary diversion.

After confirming by telephone that the cash was ready in the morning, he made his way to the bank president's secretary. With a zippered canvas duffle bag, she ushered him into the president's office.

The flustered bank executive said to Landeira, "Extraordinarily unusual for your demand of such a large sum of cash. Not easy to assemble on such short notice. I trust everything is alright."

Landeira was in no state of mind to appease the man's curiosity about the purpose of the cash. Let him speculate as to whether this was bribery, embezzlement, or blackmail.

"It involves a confidential foreign transaction where normal banking transactions are not possible," Landeira replied.

"Certainly. Do you wish to count the money before signing the receipt, Señor Landeira?

"No, that will not be necessary. Thank you for your exceptional service, Señor Lopez."

Having eaten nothing all day, Landeira stopped on the way home at a restaurant, forcing down some food. Back at his apartment, he waited for the delivery from the hardware store.

Arriving late in the afternoon by a delivery van, he and the driver transferred the items to the Buick's trunk. Parked with the trunk facing away from the street insured what he was doing could not be observed from the street. He devoted the next hour to assembling his improvised explosive arrangement. Easy enough since it only involved assembling pipefittings and hoses in the Buick's trunk using a wrench and pliers.

He practiced how to extract the heavy .45 Browning from an external zippered side pocket in the duffle bag. Surprisingly, he could retrieve it almost as quickly as from a shoulder holster. Faster than if stuck into his waistband. It allowed him to keep the gun hidden if asked to open his jacket and turn around to prove he was unarmed before drawing the gun at the right opportunity.

Nothing more to do that night except suffer through the anxiety of not knowing what Emilia was enduring. A couple of Scotches did little to settle his distress or make sleep possible.

* * * *

The next morning, he allocated to one final preparation. Should they somehow escape, they must immediately leave Cuba. He was certain this was a trap. Even if a straightforward kidnapping, why should the perpetrators leave witnesses? Given poor odds for survival, preparing for escape seemed futile. Should they somehow make it that far, the only method of escape appeared sailing to Key West, Florida.

Going through Emilia's things was difficult to decide what things might be important other than her passport and jewelry. Practical clothing, undergarments, a sweater, and a jacket for the time on the water filled a suitcase.

After gathering their belongings, he used the same ploy as the previous day to go the corporate office and sneak out the back. Taking a taxi, he stopped at a market to buy food and water. Arriving by taxi at his sailboat docked in Boca de la Chorrera, he stored the food and placed their suitcases on the bed in the berth.

A sudden overwhelming sadness swept over him. Something not experienced since the war. Fear before a dangerous mission full of unknowns. Part of his training included how to manage fear. Not something easily taught. Every person must find that key to focus on the mission and compartmentalize the fear. In this case, the fear was for Emilia. Although fatalistic about his chances of surviving, difficult to compartmentalize that also meant her death.

Leaving the boat, he agonized over what he must do next. As much as he wanted to spare Augustin and Alicia Montero the terrible the news, he had little choice. Should Emilia not survive, they must know what happened. More troubling, was lying to them about what he was planning. To them, following the kidnappers' instructions and paying the ransom would seem the best chance of saving their daughter. How could he tell them he instead planned a desperate assault? They did not know of his special training. In this situation, he even questioned if that might prove enough.

Showing up at Landeira Rum, Augustine greeted him with an affectionate hug. Entering Augustin's office, Landeira closed the door behind him. "I have some distressing news, Augustine. It concerns Emilia."

After going through the scenario, Landeira continued outlining what came next. "I have already assembled the money. I am waiting for the kidnappers to call with arrangements for the exchange of the money for Emilia."

"I will go with you," Augustin said.

"No, Augustin. Best I go alone. A second person will spook the kidnappers."

"Should we not call the police?"

Landeira shook his head. "Absolutely not. The police are stupid and clumsy. If they show up when exchanging the money, it puts Emilia's life at risk."

"Who are these kidnappers, Bart?"

"No way to tell. Criminals extorting a large ransom possible only from a wealthy company. They know of my relationship with Emilia. Her father also employed by the same corporation."

Landeira left Augustin Montero severely shaken by the news. Now facing the distressing task of telling his wife. For Landeira, a feeling of guilt about lying. Augustin would not understand why Landeira planned a violent confrontation without telling him this was likely a police or Mafia trap. Either of which possibility the result of Landeira's doing now jeopardizing the life of his daughter.

****

Late that night, Landeira sat brooding in his apartment when the telephone rang.

Sergeant Torres said, "Do you have the money?"

"Yes."

"Good. Then we make the exchange to get back your woman tomorrow night. I will call you tomorrow afternoon with instructions. Stay by your telephone."

"I want to talk to her? Make sure she is all right. Unless I do, there is no exchange."

A long silence ensued.

"Hold on."

After an agonizing delay, Emilia came on the line. Surprisingly she was not crying but her voice shaking. "Bart, is that you?"

"Yes! Are you all right? Have they harmed you in any way?"

She replied after a pause, "No." Her voice however held an inflection suggesting that was not entirely truthful. "They are treating me well. They are holding me in …"

Torres came on the line, "Satisfied? I will call tomorrow afternoon with the location to make the exchange." He then disconnected.

Another night of fragmented sleep. The morning spent with lots of coffee and a breakfast of eggs and toast to sustain him.

Waiting in his apartment the entire day was agony. You cannot willfully dispel fear only try to find your own way to manage it. For Landeira that meant running alternative scenarios through his mind. Endless repetitions of extracting the .45 Browning from the duffle bag. He practiced aiming at targets at different distances. Reciting a mantra to get as close as possible to his targets before exposing his weapon. The element of surprise gone after his first shot. No way to anticipate how many adversaries or the circumstances. Keep attacking aggressively the only plan possible.

To dispel the natural tendency to dwell on the overwhelming obstacles against success, he focused on refining his surprise offensive. They would not anticipate his concealed weapon. The first shot was his. No way to anticipate the distraction benefit of the fire or the timing of the subsequent propane explosion. Out of his control so put it out of his mind.

The telephone call came at six o'clock.

"You will drive to a location in the Cerro district. The place is a former automotive garage. Windows boarded up. Name on the sign is *Reparaciones Automáticas Cerro*. It is on Lacoste between Calz de Ayestaran and Panchito Gomez. Park in front and flash your headlights. Two hours from now. Eight o'clock."

"I understand. But here are my terms. I stay in my car until you show me the woman in my headlights outside the building. Once I see her unharmed, I get the bag with the money from the trunk. Then she walks alone towards me while I walk past her to give you the money. You check the money and I leave with her."

"Fuck you. You are playing with your woman's life. We do it my way."

"Not if you want the $100,000. Those are my conditions."

Torres fell silent for a moment before answering, "Very well, Señor Landeira. We do it your way. Come alone and show us you are unarmed before coming close. Try anything foolish and I shoot your woman."

Torres disconnected the call. From what Colonel Ventura told him, Landeira was dangerous as a cobra. Probably armed. Not the kind of man to trust kidnappers. Waiting to get the woman safely close to him before doing anything. Landeira would never get that chance. Once close enough, Torres will shoot him then the woman signaling the police waiting in several cars nearby to converge on the location. Pablo and his two associates then killed by police gunfire. Torres exempted by identification of his red shirt.

Landeira's demands held no meaning except for seeing Emilia. Just a ploy to appease the kidnappers as playing out the scenario. He intended to dictate events not submit to what he believed the kidnappers plan to kill him and Emilia. Force them to reveal Emilia's location instead of walking into some abandoned building.

* * * *

Landeira left his apartment allowing enough time to make one drive by of the location and the surrounding streets. If he and Emilia survived the encounter, they still must escape on foot into the surrounding neighborhood.

Behind the automotive repair garage there was an alley. On the other side of the alley a collection of single-story, rundown homes. Next to the garage a small grocery store, now dark. On the other side stood another abandoned building.

Driving a circuitous route of the nearby streets used up the remainder of the time. At eight o'clock, he stopped the car in the parking area in front of the garage and flashed the headlights.

Thirty seconds later, a man opened the door to the garage office with its boarded windows then stepped out looking around while shielding his eyes from the glare of the Buick's headlights. Landeira could clearly see the man holding a revolver at his side.

The man turned appearing to talk to someone inside. Landeira's heart leapt at the sight of Emilia stepping out with another man standing next to her holding her arm. Leaving the car idling, Landeira stepped out and went behind the Buick opening the trunk. Reaching in, he grabbed the duffle bag placing it on the cracked asphalt. Opening the valve to the propane tanks, he could hear the hiss of escaping gas. Opening the other valve started gasoline flowing under the trunk from the jerry cans turned upside down.

Before closing the trunk, he ignited the flare by removing the endcap then scrapping the exposed abrasive surface much the same as striking a match. Bending down he estimated the flow of the growing pool of gasoline under the Buick using the illumination of the flare. Anticipating where to place the flare to give him several seconds before the gasoline ignited, he dropped the flare hidden from the kidnapper's view before closing the trunk.

Walking to a position in front of the Buick with the headlights illuminating the scene, the closest kidnapper pointed a revolver at him and said, "Open your jacket and turn around showing you are unarmed."

Landeira did as instructed assessing the situation. Emilia was still standing outside the door with a second kidnapper holding tight to her arm and also holding a semiautomatic 9mm pistol. As Landeira completed demonstrating he was unarmed, the pool of gasoline ignited with a loud swooshing sound.

Simultaneously, Landeira extracted the Browning from the duffle bag. With the first kidnapper closest to him momentarily distracted by the developing fire under the Buick, Landeira shot him twice.

However, the man holding Emilia fired two shots in return.

Landeira released he was hit somewhere in the torso. As the man attempted to force Emilia back inside the building, she resisted then swung her arm as hard as she could to smash her fist into his groin then kicked her heel into his shin.

Distracted, the man still held her by the arm. Landeira used the moment to take aim. He needed to put the man down with a well-placed shot without hitting Emilia. The gunman in the red shirt solved the problem by shoving Emilia back into the building then turning back to take another shot at Landeira. Landeira beat him by putting a .45 caliber round into his forehead.

Ignoring his wound, Landeira rushed inside the darkened office. An open doorway led to a back area illuminated by a kerosene lantern. Expecting other kidnappers to use Emilia as a hostage shield, Landeira entered the rear storage area in a low crouching position. Ready to take fire if he could gain an opportunity to neutralize the remaining threat and save Emilia.

Two gunmen remained. One fired a hurried shot high missing Landeira bent low on one knee. Landeira placed two rounds into the man's chest.

The remaining gunman holding Emilia fired striking Landeira again.

Emilia watches in horror as Landeira fell forward stopping his fall with his left hand. Realizing he cannot risk shooting for fear of hitting her, she raised her knee and smashed down hard on the instep of the man's foot holding her around the waist. Twisting from his grasp, she came around with her elbow catching him in the side of the head. Her maneuver provided enough space between her and the kidnapper for Landeira to place two rounds into the man dropping him to the floor.

Emilia rushed to Landeira still kneeling with blood soaking his shirt. Two wounds were visible. One to the lower left side of his abdomen, the other higher up on the right near his lower ribcage.

Ignoring the wounds, Landeira had the presence of mind to realize he expended the Browning's seven-round magazine. Ignoring Emilia's ministrations, he fumbled in his pocket. Finding a spare magazine, he reloaded.

"Oh my God, Bart! You're wounded! What do I do?"

Breathing heavily, he said, "Must stop the bleeding. Help me off with the jacket. Remove my shirt and rip it up to use for putting pressure on the wounds."

Before she could do anything, from outside came a voice over a bullhorn. "This is the police. Those inside the building put down your weapons and come out with your hands raised."

Less than a minute later, the picture abruptly changed as submachinegun rounds slammed into the garage office.

"It's a police trap, Emilia! We must try to escape. They mean to kill us. Kidnapping you was just an excuse. We are meant to die along with the kidnappers."

He turned the wick down to extinguish the kerosene lantern, darkening the storage room.

"We must make a run for it. You take the bag. It is full of the ransom money." Raising his pant leg, he extracted the Walther PPK pistol. "Take this. I switched off the safety. Shoot anybody trying to stop us."

"You can't run. You're bleeding too badly," she said. Her voice amplifying her emotional ordeal after days in captivity followed by this violent encounter.

"I'll go as far as I can. Must get you away from here. Need to try to make it out the back. It is a dark night with not much moonlight. Need to escape the area among the houses across the back alley."

A great roar accompanied by the building shaking signaled the Buick exploding from the accumulated pressure of the propane ignited by the gasoline fire. If lucky, any police taking firing positions from the front got a nasty surprise. The explosion possibly rupturing the Buick's fuel tank spreading flames outward.

"I am going to crawl out first to see if I can spot anyone. You follow close behind staying very low. If I don't make it, you keep running!"

Outside two police cars were at either end of the alley with headlights pointed toward the rear of the garage. Fortunately, the light beams did not illuminate the door to the storeroom directly. Once outside, Landeira rose up to a crouch and motioned for Emilia to follow.

No police visible. Perhaps the police in the two cars went to the front of the garage responding to the explosion and growing fire now visible even from the rear of the building.

Quickly they made their way out of the glare of headlight illumination into the neighboring houses backyards. Lights began coming on with dogs barking at the commotion caused by the explosion. Looking back toward the garage the explosion spread gasoline flames even to the adjoining buildings. All the structures now fully engulfed.

Landeira struggled with every step. The pain intensifying and the loss of blood rapidly weakening him. Finding a place out of view next to car two blocks away, Emilia helped him remove his jacket and strip off his shirt. Tearing it into two pieces, she tied one piece on the wound at the ribs using the shirt-sleeves. Landeira held another folded piece applying pressure to the wound on his left side.

More worrisome was his growing fatigue. Coming down from the adrenalin rush combined with the loss of blood signaled he could not make it much further. Beginning to cough up blood meant a lung wound. Internal bleeding could collapse the lung.

After making their way to the larger street of Calz de Ayestaran, Landeira said, "I reconnoitered the area earlier. Just up this street little more than a block is a small Catholic church. Parroquia San José. Plead with the priest for sanctuary. Explain that I am a journalist. Batista's secret police want to silence me for writing against the regime. Tell him I just need to get somewhere safe to get medical attention.

"Use the priest's telephone to call Hemingway. Tell Hemingway what happened. We need him to send his driver and pick us up at the church."

"Bart, you need to go to a hospital."

"Trust me, Emilia. I go to a hospital and I am dead. This was a police trap to kill me. You were the sacrificial bait. That is why the police showed up so quickly. For some reason they want to disguise my death as a failed kidnapping."

Trying to process what Bart was telling her, she said, "Okay. Can you make it?"

"I will do my best. Keep that bag close. Inside is $100,000. We may need that to buy our way out of leaving Cuba."

Chapter 28

By the time they reached the church, Landeira was close to collapse. It was close to nine o'clock. Lights were still on in the church.

"Prop me against the side of the church out of sight around the corner. See if you can locate the priest. Do not trust anyone else. If no one is inside the church, try the rectory next door.

Struggling to speak, he said quietly, "One more thing, Emilia. If something goes wrong, get away and leave me. I may not make it anyway. Hemingway will help you get out of Cuba. Now hurry, Emilia."

Minutes later returning with the young priest, Emilia gasped seeing Bart's head slumped down on his chest barely conscious.

Looking down on Landeira and the blood-soaked makeshift bandages and jacket, the priest said to Emilia, "Get the sexton from inside the church. I need his help."

With the priest and sexton supporting Landeira, they managed get him the short distance to the rectory door. Inside, the priest shouted instructions to his alarmed housekeeper.

Settling Landeira on a bed, the elderly housekeeper took charge of doing what she could. Removing the bloody clothing, she applied pressure with gauge pads to stem the renewed bleeding of both bullet wounds caused by moving Landeira. While she stayed with her patient, she ordered the sexton to prepare a pot of hot water and bring towels.

Emilia welcomed the attention to help Bart, but knew he must get professional medical help quickly. That meant first getting him to safety. Reaching Hemingway their only hope.

"Father, may I use your telephone? If I can reach a close friend he can come and take my … my husband for medical attention by a doctor."

"Of course, Señora. Come with me."

Emilia prayed for Hemingway to answer.

Mary Hemingway answered.

"Thank God you are home, Mary. The police shot Bart. He's in a bad way. Maybe close to death. Can't risk taking him to a hospital. No time to tell you all the details but I must speak to Ernest. We need his help desperately, Mary."

Moments later, Hemingway came on the line. She ran through the brief explanation she gave to Mary, adding *they shot him for publishing material damaging to President Batista.*

"We need to get Bart to a safe place and get him medical help?"

"Where is he now? Hemingway asked.

"At the rectory of a Catholic church in the Cerro district on the south side. Parroquia San José on Calz de Ayestaran. If we could stay at Finca Vigía, we could get Bart medical attention. Then find a way to get him to his family's estate in Camagüey."

Without her asking, Hemingway said, "Gregorio and I will leave immediately. Maybe thirty minutes. Is Bart conscious?"

"Yes. Only barely. The priest and his housekeeper are doing what they can. He's lost a lot of blood. Do you know a doctor we can call?"

"Yes, of course. Mary will try to locate him while we get to you. Hang in there, Emilia. Bart is a tough fellow."

The rectory housekeeper successfully stemmed the bleeding of Landeira's bullet wounds. She gave him a glass of rum for the pain. He remained conscious although suffering painfully labored breathing while frequently coughing blood.

Avoiding revealing who was coming to help, Emilia held his hand and said, "Our friend is on the way. He is trying to locate a doctor. How are you doing?"

Landeira managed a nod while giving her a weak smile.

Seeing the headlights of Hemingway's car through the rectory windows, Emilia rushed outside to meet him.

As the big man jumped out of the car, she met him and Gregorio halfway up the driveway. "Ernest, it is best if you are not recognized. Your face is too familiar. The police are likely looking for us. I had to trust the church staff but best not to push it. Stay in the car. Keep your cap on. Gregorio and I can manage getting Bart into the back seat with the help of the priest and the sexton."

He touched her shoulder. "Very well. You bearing up okay, Emilia?"

She let out a heavy sigh revealing her fatigue. "Not really. Better than Bart though. What about a doctor?"

"Mary is trying to reach my personal physician. He is also a close personal friend. Been to the house often. My concern is about what he can do outside a hospital setting. Bart was shot twice?"

She nodded. "Once in the chest. May have hit his lung. Coughs blood. The other wound is lower down on the side of his abdomen."

Hemingway hugged her. "Well, the sooner we get him to Doctor Estrada, the better."

As instructed, Hemingway returned to the passenger seat of his big four-door Buick.

With the help of the priest, the sinewy Gregorio, the sexton, and Emilia, they carried Bart the short distance to the car. The housekeeper walked ahead with blankets and pillow to make Landeira as comfortable as possible in the back seat.

Once settled with Gregorio behind the wheel and Emilia cradling Bart's head, she said, "Drive carefully, Gregorio. Avoid potholes. A rough ride might start him bleeding again."

Making the sign of the cross, the priest said, "God be with you."

* * * *

Thirty minutes later Gregorio parked the Buick in the driveway of Finca Vigia next to another car already parked there.

Hemingway said, "Thank God. That's Doctor Estrada's car."

At the sound of the car, Mary and Doctor Estrada rushed out the front door.

Estrada opened the rear door bending over to look at Landeira's wounds. Lifting Landeira's eyelids, he said, "Mary, prepare the dining room table with blankets covered with a sheet. I will operate there. It is close to the kitchen with good light. Let's get him into the house."

Victor Estrada was a well-built man in his forties. Hemingway was still a bull of a man with muscular arms. Between the two of them, they pulled Landeira out with Emilia holding his head while they lifted him. Each held him by one arm around body and the other arm lifting his weight from under his each thigh.

Inside, Mary finished preparing the dining table. The chandelier should provide adequate illumination for Estrada to operate.

Emilia assisted in situating Landeira with a pillow under his head. He was barely conscious with his eyelids fluttering. Estrada began assembling an IV. He came prepared knowing the patient suffered gunshot wounds from Hemingway relaying Emilia's description of Landeira's wounds.

"Ernest, bring me that coat tree from the other room to use for hanging the IV bottle. Mary, I need you to fill a large pot with water. Bring it to boiling. Place a strainer inside to lift out the sterilize instruments."

Looking at Emilia, Estrada asked, "I will need some help. Are you squeamish?"

"I will do whatever you need, Doctor."

In truth, she was near collapse. Her captivity was a horrid nightmare compounded by this night's terror. Only the will power to save Bart sustained her at this point.

"Fine. Put on these surgical gloves. You will assist me."

"I have no medical training, Doctor," Emilia said looking terrified in spite of fighting exhaustion.

"I understand. I will explain as we go along but I need a second pair of hands. Ernest, can you administer the ether to put him under?"

"Just tell me what I need to do," Hemingway replied.

Landeira said weakly, "Emilia. I need you to call my two associates. Their telephone numbers are in my wallet. Tell them they are in danger from Batista's secret police. Tell them what happened. It must be about our activities as Venganza de Martí. Tell them the police shot me but I am receiving medical attention. Do not tell them where we are."

"I will. I love you," she said, giving him a kiss on the forehead.

"Everyone put on these surgical masks," Estrada said. He then handed Hemingway a surgical anesthesia nosepiece holding a large gauze pad from which to administer chloroform. "Pull a chair to the end of the table so you can hold this over his nose. When I tell you, pour in two drops from this vile. Keep it handy if I need you to repeat the procedure. Turn your head to avoid inhaling the fumes yourself. Mary, lift out those instruments from the boiling water after twenty minutes. Without touching them, dump them onto a clean towel and place them next to the patient to my right."

Once everything was in place, Estrada said, "Since there are no exit wounds I must remove both bullets then assess the tissue damage. The prognosis depends on the extent of that damage. He has lost a lot of blood. I brought three units of plasma which helps replace the lost blood volume."

Looking at everyone, "Let's begin. Administer the chloroform, Ernest. Emilia, swab a wide area around each entry wound with alcohol."

The operation took almost ninety minutes. Locating and removing the bullets early into the procedure revealed the wound to the lower part of the right lung was the most serious. The bullet smashed the seventh rib then entered the lung. The other bullet tore muscle tissue on the left side narrowly missing organs. More concerned with post-operative infection, Estrada painstakingly irrigated both wound cavities.

As a precaution, Estrada inserted drainage tubes into both wounds.

"Would have preferred doing this in a hospital operating room, but on the whole, it went very well. Barring infection, he has a good prognosis."

"Now what do we do, Victor?" Hemingway asked Estrada.

"Outside of putting him on antibiotics, nothing more can be done. You have a houseguest for a couple of weeks, Ernest. He needs rest and a lot of care. In a couple of days, we will get him standing and moving about."

"Not a problem, Victor," Mary said. "The guest bedroom is next door. The three of us can manage."

"Very well. Get the bed ready, Mary. We need to move him carefully. Fetch Gregorio to give us a hand.

With Landeira resting comfortably in the guest bedroom. Mary had Gregorio bring a camping cot for Emilia, leaving Landeira in the bed undisturbed.

Ernest put his arm around Emilia's shoulder. "He is going to make it, Emilia. You okay?"

"Ready to collapse, Ernest. I don't know how to thank you and Mary."

"Not at all, Emilia," Hemingway said.

Mary took charge seeing Emilia's condition. "You can tell us the details of what happened in the morning. Amazing you were not hurt,"

Emilia began weeping. "I was hurt, Mary. But at least I had the satisfaction of seeing the sonofabitch die with a bullet in his head."

Mary put her arm around her. "I think I understand. Take a hot shower in the bathroom next to my room. It will make you feel better. If you need anything during the night, just wake me."

Hemingway said to Estrada, "More excitement than I've experienced in years, Victor. Splendid work you did. Obviously, my friend Landeira is involved with dangerous politics. Best we keep this between us. Tell your wife I was just being a hypochondriac and needed handholding. You look like you could use a drink. I certainly do."

* * * *

Landeira rested comfortably through the night with morphine blocking the pain. Next morning, coming awake slowly he repeated Emilia's name waking her on the cot next to his bed.

She came to him touching his forehead covered in perspiration. "How are you feeling?"

"Like I was shot," he said with a weak smile."

"The doctor left pills. Penicillin for infection. These others for pain. Want one?"

"Not yet. Had a terrible nightmare."

"Could not have been any worse than what actually happened. Can I call my mother and father?"

"Of course. Tell them only that we are safe but in hiding. Batista's police are looking for us which means we must find a way to leave Cuba."

"How do we do that?" she said. "Go where? How do we get along leaving everything behind?"

"Well for starters, we have $100,000 in that duffle bag. I am not wealthy, but with my father's inheritance, I'm in good financial shape. My money is safe in the United States."

"How do we get there?"

Landeira chose not to tell her that he prepared the sailboat should they manage somehow to survive. Not sure of her reaction to his making the decision to attack the kidnappers instead of paying the ransom. His condition proved just how close they both came to dying. The immediate police response to the scene proved they were behind this.

"I think the best option is get to the family estate in Camagüey. Once fully recovered, we make our way to Santiago already largely under the control of Castro's rebels.

"Batista's hold on power is slipping. The general election in November will be a turning point. He is not running as a candidate because even with a rigged election he cannot win. Putting up a proxy candidate instead. Castro is calling for a general boycott of the election. An election without viable opposition candidates will not appease the U.S. administration. Batista cannot survive much longer. Impossible to predict what comes next. "

"Some would say it could not be any worse," she offered.

"There can always be something worse. History is full of examples."

"I am going to tell Ernest and Mary how you are doing. As for me, I am famished. Haven't eaten much for days. How about you?"

"Not sure. Propped up with another pillow and some coffee sounds good though."

Hemingway and Mary were in the kitchen.

"How is, Bart?" Mary asked.

"Awake and talking. Wants me to take him some coffee."

"I'll do that," Hemingway said.

Just then, a broadcast came over Radio Habana.

'Following an anonymous tip, last night a squad of National Police under the command of Colonel Esteban Ventura raided a clandestine cell of revolutionaries in the Cerro sector of Havana. The raid ended in a violent car bomb explosion and fire destroying several buildings. The police killed three revolutionaries while suffering the death of Police Sergeant Miguel Torres leading the assault. Torres was a veteran of eight years on the force. Several other police officers suffered injury when the car bomb detonated. According to Colonel Ventura, the police are searching for an American citizen of Cuban descent in connection to the incident. Already under suspicion for subversive activities against the government, Bartolo Landeira, a business executive with a military background remains a fugitive wanted for providing material support to the revolutionaries.

Emilia sat transfixed until the broadcast moved to another subject. "No mention of my kidnapping. Bart is correct. This was a trap by the police to kill him. I was the bait to disguise his murder."

"How does the radio report confirm that?" Ernest said.

"Because Bart shot and killed four men. There were four kidnappers, not three. I saw it all happen. The explosion came after the shootings. Sergeant Torres was one of those kidnappers. The one in charge. The others called him by name. This is Colo-

nel Ventura's doing. Those that kidnapped me were not revolutionaries, just common criminals. They spoke of nothing but the
money while they kept me in that apartment."

Hemingway exclaimed, "Sonofabitch! All this cloak and
dagger stuff now makes sense. Rumor has it this Colonel Ventura is a nasty piece of work. He must be bewildered and frantic
with you and Bart as fugitives. Blowing up the car was a masterful stroke of a practiced saboteur. Bart is a resourceful and dangerous fellow."

* * * *

Within a week, Landeira was moving about carefully using a
cane for support. Fortunately, he dodged infection. Doctor Estrada looked in every other day.

With Landeira out of medical danger, Hemingway turned to
capturing the violent incident as possible literary material. Having Landeira recount the details of events leading up to that
night, he asked endless questions while making extensive notes
like a journalist covering a war.

"Remarkable. Regardless your skills and training, a remarkable act of courage going into a gunfight against four armed adversaries bent on killing you."

"Not so remarkable when considering Emilia was more important than my life."

"I understand. Still does not diminish the feat. Reads like fiction. I was serious before when I said I should make you the protagonist of a new novel. Change some circumstances to disguise
your identity. The literary challenge becomes attempting to capture the essence of your character, Bart."

Bart chuckled. "I like your company and appreciate your
friendship, Ernest. If you write me into one of your novels, give
me a happy ending. You write tragedies. Your protagonists often
do not end well."

Hemingway laughed. "Something else is on my mind, Bart.
Although I avoid Cuban political turmoil, I understand what is
transpiring. The Batista regime is coming apart. You and Emilia

are now wanted enemies of the state. Trying to get to Camagüey is far too dangerous. You cannot fly or use the train. Driving means roadblocks. You must consider Emilia's safety.

"Therefore, I have a better solution. With Gregorio's help, I take you and Emilia to Key West on the *Pilar*. I made the trip before. We plan for a period of good weather. Leave in the early morning hours as if to get to the marlin fishing grounds by dawn. We just keep on going north making Key West by sunset."

"I appreciate the offer but if we are caught that exposes you to something you have scrupulously avoided. At the very least, deportation for you and Mary. Confiscation of your beloved Finca Vigia."

"Been taking risks all my life, Bart. Suffered through wars and plane crashes. Life is about living it to the fullest. When passion moves your heart, you must temper the impulse for caution. How well you balance that mental tug of war is the measure of a man. What do you say?"

Bart extended his hand. "Thank you, Ernest. I have come to love Cuba as you do, but there is no way Emilia and I can remain here until something changes."

Gregorio picked up their few belongings stored on the sailboat by Landeira before the incident. Hemingway promised to look after Landeira's beloved *Elegante Bellezza*. They must abandon everything else.

One week later, they left Finca Vigia in Hemingway's Buick in the early morning hours before sunrise. Gregorio drove with Hemingway and Emilia seated in the back seat. With circumstances in Havana increasingly unsettled and Hemingway a recognizable figure, they could take no chances if stopped by random police or army roadblocks looking for revolutionaries. Landeira therefore rode uncomfortably in the trunk.

Mary Hemingway flew on ahead to Key West to meet them. Also wanted by the police, Emilia held Mary's Cuban residency documentation should she need to show identification on the way to Hemingway's boat docked in the fishing port of Coljímar. They planned a grand celebration with an extended

stay at Hemingway's Key West house while Bart Landeira and
Emilia Montero fully recuperated.

Epilogue

B art Landeira and Emilia Montero remained in Miami following their escape from Havana in late summer of 1958. They
watched as the Cuban revolution moved into its final phase. Fidel Castro's 26 July Movement gained recruits while the demor-
alized Cuban Army rapidly disintegrated as a cohesive military
force following Batista's failed Summer Offensive in August.

The end came swiftly as the dictatorship collapsed. The 1958
election in November resolved nothing. Andrés Rivero of Batista's Progressive Action Party won the counterfeit election with
an estimated voter turnout of only 50 percent. No candidate represented the revolutionary movement. Calling for a boycott of
the election, Castro went further by threatening the lives of anyone voting. Rumors circulated about the United States secretly
supporting Rivero to maintain its influence by continuing the
status quo.

Weeks later, with no advance warning, President Fulgencio
Batista departed Cuba in a military aircraft from Camp Columbia outside of Havana bound for the Dominican Republic on
January 1, 1959 at 12:53 am. President-elect Rivero fled with Batista without ever taking office. The Cuban Army immediately
laid down their arms all across Cuba. The following day rebel
columns under the command of Che Guevara and Camilo Cienfuegos entered Havana to cheering crowds. Fidel Castro arrived
in Havana on January 9.

General Eulogio Cantillo temporarily assumed the presidency after Batista fled the country. A futile effort following the total collapse of all the former Cuban security forces resulted in his immediate arrest. Castro appointed Cuban lawyer and politician Manuel Urrutia as president of a provisional government. Urrutia served only seven months before resigning after disputes with Fidel Castro over nationalization policies and Castro's political shift toward Marxism. Fidel Castro assumed the presidency in July 1959.

Cuba rapidly moved into the sphere of the Soviet Union, which recognized the strategic importance of Cuba's geographic proximity to the United States. Within the next couple of years, momentous events would dictate United States-Cuban hostile relations that still remain to this day. First came the monumentally ill-conceived CIA-backed Bay of Pigs invasion by Cuban exiles in April 1961, easily repelled by Cuban forces.

The tense nuclear standoff of the Cuban Missile Crisis followed over a period of two weeks in October 1962. Fidel Castro and Soviet Premier Nikita Khrushchev conspired to deploy medium range nuclear intercontinental ballistic missiles in Cuba. Photographed by high-altitude U-2 U.S. spy planes, U.S. President John Kennedy deployed a naval blockaded of Cuba. The tense military standoff as Soviet warships prepared to challenge the blockade brought the world closer to World War Three then at any other time. The collapse of the Soviet Union in 1991 did nothing to diminish the longstanding hostilities between Washington and Havana.

With Cuba transformed into a Soviet-aligned communist state, Bart Landeira and Emilia Montero never returned to Havana. The nationalization of the large landholdings and corporations dismantled Landeira Grupo. Landeira Rum came under state control. With their daughter fleeing Cuba and their son dead, and Cuba turned communist, Augustin and Alicia Montero also chose to leave Havana a year later. They had the means since Landeira convinced them to place the proceeds of the sale of Montero Rum in U.S. investments and U.S. bank accounts.

Having contemplated leaving Havana for some time, it was only Emilia that held Landeira there. Now with her parents in Florida, they were both free to pursue a new life together elsewhere. A career in foreign journalism no longer fit the new life he envisioned with Emilia. With mutual backgrounds in business law, an idea came to Landeira. Having once briefly visited the island of Antigua in the Leeward Islands of the Caribbean, he recalled falling in love with its many pristine beaches. The easygoing life style similar to Cuba. Many foreigners of wealth appreciated the charms of Antigua as evidenced by luxury homes and expensive yachts. A British colony, he read in the Financial Times of recently enacted favorable tax laws similar to those in the British colonies of Bermuda and the Cayman Islands. Tax laws attractive to foreign investors. The term *tax haven* coined to describe legal mechanisms to reduce taxes in the home country for corporations and wealthy individuals.

The thought of transplanting to Antigua and developing a tax consulting law practice in partnership with Emilia sounded more interesting than staying in Florida. A magnificent location for a sailor. A stable political environment. Since becoming friends with Ernest Hemingway, he began writing fiction making Antigua the perfect working environment.

The irony of entering into a legitimate form of essentially his father's career was not lost on him. Given a different time, different circumstances, their relationship might have turned out differently.

Not only did Bart and Emilia go to Antigua, they married, acquired licenses to practice law in Antigua, and opened their legal consulting business. Augustin and Alicia moved to Antigua within a year, Augustin purchased an Antigua rum distillery with the money received from his prior sale of Montero Rum. Renamed Montero Antiguan Rum he intended to replicate his acclaimed Cuban Montero Rum.

Bart Landeira began his first novel. The setting, 1950s Cuba. The working title *Havana*. A troubled time and place full of intrigue, adventure, and romance with no shortages of villains.

Afterword

The following provides a brief summary of what happened to the actual historical figures featured in the novel *Havana*:

Fidel Castro:
Castro ruled Cuba as a communist government but one with the imprint of his singular personality until 2007 when he turned over the presidency to his brother Raúl because of failing health. Since 1959, he weathered the economic impact on Cuba following the collapse of the Soviet Union, while never reconciling with the United States. Fidel Castro died in 2016 at the age of 90.

Fulgencio Batista:
Refused exile in the United States as too great an embarrassment, Batista lived out the remainder of his life in Portugal. He died of a heart attack in 1973 at the age of 72. Later information alleged his death occurred only two days before a planned assassination attempt on orders from Fidel Castro.

Rafael Trujillo:
Trujillo ruled the Dominican Republic for 31 years from 1930 to 1961. Serving two non-concurrent terms as elected president, he ruled as dictator for the last 9 years. Recognized as the most brutal of the many Latin American dictators of the era, Trujillo extended his state terrorism to assassinations in foreign countries. As poetic justice, Dominican military officers assassinated Trujillo in Ciudad Trujillo in 1961 at the age of 69.

Esteban Ventura:
Ventura fled Cuba on the same flight transporting Fulgencio Batista. The United States accepted Ventura into exile along with other notorious murders from the Batista regime. Cuba turning communist discouraged pursuit of those responsible for mass murder under the Batista dictatorship. Ventura lived quietly in Miami, Florida until his death from natural causes in 2001 at the age of 88.

Meyer Lansky:
Lansky fled Cuba a day before Fidel Castro triumphantly entered Havana. With all the casinos looted and damaged, Castro outlawed gambling wiping out Lansky's asset base and revenue streams. Lansky retired to Miami, Florida where he died of lung cancer in 1983 at the age of 80. His documented net worth was almost nothing. While the FBI believed Lansky amassed a fortune of $300M in hidden bank accounts, they never recovered any money. Whether such a fortune ever existed still remains a mystery.

Santo Trafficante Jr:
The Castro government expelled Trafficante from Cuba, and like Meyer Lansky, seized his Cuban business assets soon after coming to power. After returning to Tampa resuming organized criminal activity there, Trafficante became associated with the CIA and participated in many of their failed attempts to assassinate Fidel Castro. Trafficante died in 1987 at the age of 72 in a Houston hospital where he had gone for heart surgery.

Ernest Hemingway:
Suffering depression and memory difficulties affecting his ability to continue writing after receiving electrical shock treatment at the Mayo Clinic, the Nobel Laureate committed suicide at his home in Ketchum, Idaho in 1961 using his favorite shotgun. He was 62. To this day, his Cuban home, Finca Vigia outside Havana, and his former home in Key West, Florida survive as museums.